THE CUMBRIAN CABAL

Geraldine Pewtress

HAMMERTON PRESS

ISBN: 0 9540960 0 2

This book is a work of fiction and is entirely a product of the author's imagination. All characters are fictitious and any resemblance to actual persons, living or dead, is purely coincidental.

British Library Cataloguing in Publication Data.
A catalogue record of this book is available from the British Library.

Published by Hammerton Press 2001.
Hammerton Press, Piercy End, Kirkbymoorside,
York YO62 6DQ.

Printed and bound by Bookcraft, Westfield Trading Estate, Midsomer Norton, Somerset BA3 4BS.

AUTHOR'S NOTE

The characters and events in this book are all fictitious, and intended to be taken like Life itself - not too seriously.

ACKNOWLEDGEMENTS

Were it not for my husband's endless patience in helping me use a computer, 'The Cumbrian Cabal' would never have been written. Nor would it have had a cover without his painstaking technical work, accurately positioning the original photograph, text, fonts, inset sketch, correct spine width etc.

Excerpt from the Folk Song *"Nothing Worthwhile Comes Too Easy"* on Page 58 is reproduced by kind permission of Rex Brisland, Arbris International, 1 Farm Close, Birstall, Leicester, LE4 4EG.

The book described on Page 246 is *"The Hiding Place"* by Corrie ten Boom, a truly inspirational book first published in 1971 by Hodder & Stoughton and still in print.

Danny's description of the affectionate bond between seamen on Page 249 is attributed to my cousin Hughie, who was in fact talking about my own father.

As far as I am able to ascertain, formal permission is not required in order to quote the excerpt from *"The Song of Hiawatha"* by Henry Longfellow on Page 194, or from the traditional song *"The Leaving of Liverpool"* on Page 251. All reasonable efforts have been made to secure copyright permission for material published in this work, and Hammerton Press wishes to apologise for any inaccuracies or omissions with regard to the recognition of copyright holders given above.

For my dearest Jim, with all my love.

ONE: COMMON GROUND

If he didn't get to sleep soon, fretted Len as the jumble of thoughts whirling around his overtired brain (despite having done enough deep breathing exercises to prepare for an assault on Everest) spiralled towards meltdown, the Inspection Committee arriving next day to decide Beckside's fate would be greeted by the senior member of staff resembling one of the Undead after a hard night at the morgue. And just to add to the all-important first impression of bright-eyed efficiency, step forward the supporting cast whose idea of animated enthusiasm was an indifferent stare. The Seasonal Assistants from hell.

For most of the twenty four years he and Kate had run Beckside Youth Hostel they'd enjoyed very good working relationships with their staff, some of whom had remained with them for several seasons. But this summer it looked as though the place was set to become a war zone. And lined up to face him on the battleground were two separate Fronts, each requiring a different response and strategy, and each potentially lethal. The hostel was struggling for its very survival - that was Front Number One - and the army on whose support they needed to rely in the coming *guerre à mort* was currently engaged in its own unspoken, and apparently motiveless, wearing-down campaign of sullen apathy and sly disobedience. And that was Front Number Two.

So far he'd overlooked it, partly because Kate had, as usual, made excuses for them - they were young, and adapting to unfamiliar routines etc - but mostly because he had enough experience of human nature to know that direct confrontation would merely be met with jubilant glee, widen the chasm even further, and achieve nothing. His colleagues had laughed when, on a recent Harmonious Staff Relations Course where everyone was asked to describe their staff, he'd summed up the latest recruits as Lord Snooty meets Lucretia Borgia with PMT, but it was no joke living in this atmosphere day after day, and things had to either improve very soon or end in an acrimonious parting of the ways.

So - how to inject them with a sense of urgency about the coming Inspection? A rousing pep talk? "Remember, Beckside's future is at stake! Things are desperate financially, and a bad report from the Death's Head Squad means definite closure..."

Unlikely. As long as there were sufficient funds to pay their salaries for the next few months, Beckside's future had as much relevance in their present lives as the question of whether they'd need zimmer frames when they were ninety.

Wheedling emotional blackmail? "You wouldn't want to inconvenience backpackers from all over the world by allowing Beckside to close, would you?..."

Even more unlikely. Anna expected every living creature with whom she came into contact, from the Inspection Committee to the hostel cat, to ensure her comfort and convenience in life took priority over all other matters, and the only inconvenience to concern her would be her own. As for Oliver, he doubted the lad was capable of a sense of urgency about anything other than where his next bar of chocolate was coming from.

Beside him, Kate sighed in her sleep. Three o'clock chimed on the distant village church clock. Perhaps he should get dressed, go downstairs, and start the monthly accounts, which would probably refuse to balance on the very day it was vital to dispose of them speedily in order to concentrate on the Inspection...

At 6.30AM, despite two alarm clocks screeching at maximum decibels and Kate nearly dislocating his shoulder as she shook his arm, Len was almost comatose. His planned session of calm meditation after a night of empowering, refreshing sleep, psyching himself to conquer whatever disasters waited to strike during the day, was instead spent burrowing deeper under the quilt to shut out Kate's voice reminding him sharply that seventy-five breakfasts wouldn't cook themselves, and had he forgotten the Inspectors were coming today?

Apart from Oliver writing off a year's supply of dishcloths by soaking them overnight in undiluted bleach, the first part of the morning presented no headaches other than the one raging in Len's own skull. It was the second half of the morning, when preparations for the Inspection must start in earnest to ensure the building gleamed like the boardroom of a multi-national business empire (and staff personality clashes and tensions simmering just below the surface most likely to erupt) that would need handling with the sensitivity of a bomb disposal expert, and although Len's diplomatic skills had been honed in the school of hard knocks, he was quite happy to try old-fashioned bribery if it would bring about the required result. So, when the hostellers had all left for the day and the staff sat down to their mid-morning tea break, he opened a packet of chocolate biscuits and nudged the contents towards Oliver.

'Now the first place they'll look is, toilets. So we want them all to outdazzle the mirrored sun, don't we. *Don't we?*' he cajoled as Oliver's unresponsive face regarded him with its customary blank stare. The ideal rest-cure after a sleepless night: headbutting a reinforced concrete wall.

And he may as well give up before he started where Anna was concerned. Whatever the alchemic formula to penetrate that alabaster surface and tap into any seams of goodwill lying far beneath, it certainly wouldn't comprise of anything as straightforward as chocolate biscuits.

He sighed and spread his month-end accounts on the table. Because regardless of raging headaches, nervous exhaustion, and worry over make-or-break Inspections (quite apart from the day-to-day responsibilities of running of a seventy five bed Youth Hostel) accountants, like menacing volcanoes of old demanding a succession of live virgins tossed in at regular intervals, expected the accounts to be done on time.

And to balance.

As his pen moved haltingly down a column of figures, returned to the top, and began its descent again, Anna clacked in, still wearing the high-heeled strappy sandals he'd earlier complained were starting to make the floor look as if it had suffered a severe attack of acne.

'If that washing machine you promised isn't here by noon, I'll have left by five past,' she informed him coolly. 'I have no intention of washing any more of these disgusting rags by hand.'

She hoisted onto her left hip a laundry basket overflowing with sodden tea towels, slammed the kitchen door with a flick of one foot that bore the hallmark of a world-class expert in the art of unspoken insults, and click-clacked down the Reception Area, a trail of drips marking her progress.

Len flung the door open, conscious he'd almost wrenched it off its hinges and would be lucky if it opened or closed again at all.

'Slam this door when I'm half way down a column of figures again, milady, and it'll be the last thing you'll ever do!'

She ignored him.

As he started in pursuit - nobody treated Len as an ineffectual fool, even though he often privately felt like one - Oliver's lanky frame unfolded from the porch bench on which he'd obviously been lounging, and, postponing the joust for supremacy with Anna, he confronted this even more infuriating insolence.

'Kate said it was OK to have a little rest if I got tired, because it's still all new.' Oliver got in first, breath laden with chocolate, tone resentful. (Fetch this, carry that, lift dat barge, tote dat bale - and now skivvy for the poxy Inspection as well! The Job Description bumf had spoken in glowing terms of varied, fulfilling work, and interesting people he'd meet; Oliver was already phrasing a complaint to some benign Head of Operations who would award generous compensation for his disillusionment.) 'I've only been here a couple of weeks.'

'Got tired? At your age?' Len stared at him. 'When I was eighteen I'd been at sea three years, frozen to the bone in the North Atlantic and expected to work, seasick or not!'

Oliver stifled a yawn, which was his usual response to decrepit geriatrics rambling about harsh conditions endured during their youth, and studied the steam swirling from disinfectant in the bucket.

Len paused as the front door creaked shut behind Anna. '- *And you only had a tea break ten minutes ago!'*

The temptation to really let rip with some justifiable riot-reading would probably result in a phone call to Mummy, who'd swoop in like an avenging valkyrie just as the Inspection was taking place and accuse him of brutal and merciless slave-driving. Which wouldn't do much for the spirit of co-operative teamwork on which such emphasis had been placed at the Harmonious Staff Relations Course. So - for now - he'd concentrate solely on getting the work done.

'Wherever I look, there you are, slumped motionless. Except for your jaws. You should be supercharged with energy, the chocolate you guzzle! Now *move!*'

Braced for a variation on this morning's performance when Len had discovered the entire stock of dishcloths dissolved into ribbons in the sink (they'd told him to soak them overnight in bleach, and he had. How was he supposed to know you had to dilute the stuff?), Oliver hid a triumphant smirk, gathered his mop and bucket, and slouched along the Reception Area.

This had been a dark and gloomy wood-panelled Entrance Hall in the days when the old Lakeland stone house was a private residence set in its own grounds overlooking the lake, and during the forty years it had served as a Youth Hostel it hadn't changed much. A few homely touches had been added - a cluster of institution-type easy chairs grouped around a coffee table, several posters, a notice board advertising local tourist attractions, a stack of ancient Reader's Digests, out-of-date magazines and children's Annuals in a small bookcase, and some musty hardbacks, undisturbed for years, propped against a spindly plant on the window ledge.

Len shepherded him to the wide oak staircase, indicated with an unceremonious jerk of his head the Washrooms waiting to be cleaned on the first floor landing, and turned to re-grapple with his accounts. The kitchen door was given another eloquent slam.

And Oliver, raising his middle finger at it, slumped to the bottom step to resume his interrupted Rest and Recuperation.

'No wonder they suspected you when they found that note about electric cattle prods in the Suggestion Box on the Harmonious Staff Relations Course,' remarked Kate when the door stopped reverberating once more. 'But then of course they've never met Oliver. It can be a bit difficult to get through to him at times.'

'Get through to him? You can't even make contact with him!' snorted Len. 'Know-it-all whizz-kids droning about motivating staff... they want to try it in real life, and motivate him!'

The band of pressure circling his forehead tightened another couple of notches. He filled a glass with water, fumbled in the Medical Cupboard for the paracetamols, swallowed a couple, leaned against the cooker, then flinched as a gas tap dug into his back. He still missed the Aga with its huge old kettle perpetually simmering on the firelid, under which, in a fit of drunken hilarity

9

soon after he and Kate had arrived as idealistic young wardens from Liverpool all those years ago, they'd scrawled their own succinct summary of The Universal Cookery Book: IF IT'S BROWN IT'S COOKED, IF IT'S BLACK IT'S ***! This advice had burnt on, instructing countless staff in the finer points of *haute cuisine* over the years, until the kitchen was modernised. ('Vandalised, more like,' Len had commented as he stared, unimpressed, at the soulless, sterile 'Food Preparation Area', all stainless steel and clinical white tiles, that had once been their warm, friendly kitchen.)

Outside, a van's doors slammed. Before Len could safely re-position the papers spread in orderly piles on the table, the fishman was dumping a crate of cod down next to them, showering everything in range with fish-water.

'Eighty fillets, including one for the cat, was it?' He bustled to the door, announcing over his shoulder: 'And I've got the washing machine in the van as well. Forty pounds, OK?'

Len flicked fish-water from the greengrocer's bill. 'If that old kleptomaniac thinks I'm paying forty quid for some broken-down heap of rust -'

Kate sighed. 'Are you trying to win the Obstreperous Old Git Of The Year Award? Listen to yourself, Len! D'you know what you sound like?'

'I know what I'll sound like when we're redundant as a result of this Inspection!' Len massaged his forehead as an endless list of things to be done before The Committee arrived at five o'clock unfurled before his eyes.

Kate, in the unflattering navy blue nylon overall "they" insisted she always wore, her face red from kitchen heat, her hair tied back in an elastic band, pushed away the crate of staring fish, perched on the edge of the table, and stroked back his hair in a gesture of exasperated tenderness. Her grey eyes had retained the gentleness and humour that had first attracted him, and as he stared into their depths, ignoring the lines that had accumulated around them, the frenetic sense of urgency about the Inspection receded as he saw again the clear, expertly made-up eyes of a stunning twenty year old girl on the day they got engaged.

He hadn't planned to get engaged, let alone married. Life was too good, freedom too precious. And yet, somehow... It was one of those sights imprinted on his mind forever, Kate teetering along in white stiletto heels and the cheong-sam he'd bought on a Far East trip because on his last night ashore they'd been to see *The World of Susie Wong*, and she'd fancied herself in a cheong-sam, and he'd said she'd never dare wear it, so of course she had to prove him wrong. He'd presented it to her on his next first night home, all wrapped up in fancy paper, and she'd put in on there and then. Well, not quite there and then. In fact it had spent most of that evening on the floor.

The tension relaxed, the frown lines faded. Len was twenty three again, a carefree sailor with the world in the palm of his hand; tall, dark and handsome as any women's magazine hero, and he knew it. Liverpool had just won 2-Nil, they were going to a party that night, and he'd given her a wad of notes (she'd got through her own wages days ago) to buy a dress while he was at the match. He'd waited for her under Lewis's statue, wondering if she'd have enough left to pay the fare home. They were a good Line to work for, the Blue Funnel Line, or Blue Flues as they were known locally, and it was just as well because Kate spent money like a banknote forger's floosie.

When she finally arrived she'd dumped her parcels on him and hoisted herself onto the bus. And that was another indelible sight; Kate, boarding a bus in a tight skirt and tottering upstairs as the vehicle lurched and jolted its way to the Pier Head.

Of course, the ferry had just left, a howling gale was tearing up the Mersey, and tendrils of hair, which she'd had piled up on top of her head at some posh hairdressers, were starting to come down, and by the time the next ferryboat arrived the whole lot was blowing round her face and she'd had enough of the cheong-sam and wished she'd worn jeans like everyone else, especially when her stiletto heel caught between the planks of the gangway and broke. And the swell lifted the gangplank and she'd lost her balance, and he'd caught her and steadied her. And that was when he'd proposed, with the wind whipping away his words, up the river and over the docks and warehouses...

'You've gone all glazed-eyed again!' She was digging him in the ribs, and the kitchen came back. 'Did you hear me? I said, let's get the washing machine in.'

'Stuff the washing machine, let's go upstairs.' The words were so soft Kate wasn't sure if she'd actually heard them.

'You what?' She gaped at him open mouthed.

Back came the month-end accounts that wouldn't balance, the fishman demanding money with menaces for a clapped-out wreck, Oliver skulking off with his purloined chocolate while the place resembled an overflowing dustbin, and the Inspection, with its impending sense of doom, looming ever nearer.

In silence he made out a cheque for forty pounds.

Anna paused on her way outside with a second basket of tea towels to watch Oliver swish a mop carelessly over the front doorstep.

'If Len sees this step,' she warned, 'You'll probably get that mop water thrown all over you, because it's dirtier now than it was to start with.'

Oliver leaned on the mop handle and surveyed the filthy rivulets of water dripping down the step. 'I hope he does. Should be worth at least a five figure sum in compensation. I've got my list of complaints ready for these Inspectors the minute they walk in the door.' He sloshed another mopful of almost black water along the step. 'I couldn't stand this until September, I'd end up as screwy as he is. How long d'you reckon you'll stick it?'

'Long enough to win a bet.' Anna pushed back a waterfall of liquid-honey hair framing flawless skin and delicate features.

Oliver wondered whether she was joking, and decided she wasn't. It was difficult to know what to make of Anna. Other than that she was twenty four, had been to an Art School in London, and sold paintings in London and Cornwall, she gave very little away about herself.

'You mean, you won't be here long then?' Better consolidate his position of confidante and ally while she was in a talkative mood; the way things were going, he'd need someone to gang up with against Len and Kate.

'I'll be here until October.' She sat on the wall and looked down at the lake, shimmering in the spring sunshine. The road running alongside it was quiet now, but in a few weeks would be full of cars inching their way towards the car park as the village swarmed with visitors. All homing in on the Art Gallery, if Anna had her way. She'd taken her first batch of paintings in during the week; they should be framed and on display for sale by now.

'Oh, right.' Oliver absently swung another mopful at the step, watching swathes of bubbles glisten in the sun before they disappeared into the porous stone. 'Is that the bet? You'll last until October? What'll you win if you do it?'

'A week on a very exclusive island in the Great Barrier Reef.'

'Oh, right.'

'That's the starting point. I intend to paint my way around the world. A sort of global watercolour tour. A friend's suggested I turn it into a book. He's a publisher.'

'Oh, right,' said Oliver again.

'Meanwhile, I wanted to paint in the Lakes anyway, and this saved the hassle of finding somewhere to rent.' She indicated the door. 'Misfits Anonymous in there are just a couple of dumbos to be put up with until I've built up a Cumbrian folder.'

Oliver nodded, aware this was the cue for giving his own reasons for being here. Which were far more simple.

During the latest blazing row with his father over the volume of "that intolerable torture" thumping down from his bedroom, he'd been given an unequivocal choice: either he took himself, his amplifiers, and that infernal cacophony to the wilds of Siberia, or the entire rats' nest of tapes would be dumped down a disused mineshaft. As this ultimatum presented a very convenient excuse to avoid taking 'A' level exams, with their ensuing disastrous results, he made his decision there and then: he'd seen an advert for resident Youth Hostel Assistants, and rather fancied the idea of idling away a few months in a nagging-parent-free zone. A limitless procession of more exotic nubile females than the local lot at Oak Road Comprehensive wouldn't go amiss, either.

His mother, at first nonplussed at this decision ("But darling, what about your 'A' levels?"), then fiercely proud ("So enterprising! And so... innovative!"), veered back to mystified incomprehension that her son wanted to be left at Beckside at all when she heard Len and Kate outline the duties of a Seasonal Assistant.

Over coffee, scones, and pleasantries, she directed the conversation towards Oliver's numerous talents and skills. He'd be such an asset, she assured them. So enthusiastic, and so *helpful*! No, she didn't know what the job entailed, but Oliver loved meeting people so he was bound to be indispensable, wasn't he? Helping folk to climb mountains, or whatever they did. She flashed a bright smile at Len. 'And he's terribly interested in birds and things,' she added vaguely.

But as Kate was listing specific tasks ('You mean he'd have to empty the bins in Ladies' Lavatories? But surely you have cleaners in to do all that sort of thing?... *He's* the cleaner?... Oh! Well I'm sorry, but I really couldn't agree to... er...') his horrified mother signalled with much dramatic eye-play that her son should accompany her outside. Alone.

'Darling, are you *sure*?' she'd protested anxiously. 'Because quite honestly... And I thought they had cleaners to do all that! Don't you think you should come home with me and take your 'A' levels?'

'I can't let them down now,' mumbled Oliver, avoiding eye contact, and his mother gazed at him fondly. So noble! And so unselfish!

'Oh darling... but the *moment* you realise you've made the most ghastly mistake, ring me. I'll collect you straight away. It's not what I'd envisaged at all!'

It wasn't what Oliver had envisaged at all, either.

So, conveniently ignoring his own reasons for being at Beckside, he summed up his superiors in a succinct three-second psychoanalysis: 'Yeah. Dysfunctional Liverpudlian cretins, not a brain cell between them!'

He shook his head pityingly. How reassuring it was, and what a sense of superiority it gave one, to know, with absolute and infallible certainty, as one did at eighteen, that one would never end up a pathetic old relic from a bygone age oneself.

The Office was positioned at the far end of the Reception Area, between the kitchen and the stairs, with its door in the far corner under the stairs. The illogicality of this - despite Len's demented pleas over the years for a doorway to be knocked through the adjoining kitchen wall - meant that during the hours the Hostel was closed, as now, the door was left open to save fiddling with keys each time someone needed to gain access.

Behind a glass hatch, which opened as required, a wooden counter held the Register, Booking Diary, file containing correspondence, a chewed ballpoint attached to a string, and Len's "Liverpool Pilot Boat, Maritime Museum" mug, full of assorted felt-tips that no longer worked and pencils that needed sharpening. The Office was also The Shop, and sold postcards, maps, guidebooks, sweets, lemonade, baked beans, peas, stew, tinned fruit, rice pudding, evaporated milk etc, and coffee, teabags, sugar, dried milk - provisions for those wishing to prepare their own meals in the Self-Caterers' Kitchen.

Oliver, sneaking in the front door behind Anna, listened to ensure the fire-breathing guardian of The Shop's treasure was safely ensconced in the kitchen, then darted in and grabbed a handful of chocolate bars.

'No wonder he asked if you've got worms,' remarked Anna, eyeing his skinny frame. 'Be careful he hasn't rigged up that Poets Corner Reject as a guillotine.' She nodded to a large painted board above the Office, and quoted aloud:

"WELCOME TO BECKSIDE"

A warm and friendly Welcome
Whoever you may be,
And however you have travelled,
By land, or air, or sea.

You'll find good food and warmth here,
You'll meet friends old and new,
Your hosts are Len and Katy,
And all their friendly crew.

So hikers, bikers, backpackers,
Exploring far and near,
Spend a night or two with us, you'll find
Good company and cheer!"

'Funny to think we're the friendly crew,' commented Oliver, unwrapping his plunder.

'Even funnier to think of them as loveable old characters, all jovial banter and merry laughter in the Common Room.'

'Yeah...' Oliver selected an indelible marker from Len's pencil-mug and eyed the Welcome sign thoughtfully. A series of squeaks accompanied the transformation as he filled in the space between the lower and middle strokes of the first E in BECKSIDE, then added another couple of strokes down the sides to form a bold, square A.

He stood back, admiring his handiwork. 'There! That's a better name for this dump. And I'm going to tell these Inspectors what that crabby old bat's really like, as well. Roll on five o'clock!'

Len's pen hovered over a niggling discrepancy, then clattered onto the table. 'Why bother? They're going to close us anyway...'

Unemployed and homeless, at forty seven years of age. Which meant, back to Liverpool, cap in hand to the Social Security. All the council houses in this locality had long since been sold off and turned into astronomically priced holiday homes, and when he and Kate had been young enough to apply for a mortgage, their joint salary meant the Mortgage Arranger could offer nothing more constructive than a pitying look. So there was no hope of continuing to live in the area where they'd put down roots over the last twenty four years.

He needed some fresh air.

He screwed into a ball the memo from Head Office exhorting all staff to submit month-end accounts *promptly* as well as accurately, aimed it into the waste bin, headed for the back door, glanced at the washing machine clanking its way through yet another load of tea towels in the utility room, detoured in, and gave it a therapeutic thump. The clanking sputtered to a reproachful silence; the mechanism refused to re-start.

Just to add to the rest of the day's problems, the instrument panel now dangled drunkenly from one screw.

Five o'clock chimed on The Office clock, and a colourful mix of hikers, mountain bikers, outdoor pursuits enthusiasts, families, a University walking group, and backpackers of all nationalities swarmed noisily into the Reception Area.

And in the far corner the Inspection Committee were also assembling, greeting each other with pleasantries and small talk.

Oliver, sent by Kate to check the numbers for tomorrow's packed lunches, lolled against The Office counter as he waited for Len to take a brief moment from booking in new arrivals, and studied the all-powerful deciders of Beckside's fate. Len had explained that a clutch of volunteers, sharing in tandem with paid officials a dwindling but nevertheless significant portion of power, made up a Committee who met at regular intervals, discussed policies, and periodically undertook such tasks as

Hostel Inspections, and he was curious to see them.

Holding court at the centre of the orbit was an expensively-suited, portly figure of authority, accompanied by an impeccably coiffured wife. The lesser satellites gravitated respectfully around them; a cadaverous male enveloped in an ill-fitting jacket, a stooped man in his thirties with straggly hair and a badge saying "Brian" on his pullover, and a teenage girl with an anxious expression, nervously chewing a clump of hair.

Oliver's eyes, however, were drawn in repelled fascination to what, to him, appeared to be a potato-shaped gargoyle in a pillar-box red skirt and puce blouse, slumped in an easy chair, apparently deep in thought. Canary yellow frizz like a mass of unravelling plastic panscrubs framed a florid face, the features long since blurred into fat, the mouth petulant, the complexion coarse, the chins multiple, the eyes pig-like. His eyes travelled furtively downwards. The blouse stretched across large breasts encased in a corset-like uplift bra, the straps digging into fleshy shoulders bulging over the confines of the undergarment; the mini skirt strained over massive thighs, crossed to display overweight legs and podgy feet in ancient white high heels.

Her eyes flickered towards him as she became aware of his scrutiny. He gulped, aware he'd been staring like a rodent hypnotised by a swaying snake, and turned to Len (wrist now swathed in a bulging bandage) who was scribbling the packed lunch numbers on a scrap of paper.

'...And tell Kate it'll be All Stand for Their Worships the Judges any minute now.'

'Oh, right.' If Anna ever wanted to do a study of a condemned man she wouldn't find a more apt model than Len's haggard face, thought Oliver, and added awkwardly, 'Headache better now?'

The front door opened with its habitual eardrum-imploding screech.

'It was.'

'Oh sorry. I forgot. I'll oil it tomorrow,' promised Oliver.

'It's not the door, it's what's coming through it.'

What was coming through it tripped over a trailing shoelace as he transferred four carrier bags to one hand and adjusted a pair of glasses sliding down his nose with the other. One of the bags dropped. There was a smash of glass.

Oliver stared at the newcomer's frizzy ginger hair, once-white shirt now adorned with the remains of several meals and buttoned up wrongly at the neck, filthy shorts fastened with a safety pin, and plump white legs, devoid of muscle, disappearing into mud-encrusted trainers.

'I see what you mean,' he giggled. 'D'you want me to get you another aspirin, for when Beau Brummel and his matching designer hand-luggage finally makes it to the desk?'

'Shush, they'll hear you!' snapped Len. 'I don't need you antagonising the Inspection Committee before they even start!'

Oliver's grin was replaced by a look of incredulity. '*He's* not one of them, surely?'

'Formal introductions will take place later, but yes. Dud's on the Committee,' confirmed Len grimly.

The Judges had now all arrived. The Assizes were about to sit.

The object of Oliver's scrutiny was indeed deep in thought as she watched Len clear away the broken glass, pickled onions, and pool of vinegar corroding its way through the lino.

Her mother, Bridie, had been dropping heavy hints about "that Dud one" taking his time popping the question, wasn't he, and it was about time he did pop it if you asked her, because he was quick enough at popping other things, if Mona got her meaning. And if she knew anything about men - and she did - that gossoon was only after One Thing, and since he'd long since got it he was probably scenting the air elsewhere right now. So if Mona wanted a return on her outlay - because she'd put in enough time and effort, hadn't she - she'd better get him up the aisle quick. He was the type to be forever casting his eyes round, that one. Well, once Mona had the lines in her mitt and the ring in the pawnshop, he could be off a-whoring wherever he pleased and bad cess to him; by then she'd be legally entitled to half the house, his dimwitted old mother would be banished to Sheltered Accommodation, and the goose dispatched daily to work while his master ("mistress" didn't sound quite right in this instance) accrued a limitless supply of Golden Eggs in the form of the joint account.

Yes, thought Mona. She'd invested *more* than enough time and effort, sucking up to that snotty Chairman to get herself invited onto The Committee instead of forever being tolerated as a "guest." Talk about always the bridesmaid, never the bloody bride... She eyed Dud speculatively. He might be a numbskull, but he was a well-paid numbskull with a steady job in the Inland Revenue, and he was not going to slip the leash.

It was time to bring him to heel.

Len, once again immersed in the queue, glanced up as Dud materialised at the head of it, grinning matily at an Australian backpacker currently booking in.

'Mind if I barge in a mo, mate? Just want a quick word with old Len here... Suppose we'd better keep Kate happy and have a cup of tea before we start, Len. I know how upset she gets if we don't let her make a fuss of us. Oh, and Major Pratt says, there's no need for you to accompany us on the Inspection, we'll just mooch round on our own. We'll be finished at seven, in time for the meal. I'll jot down notes of all the faults we find, then write them out properly before the Committee Meeting next weekend, when we'll be announcing the decision on Beckside's future.'

'It's not next weekend, Dud. It's the one after.'

'Oh, I think you'll find it's next weekend, Len, old friend. One thing about me, I never get my dates wrong. Got it in my Hikers Diary... it's here somewhere.'

He rummaged in the first carrier bag, then the second, then started on the third. The queue watched in bemused silence.

'No, tell a lie, it's here!' He straightened triumphantly and delved into his shirt pocket. A puzzled frown appeared. 'Now that's strange! Definitely here somewhere. Hang on a mo.'

He rustled into carrier bag number four. 'Because I did something a bit silly, once. I went to the wrong venue. Ha!'

'Is there a charge for the entertainment?' asked the Australian.

Len reached under the counter and produced a typewritten list of dates. 'Look. It says here, Dud. The fourteenth.'

Dud peered at the list. 'It isn't, is it? Are you sure? I thought it was next weekend. Has Dottie typed it wrong?'

'Definitely the fourteenth, Dud.'

'Oh. Oh well, as long as you're sure... By the way, my button's gone on my shorts. Kate'll have time to sew it back on before we start the Inspection, won't she?'

'Does it look as if I've got time to sew a button on his shorts?' glared Kate, banging a pan down on the cooker.

Anna, methodically working her way along rows of paper bags containing the clingfilm-wrapped rolls for tomorrow's packed lunches, tossed a packet of crisps, chocolate biscuit, cereal bar, and an apple into each one. Further along the table, Oliver was topping up tomato sauce bottles from a gallon drum. Both appeared totally engrossed in their tasks; both, Len knew, were listening in rapt attention.

The silence intensified. Kate mutinously tipped frozen peas into the pan.

'Why can't he sew his own button on?' asked Anna. 'In fact, why can't they get their own tea in the Self-Caterers' kitchen? We've got enough to do in here, preparing seventy five meals!'

'That's not the way it works, Miss Clever-Clogs,' Len told her shortly. 'It might happen in 2000AD - although I doubt it - but not in the 1980s. Right now, as far as they're concerned, that's what the kitchen low-life's here for, so you'd better get used to it. Anyway, last time Dud went down to the Self-Caterers Kitchen in the middle of the night to make himself a cup of tea, the fire alarm woke the whole hostel and we had to drag the doctor out of bed to see to his scalds. It's easier to just do it ourselves.'

'Funny, though.' Kate jabbed a frozen lump of peas with a wooden spoon to break them up. 'How they're always harping on about not fussing over them, they just want to be one of the gang, don't stand on ceremony - I've a good mind to take them at their word for once, give them a needle and cotton and a couple of teabags and let them get on with it.'

'Kate, this is the Inspection Committee we're talking about. You know, the ones who'll be deciding our future tonight,' Len reminded her impatiently.

'I know. That's the whole point. Tea bags are there, milk's over there, sugar's over there, biscuits are -'

'Pack it in, Kate!'

'It's us that'll be getting packed in, Len!'

It was Kate's turn to face the futility of all today's desperate, clutching-at-straws efforts. Beckside's closure, although not yet formally announced, was a foregone conclusion. By the end of the year she and Len would be on the doorstep, surrounded by their belongings in cardboard boxes and bin-bags; Oliver would have long since enrolled at college to train as a whizz-kid and join some organisation as a highly-paid executive (probably this one, knowing their luck, if Beckside did survive), and Anna, after her brief research into the slave classes, would continue a life of fulfilment and ease, with Kate and Len filed away for use as amusing anecdotes at dinner parties: "Have you met Anna? Do get her to tell you about the time she worked in a Youth Hostel, it's an absolute *hoot!*"

She turned back to the frozen peas. If she had to go down, she'd go down fighting. And with self respect.

'Tell him I'm busy. There's a needle and cotton in The Office.'

Len glanced at Anna and Oliver, apparently concentrating furiously on their tasks, then turned back to Kate.

'Have you taken leave of your senses?'

'No. I'm finally beginning to come to them,' Kate said calmly.

A gurgling sound erupted from the tomato sauce bottles as Oliver, eyes now swivelling from Len to Kate and back like a Wimbledon spectator, lost concentration. Tomato sauce overflowed down the bottle and cascaded onto the table.

'Are you supposed to be filling those bottles or seeing how much you can waste?' snapped Len.

'Oh, what does it matter.' Kate sounded as if she was past caring. 'For all we know, there's an estate agent hammering a For Sale sign in the garden right now!'

'I thought it was leased from some old man?' said Anna.

'Well in that case, they couldn't sell it, could they,' contributed Oliver helpfully.

Len rolled his eyes to the ceiling. 'Could I get a word in while you Philadelphia lawyers mull over the legalities? They're sitting out there waiting for this tea!'

'Knickers to their tea,' said Kate.

'Is this some sort of Mid-Life Crisis, or what? For heaven's sake Kate, it's only a button on a pair of shorts!'

If only it was, thought Kate, deliberately unbuttoning the detested navy blue overall which so successfully conveyed the intended image of sober, mature responsibility, to reveal the normally hidden vibrant love of light and colour beneath; a floaty Indian skirt in vivid blue with gold threads running through, and a low-cut delicately embroidered gypsy blouse.

'That's not worthy of you.' Her voice was deadly quiet as she hung the overall behind the door. 'You sound more like Dud, patronising me. And no. I'm not having a Mid-Life Crisis.' The elastic band was pulled off, the hair shaken free. 'This isn't even Phase One of a Mid-Life Crisis, Len. When I'm good and ready to have a Mid-Life Crisis, I'll have a Mid-Life Crisis *nobody's* going to forget!'

The back door slammed behind her. Oliver's glance at Anna conveyed quite plainly that in his view they'd both ended up working in a loony-bin.

Major Pratt sat exchanging pleasantries with his acolytes in the Reception Area.

'Taking their time with this tea, aren't they. While we're waiting, a quick reminder - have you all remembered to claim your travelling expenses?'

There was a murmur of assent. It seemed everyone had remembered.

'Nobody overlooked claiming expenses? Oh good. By the way, how's Albert? Anyone heard?' He rubbed his chin as a thought occurred to him. 'Did we send him a Get Well card?'

Brian flicked through the Minutes of the Last Meeting, which he always carried around with him for reference.

'There's nothing mentioned here...'

'Do you think we should send one now, darling?' suggested Eloise's thoroughbred English tones, 'So we can be sure?'

'Bit wasteful if he's already been sent one,' objected Brian.

'But supposing he hasn't?' stammered Babs, concern for Albert overriding her nervousness at speaking in the presence of such illustrious superiors.

'Well surely the simplest thing,' said Major Pratt crisply, to indicate he hadn't intended a brief, courteous enquiry to end up dominating the conversation to the exclusion of all else. They'd be starting the Inspection as soon as they'd had the obligatory cup of tea (when it finally arrived. What on earth were they *doing* in that damn kitchen?) and he wanted to emphasise the sort of thing they should be on the look-out for. 'Would be to just send another one. Now, one or two points I'd like to -'

'But if he gets two, he might wonder why, and he might think we've sent a second one because we can't remember whether we've sent one or not, so we're sending another just to make sure!' Babs couldn't bear the thought of Albert suspecting that nobody remembered whether they'd sent him a Get-Well card.

'Well we are, Babs!'

There was a loud belch. Mona massaged her solar plexus. 'Pardon.'

Eloise glanced discreetly downwards. One tried to overlook the coarseness and vulgarity, but having been educated at a convent where it was considered an affront to modesty to even cross one's legs, so that even now she invariably sat with one elegant ankle positioned behind the other, she wished Mona would alter that unladylike mode of sitting with her legs wide apart, so that the view from the opposite group of chairs was startling, to say the least.

'Surely it's better to send two cards than none at all, Babs?' she coaxed gently.

Major Pratt tutted. Albert's Get-Well card had occupied more than enough time already. 'You're right, darling. Best just send another one, then we can leave the subject. D'you think you could attend to that for us, Babs? Choose a suitable one? Now, one or two points -'

'What sort of card would you suggest?' blinked Babs. 'A humorous one?'

'*No*. Not for haemorrhoids... Now, I want to -'

'We'll leave the choice to you, Babs,' murmured Eloise with an encouraging smile.

'Don't forget to fill a form in to claim the amount back,' added Major Pratt, a touch of impatience creeping into his voice. 'Now, one or two points I -'

'How much should I spend?' wondered Babs nervously.

'What?' barked Major Pratt, impatience turning to irritability.

'Erm, on the card,' floundered Babs. 'Should I go up to a pound, or stick to... erm, around fifty pence?'

'What do you think, darling?' Major Pratt hadn't a clue how much Get-Well cards cost.

'Well quite frankly, where on earth would one *get* a card for fifty pee?' pondered Eloise. 'I think up to two pounds, darling.'

'You can get nice ones for seventy-five pence on the market,' contributed Dud.

'Oh good lord, just get a suitable one, not too expensive!' snapped Major Pratt testily. Good heavens, he was as concerned as anyone else about Albert's haemorrhoids, but they'd be discussing Get-Well cards all night if he didn't chivvy things along. And that was another thing. He glared at the kitchen door. 'And where's this tea? What on earth are they *doing* in that damn kitchen?'

Len, calling down the wrath of heaven on Dud's shorts as he plonked the teapot on the tray, broke off as Major Pratt's head appeared around the door.

'Everything A-OK, Len?'

'Yes. Fine. Just bringing the tea now.'

Major Pratt glanced at Anna and Oliver, who stared silently back. As soon as the door closed Anna turned on Len.

'What did you tell him everything's fine for? It couldn't be much worse, could it. Kate's just walked out! Am I supposed to cope with seventy five three-course meals on my own? Because if I am, I'll be joining her!'

'And I'll be following behind,' nodded Oliver.

Len added teaspoons to the tray. 'I think it's time we did a bit of straight talking. First of all, Kate hasn't walked out - '

'Oh. You mean we dreamed all that?' challenged Anna. Slumming it in a Youth Hostel for a few months was one thing; finding herself in a nuthouse another altogether.

'- She just needs a bit of space for a few minutes, that's all.' Len's voice was quiet. 'It's touch and go whether or not they close us at the end of this year. She's frightened and worried.'

There was an uncomfortable silence. He could almost hear Anna's thoughts: More fool you. Slave-labour for twenty four years, then end up destitute and about as highly thought of as a container of nuclear waste.

Again Major Pratt's head craned round the door.

'Is there some problem with this tea, Len?'

'Just coming now,' Len assured him, tipping digestive biscuits onto a plate. 'And while we're at it,' he went on as the door was (yet again) closed none too quietly, 'I know you're only here for the summer, but as long as you *are* here, let's start showing a bit of loyalty to each other. You keep your traps shut about Kate and give us some support tonight, and we'll do the same for you if you need it, during the season. Because sooner or later you will. If you intend staying?' He looked at them. Might as well bring things to a head, here and now.

Anna gave a languid shrug. After a moment, Oliver nodded.

24

'Well, that's cleared the air a bit. Right. Take the tea out, Anna.' He added some ginger buns from a plastic container. 'They can have these buns you put too much ginger in, as well.'

'That'll put them in a good mood for the Inspection, won't it. What are they like anyway, these VIPs?'

Len hesitated. 'Er... on second thoughts, not you. Oliver can take it. Dud's got a horrible habit - well, he's got quite a few - but every year he gets an obsession about one of the female staff somewhere and he's never off the doorstep. We don't want him fancying you, and dumping himself on us every weekend.'

'What if he fancies me?' said Oliver.

'Don't be silly.' Len opened the door, propelled him into the Reception Area, and nodded towards the Inspection Committee. 'Over there, sitting in their coven round the coffee table.'

The door closed behind him.

'And don't forget,' Len hissed through the crack, 'No blabbing about what's happened in here.' He affected a self-righteous whine. '"*Kate's thrown a menopausal tantrum and walked out!*"' Let's start again, shall we. If we want to survive the summer, let's at least try to get on, stick together in a tightly knit bunch. Because what you both still have to realise is, we're up against the tightest bunch of nits you're ever likely to meet!'

'Oh you're here, are you?' remarked Dud as Oliver lurched unsteadily towards them. 'Thought you must have all gone to India to pick it!'

The group eyed the refreshment tray without enthusiasm.

'Now you must be Oliver?' guessed Major Pratt, as Oliver positioned cups on the coffee table.

'Yes, that's right.'

'Where's Kate? Busy, is she?'

'Er... Yes, that's right.'

'Well, introductions, I think. Of course we're not all here -'

'No, so I see,' Oliver couldn't resist saying.

Major Pratt shot him a long look. 'Because this is an Inspection, as opposed to a full Committee Meeting,' he continued smoothly, and motioned in turn to his companions. 'My wife Eloise... young Babs... Wilf, doesn't say a lot, but misses nothing...' Oliver glanced at the hooded, lifeless eyes, and gulped. '...Brian, as per the badge - well done, Brian, we should all follow your example, I'll bring it up at the next Committee Meeting... Dud... His friend, Mona, will be back in a moment, she's just gone to the, er... She isn't actually on the Committee, she's just, you know, come with him for the weekend. And I'm the Chairman for my sins. Major Pratt.'

'How d'you do?' muttered Oliver.

'Believe you've got a bit-of-all-right working here this year?' probed Dud.

'Yes, that's right.'

'Anna, is it? Bit of an artist, like?'

'Yes, that's right.'

'Yer fornicating imp-outa-hell, yer!' Mona, scattering terrified hostellers right and left, bore downstairs towards the stunned assembly, jabbing a sausage-like finger in Dud's direction. 'Didn't I warn yer? DIDN'T I BLOODY WARN YER? You start that lark again with yer wandering eyes *an' I'll pulverise the crown jewels on yer to giblets!'*

Brian's instinctive giggle tailed off as he realised she wasn't joking, and Major Pratt shot a pained glance at his wife. It was going to be one of those evenings, was it.

'I... all I said was... I just...' squirmed Dud.

Eloise immediately took the situation in hand, turning to Major Pratt with a gracious smile.

'Darling, I was thinking. You know I said I must pop back down to the shops - the Gallery, actually, which is open until seven o'clock?'

Major Pratt suppressed the puzzled contradiction he was about to voice with a politely-interested grunt.

'Well, *would* you mind terribly if we ladies abandoned you, and whizzed down there now? We'd be back in time for the meal. Poor Mona obviously needs to unwind, don't you dear, and we could help Babs choose Albert's card... No, I insist, Mona, you *must* come with us. You have such... *exuberant* taste, I'm sure that between us we'll find the very thing. And we can have a coffee. They do the most heavenly chocolate cake...'

Mona surveyed the refreshments on offer here. Most Youth Hostel wives competed to outdo each other with trolleys crammed full of dainty morsels; the best this bloody lot could manage were a plate of shop-bought biscuits and a batch of God-knew-what that had obviously gone wrong.

And Major Pratt belatedly took his cue.

'Of course, darling. Don't forget the receipt to claim back expenses,' he reminded them with a benevolent smile.

'After all,' Eloise nodded reassuringly at Babs' nonplussed expression as she guided her towards the front door with Mona, 'I'm sure the menfolk will winkle out anything that needs attention. We don't *all* need to traipse round searching out missing washroom plugs and things, do we?'

They were gone.

Major Pratt looked up at Oliver, then pointedly at the teapot and cups. Oliver stood with aggravating incomprehension.

'Well, I'd better get back,' he said as the pause lengthened, helped himself to a digestive, and dawdled back to the kitchen.

'Not very bright, is he,' remarked Dud when the door closed. 'Didn't seem able to say anything except, "Yes, that's right".'

Wilf nodded disapprovingly.

'Didn't even pour the tea!' complained Brian.

'That was Dumb Insolence, Brian,' said Major Pratt grimly. 'I never tolerated it in the Army, and I've no intention of tolerating it now. And he was quite secretive - furtive, almost. As if he'd got something to hide. Especially when Kate's name was mentioned... Did you see the way he kept edging towards the kitchen?'

Wilf nodded suspiciously.

'One would almost think there was something he didn't want us to know about. Never mind. Whatever it is, we'll dig it out during the Inspection. And as we all know, Beckside is due a particularly thorough one this time...'

Oliver flopped onto a kitchen chair and exhaled loudly.

'What's the matter, Oliver?' grinned Len. 'Smitten by the lovely Mona? I bet you didn't realise there were perks of the job like meeting busty blondes in mini-skirts, did you?'

'I didn't realise I'd meet the weirdest collection of spooks outside the Addams Family,' admitted Oliver with feeling.

'I suspect that by the time September comes,' murmured Anna, 'The Addams Family might seem boringly sane and normal.'

'Long as that, huh?' Len raised a wry eyebrow. 'I hadn't realised you're such an optimist!'

A hearty female in a tweed skirt, blouse fastened at the neck with a Cairngorm brooch, ankles hanging over stout brogues, smiled at the foursome huddled round the refreshment tray.

'This is what I like to see. New friends, companionship, hikers' tales at the end of the day... That's what hostelling's all about!'

'How true,' agreed Major Pratt gallantly. 'Would you care to join us?'

'Well, why not. Thank you.'

She lowered her broad haunches into a sagging easy chair. Major Pratt poured her a cup of tea.

'What a delightful old building this is,' she enthused, looking round at the panelled walls and wide staircase. 'I wonder what it was like to live here when it was a private residence? Just imagine, children might have sung carols around a Christmas tree in this very spot!'

'Ah, yes. Gracious times. Although latterly it belonged to an old lady who lived on her own for years. Almost a recluse,' Major Pratt confided. 'When she died she left it to a gentleman in Glasgow. He leases it to us.'

'We're on The Committee, that's how we're in the know,' added Dud importantly, selecting the largest bun on the plate.

'Oh really? How interesting. You obviously know a lot about the building then?'

'Yep. We're here to inspect it, love.' Dud took a large bite into the bun and burst into a fit of coughing, spraying her with cake crumbs. 'Hell's teeth! Lot of ginger in these cakes, isn't there!'

'And what do you inspect, exactly?' She flicked surreptitiously at her skirt as Dud, eyes streaming, gulped for breath.

'Oh, we, you know, make sure the place is up to scratch, all the equipment in good working order, that sort of thing.' Major Pratt selected a bun, sniffed at it, frowned, and returned it to the plate.

'Ah, you mean like the tea towels. I noticed a girl bringing them off the clothesline as I came in. I wondered if it was the light, they all looked a bit dingy. As though she hadn't done a very thorough job washing them.'

'Make a note would you, Dud. Tea towels - a bit dingy. Not washed properly. Did you notice them, Wilf?'

Wilf nodded solemnly.

'Because that's the sort of thing we're after. And -'

'Tch! Pen's run out!' Dud pressed on the point until it tore a hole in the paper. Wilf passed him a ballpoint.

'I always like to iron mine. They look so much fresher, don't they,' went on the lady pleasantly.

'Tch! Ink's leaking in this one!' grumbled Dud, wiping an inky smear over the length of one page.

She handed him an irreplaceable heirloom Conway Stewart fountain pen. 'Would you like to use mine? No, really; I'll get it back later, when you've finished.'

'How kind,' murmured Major Pratt. 'Have you got that, Dud? Suggestion: tea towels would look fresher all nicely ironed.'

'Must be fascinating, running a Youth Hostel, I always think,' expounded their guest, sipping at her tea. 'Meeting people from all over the world and chatting to them... Do the Wardens actually get paid, or do they have a proper job during the day?'

The phone rang in The Office. Len appeared from the kitchen, a bunch of keys in his hand.

'Here's Len now, you can ask him yourself. You get paid as well, don't you Len!' quipped Major Pratt jovially.

'Do you really? What pleasant lives some people lead, free from all stress and worries,' she burbled. 'Sailing along, not a care in the world, and getting paid as well!'

'Um,' said Len.

'And how marvellous, living in a beautiful old house like this.' She leaned forward with polite curiosity. 'Tell me, what are your private parts like?'

'Um...'

'Do you inspect the Warden's private quarters while you're here?' she enquired earnestly of Major Pratt.

'Not unless they've got something wrong with them, that they want to show us. Any, you know, problems.'

'Problems?' She gave a neighing laugh and eyed Len archly. '*You* don't know the meaning of the word!'

Len selected a key from the bunch and opened The Office door. 'Sorry, I must answer the phone.'

It stopped ringing.

'They even get their food provided, don't you Len,' went on Major Pratt as Len emerged and locked the door again. 'Last time I was here they were all sitting eating one of those pies with an egg in it.'

Beat that for considerate employers; we actually eat. 'Somebody'd left it behind, we were using it up,' explained Len aloud.

'Yes. Well, Len, I suppose we'd better make a start. Justify our expense accounts, what.' Major Pratt finished his tea. 'We won't wait for the womenfolk, you know what they're like when they get to the shops. Eloise's been looking forward to this Inspection for weeks, she loves being let loose in this village. Especially the Gallery.' He stood up, inclining his head to the lady. 'Will you excuse us?'

'Yes, of course,' she said, replacing her cup on the tray. 'I mustn't hold you up! I'll take the tray back to the kitchen!'

'No, no, don't you bother,' waved Major Pratt. 'Kate'll get it. She enjoys pottering round doing her little tasks, doesn't she Len? Loves fussing over us all!'

'Um,' said Len.

The lady hiker watched admiringly as the Inspection Committee drifted towards the stairs.

'Aren't they *wonderful*,' she breathed, eyes shining like a besotted teenager in the presence of pop idols.

'Um,' grunted Len again, mopping up slopped tea, spilt sugar, crumbs, and a half-eaten ginger bun on the floor.

It was nearly 7.15PM.

Kate still hadn't returned. The first course had been served, the soup pan, as tradition demanded, left in the dining room for those who wanted second helpings, and the main course ready to go into the Dining Room, when Oliver sidled into the kitchen clutching a handful of papers.

'Where've you been?' snapped Len. 'It doesn't take all night to tell someone we'll ring them back soon as the meal's served!'

'There were some old bits of paper lying around in the Reception Area, so I stopped to tidy up a bit, like you said, with the Inspectors being here. I thought they were rubbish - I was going to throw them in the bin - then I noticed what they were.'

'Well, what are they?' asked Anna, eyeing with distaste the crumpled, dirty pages, obviously torn from a poor quality exercise book and covered in a riot of scribble, crossings out, ink blots, and smears of ballpoint ink.

'The notes from the Inspection.'

The kitchen went very quiet.

Oliver dropped a fountain pen and two ballpoints on the table. 'These were with them.'

Anna looked at Len. 'We're not supposed to see these notes, are we?' Then, in the next breath: 'What've they put?'

'Give us them here!' said Len shortly.

Oliver obediently handed him the papers. Len scanned through them and looked up, frowning. 'What's all this about the Welcome sign vandalised by obscene graffiti?'

Anna craned round his shoulder, quoting aloud, '"Tea towels look as though they haven't been washed properly. Suggestion, underlined. They would look much fresher all nicely ironed." IRONED??!! *If you think I'm -*'

The door swung open. All three instinctively turned to face the intruder.

Oliver froze as he saw Dud grinning on the threshold; Anna closed her eyes. When she opened them, the papers had been crumpled into a ball behind Len's back.

'Hi gang! Didn't have time to pop in earlier, but I've just realised I've lost all my notes and Wilf's biro, and some old bird's fountain pen!' Dud bumbled amiably into the room, adjusting his glasses and adding another crop of fingermarks to the lenses. 'Probably left them in the Men's Lavs or somewhere, so I thought, I'll get them between courses... Where's Kate? Run off with the fishman? Ha!'

All three stared at him wordlessly.

'Good excuse for a quick shufti at the bint as well, Len,' he continued in an audible aside, his eyes moving down the full length of Anna, taking in the butcher's apron tied twice round her waist, denims, bare feet in Scholls (she'd finally changed the strappy sandals), and back up to her expressionless face.

Len, taking full advantage of this concentrated scrutiny, slid to the table and quietly scooped the pens into his pocket.

'Oh, yes, very nice. *Very* nice. I approve. Mind you, I prefer them with a bit more up front, myself, and a nice low-cut dress - I like 'em to know who wears the trousers, Len - but if you play your cards right, Anna is it, I might just take you down the pub with us later!'

The atmosphere, predictably enough, plummeted from freezing to Polar, and Len, for once, found himself a powerless bystander. Curiosity battled with self-preservation; the unmissable spectacle of Anna's reaction to this glamorous invitation set against the equally compelling urge to hustle Dud from the kitchen before he discovered his missing notes clutched behind Len's back.

Anna, however, said nothing. Or at least, nothing verbally. Her body language said it all as she gave Dud a stare every bit as insolent as his own, eyeing him in turn from head to foot and taking in every detail - *every* detail, thought Len, amused - then turning away in contempt, clearly signalling that the adversary wasn't even worthy of retaliation.

'Oh, playing hard to get, eh?' winked Dud archly.

Again there was silence. It began to dawn on Dud that they were looking at him a little oddly. What was the matter with them all? You'd think they'd been struck dumb! He began to wonder what he'd accidentally stumbled on here. Major Pratt was right, this lot were definitely up to something. And it concerned Kate. Oliver had gone all shifty when he brought the tea out, when Kate was mentioned...

'So where is Kate then?' He deliberately targeted Oliver, who gulped.

'She's just popped out for - er... for - for a minute.'

Popped out for a minute? With the main course waiting to be served? Had she been at the sherry bottle? Was she lying drunk on the larder floor? There was something decidedly fishy going on here, and Dud intended to find out exactly what it was.

'Where to?'

'She's just -' began Len.

'I'm here, Dud.' Kate materialised in the doorway, fastening her overall. Her voice was subdued.

'Oh, hi, Kate! Looking more ravishing than ever,' gurgled Dud roguishly. 'Must be that overall, you know the effect it has on me. Have this woman bathed, perfumed, and taken to my tent! No, I thought maybe you'd gone gathering mushrooms for the soup - I was just going to ask Len if you knew the difference between mushrooms and toadstools! Ha!'

Len and Kate glanced at each other. It lasted a second, it said a lifetime, and it left Oliver, who intercepted it, feeling like some crass tourist trying to analyse the Mona Lisa's smile.

'We're just about to serve the main course, Dud,' hinted Len.

'You can serve *her* up as the main course any time!' Dud simpered flirtatiously at Anna, who ignored him. 'Well, better find my notes, or my name will be mud, because I'm the only note-taker and we haven't time to go round again. We're going down the pub as soon as we've finished the meal. It's Major Pratt's birthday. I've organised a kissogram girl as a surprise!'

He headed for the door, caught his sleeve on the handle, disentangled himself, and vanished.

'That means she'll turn up next Saturday and wonder why there's nobody there, probably,' said Len, and looked at Kate. 'You OK, love?'

'Was he real?' gasped Anna.

'He's real all right. You want to try sniffing him close up. Or rather, you don't,' said Oliver. 'Unless BO and stale cigarette smoke turn you on?'

'And he's... *he's* on The Committee? He's one of these people you call the high-ups?' said Anna incredulously.

'Yes,' confirmed Len.

'And HE'S been inspecting US? That...?' Her face was a mask of disbelief and revulsion.

'Oh, you do actually get stuck for words sometimes then?' commented Len wryly, and turned back to Kate. 'She's not the only one to be knocked speechless. Look at this.' He handed her the notes. 'No, on second thoughts perhaps you better hadn't. You might turn right round and walk out again.'

'What are they?' Kate frowned at the assortment of papers.

'The notes from the Inspection. Oliver found them, lying round in the Reception Area. Beyond belief, isn't it.'

'Nothing's beyond belief to me after the last forty five minutes.'

'Why? What happened? Where've you been?'

Kate stared unseeingly at the papers, feeling utterly foolish and stupid, aware they were watching her, awaiting a logical, reasonable explanation for an illogical, unreasonable act. Len looked even more harassed than usual; the other two looked unsure what to make of her at all.

If she could just be on her own with Len... If they could escape for five minutes, go up to the flat, just the two of them, and he'd put his arms around her, and she could pour it all out, and he'd stroke her hair and his very presence would make

33

everything all right... She never felt foolish or ridiculous with Len. They'd been through too much together. But it was different trying to explain to Anna and Oliver. She knew they already thought of Len and herself as neurotic figures of ridicule - and she'd just proved them right.

After all, she was forty five years old. She was supposed to be wise, mature, responsible; the one in control, the one who stayed dependable and dignified whatever the circumstances, the one who was expected to shrug off the pain of failure, wasted years, disillusionment, and mask with a facade of saintly patience her hurt and resentment at seeing Len constantly belittled, undervalued, and unappreciated.

'I - I walked down to the road and started hitching. I decided I'd get in the first lorry that stopped.'

Anna and Oliver glanced at each other. They'd ended up in a nuthouse all right.

Len took her hand. 'I hadn't realised things were that bad, love.'

'Oh, it gets worse,' Kate assured him. 'I'll give you three guesses who stopped.'

'Lord Lucan, going the other way?' suggested Oliver politely.

'Tom Cruise?' Anna was starting to find the situation amusing. It wasn't her problem if seventy five people sat drumming their fingers in the Dining Room while the staff conducted guessing games in the kitchen. 'No, couldn't be him. You wouldn't be still here.'

'Eloise, knowing our luck,' muttered Len. 'Coming out of the Gallery laden with trinkets just in time to see you - in that low-cut gypsy get-up of all things - thumbing lorry drivers.'

Kate shook her head. 'The fish man, on his way home.'

'What did he say when he saw you hitching a lift?' grinned Anna.

'He didn't get the chance to say anything. Before he realised what was happening I'd leapt in beside him and exploded about, well, er, everything. I think he was waiting for my fingers to close round his windpipe any second. So -'

'So he drove you straight round to the nick?' nodded Oliver.

'- So -' She glanced at Len. That look flashed between them again, noticed Oliver. 'He's collecting the washing machine tomorrow. And he was so apologetic about it suddenly conking out mid-cycle and the instrument panel mysteriously dropping off, he's bringing us a free salmon as well. As well as a full refund, I mean. In cash; he'd already banked the cheque.' She reached into her overall, produced a wad of notes from her gypsy blouse, and waved them seductively at Len.

'Well, get one that works next time,' said Anna. 'Preferably one that does its own ironing as well. Have you seen what they've written about the tea towels?'

Kate skimmed through the papers. The smile vanished.

'Mm. Shame he's lost his notes, isn't it. I think we ought to help him out a bit.'

'Eh?' said Len.

'Think about it.' She flicked over a page. 'It's a chance in a lifetime. He'd never admit to the others that he's mislaid his notes, and Corporal Clott and his KGB are all too busy searching out faults to notice what he's put. And he's the last one to remember what he's written anyway; hc'd never notice an odd item missing here and there, and a slightly different one in its place...'

There was silence. All four looked at each other speculatively.

Anna picked up the fountain pen and examined it. 'This is obviously the pen that's been used, the same turquoise ink,' she said tentatively. 'The blots would be no problem. Or this hole in the paper. Or the smears made by the ballpoint.' She looked at Len. 'I'll have a go at it if you like. It's pretty easy, characterless writing to copy....'

'It's the same cheapo exercise-book paper as the Menu Book,' encouraged Oliver.

'And I can guarantee he hasn't cracked on to Major Pratt yet that he's left that woman's pen lying around,' added Kate.

'And the last people on earth he'd suspect of daring - let alone having sufficient intelligence - to substitute a Revised Edition while they're down at the pub,' considered Len slowly, 'Would be the doltish, moronic paid staff...'

All four looked at each other, each wondering whether the others were just being flippant or were actually serious. The whole thing was preposterous, too far fetched to be true. And yet... and yet that in itself was the very reason it might actually work!

Kate got out the Menu Book from the kitchen table drawer,

tore out a few pages, and handed them to Anna. 'Here, Picasso. Get busy as soon as we've served the meal.'

'Don't be silly!' Len made a token blustering protest. 'I wasn't being serious!'

'I was,' said Anna calmly.

Len's stance on moral high ground faltered to a half-hearted quibble. 'Kate! What if these two get drunk at the Assistants' Convention and blab it all out?'

'They couldn't very well, could they. They'd be as guilty as we are.' Kate's smile returned. 'In fact, it's one thing all four of us would have in common.'

'Yeh,' agreed Len caustically. 'That'd look good on the Harmonious Staff Relations Course assessment form, wouldn't it. Question: What do you feel you have in common with your staff? Answer: We're all a bunch of crooks and felons!'

'In fact maybe we've got enough common ground to actually get us all through the summer?' went on Kate, ignoring him. 'What d'you reckon?'

Anna gave one of her expressive shrugs. She'd already decided to survive the season by fair means or foul, but it was so much less effort to ensure Life did as it was told with a beguiling smile than a blazing row. And if the fair means didn't work out, there was always the foul. She was well capable of handling Kate and Len if need be. Especially armed with this useful snippet of knowledge, should any gentle manipulation be required to make sure life at Beckside fitted in with her personal requirements. Such as, time off as and when she wished, that sort of thing.

Oliver also nodded. The prospect didn't fill him with enthusiasm, but the alternative was even more bleak. He'd give it a couple of weeks anyway (say until 'A' level exam time was safely past), and see what happened when the forgery was discovered, as it was bound to be. Should be interesting, being a witness at Len's Industrial Tribunal... In fact, *he* would have the power, if he chose to exercise it, of deciding if and when it *would* be discovered! Hmm. With this explosive arsenal held over Len's head, life at Beckside could become rather pleasant. Amusing, even. There was already an accumulating tally of scores to be settled.

And he could always ring his mother when he got bored with

the whole thing. He even had the ideal excuse for leaving: "I discovered that Len and Kate were nothing but criminals," he'd explain virtuously. "They actually bullied me into a conspiracy to forge an Inspection Report, against my will!"

So yes. For now, he'd play along with the old pals act.

In the Dining Room, as they waited for the main course to appear, Eloise passed Albert's Get-Well card around the table for everyone to sign, and Major Pratt opened the additional token birthday present his wife had bought on impulse at the Gallery - an expertly painted watercolour of the Langdale Pikes by Anna Somebody-or-Other.

'Oh, it's beautiful,' gushed Babs.

'Yes, it'll co-ordinate rather well with the new suite in the conservatory,' agreed Eloise, pleased, as she entered her own neat, precise signature under the card's flowery verse.

Mona looked at the painting critically. It was all right in its way, she supposed, although if Lady Snotty-Britches had taken the trouble to ask, she could have told her where you could buy a set of two pictures for £2.99: Tarn Hows, *and* Derwentwater from Ashness Bridge. They didn't have posh frames like this rip-off effort, but what was wrong with white plastic ones? Anyone daft enough to pay ninety bloody quid in that la-di-dah Gallery had more money than sense, and deserved all they -

'Tch!' Major Pratt, having signed Albert's card with an imposing flourish and passed it on to Brian, glared impatiently towards the kitchen. '*Another* infernal delay! Where's the Main Course? What on earth are they *doing* in that damn kitchen?'

Kate was having her nightly soak in the old discoloured enamel bath, listening as The Corries sang the haunting 'Flodigarry' on an ingenious stereo system Len had rigged up from the sitting room next door, and staring out of the open window at the night sky. They never bothered to draw the curtains, except during the winter months to eliminate some of the draughts; nobody could see into dormer windows three floors up except the house martins that swooped and dived and chattered as they fed their young.

It had its good points, living up here in their eyrie in the old servants' quarters. But it had its drawbacks too, especially when the boys had been small, and they and their paraphernalia had to be lugged up and down three flights of stairs every time they went in or out, even into the garden. And it was very cramped, especially here in the bathroom where you had to flatten yourself against the wall in order to close the door.

"One day," Kate had vowed, years ago, "When our ship comes in -" (it had been in the days when people still said that) "I'm going to have a bathroom like a baronial hall!"

Some chance of that now. They'd be lucky to have a bathroom at all soon. Even sooner if The Committee ever sniffed out today's nefarious plot. She must have been mad to have suggested such lunacy. It had been reaction to the stress of the Inspection, they'd explained to Anna and Oliver. (Or else we're going through a phase. Guilty as charged, Your Honour, but we've had a deprived adulthood you see, m'lud.)

The forgery was still on the kitchen table, where Anna had left it. It was good; in fact it was faultless. But Dud wouldn't - couldn't - be *that* gullible, and they couldn't risk involving Anna and Oliver in instantly-dismissible Industrial Misconduct.

And Len, despite the uneasy truce, still didn't quite trust either of them. Even if direct blackmail seemed extreme, it could be unwittingly blurted out in an unguarded moment, and within days the gossip circuit would be abuzz with rumours, and some sanctimonious pillar of righteousness would see it as their bounden duty to pass it on to The Committee. So they'd told Anna and Oliver to regard the whole thing as a joke, a laugh, a bit of fun to lighten tension, ease the day's stress, and hopefully improve working relationships. The authentic notes lay in The Office, to be handed over in the morning.

The water was cooling. She reached forward to add more hot water, catching her hand on the chip in the porcelain inset in the tap where Tony had dropped his SAS dinghy on his sixth birthday.

She and Len were very proud of their sons, and had a good relationship with both of them. Tony was in the Army, half way through a tour of duty in Northern Ireland. Kate's blood ran cold at the thought of her twenty year old son driving armoured vehicles around Belfast and swarming up and down ropes dangling from helicopters over Crossmaglen. Not that she knew much about it - he kept pretty cagey about the whole thing, which she found even more frightening. And Mike; Mike had turned out to be the brains of the family (heaven only knew where he got them from), got a good Degree in Civil Engineering, and was currently working nights in a factory until he found a job in his chosen field.

Len came in and perched on the rim of the bath, yawning. She smiled lazily up at him. The water looked inviting; Kate looked inviting. One thing about the ancient, chipped enamel bath: you could fit two adults in. Only just, but that was enough. He undressed and lowered himself into the water.

It had been a long, exhausting day.

The fragrant steam from Kate's aromatherapy oil was taking effect.

As the tension seeped slowly from Len's weary limbs, footsteps crunched along the drive. A drunken cackle floated up from outside the front door, where Dud was obviously fumbling with the spare key Len had lent them. They heard a clink as it dropped on the step.

'Blast! It's bounced into the bushes!'

'Shh!' hissed Major Pratt.

'S'all right,' Dud assured him in a clearly audible aside. 'Nobody'll hear us. Good job the girlies got tired and came back early, wasn't it? They'll be dead to the world by now!'

'We'll find it in the morning,' decided Major Pratt. 'Better attract Len's attention. He'll let us in. Look, there's a light on in their bathroom. Pass me a pebble.'

'I'll do it!' volunteered Dud, and Kate and Len instinctively braced themselves for a rock to hurtle through the window.

'No, on second thoughts, we'll try calling first... *Len!*'

'LEN!' Dud joined in enthusiastically. There was another drunken giggle, and a loud burp. 'Ooh, I fancy some tea and a big plate of chips,' his carefree voice informed the night as Len climbed out of the bath with murder in his eye.

Later, when he thought about it, Len pinpointed that precise moment as the one when he knew he'd present Dud with the fraudulent set of notes after all.

A relentless drum percussion solo continued on the front door as he dripped downstairs, a towel tied round his waist. Dud's pasty face grinned at him as the door swung open.

'Get the kettle on, Len!' he greeted, rubbing his hands. 'And the chip fryer! I'm in the mood to make a night of it! Anna still up? Wouldn't mind doing an Inspection on *her*, check all the equipment's in good working order!'

'Well, Brian and Wilf and I will wish you two night owls adieu,' said Major Pratt as Len re-locked the front door. 'They take so much out of one, these Inspections. Poor Eloise was absolutely exhausted!'

Len bit back the obvious comment. It would achieve nothing to remind Major Pratt that Eloise had been enjoying chocolate cake, coffee, and selecting which painting to purchase while the Inspection was taking place.

Dud fidgeted restlessly until the other three departed upstairs. When they were safely out of earshot, he murmured: 'By the way, Len old chum, I don't suppose the Inspection notes turned up anywhere, did they?'

'As a matter of fact,' said Len, unlocking the kitchen door. 'They did. And a Conway Stewart fountain pen and two ballpoints as well.'

'Oh, great,' nodded Dud in relief as he saw the notes on the table, and dropped his voice to a confidential, man-to-man whisper. 'No need to actually mention this to anyone, is there?'

'Don't worry. I won't tell a soul except Kate. And I can promise you nobody will ever hear a word about it from her.'

Dud cleared his throat. 'Not even, er, Anna and Oliver?'

'Especially not Anna and Oliver.' Len's face was an expressionless mask as he watched Dud pick up the forged notes. 'I know nothing about any lost notes. In fact as far as I'm concerned, this conversation never took place, and I'll deny all knowledge of it in the future.'

'Not a bad old stick, are you, Len!' Dud put an affectionate arm around Len's shoulder without even a glance at the papers.

Len politely shook it off again. 'Well, you know what they say. One good turn deserves another, eh?'

Before Dud quite realised how it had happened, he found himself standing outside the kitchen door as Len re-locked it.

'What about my tea? And chips? Special treatment for the Committee, Len, old pal?'

'You've just had it, Dud. Old chum. Now I've got one last little job to do while I'm downstairs, so I'll say goodnight.' Len unlocked The Office door. 'Have fun.'

Dud meandered disconsolately towards the stairs with the bogus Inspection Notes. And Len ripped up the genuine article, watching with satisfaction as the fragments, too small for Anna or Oliver to identify which version had been destroyed - no need for them to know anything about the latest change of plan in case either of them got any bright ideas later on, and anyway responsibility for this villainous skullduggery must be solely his - fluttered into the waste bin.

Whether unemployment resulted from redundancy or ignominious dismissal, other than a pittance of severance pay he had very little to lose. He could either go out with a whimper (and like Kate, his response to that was ta, but na), or all-hell-let-loose pandemonium. But there was a third possibility: this, although by far the most pivotal, wouldn't be the first time the juggernauts of power had been unknowingly outmanoeuvred by a combination of ex-seaman Liverpudlian savvy, a refusal to be floored by life's knocks, and a readiness to exploit whatever opportunities fate may provide. Like this one. So let's see if the Inspection Committee were as clever as they thought they were.

Yeah. Let's go for broke.

The building was quiet, except for its own familiar night-time creaks as the central heating system cooled. Len trudged back up the narrow stairs to the flat, locked the door, leaned his head wearily against it.

Kate appeared noiselessly behind him. Her hands reached around his waist, gently loosening the knot in the towel until it lay discarded on the floor. He turned, looked into the unusual slate-grey eyes; eyes that could soothe him, eyes that could excite him.

And as he allowed her to lead him wordlessly into the bedroom, the expression of haunted desperation that the world assumed was all Len's face ever wore was replaced by a smile so tender, so magical, that her heart felt as though it would physically melt with love and desire.

Life can deal out days of undiluted awfulness at times, but it has its compensations.

TWO: THE PERILS OF PASSION

The inevitable had happened. Dud, consumed by obsessive infatuation the moment his eyes locked on to Anna, had escaped Mona's clutches and sneaked off to Beckside the following weekend to woo his intended conquest.

To spare herself the bother of repeatedly fending off this tiresome ardour with icy (and ineffective) sarcasm, Anna responded by totally ignoring his presence whenever it was impossible to avoid him. It was obviously going to be a long and extremely tedious forty-eight hours...

The Saturday morning breakfast queue, unruly and jostling, snaked out of sight through the Dining Room door against a cacophony of screams and yells which rendered coherent thought impossible. Kate was doling out fried eggs, tomatoes, sausages and bacon, Anna served croissants, and Oliver, in a state of zombie-like automatic pilot, ladled beans onto toast as a procession of plates passed in front of him and a horde of rioting children fought to get to the front of the queue.

'I'm not allowed beans. They give me a farty arse,' a childish nasal Liverpool accent informed him above the tumult. Sleep-encrusted eyes peered through a thatch of uncombed hair; grubby hands held two plates waveringly over the breakfast selection.

'Not only that, he peed his bed last night,' sniggered the child behind him.

'Shut it, you!' The bedwetter, detailed to collect the headmaster's breakfast while the headmaster was engrossed in The Independent at his table, laid both plates on the counter and gave the informer a hefty push.

The informer stuck out a retaliatory foot and tripped the bedwetter, who stumbled. The headmaster's plate, now laden with its full complement of Traditional English Breakfast, tilted; the fried egg slithered to the edge and dangled over the rim, the sausages rolled onto the floor, the tomato splattered on top of them. The next child in the queue, who had just finished picking his nose, scooped them up, dropped them back on the plate, then dragged the egg back into position with his fingers.

Kate tried to ignore the white light pulsating behind both eyes. A full-blown migraine was very definitely swooping in for the kill unless she could avert it in its early stages, which, given the pandemonium reverberating around the building, seemed unlikely. And she couldn't allow herself to be laid low by a migraine today. Tonight's meal had to be exceptional.

'Throw it in the bin. There. *There*, right in front of you.' She refilled a clean plate. 'Give him - UGH! *Take it off!*'

Anna and Oliver looked up, startled.

'It's all right Kate, it's not real dog-dirt,' chortled Dud, positioning the offending item next to the headmaster's bacon.

The children giggled delightedly, sensing confrontation.

'Good, isn't it?' beamed Dud. 'Really lifelike!'

Kate felt sick. The thing was indeed lifelike.

'Take it off, Dud!'

Like Caligula turning to an arena of spectators looking forward to a particularly juicy slave pitted against a ravenous lion, Dud addressed the milling children. 'What d'you think, kids? Do we take it off?'

'NO!!!' came the thunderous response.

'There you are, Kate. Don't be such a spoilsport. Come on - hide it under his fried egg. Let's see what he does!'

Amidst howls of outrage from the cheated audience, Kate flipped the local novelty shop's best seller off the plate. The headmaster frowned, trying to concentrate on an article about the breakdown of law and order.

'Oh, I might have known.' Dud's tone was ruefully playful, reinforcing his role of fun-loving Good Old Uncle Dud and Kate's as Miserable Old Killjoy. 'Only a bit of fun, wasn't it?'

'YES!!!' Again came the roar, threatening this time. Their appetites had been whetted, their bloodlust roused, and *she'd* deprived them of the spectacle of Old Hairy-Conk discovering a lump of dog muck nestling in his breakfast. And the best of it was, he couldn't very well unleash a tirade of fury (or if he did, it would be doubly entertaining) when the culprit was another adult grinning at him in friendly fashion and waiting for him to appreciate the joke.

Kate looked down at the fried eggs. They stared back, row upon row of bilious, greasy yellow eyes. Some adults found this

43

kind of practical joke hilarious; she knew instinctively that the headmaster wasn't one of them, and that a vitriolic letter of complaint would be despatched to Head Office.

'But then that's the trouble with you, Kate,' diagnosed Dud. 'No sense of humour. Has she, kids?'

'NO!!!' came the bloodcurdling roar of agreement.

'And Len's just as bad. I floated it in his mug of tea this morning while he wasn't looking. I thought, hello, we'll have a bit of fun here. You should have heard him! Grumpy old devils, arn't they?'

'YES!!!' again roared the breakfast queue.

The headmaster looked up irritably. The commotion appeared to be actually increasing, if that were possible, and centred around that nitwit who'd barged in when they were distributing the children's cocoa last night and insisted on telling ghost stories, so terrifying a couple of the more homesick and nervous souls, and over-exciting the bloodthirsty majority, that it was 3AM before any of them went to sleep. He scowled around the dining room. Bachelors of his years didn't need School Governors' fatuous suggestions about "Getting to know pupils informally, outside the school environment" or "Trips to the countryside being so beneficial for inner-city children". Might be beneficial for them, but he doubted it was doing much for those bemused-looking individuals patiently waiting their turn in the queue while the rabble surged heedlessly in front of them.

And it *certainly* wasn't beneficial for him.

Had Dud stuck at being smitten with a hopeless passion for an unattainable goddess, his adoring glances and wistful sighs from afar (and they were the key words, *from afar*) would have suited Anna's purposes quite well. It never did any harm to have a well-disposed figure of authority in reserve, a useful trump card to play should the need arise; Kate and Len not toeing the line regarding time off as and when she wanted it, for example.

But that didn't mean he was free to put his ideas into practice.

'I don't want that mangy-headed spook anywhere near me when I'm sunbathing in a bikini this afternoon,' she warned, when they'd returned to the kitchen.

'No. Mona wouldn't be too happy about it, either,' agreed Len solemnly. 'She'd be getting the tar and feathers ready right now

44

if she thought you had designs on Dud's virtue.'

Anna looked at him sharply. Dud's nauseating presence was bad enough without Len treating it as a subject for humour.

Kate was massaging her temples. 'Stop teasing her, Len. What Mona'd do if she caught Dud with Anna in her bikini is the least of our worries today -'

'It might be the least of yours!'

'- It's this French group tonight that's important.'

In addition to the trauma of last weekend's Inspection, there was another trial to endure that would influence the decision on Beckside's future. The Chairman's wife's old school French penfriend, a Cordon Bleu expert of unparalleled excellence, was bringing a group of students on a tour of the UK to study different markets, and Major Pratt had suggested Beckside as an example of catering on an extremely limited budget. The inference, though unspoken, was clear: an unofficial report on the quality of Beckside's meals, according to the favourable (or otherwise) opinion of the Cordon Bleu paragon, would be taken into account as well as the official Inspection report.

'And due to your economising,' went on Kate bitterly, 'We've got hardly any frozen food until the delivery on Monday.' Her migraine was worsening despite the usual Mind Over Matter attempts to ignore it. 'Oh, my head. Let's have a quick brew. A cup of tea will sometimes stave it off if I catch it early enough...'

The phone rang. Nobody moved.

'Your turn to answer it, Anna,' Len reminded her.

'I've only just sat down, why can't Oliver go?'

'I've only just sat down as well!'

It stopped ringing. Dud's voice floated towards them.

'Now look what you've done, squabbling!' said Len, annoyed. 'Given him the excuse he wanted, to come in here!'

Almost immediately, as he'd predicted, Dud was in the kitchen leering at Anna, who, with an icy glare, got up to make the tea.

'Len, I answered the phone.' Dud managed to sound reassuring, patronising, and disapproving all at the same time. 'Some woman in the village. The postman's delivered a Hostel letter to her by mistake, she'll pass it in this evening... oh, just having a fly cup of tea, are you?'

'Kate's got a migraine,' explained Len shortly. And no wonder. Trust *Dud* to appear this weekend, with his stupid infatuation for

Anna and his even more stupid practical jokes. When he'd arrived unexpectedly last night, Len had at first feared a furious denouncement following the discovery that the Inspection notes had been swapped for a more flattering version, but it was immediately obvious that Dud hadn't even looked at the notes he was supposed to be writing up in time for next weekend's Committee Meeting. Len, however, was still on edge that he was on the premises at all. They had enough to worry about, ensuring tonight's meal would be perfect in every way, without the added threat of Dud finding it hysterical to repeat his jolly jape and adorn the French spy's dinner with what he'd plonked on the Headmaster's breakfast plate, or hide a whoopee cushion on her chair.

'Oh, go on then, since you've twisted my arm,' grinned Dud, closing the door. 'You should have migraines more often, Kate! Actually, I'm glad I've caught you, Anna, because I haven't had a chance to say, now don't be nervous of me while I'm staying here. I mean, with me being on The Committee, like. Because I'm going to just muck in and be one of you on this visit.'

'My my. The Gods descending from Mount Olympus for a token mingle with the mortals... How egalitarian,' murmured Anna.

'Well, I don't want you to feel, you know, that I'm a bit superior or anything,' continued Dud kindly.

'Don't worry. I won't.'

'That's right. Just think of me as one of the gang. I might be on The Committee, but that doesn't mean I'm above having a bit of a giggle. Kate knows that, don't you Kate.'

'Yes,' said Kate flatly.

The door opened; the postman tossed a bundle of mail to Len.

'Ah, the winged messenger in his hobnailed boots. Excuse me, you've delivered -' began Dud, but the postman was already sucked back into the melee in the Reception Area. 'Oh well, she's bringing it round this evening. Anything interesting, Len?' He eyed the letters with relish.

Len flicked through the pile, separated personal mail from Hostel business post, and distributed it. Nobody, except himself, noticed Kate's face as he handed her a large brown envelope. And to make sure nobody did, he deliberately allowed a wad of typewritten papers to spill from the Head Office envelope.

'Certainly is. Memos, Minutes of Meetings, Highlights of Minutes of Meetings...'

It worked.

'Ah. Can I take a look-see at the last Committee Minutes?' asked Dud, reaching for the assortment eagerly. 'Check Dottie got it all down... Yes. Here we are. "The Committee recorded its thanks to Dud for installing a new draining board at Wayfarers Hostel."' He leaned back with a smug smile.

'What's this next bit?' asked Len, craning over and also reading aloud. '"A minor adjustment will ensure it slopes inward to the sink instead of the opposite way, as at present."'

'Oh, they can stick a bucket underneath for the time being.' Dud was staring at the mottled pastel pink writing paper Anna discarded on the table as she unpinned a cheque from its accompanying typewritten note. The neat, precise handwriting was vaguely familiar.

'Not being nosy or anything Anna, but is that from Eloise?'

Anna, scanning the business letter, didn't even hear him.

'Aha. Yes, it is! I recognise the printed address at the top,' declared Dud triumphantly. 'Do you know her, Anna?'

'Who?' She looked up, irritated.

'The Chairman's wife. Mrs. Pratt. Eloise if you're well in, which I see you are, because that's what she's signed it.'

Anna glanced at the pink notepaper.

'Oh that. It's from some woman who bought one of my paintings from the Gallery last weekend. She left it with them to forward with the cheque. Not that it's any of your business.'

'Was that *your* painting? That watercolour Eloise bought for Major Pratt last weekend?'

Anna shrugged.

'How much did she pay for it?' asked Len curiously.

'Len!' exclaimed Kate.

'It's OK, it's no secret. There's a couple of my paintings in the window anyway, with the price marked. Ninety pounds, that particular one was. They decide the price, then deduct commission and framing expenses.'

There was a pause.

'I'll sell a few in the Hostel Shop for you, if you like,' offered Len casually. 'How much commission do they charge, exactly?'

'You're joking!'

'No I'm not.'

'What does she say in the letter?' Dud was trying to read it upside down. '"...Delighted with the painting... would love to meet you... like to invite you to our home, to see how wonderful it looks in the conservatory..."' He could hardly contain his excitement. 'Wait til I tell them who the artist is! Isn't it a fantastic coincidence?' An idea suddenly occurred to him. 'Tell you what - I'll take you there on the Honda, Anna!'

Anna's eyes flickered coldly towards him. 'Firstly, that was private correspondence you just read out. And secondly, if I intended going, which I don't, the last person I'd want to take me - *on a Honda?!* - would be you.'

Kate closed her eyes. It was one thing for Dud to fraternise with the proletariat whenever the mood took him, but quite another for the proletariat to elevate themselves to the level of a Committee member. Kate knew he'd immediately pull rank, like Royalty when one of the subjects becomes a bit too chummy. In his younger days he'd hero-worshipped The Committee (Len had once come close to losing his job when he'd jokingly called Dud a Committee Groupie), and he naturally expected others to be similarly awestruck now.

'Ah, that's because you're not one to blow your own trumpet, are you Anna.' Dud smiled tenderly at Anna, and Kate and Len gaped at each other openmouthed.

'It's because I don't want to make polite small talk with some boring old bat just because she's bought one of my paintings.'

Len, observing Dud's body language, shook his head at the helpless absurdity of the infatuated male. The more contemptuously Anna treated him, the more conciliatory - not to say grovelling - Dud became. Anyone else would be sharply informed that Eloise Pratt was *not* a boring old bat, but an elegant and accomplished dinner party hostess, renowned for her tasteful flower arrangements cascading over crisp linen napkins and Waterford crystal, who lived in opulent splendour in a secluded mansion overlooking the golf course and neighbouring clubhouse, where Dud rather fancied hobnobbing with Major Pratt and his affluent band of bon-viveurs, downing a few whiskies and sharing masculine banter after a companionable round of golf.

Of course the real reason for her reluctance, thought Dud

indulgently, was insecurity. Under that ice-cool, hard-bitten exterior she was really just a timid little fawn who needed a protective, broad-shouldered male.

'It's only natural to be a bit shy about it,' he nodded understandingly, 'With your artistic nature, sensitive and gentle.'

'Sensitive and gentle! Huh!' snorted Len.

'You and Kate wouldn't understand artistic temperament,' Dud told him witheringly, 'But that's the reason she's a bit highly-strung now and then, isn't it, Anna. It's understandable, stuck in this claustrophobic kitchen,' He leaned to one side, scratching his left buttock judiciously. 'Like some exotic butterfly kept captive when she should be a free spirit roaming wild on the fells, creative juices flowing -'

Kate looked up. 'And what about me, stuck in a claustrophobic kitchen?'

'Well it's different for you,' dismissed Dud. 'It's not as if you've got any artistic talents, is it. You've got no creative juices to flow!'

He paused. They'd somehow drifted from the subject of Anna's trip to the Pratts. Still, he wouldn't steer the conversation back right now. He'd do that tonight, over candlelit dinner.

Of course, he hadn't actually, definitely, arranged "tonight" yet, in spite of lurking in various likely ambush-points to speak to her privately. He'd given a lot of thought to what they'd do - apart from the obvious, and that might be better postponed until the second date to press home the "Soulmates Destined For Each Other Since The Beginning Of Creation" angle - and decided to take her to a newly-opened, extremely upmarket restaurant overlooking the lake. She was the sort who wouldn't dream of dining anywhere but the most expensive joint in the locality. (And, as of now, so was he.)

But the curious thing was, no matter how cunning his ruses to get her on her own, she always seemed to be either nowhere in sight or surrounded by others. Funny, that. But they could sort out the Pratt visit details later. Best let the subject drop for now.

'Anyway,' he continued instead, looking at Kate. 'You've been very quiet since the post came. You going to open that envelope? You've been staring at it long enough!'

'No.'

'Oh, that sounds interesting. Private, is it?'

49

'Yes.'

'Large plain brown envelope... Not one of those exotic underwear catalogues, is it? Go on, Kate, open it, we'll all help you choose!'

Kate stared fixedly at her envelope.

'Oh good grief, you're not going to start blubbing into your tea, are you?' derided Dud, delighted at having discomforted his victim. 'Like I said at breakfast - the trouble with you is, you've got no sense of humour!'

'And the trouble with you is, you think you have.' Len's voice was loaded with contempt.

Kate began clearing away the cups. This interlude, far from curing her migraine, was worsening it. 'Er - if you've all finished your tea...?'

'You mean, you and Len want to look through this naughty catalogue?' smirked Dud, reaching to rescue his mug. *He'd* decide when he'd finished his tea, thank you very much.

'I mean,' Kate got there first and deftly moved it out of reach. 'It's time for me to be stuck in a claustrophobic kitchen like a captive butterfly and do some work, Dud.'

And Dud, who didn't take kindly to being outmanoeuvred, or having his flirtatious banter with Anna being abruptly curtailed, mentally chalked up this insubordination to be punished later.

It was just after 10AM. The Hostel had officially closed, the unseen work begun. A thorough cleaning of the building took place every day; deliveries of bread, fresh fruit and vegetables, eggs etc were stored away, books balanced, future bookings acknowledged, monies banked, correspondence answered, and so on. There were still a few stragglers in the Reception Area, putting on boots, poring over Ordnance Survey maps and munching Kendal Mint Cake, but most hostellers had now left for the day.

Dud sidled up to The Office, where Len was attending to advance bookings.

'Just wanted a private word, Len, man to man, like. Thought I'd sound you out about tonight.' He selected a postcard from the stand, absently flicking the corners. 'You know I've got the hots for Anna, don't you?'

'Oh?' responded Len cautiously.

'Yes, so no problem about letting her have the night off, like, is there?'

Len looked at the postcard in Dud's hand, now being twisted into a cone. Anyone else would have long since understood and accepted the message Anna had so clearly spelled out.

'What about Mona?' he parried.

'What about her?'

'Well, I thought -'

'You let me worry about Mona,' winked Dud.

'I meant, she's been known to get a bit short-tempered about you casting your eye round, hasn't she. What if she were to turn up unexpectedly?'

'She won't.'

'Are you sure?'

''Course I'm sure.'

'Oh.' That meant she was probably on the next bus.

'Anyway, like I say, I'm ready for a more classy type of bint now.'

'Oh,' said Len again.

'Yeah. And I reckon Anna's up for it, secretly, under all this haughty touch-me-not act. What d'you think? Be honest, Len.'

Len pretended to consider.

'Well if you really want me to be honest,' he said eventually, in what he hoped was a tone of brotherly confidentiality, 'I'd say forget it, Dud.'

'Forget it? What d'you mean? Why?'

Len chose his words with care. 'Well, as far as Anna's concerned, men are things in white dinner jackets with theatre tickets, and -'

'You just don't listen, do you Len. I *told* you, that's the attraction. She's class. And she's got spirit as well. Did you hear her answer me back? I like that, Len. I like to tame 'em. She's not overawed by me being on The Committee, either.'

'Oh, I don't think Anna's overawed by the Committee,' Len agreed, a trifle too readily. 'But she's very, er, upmarket, and -'

'I wasn't going to invite her to the Bus Station Cafe for sausage and chips, Len!' said Dud loftily. 'No, I thought that new restaurant that's just opened down by the lake. You know, that really posh place?'

'Oh, Anna's already been there.'

'Already been? Who with?'

'One of her old boyfriends stayed here during the week. He knows the proprietor. He took her there the night it opened.'

'Oh he did, did he?'

'Yes.' Len tactfully returned to the Booking Diary.

'Hm. I can see I'll have to make sure she knows what's what. Anyway, about tonight, Len, you'll let her have the night off then?'

'If Anna wants the night off to go out with you, Dud,' Len looked up again, his face expressionless. 'I won't stand in her way.'

'That's all I wanted to know,' said Dud crisply, replacing the now mauled and filthy postcard in the rack. 'Think I'll buy one in the village, Len. They're a penny cheaper there!'

Like all old buildings, Beckside had its own familiar creaks and noises which could only be heard when it was empty. Len stood listening in The Office for a moment; the house itself always seemed at peace during its closed hours, sharing with him quiet companionship after the turmoil. The Reception Area was deserted. Oliver was sweeping the first floor dormitories, Anna hanging tea towels outside. Of Dud there was no sign, but Len knew he wouldn't be far away because it was Official Tea Break in five minutes.

He padded noiselessly to the kitchen. Kate was sitting at the table, staring into space, brown envelope in her hand.

'They rejected it then?' he guessed sympathetically.

'Yes, they rejected it. And how, they rejected it!'

'That bad, eh?'

'Worse. I feel so ashamed.'

'Ashamed? Why?'

'Because obviously I've written a load of drivel.'

'Oh come on! It's better than some of the rubbish you see on TV.'

'That's just it. It's not even *as good as* some of the rubbish you see on TV is it, because it's just been rejected!' Impatiently she blinked away tears. 'How pathetic, scribbling away for hours on end, thinking I was capable of writing a play!'

'There's nothing pathetic about having a go at something, even if it doesn't work out,' Len pointed out quietly. 'What's pathetic is not having enough guts to even try. Everybody gets rejection slips, Kate. People paper bathrooms with them when they're famous.'

'I don't want to be famous! And I don't want to have to see this on the bathroom wall every time I go in!' Kate paused as the back door banged. 'That's Anna. They'll all be in here in a minute... I couldn't bear it if they found out about this. Dud'd never stop laughing.' She mimicked his disparaging scorn: '"It's not as if *you've* got any artistic talent, is it. You've got no creative juices to flow!"'

'They won't find out. Anyway, Superstud's in no position to laugh at anyone. He'll know what rejection feels like himself very soon; he thinks he's going to wine and dine Anna at that posh new place down by the lake tonight!'

He'd hoped to make her smile. Instead, he made things worse; migraines always triggered a childish unreasonableness in Kate which she found impossible to be jollied out of.

'I wish someone would take *me* there. Just once...'

'Kate, d'you know dinner for two costs best part of a hundred pounds at that place?'

'*Yes!*'

'Even Anna said it was expensive.' He glanced towards the back door. 'I could throttle her. All the profit Beckside could make, selling her paintings in The Shop, and she wheels them down to that snobby Gallery!'

'I was thinking of the fulfilment she must get from painting them,' mused Kate wistfully.

'Fulfilment? Her? She just churns them out, no effort at all. Tourist tat, she calls them!'

Kate looked down at her hands. Churns them out. Tourist tat. No effort at all. She'd given every last ounce of effort she had, and achieved precisely nothing. Worse than nothing; at least before she started there'd been a sliver of confidence, secret optimism for a dream she'd hardly dared formulate.

The throbbing behind her right eye intensified. She'd be vomiting in a minute. When the phone conveniently rang she seized the excuse to escape from the kitchen - then blinked in amazement as she opened the door. Dud, who considered it beneath his dignity to even know where the brushes were kept, let alone how to use one, was sweeping the Reception Area.

Kate was so astounded by this spectacle, it wasn't until she'd actually lifted the receiver that she remembered she'd left her envelope in the kitchen.

Dud had timed his manoeuvre with care. Anna had to pass him to get to the kitchen for Tea Break. He swept up and down the same stretch of floor, followed by a cloud of dust that billowed up, settled, then rose once more as he progressed back and forth. She'd see him sharing the workload (just like them!), and insist he joined them for tea break. Then, as they strolled to the kitchen, he'd finalise the arrangements for tonight.

He slyly swept a cloud of dust into The Office so Kate would close the door; didn't want *her* earwigging his plans! She was embroiled in a conversation regarding the travel arrangements of a group of Norwegians who obviously didn't understand much English. Good. That'd keep her occupied for a while.

He turned and re-swept his way back to the kitchen. Better look industrious; Anna would be here any moment now.

Anna sat at the kitchen table sipping tea, engrossed in a book Len had lent her. Len, also sipping tea, had vanished behind his paper. Both looked up as Oliver stumbled in, almost choking with laughter.

'Stupid nit's just broken his foot with the brush!'

Anna and Len glanced at each other, then, in joint accord, returned to book and newspaper as the casualty limped in. Dud gaped at Anna, who, becoming aware of the scrutiny, looked up with a blank stare.

'How did you get in here?' he demanded.

The blank stare intensified. 'Through the door.'

'Which door?'

'That door,' she enunciated with insulting clarity, nodding towards the back door. 'Can I go back to my book now, or do you want to know which way I turned the handle?'

'Oh! Er, no, no, I just, er,' mumbled Dud, and sat down.

Anna returned to her book.

'How's your foot, Dud?' asked Oliver innocently.

'Yes, what was all that about?' Len looked at him curiously. 'You hit your foot or something?'

'I wasn't concentrating. I was thinking about something else.'

Dud cast a soulful look at Anna, which was wasted as she wasn't listening. 'I thought I saw a mouse so I bashed it with the brush.'

'A mouse?'

'Yes, but it was my foot. I thought my shoelace was its tail, like.'

Len shook his head, perplexed. Not much difference between a Size Eleven trainer and a mouse, is there. And the clot had probably broken the brush as well. Or, as Oliver said, his foot.

'D'you need First Aid ?'

'Depends who's going to administer it.' Dud leered at Anna, who was oblivious to the conversation.

'I'd better log it in the Accident Book,' decided Len.

'No, don't bother with that. Don't need to make a big thing of it. No, all I need is a bit of sympathy from the right person.' Again Dud tried, unsuccessfully, to attract Anna's attention. 'Oh, I can see we'll get nothing out of you once you get your nose stuck in a book, Anna.'

No response.

'Must be good,' he persevered doggedly. 'I like a good read myself. Occult, I like. How about you, Len?'

From behind the sports page, Len answered, 'No. If I want a good fright I just look at our bank balance.'

'Oh, ha!' guffawed Dud, determined to kick-start a lively tea-break conversation. Yes. An intellectual literary discussion would be the sort of thing she'd enjoy. 'So is it good then, Anna?'

No answer.

'You enjoying it?' he persisted.

Oliver dug her in the ribs. 'Dud says, are you enjoying the book?'

Anna looked up. 'I was.'

'Just finished a good one myself,' he informed her as soon as she looked down again. 'Erm, oh heck. Forgot the name. Oh, what was it now?'

Anna flicked over a page.

'So what are you reading, then?'

Silence.

'What's it about?'

Len's nerves were starting to fray. 'It's mine, actually. It's about someone who rowed across the Atlantic single-handed.'

'Oh. Takes all sorts, doesn't it,' said Dud, unimpressed.

Oliver, finding this tea-break a diverting entertainment after a tedious morning, again mischievously nudged Anna.

'Dud says, it takes all sorts, doesn't it,' he relayed innocently, nodding at the book.

'It'd take someone a lot more interesting than him,' she agreed, 'To do what this guy's done.'

'Well somebody's got to send out the Tax forms, Anna. We can't all go rowing over the Atlantic, can we.'

The silence lengthened.

'That why *you've* got the book, Len? Get a few tips for when you and Kate row down the Mersey into the sunset?' grinned Dud. 'And that might be sooner than you think. We'll know next weekend whether Beckside will close or not, won't we. Far as I recall, the Inspection report wasn't all that glowing, was it?'

'I've no idea.' Len flashed a warning glance at Oliver.

'No,' acknowledged Dud. He probably hadn't. Anyone else but Len, who through a stroke of luck (and yes, he was man enough to admit it, perhaps just a tad carelessness on his part for losing the things) had been in possession of confidential Inspection notes concerning his future, wouldn't have been able to resist a sly skim through them. But not Len. How was it Major Pratt had summed him up? "Congenitally - and more important, cerebrally - incapable of deceit, old Len." Yes, that was Len all right. A bit dim, but straight as a die. No deviousness in him. Incapable of subterfuge.

'But to come back to the book. I was on the Western Ocean run myself when I was seagoing,' Len was continuing smoothly. (If Dud hadn't known Len better, he'd have suspected it was a deliberate drawing away of the topic from the Inspection Report.) 'And anyone who's ever seen an Atlantic storm would have a lot of respect for the author. I certainly have.'

'Oh, we all know you've seen Atlantic storms,' groaned Dud, deliberately misunderstanding. He leaned confidingly towards Anna. 'Never let Len start about the sea. You can never shut him up once he gets going.' A stimulating discussion at which he could sparkle and impress her with effortless wit was one thing; this wasn't what he had in mind at all, and he for one had had enough of heroic journeys across the Atlantic in rowing boats. Come in Number Five, your time's up. 'Anyway, I'm getting a bit bored with Confessions of an Atlantic Rower -'

'*I'm* getting a bit bored with *you*,' announced Anna coolly. 'And I'd like to continue reading, if you don't mind. Because he isn't boring me.'

'- Now me, you see; I like to think I've done some good in my own modest way, serving on The Committee. Oh, I could write a book about it.'

'Could you,' yawned Anna. 'Well, no time like the present. Plenty nice quiet dormitories upstairs you could sit in, to start it.'

Silence once more. She could be a bit prickly when she wanted; that artistic temperament again. Time to lighten the atmosphere a bit. Dud's eyes slid to Kate's envelope on the work surface... Yes. Time we all had a bit of a laugh.

'I see Kate's left her catalogue behind,' he grinned, reaching for it. 'Shall we all have a look?'

'*Leave it alone.*' Len's voice, though quiet, was like a whipcrack.

To be fair to Dud, he had no intention of actually opening the envelope. He just wanted to throw in a bit of good-natured ragging, the sort of jocular banter that was the normal currency of communication between old and close friends, for Anna's benefit. And to change the subject from swashbuckling Conquerers of the Atlantic, of course.

It was just unfortunate that as he leaned sideways in his chair and picked up the envelope - by the wrong end - a sheaf of papers fell out of the other end and spread all over the floor.

'*Have you got some sort of death wish?*' Len sprang from his chair like a deranged jack-in-the-box and knelt to gather the scattered pages of Kate's play.

'Temper, temper. What is it, anyway?' asked Dud with friendly interest, joining him on the floor. He picked up one of the papers, adjusted his glasses, scrutinised it.

Len snatched it from him. 'ARE YOU DEAF? I said it's Kate's, *it's private,* LEAVE IT ALONE!'

Dud picked up another sheet. 'Is it a script?... a play? Has Kate written a play?'

'*I'm warning you.*' Len's tone left no doubt he was deadly serious. '*If you don't leave that alone *you'll be wearing your bollocks tied round your neck as medallions on your chest!*'

Nobody heard the door open.

Len had missed the rejection slip under his chair. Dud reached for it, grinning. 'Oh, look at this! Kate's tried to write a play, and it's been rejected. They've sent it back. It's no good!'

Len, suddenly aware of a movement by the door, looked up, straight into his wife's stricken face.

The curtains were drawn, and a bowl to vomit into, should the need arise again, lay on the bedside table. Len opened the door quietly.

'Are you awake?' he whispered.

Kate hadn't the energy to make the obvious retort.

'Anna asked me to give you this.'

One eye flickered open. Len was holding an exquisite watercolour of the view from the garden. The fellside, covered in bracken, dropped away to the lake below, and drystone walls snaked up the opposite fells to a skyscape of blue-black thunder clouds from behind which the sun, obviously about to emerge, sent a shaft of light onto the dark emerald lake.

It was a view Kate had grown to love deeply over the years, and one that held many memories. She'd nursed her sons when they were babies in that sheltered and private corner of the garden, separated by the yew hedge from the main grounds. They'd played there in childhood, mended bikes in teenage years, and sat in the sunshine revising for exams as they got older. Tony had brought his first serious girlfriend, and they'd all held a party. A barbecue. A real one - two logs, with the fire in between, and kebab skewers balanced on the logs to grill the food. And Len had managed to set a nearby bush on fire...

It was a small painting on excellent quality watercolour paper. Anna had obviously painted it during the week when they'd had a brief but violent storm. She'd captured the mood perfectly; it had clearly been painted for her own pleasure rather than "tourist tat" to be sold through the Gallery. Dark green ribbon attached a second sheet underneath to form a greetings card, on which was written in gold lettering the words of a Sixties folk song Kate guessed Len had dictated:

"Nothing worthwhile comes too easy,
There's always some suffering and pain.
But there's always more warmth in the sunshine
When it follows soon after the rain."

It had been signed by Len, Anna and Oliver. Underneath, Len had added a private message of his own.

'Oh, it's lovely,' she whispered, moved. She had thought she was too low to derive solace, let alone pleasure, from anything at present, but she was wrong. 'I'll get it properly framed.'

'Yes. Must be worth ninety quid at least,' agreed Len, pleased. 'Now go back to sleep, and don't worry about tonight's meal.'

Kate was already drifting downwards into the refuge of sleep. 'I'm past worrying. In fact I'm past caring. Tell Anna to stick to anything easy and straightforward; fish fingers, or something they can't have any disasters with. And trifle, which they can do in advance. Not what I'd intended, but at least it's safe. Nothing can *possibly* go wrong with that...'

It is difficult, but possible, to cook a three-course meal for seventy five people on your own, provided the meal is relatively straightforward and you have no interruptions. What you don't want cluttering up the kitchen while you're trying to do it is a hand-wringing penitent bewailing his remorse.

But Dud believed in grasping Life's opportunities, and this one meant he could appear as a dependable and much appreciated extra pair of hands ("Oh Dud, *would* you?" he'd envisaged Anna murmuring gratefully when he'd insisted on taking Kate's place by way of atonement. In fact she'd maintained that enigmatic silence he found so bewitching). Every bit as cosy as that exclusive restaurant, not to mention the money saved - he hadn't realised how astronomical the prices were until he looked more closely at the menu in the brass case outside the door, and then he'd nearly fallen through the pavement. Quite apart from the fact it was all in French.

So he'd hastily assumed a contrite concern for Kate. He did in fact feel a certain measure of genuine regret; poor thing, suffering from delusions of intelligence. But then everyone knew the female mind was apt to play strange tricks at Kate's age...

He hadn't realised there were so many mathematical calculations when he'd taken it upon himself to override Len's instructions and change the menu from baked potatoes (which he personally disliked) to instant mash (which he loved). He studied the instructions on the tin of potato powder, and filled a five-gallon pan with boiling water from the urn. Then, still unsure how much powder to add (what a complicated method! Surely there was a simpler way of doing things? He'd bring it up at the Committee Meeting next weekend. "The whole process came to light as I was standing in for Kate, because she had a migraine - yes, fortunate for her I just happened to be there, wasn't it..."), tipped in the entire tinful.

Seems to soak up the water quickly, doesn't it, he thought in surprise, jabbing ineffectively at the resultant cement-like concoction. Must need a bit more water.

It needed a lot more water. Dud made several trips to the urn. Mashed potato billowed from the pan, the wooden spoon ground to a halt, and blobs of potato detached themselves and spread over the entire area.

He hoped Anna appreciated all this effort! He looked across to give her a reassuring smile, and was surprised to see her arranging fish fingers on baking trays.

'What are you doing that for, Anna?' Abandoning his potato, he went to investigate.

'How else would you suggest they go in the oven?'

'They don't need to go in the oven.'

She looked at him in amazement. 'Oh. We're serving them frozen, are we?'

'I mean, why put them in the oven when we spent all that money on a new fryer?'

'Kate always does fish fingers in the oven.'

'Tch! They make all this fuss about needing a new fryer, then what do they do? They do the fish fingers in the oven, because they've *always* done them in the oven! Silly old fool's probably frightened of it. You know, all the technology.' He strolled over to the deep fat fryer. 'I've always fancied a go at one of these things. Let's try it out. Frying Tonight!'

'Why not just stick to a system that works?'

Dud regarded her with mock reproach.

'Because,' he explained patiently, switching on the fryer with a flourish, 'If nobody ever tried anything new we'd never have invented the wheel and we'd all still be living in caves, wouldn't we Anna.'

It was obvious to Anna that three hundred fish fingers dunked into a deep fat fryer would result in catastrophe. But although

Len had sympathised when she'd protested earlier about being stuck in the kitchen with "that repulsive maggot", he'd quietly reminded her that whilst on a personal level she was free to say what she wanted, there was a limit to what she could say to Dud in a professional capacity. She was a Seasonal Assistant, he was on The Committee, so she was at the bottom of the pecking order whilst he was at the top. Which was why she'd given way on the instant-potato issue.

'Why not,' she suggested diplomatically. 'Concentrate on your potato, and leave the fish fingers to me?'

'Because, just for once, we're going to have some efficiency in this kitchen.' As he waited for the red light to indicate the fat was sufficiently hot, Dud glanced at the potato pan surrounded by its concentric blobs of varying sizes (yes, he'd certainly recommend they looked into ways of improving Beckside's catering methods next weekend), then his eye moved on to the soup Len had made earlier. If instant potato was any example of the inept way they did things here, he'd better check on that... He stirred, sniffed, tasted it with an ostentatious slurp.

'Oxtail. Bit unimaginative, isn't it. Don't get me wrong, they do their best, old Len and Kate, but neither of them have much pizzazz, like, have they.' He disappeared into the larder and emerged with a container of tomato soup powder which he tipped liberally into the pan.

'*You're supposed to mix it with cold water first!*' cautioned Anna, too late.

'Brainwashed you as well, have they.' Dud nodded complacently. 'Just a big con to make everyone think the job's more complicated than it really is, all this "*Must* do the fish fingers in the oven, *must* mix the soup powder with cold water, *must* -*" Oh look, the fat's hot enough now.' He swept the fish fingers into the fryer. 'Oh. They don't seem to quite fit, do they,' he observed after a few moments. 'Never mind, the fat's starting to bubble up now.'

The fat was indeed starting to bubble up. It spat and hissed; a pall of black smoke spread over the kitchen.

'*Switch it off!*'

'Oh stop fussing, woman. It's supposed to do that!'

A buxom girl in denim shorts and low top loomed through the smoke, and drawled in a seductive American accent: 'Are you

Oliver? The light bulb's gone in the Bike Shed. The Warden said, go get Oliver to see to it.'

'Hey up!' Dud rubbed his hands. 'You want anything seeing to in the Bike Shed, babe, forget Oliver, *I'm* your man. Name's Dud. I'm on The Committee.' He headed for the door. 'Back in a mo, Anna - duty calls elsewhere!' (And very conveniently too. He was dying for a fag.)

Oliver appeared in the doorway, blinking at the smoke-filled kitchen.

'Missed out there, pal!' hissed Dud as he squeezed past and hurried after the denim shorts.

'What's happened? Where's he going?'

'To electrocute himself, with luck.' And probably plunge the entire building into darkness just as the smoke alarm goes off, Anna added silently as she switched off the fryer and raised the baskets onto their rests.

The extractor fan whirred gallantly, but smoke was drifting ever nearer the alarm on the ceiling. As she tried without success to waft it in the opposite direction, Oliver stared, mesmerised, at the fryer baskets containing three hundred fish fingers congealed into two solid lumps, from which oil dripped with hypnotic regularity onto the peeled-off coatings of breadcrumbs now floating as blackened flotsam in the bubbling cauldrons beneath.

Len's attention was taken up with booking in the group who had just arrived when Oliver, having lost both toss and ensuing argument, trudged sullenly to The Office to inform him that the Main Course on tonight's menu was now off.

A shrill French voice was complaining that her party was travel-sick, exhausted, hungry, and didn't think much of the weather. (During the afternoon a bank of cloud had drifted in and obscured the warm spring sunshine, its accompanying drizzle becoming increasingly heavy. The long overdue rain was now making up for its absence with a vengeance, and looked set to continue without let-up for the next week.)

'Does it *always* rain here?' The French accent, obviously cultured and well-educated, was petulant.

'No,' said Len cheerfully. 'It's been lovely until today.'

'What it has been like until today is irrelevant!'

'Never mind. You'll feel better after a good meal.'

'I hope so.' The Frenchwoman sounded doubtful. 'My students are most interested in learning about catering for different markets -' She indicated a queue of bored-looking teenagers lolling against the wall, '- Which is why I specifically asked Madame Pratt to suggest where she felt we might be served an excellent example of what can be achieved by imaginative utilisation of a limited budget, so my students will see how flair and talent can compensate for financial restrictions. I also made it clear I wish to dine in a civilised and peaceful environment, which I consider vital to the digestion -'

A faint approaching buzz suddenly erupted to a deafening roar. The front door was punched carelessly aside, the Reception Area flooded by the screaming, racing, fighting horde of urchins who had reduced breakfast to chaos.

'Ay mister, is it chips tonight?' greeted the bedwetter.

'*Chips!*' groaned the woman with an expressive Gallic gesture of despair.

'Because if it isn't,' a second child stared threateningly at the newcomers, 'Me and the team'll be taking this place apart.'

The bedwetter reappeared from behind the Frenchwoman's spindly legs to inform Len of his culinary requirements. 'Ay, I'm not to have peas, they give me the trots. Soup gives me the trots as well.'

'What's soup?'

''Aven't you never 'ad soup, Daz?' The bedwetter wiped his nose with his hand and smeared the result on his trousers.

The French leader was beginning to wonder why on earth Eloise had recommended this place. She supposed the area was nice enough - what one could see of it through the rain - but she certainly hadn't bargained on some third-rate establishment in the charge of an inept bumpkin who had probably never eaten anything but chips in his life, and overrun by delinquent slum children. It was obvious the place had gone downhill since Eloise had last stayed here, because if Eloise had known the true state of affairs she'd never have suggested it for their overnight stay. Well, she would most certainly inform her and Major Pratt of her disappointment and dissatisfaction when she telephoned them later this evening.

Oliver (convincing himself that the reason he'd said nothing until now was purely courtesy; waiting for a suitable break in the conversation) knew he couldn't delay breaking the glad news to Len much longer.

'Er, Len...'

Len looked up impatiently.

Losing not only his nerve but his voice, Oliver's mouth gaped unproductively open. Anna had advised imparting the news with discretion and diplomacy to avoid the entire hostel learning that tonight's main course had just been incinerated beyond recognition, which wouldn't help matters. He cast around for some suitably cryptic yet enlightening phrase. None came.

The French leader subjected him to a disparaging scrutiny; her yawning charges fixed him with a vacant stare.

'What's the matter with you?' snapped Len.

One of the urchins gave a loud burp. The entire group dissolved into sniggers, which quickly turned into wild hysterical laughter. The French teenagers stared impassively at the culprit, then one of their number, a swarthy, handsome individual of about fifteen, took up the challenge and issued a louder, longer, and infinitely more offensive burp.

And then it happened.

The headmaster of the Liverpool schoolchildren, having panted up the drive in an effort to, if not "lead" his charges, at least catch up with them, tottered in the front door, clutching at his chest and wondering if this chaotic pounding of his heart was the onset of a cardiac arrest. How long would it take an ambulance to reach this benighted place? Where was the nearest hospital, anyway? He saw himself gasping his last breath in the ambulance as it bumped and jolted its way to distant Carlisle. And he hadn't got around to adding that codicil to his will yet...

He sank into one of the easy chairs, cursing the School Governors who'd thought up this ridiculous idea - then opened his eyes in surprise. A husky French voice was enquiring with concern if she could help. The headmaster gazed up into the hooded brown eyes, all thoughts of cardiac arrest swept unexpectedly away by a strange melting sensation that was causing his heart to pound just as fearfully, but for a different reason entirely.

Mr. Miller, who all his adult life had poured scorn and ridicule on the notion of love at first sight, found himself in the unbelievable situation of having to eat every one of his scathing words. Because Mr. Miller's flintlike heart had, in that brief instant, overruled his sensible, mature, sober head, and years of logic and reasoning were effortlessly felled by that age-old adversary, emotion. He was staggered to find he'd fallen in love.

At first sight.

And the French leader, who, after a brief disastrous marriage at eighteen had lived contentedly alone for the past thirty years, also found her heart beating faster as she introduced herself.

'Mireille Lesage,' she informed him, fluttering her eyelashes.

'Edward Miller,' he replied, gazing up spellbound at the sallow face, oblivious to the sniggers of their respective charges.

And the world stood still for both of them.

Except that in reality, of course, the world continues to revolve, and their private capsule of bliss was abruptly punctured when one of the urchins shrieked: *'Ay! Look at that smoke coming from under the kitchen door!'* And to the ensuing pandemonium was added the smoke detector's eardrum-imploding screech.

Kate, two floors up, was dreaming. It was New Years Eve, and the River Mersey was welcoming in the New Year in its own inimitable way. Foghorns blared from the Landing Stage; tugs, ferries, and Pilot boats moored alongside sounded hooters and sirens; cargo vessels and liners lying at anchor in the deep central channel whooped joyously. The Mersey was once again alive and noisy.

One siren in particular seemed to go on and on... Kate surfaced almost to consciousness. Then the high-pitched wail abated, the river became quiet again, and she sank once more into deep, heavy sleep.

Dud groped his way into the kitchen.

'Where's all this smoke come from?' (Had he left his fag in here? No, he definitely remembered throwing it on the Bike Shed floor, so that was all right. Nothing to do with him. Safe to be judgemental, critical, righteously angry.)

'The deep fat fryer,' said Anna succinctly.

'Oh.' (Better hold fire with the judgemental anger for the moment.) 'Is it faulty then?'

'Not as faulty as the cretin who put them in it,' fumed Len.

'And what's all this mashed potato doing here?' He nodded at the overflowing potato pan. 'I said *baked* potatoes! We only ever use instant for shepherd's pie. In any case, we're expecting seventy five for the evening meal, not seven hundred and fifty!'

'Oh, you can always make potato cakes or something with the surplus.' Dud airily dismissed such trivia. Inclined to fuss at times, old Len.

'Potato cakes? Look at it! Caked all over the cooker, all over the floor, everywhere!'

'D'you think perhaps you're over-reacting a bit?' chided Dud, stepping in a large blob of potato. 'All this hoo-ha about a bit of extra potato! Not as if it's going to be wasted, is it?'

Oh, it won't be wasted, thought Oliver with feeling. We'll all be living on mashed potato from now til Kingdom Come.

Len was acutely aware that holding an inquest into who was to blame for what was merely wasting time he didn't have. The ultimate responsibility for producing an edible meal for seventy five people out of this debacle was his, and there'd be an even bigger inquest - with him as the subject - next weekend if he didn't come up with something. He turned back to the disaster in the fryers; three hundred fish fingers fused into two useless misshapen fish footballs, and no time to cook anything else, even if they'd had anything else to cook. It was now 6.55PM. The meal was due to be served at 7PM.

He stifled a hysterical urge to drag the fingers back an hour on the cheerfully ticking clock. Unless a kindly Fairy Godmother appeared with a magic wand, it would be necessary to fall back on tinned corned beef kept in reserve for only the very direst of dire emergencies - which, in twenty four years, had never actually happened until tonight. A vision of Eloise's impeccably made up face flitted before his mind. Oh God... Corned beef, at the Youth Hostel she personally had recommended for its excellent meals. He wondered what the French for corned beef was. Hopefully there wouldn't be a translation, because it didn't exist in Cordon Bleu circles. (It *certainly* didn't exist in Eloise's circles.) Perhaps they'd think it was some quaint mouthwatering local pate they'd never seen before? And perhaps they wouldn't...

He dispatched Oliver to the larder. Fortunately there was a thick meaty soup. He glanced at the back burner, on which he'd left simmering a nutritious but unremarkable pan of oxtail soup of the correct consistency, and correct colour.

A covering of bright red lumps now floated all over it.

'What-have-you-done-to-the-soup?'

'Oh, we added some tomato soup powder to it,' explained Dud carelessly, scraping potato off the sole of his trainer.

'WHAT FOR?'

'He thought it looked unimaginative,' said Anna flatly.

Len's response to this was an indistinct obscenity paraphrased around an enquiry as to it whether Dud considered it looked sufficiently imaginative now? He skimmed off the surface layer into a bowl, and glanced round for the trifles which Anna should by now be sprinkling with chopped nuts and chocolate flakes.

'Where are the trifles? Have you finished them, Anna?'

'No. I couldn't find them.'

'Couldn't what?' How could anyone not find seventy five jellies in sundae dishes?

Oliver emerged from the larder before he could pursue the matter further, and stuttered in a sepulchral whisper: 'There's, there's no corned beef. It's, it's gone. I remember now. Kate gave it to a group who wanted to make packed lunches.'

Len spun round. 'If you're trying to be funny -'

One look at the lad's face was enough. He wasn't joking.

To serve a main course of corned beef was shameful enough at the best of times. To serve it tonight, knowing a report on the meal would be relayed to Major Pratt (and then circulated scathingly on the gossip circuit, which would destroy Kate) was even worse. But to find himself, less than five minutes before the meal was due to be served, without even corned beef to fall back on was beyond any Warden's worst nightmares.

'I'm glad you mentioned the jelly,' said Dud brightly. 'It hadn't quite set, you see, so it's in a pan in the freezer to finish it off.'

Len stared at him. Kindly Fairy Godmother, please fly through the window quickly, before I end up on a murder charge...

'It hadn't quite set?'

'No.'

'And it's in the freezer - in a PAN?'

'Yes. I didn't have time to ladle it into sundae dishes, Len,' explained Dud. 'I had to ring Major Pratt, to tell him it was Anna who painted his picture. He was amazed!'

'He's going to be even more amazed when he hears about

tonight,' said Len grimly. 'A plague of starving locusts swarming into the dining room with Madame Cordon Bleu and her Stasi heading the queue, and - just to re-cap - we've got no fish fingers, no corned beef, the jelly's in a pan in the freezer 'cos it hasn't quite set, and we don't recommend the soup much either.'

He prodded the welded-together monsters with a wooden spoon, silently pleading for inspiration to strike. Desperation struck instead; Len was ready to try anything. Mash what was left of the fish fingers with milk and marge, add that left-over rice from yesterday, stick a slice of tomato on each portion, spread it on trays and do it in the oven, and it *might* be ready by quarter past… He sent Oliver back to the larder for the tomatoes.

'Good idea, Len!' approved Dud. 'We could tell them it's kedgeree, couldn't we!'

'Yeh. We could tell them it's fresh salmon sent down from Balmoral while we're at it, couldn't we,' nodded Len. Mangled fish fingers hidden under slices of tomato, and tell them it's kedgeree... Oh God. 'I need a drink.'

He groped for the Medicinal Purposes Only brandy in the medical cupboard. There'd be a French translation for kedgeree all right, but he doubted the Cordon Bleu maestro would use it when she was describing tonight's meal to Major Pratt.

'What's this?' demanded the bedwetter with a critical stare at the soup pan.

'Oxtail soup.' Len attempted a genial smile.

'What's tail?' The urchin screwed up his face in revulsion, and informed his contemporary at the table: 'Ay Daz, that stuff you're eating's made out of things' tails!'

Daz instantly spat out a mouthful of soup, spraying the child opposite, who hurled a slice of bread in retaliation.

'Are those red bits,' wondered his neighbour. 'Blood, from when they chopped their tails off?'

The soup-spitter crumbled the bread into a ball and threw it back. His opponent ducked. The missile sailed over him and hit the shiny bald head of an elderly hiker at the next table.

Len took a leaf out of the Headmaster's book and pretended not to see, left the pan for anyone who wanted seconds (there wouldn't be many; most of the diners had taken one look at the soup and opted for fruit juice, unaware the spurned oxtail soup would turn up again the following night as gravy), and returned to the kitchen for an update on the "kedgeree".

As soon as he opened the door he sniffed suspiciously. 'What's been going on in here?'

'We've had a slight mishap. Nothing to worry about,' Dud reassured him.

Len held up the brandy bottle. It was empty.

'Dud knocked it over,' explained Anna. 'It's in the kedgeree.'

'Only a tiny drop went in. It'll all have evaporated while it's cooking,' soothed Dud.

Len was aghast. 'There's young kids in that Dining Room. There may be alcoholics as well, for all we know!'

'Oh, stop fussing, Len!' He could be like some nagging old woman at times, thought Dud impatiently. What did it matter if a drop (well all right, half a bottle) of brandy went in the kedgeree? 'Now, where were we? Oh yes. I'll drain the cabbage, Anna. Your delicate little artist's hands can't manage that big pan, and we don't want any accidents, do we.'

He staggered to the sink, balanced the pan on the rim, and tipped it forward. The lid fell off and clattered along the draining board, the pan slipped out of control, the contents flopped on top of various utensils soaking in sudsy washing-up water, and the overflow slid down the sink unit onto the floor. In the terrible silence that followed, a forlorn and reproachful dripping settled into a steady rhythm.

Dud stared at the devastation on the floor. '*Oh, hell's teeth*! Maybe we could salvage some of it... Where's a jug?'

'Salvage it? In a jug?' Len could hardly believe his ears. 'And what if Madame Cordon Bleu comes in and finds us all shovelling cabbage off the floor into serving tureens?'

As he spoke a distant chorus of voices broke into song to the tune of "O Come All Ye Faithful", accompanied by cutlery banged enthusiastically on the tables. It grew swiftly louder and more insistent: "Why are we waiting, *why are we waiting,* WHYYYY ARE WE WAAAIIIT-ING?"

Len saw them look at him expectantly, waiting for him to whip away the conjurer's cloth and produce, by some skilful sleight of hand, some magic incantation, a pan of steaming hot vegetables for seventy five people. Voila! Not like that, like that!

But magic incantations need kindly Fairy Godmothers to utter them; the incantations Len was uttering were more likely to summon Lucifer from the underworld. He saw himself, in slow-motion, hand Oliver the keys to The Office. A high-pitched voice (surely it wasn't his?) croaked: *'Bring a case of peas.* HURRY!'

As Kate never served tinned vegetables, and there was no time to cook other frozen ones even if he'd had any to cook, there was no instant solution conveniently waiting. This meant opening about fifty of the small tins of peas sold in The Shop.

He searched wildly for the seldom used tin-opener. As tins were torn open, the contents tossed into a myriad of pans and spread on every available burner, including the Self-Caterers' Kitchen, Len, fearing a riot in the Dining Room, decided someone must put in an appearance. His eye fell on Oliver, and he refused to be swayed by any entreaties.

'I can't do it!' protested Oliver in panic. 'I hate going into rooms full of people!'

Len didn't even pause from his task. 'Didn't your mother say when you started work what an asset you'd be, because you love meeting people?'

'Yes, but -'

'Well then. Here's your chance. *Take the mint sauce in.*'

The ability to look poised and confident as one enters a room of seventy five people impatiently awaiting a delayed meal is a life-skill not easily mastered at any age, and one that Oliver, at eighteen, had no wish to acquire. He tried to slink, phantom-like, into the Dining Room, but as he was carrying a tray containing bowls of some concoction obviously intended to accompany the meal, and curiosity was running high as to when the meal would actually arrive - and until it did, Oliver and his tray provided the sole focus of attention - the uproar continued with an increasing malevolence: "WHY-Y-Y ARE WE WAITING?"

The soup-spitter snapped his fingers. 'Ay you! Manuel! What's the hold-up? Are we ever going to get any dinner, or wha'?'

'Yes, it's coming now,' placated Oliver. 'We don't like... er... rushing people between courses.'

'They've probably had some of their own soup and they're all lying dead on the kitchen floor,' guessed his companion, scrutinising the bowls. 'What's this supposed to be?'

70

Oliver placed one of the bowls of mint, mixed with sugar and vinegar by Anna earlier, on the table. 'Mint sauce.'

This information was received in silence. A critical inspection took place.

'He's barmy,' came the verdict from the group's own personal Egon Ronay, whose elder brother's job in a hamburger bar qualified him as culinary advisor to the rest. 'Mint sauce is dark green stuff in a jar. He's giving us chopped-up hedge leaves!'

Fortunately for Oliver, the diners were distracted by the arrival of the trolley, and all eyes swivelled sharply to the trays of "kedgeree" Len was placing on the serving counter, next to several pans of peas and tureens of mashed potato (which had been topped with cheese, grilled to a light golden brown, and garnished with a sprig of fresh parsley).

'Oliver, check the peas in the kitchen. Dud'll serve in here with me and Anna. Have the next lot ready,' ordered Len urgently, and Oliver thankfully scuttled out.

'What's this?' demanded the delegation of eagle-eyed waiters, inspecting the kedgeree.

In fact, the whole thing had turned out remarkably well. It looked and smelt appetising and delicious; succulent white fish with rice and golden flecks of breadcrumbs mixed in (the coatings trapped in the centre of the disintegrated lumps had escaped being incinerated), topped with sliced tomato and segmented into generous portions.

'It's, er, "Beckside Kedgeree". It's very nice, you'll like it,' Len told them, adding under his breath, 'I hope.'

'*Wha'*?' The delegation had never heard of kedgeree.

'What is it?' came the impatient enquiry from table to delegation.

'Porridgy or something,' shrugged the spokesman.

'PORRIDGE! Ugh! Yeuch! Eeargh!' came the predictable chorus of revulsion and disgust.

'*It's not porridge*!' said Len desperately, fearing the entire meal would be consigned to the waste bin. 'It's, it's - fish!'

'Thought it was supposed to be fish fingers?'

'Fish fingers are off.'

'The soup was off, but that didn't stop you giving it us!'

'I told you peas give me the trots!' accused the bedwetter, frowning at the pans. 'Thought it was supposed to be cabbage?'

'Cabbage is off as well,' said Len shortly.

'Everything's off in this dump.'

A running battle commenced on the two nearest tables, with mashed potato providing the ammunition.

'Will you lads stop flicking potato!' called Len. 'Look! You've just hit that lady!' And of course we can all guess who it'd be, can't we... He watched as the French leader, accompanying the Headmaster to a table as far away as possible from both groups, indignantly wiped a glob of potato from her well-cut gored skirt.

'Did you hear me! I said *stop flicking peas round!*'

'You didn't, you said stop flicking potato round,' jeered the strategist of the winning side, aiming another pea at his opponents.

'Well stop flicking *anything* round!'

'I don't know why they bother putting it on plates at all. It'd be so much easier to have one big trough and just pour all three courses in it at once,' remarked Mr. Miller to his lady-love, who responded with a Gallic shrug of agreement as they chose a table of intimate isolation in the far corner, ignoring the chaos all around them.

'We're out of peas,' announced Dud, collecting the empty pans and trotting to the kitchen.

'Ay! He's going for more peas!' noted the battle strategist. 'They'll get fresh ammo!'

The vanquished on the opposing table performed a selection of Haka-like insulting gestures to inflame the enemy as they waited for the cavalry to arrive back with the reinforcements. The victorious table quite obviously could not allow the cavalry to get through.

'Let's ambush him on his way back!' whispered the second-in-command, and the entire table, apparently developing an urgent need to visit the Men's Washroom, rose in unison and trooped purposefully from the room.

'Chop chop, Oliver,' chivvied Dud, bustling into the kitchen.

'Are you sure you can manage all those pans at once?' cautioned Oliver as Dud scooped a fistful of pans from the cooker like a Bavarian barmaid at a beerfest, and got his answer as they clattered to the floor, disgorging a torrent of bouncing peas over the still-damp spot vacated by the cabbage.

Dud cradled his hands between his knees. 'OW! Stupid fool, you let the handles get too hot!'

'There's more in the Self-Caterers' kitchen,' gabbled Oliver as Len's voice shouted from the Dining Room: 'Bring those peas in here! NOW!'

Dud's footsteps receded down the Reception Area, then stopped as the phone rang. Oliver, clearing up the green skating rink the floor had metamorphosed into for the second time, heard Len's voice, hoarse and desperate:

'I said *hurry-up-with-those-peas!*'

He tested the latest batch with his finger. They weren't boiling, but they'd do; the situation was obviously urgent in the Dining Room. As he drew level with the phone, Dud placed his hand over the receiver and hissed: 'Hell's teeth! It's Mona!'

From the Dining Room Len's voice roared: 'Will you GET IN HERE WITH THOSE PEAS!'

'Coming, Len!' answered Dud with relief. 'Have to go, dearheart. Ring you back later!'

Sneaking the receiver back on its cradle as though it were an unexploded bomb, he grabbed the pans from Oliver and ran towards the Dining Room.

And Oliver, hurrying to the Self-Caterers' Kitchen to rescue a collection of blackened pans with shrivelled remains of peas burnt irremovably on, froze in shock as a chorus of blood-curdling warcries and hair-raising shrieks rent the air, followed by a terrified scream and the sound (rapidly becoming quite familiar) of pans clattering once more to the ground.

When Len raced into the corridor at what sounded like murder being done, all he found at the scene of the crime was the victim slumped dazedly against the wall amidst a sea of processed peas.

Before Dud had even realised what was happening the crack SAS Sabotage Force had struck, hidden round the corner until Authority was safely engrossed in tending the casualty, then, panther-like, re-crossed enemy lines into the Dining Room and resumed their seats. By the time the headmaster had been prised from behind his barricade to carry out an investigation, indisputable identification was impossible, and the perpetrators sat munching their kedgeree with innocent relish.

'Make him a cup of tea,' Len instructed Oliver in a tone

noticeably lacking in sympathy as he assisted the overwrought victim to the kitchen.

'I need something stronger than tea, Len,' groaned Dud.

'Pity you spilt the brandy in the kedgeree then, because there's none left.'

'Put plenty sugar in it, Ol,' quavered Dud as Oliver, shoulders shaking as though in the grip of an uncontrollable coughing attack, tossed a teabag in a cup and filled it from the urn. 'I've had a terrible shock.'

'Oh don't be such a spoilsport, Dud. It was only a bit of fun!' mimicked Len in a faultless imitation of Dud's voice at breakfast. 'Where's your sense of humour?'

'Don't get me wrong Len, I'm the first to appreciate a joke -'

'Just as long as it's not against you,' nodded Len, and Dud abruptly changed the subject; a timely reminder to the paid staff that whilst humour was all very well in appropriate circumstances, disrespect towards a Committee member would not be tolerated.

'That was Mona on the phone,' he announced sternly. 'She wants to book in for the Committee Meeting next weekend.'

'Oh,' said Len, more concerned about tonight's dessert. If they had any dessert. If the kindly Fairy Godmother, who'd obviously been busy elsewhere earlier, would at last ensure that nothing else went wrong. They'd had disasters before - all Hostels did from time to time - but never on this scale, involving all three courses at once. But enough of defeatist talk and pessimism! Everything was going to go right from now on. Wasn't it, kindly Fairy Godmother?

Behind him, what sounded like a chained giant being dragged from the larder shuffled to a stop. He turned to see Oliver manhandling a five-gallon pan of curdling green slime which sloshed over the sides to form dribbles of vile-looking mucus.

'Here's the dessert,' announced Oliver succinctly.

'I thought, instead of ordinary lime jelly for the trifles, I'd make milk jelly,' explained Dud. 'So I added some tins of milk.'

'Let me guess,' murmured Len pleasantly. 'You didn't add the milk *as well as the full amount of water*, by any chance?'

'Ah. Think you might have something there, Len old friend.' Dud attempted to lighten the atmosphere. 'Never mind. Worse things happen at sea!'

'I can assure you they don't,' said Len with feeling.

He reeled towards the larder. Dear kindly Fairy Godmother, *please* let there be enough ice cream in the freezer. Any sort, as long as there's enough. And some catering-size tins of fruit salad to go with it. Or pears. Or peaches. Or ANYTHING. Because, he remembered in panic, the wholesale delivery, like the frozen food, wasn't due until Monday, and there was precious little tinned fruit in The Shop except for what didn't sell well, due to his policy of cutting down on non-essential stock and re-ordering only when necessary.

He'd reached the point of expecting the shelves to be bare - in fact the sight of a line of tinned fruit would have reduced him to tears of hysterical gratitude - but that didn't lessen the awful sensation of his intestines knotting themselves into macrame hangings as, yet again, he was faced with producing an array of epicurean victuals for seventy five people out of thin air.

The entire race of kindly Fairy Godmothers must be occupied with some (other) global-class catastrophe tonight...

It was over.

Len tottered back to the kitchen, fell into a chair, and reached for the brandy bottle. All the years they'd kept the stuff for emergencies, and now, when he felt as surreal as one of those watches in a Salvadore Dali painting and in need of a drink as never before - not a drop. He was unsure who'd been more taken aback at the sight of the dessert he'd just served; himself or the astounded diners. What a colour co-ordinating analyst would have made of the startling visual combination might make interesting reading; all he knew was, he never wanted to go through another night like this as long as he lived.

The phone rang. He heard Anna answer it, and looked up as she came in.

'Len, I know I'm on Shop duty tonight -'

Here we go, thought Len. Nothing's for nothing where Anna's concerned.

He was right.

'- But could I swap with you and do tomorrow night instead? There's a group of friends staying in Keswick for the weekend. It's someone's birthday, there's a party.'

The resilience of youth, marvelled Len. All he wanted to do

was fall into bed next to Kate and forget tonight ever existed.

'That reminds me. Did Dud say anything?'

'Dud? What about?'

'Tonight.'

'What about tonight?'

'I think he wanted to ask you out.'

'Well he's going to be disappointed then, isn't he. And the answer would still be no, even if I wasn't doing something else. So, OK if we swap then, and I'll do tomorrow night instead? He's picking me up at nine o'clock.'

Len had been young himself once. 'Aye, go on then,' he sighed, dropping the empty brandy bottle in the bin.

Dud had had enough of kitchen work. He'd done his bit, taken the reins, steered them safely through the crisis. He could now relax, leave them to tidy up the loose ends such as cleaning the kitchen, scrubbing the pans and cooker, and other menial tasks.

And then… he'd inform Anna that he was whisking her down to the pub. No arguments! She deserved a treat after her valiant little attempts to help.

'Give me the dosh and I'll bring you another bottle of brandy back from the pub, Len,' he offered as he watched Len open The Shop for the evening session. 'I'm taking Anna for a drink as soon as she's finished.'

'Well actually, Dud,' answered Len. 'I think she's made other plans.' He explained that a friend would be calling for her to join a party.

'A friend, eh?' Dud rubbed his hands. 'And a party? Better and better, Len. Sounds good to me.'

'No. They're - *they're* - going to a party, you see, Dud.'

'Yes, I heard you, I'm not deaf. Or stupid. Keswick, eh?'

Len tried again. 'Some friends are up for the weekend, and -'

'Oh, get to the point, Len!' Inclined to ramble on like some old washerwoman at times, was Len. 'Is how we'll get there bothering you? I know I can't fit Anna *and* her friend on the back of the Honda; I'll go with them in the car!' (Len could be so dim sometimes! Or jealous. Poor old codger was past it, whereas Dud, natural-born party animal, original Life-and-Soul, Party Tricks Inc, Practical Jokes a Speciality, would be orgying the night away with two nubile wenches.)

'If it's the friend I'm thinking of, it's a two-seater.'

'Oh.' Dud's face fell, then brightened. 'Well, I'll follow on behind.'

An intriguing picture flitted across Len's mind; Dud, turning up on the doorstep, an unwanted and uninvited guest at Anna's friend's party.

'Mm,' he conceded. 'If you're invited you could.' He paused to let that sink in, then added artlessly, 'Have you been invited, then?'

'Not yet,' replied Dud, undaunted. 'Actually, before I see Anna, I suppose I'd better ring Mona back. Get that over and done with.' Unless, of course, he could get Len to fob her off? He eyed him speculatively... No. Len wasn't capable of hoodwinking even the dimmest fool about anything. Couldn't con a halfwit. Which was as it should be, of course, but meant that if there was ever any jiggery-pokery or devious dealings to be done, you could count him right out.

He dialled the number.

'Hello?' croaked an quavering voice, and Dud groaned. Trust the old bag's even older bag of a mother, Bridie, to answer. He hoped she had her teeth in, or everything would take twice as long, and he only had twenty pence.

'Is Mona there? It's Dud.'

'Who?'

'*Dud.* Is Mona there?'

'Eh?'

'IS MONA THERE?' he screamed, glancing at Len, who was spacing out the remaining tins of peas along the shelf to fill out the gaps.

'Wait yet now, til I turn the wirelecl off.'

And get your teeth in while you're at it, thought Dud irritably. There was a pause as the crone plodded off, then returned.

'Now. What icl it you're wanting?'

'IT'S DUD, I WANT TO SPEAK TO MONA!'

'Ah, it'cl yourclelf, icl it, Dud. Well clee'cl gone out. Clee claid, ring back at nine o'clock.'

The phone was replaced with an abrupt clunk. Dud listened to the dialling tone, blinked, then replaced the receiver.

'What time's Anna going?' he asked casually.

'Nine o'clock,' answered Len, equally casually.

Hm. Should be OK. He'd give Mona a quick ring just before they left, and then - the night was his. And Anna's. And the friend would probably be very tasty as well. And Dud was man enough to satisfy both of them.

He'd pop to the kitchen now to invite her to the pub, so she in turn would invite him to the party, then go and tart himself up.

He stopped at the kitchen door. On second thoughts, he'd get changed first, *then* issue the invitation, because it sounded as though they hadn't finished the washing up yet. Didn't want to get lumbered with that!

Kate woke up and lay quietly for a few moments, savouring the absence of pain. The long sleep had done its work; her migraine had abated.

She glanced at the clock - ten to nine - dressed, splashed her face, and went downstairs, just in time to see Anna, looking stunning in a pale green silk shirt and white jeans, a long black scarf tied round her waist and another tying back her hair, swinging out of the front door with a tall, bronzed Greek god in dark denims and a dark green shirt.

Len and Oliver, in The Shop, were also watching the departure with interest. And Dud, who had apparently been lying in wait, was almost hopping with rage.

'I thought you said it was a friend!' He rounded furiously on Len as the front door closed.

'I did.'

'Yes, but I thought you meant a *friend!*'

'I did mean a friend.'

'You didn't say what sex he was!'

'You didn't ask.' Len smiled as Kate came across to join them. 'Hi there. You look a lot better!'

Dud glanced round peevishly. 'Oh. You've turned up, have you. Now all the work's done.'

'She had a migraine, if you remember,' Len reminded him.

'Tch!' tutted Dud. If anyone deserved to be cosseted because they had migraines it was him, because this was enough to give anyone one! You nip off for five minutes with the American bint in the Common Room while Anna and Oliver drudged in the kitchen, and when you returned the place was deserted. Anna had gone to get changed, which meant hanging around the

Reception Area waiting for her. Which was a bit undignified and not part of the plan at all. And after all that, she swans off with someone else!

This was Len's fault. He should have subtly conveyed to her that Dud had plans for tonight. Because of course Anna was unaware, when she agreed to go to the party with the unknown nuisance who had just wrecked the entire weekend, that *Dud* intended taking her out. But then, subtlety had never been Len's strong point...Oh well. Obviously it was the Yankee consolation prize for tonight. Still, the groundwork had been put in; Anna had been really impressed with him pitching in and helping, you could tell. Must remember to make sure it was noted in the Committee Minutes next weekend!

Better get back into the Common Room before Miss All-America went out as well. He'd ring Mona later; the public phone was in use now. He glanced across to where Madame Lesage and Mr. Miller, gazing into each others' eyes, drooled into the receiver.

'Yes, it has been the most *marvellous* evening, Eloise,' Madame Lesage was assuring her friend enthusiastically. 'I can't tell you how happy I am that you suggested Beckside for our stay! I'm so glad we didn't go anywhere else!'

As she rang off with another round of effusive compliments, Mr. Miller strolled across to Kate and Len.

'That was a most unusual meal tonight,' he remarked amiably.

'Could we have the menu as a momento of our visit?' requested Madame Lesage, joining him.

Kate looked pleased. 'Yes, of course,' she agreed, guessing this must be Eloise's French penfriend, although she wasn't sure about the balding companion whose arm the woman clung to as though fearing he might blow away. 'What a nice idea. I'll ask our Assistant to write it out for you. She does calligraphy.'

'Thank you. And - I promise to understand if you insist on keeping this a secret - may we also have the recipe for the main course? We collect examples of recipes that are -' She looked enquiringly at her companion.

'Peculiar,' he supplied obligingly.

'Yes. Peculiar to the locality.'

'Oh. Don't you have fish fingers in France then?' asked Kate, surprised.

The French leader laughed politely at this feeble joke, then recalled Len saying earlier that his wife was unwell. She had obviously forgotten what she'd served. 'Your regional version of kedgeree, with the merest hint of brandy in it.'

There was a pause.

'Regional version of... with the merest hint of *what* in it?' repeated Kate, puzzled.

'Was it flambéed in brandy?' asked Mr. Miller with polite interest.

Kate blinked at Len, who refused to meet her eye.

'Flambéed in...?'

'Most imaginative, anyway. And all that trouble you took, to ensure the peas were served really hot.'

'Peas?' Kate frowned openmouthed at her husband, who focused his eyes on a stain on the wood panelling where someone had shaken a tin of cola that had sprayed all over the wall. What were they talking about? They didn't *have* any peas until the frozen food delivery on Monday. That's why they'd served cabbage.

'But the most adventurous course, we felt, was the pudding,' continued Mr. Miller, wishing the Warden's wife would stop this irritating habit of repeating everything he or Mireille said. And that vacant look - it was like trying to hold a conversation with one of his Remedial Class children.

'Adventurous? Trifle?' echoed Kate faintly.

'Prunes,' reminded Madame Lesage tactfully. 'With mint choc chip ice cream.'

'PRUNES?'

'Yes. I thought it a most, er… unorthodox combination of colour, texture, and flavour...'

Len kept his eye firmly on the cola stain.

'But, as I've just told dear Eloise,' continued Madame Lesage, smiling coyly at Mr. Miller, 'We will both remember Beckside - and tonight's meal - for as long as we live. Won't we, cherie?'

'The one as unforgettable an experience as the other, dearest,' agreed Mr Miller drily.

'Right!' said Kate grimly. 'What's been going on?'

Len took a deep breath. 'Well, I know this is going to sound a bit far fetched...'

And it did.

'Are you making this up?' she demanded, as Len described how Eloise's middle-aged penfriend and the inner-city Headmaster took one look at each other and abandoned themselves to white hot passion, oblivious to the sniggering of both sets of gawping youngsters.

Dud approached from the Common Room, carrying an envelope.

'Some woman's just brought this,' he announced. 'The one that rang up this morning. I found her by the french windows, lost. It's that letter the postman delivered to her house by mistake.'

It was addressed to Kate. She opened it, skimmed through, blinked, re-read it, blinked again.

Dud hovered expectantly. 'Not *another* rejection I hope, Kate?'

'No,' said Kate slowly. She looked at Len, took in the lines of strain and worry, knew she'd been responsible for causing some of them. Well, this might just take one or two away, if only temporarily.

'Remember that competition in the free newspaper? To write a poem advertising that posh new restaurant that's just opened?' She smiled guilelessly at Dud. 'You know, the one Anna went to during the week?'

'No,' said Len, mystified. She was always going in for competitions. He couldn't keep track of them all.

'Yes you do, I told you. You grumbled about wasting a stamp.'

Len shook his head, still none the wiser.

'Well... I've won!'

Len, Oliver, and Dud all stared at her openmouthed.

Dud was thinking, Kate, won a POETRY competition? Never! They must have made a mistake.

Len's thoughts ran along similar lines - We don't win things. We've never won anything in our lives.

Oliver, remembering the Poets' Corner Reject hanging above them, decided privately that Kate's must have been the only entry.

'What's the prize?' asked Len curiously.

'I told you that as well. A meal for two. At the restaurant. Tomorrow night. Just as well you swapped with Anna, wasn't it?'

Madame Lesage and her group, and Mr. Miller and his group,

had at last departed, with much theatrical wrenching apart and fervent promises to reunite as soon as they'd dumped their charges - he in Liverpool, she in Paris - and much flowery protestations of indebted gratitude to the best Youth Hostel in the Lake District - the whole country - the entire globe! (As they'd be sure to tell Major Pratt and Eloise.)

Dud's departure hadn't been quite so ecstatic. As the staff, dutifully lined up to wave him off, mumbled insincere farewells, he remarked ominously: 'I'll see you all next weekend at the Committee Meeting, when we find out Beckside's fate.' Then, with a last soulful look at Anna, he opened the throttle and slewed and skidded his way down the drive, missing the gatepost by a fraction of an inch.

The engine sputtered and died, revved, died, revved again. A cloud of smoke rose above the trees, marking the motorbike's uncertain progress to the summit of the hill, then, as the descent down the far side began, gradually faded away.

And Beckside's staff heaved a collective sigh of relief.

Although it rained for most of the following day, the clouds broke up and dispersed towards evening, and the sun was now setting behind the hills overlooking the lake. It was pleasantly warm on the terrace.

Kate selected another strawberry dipped in chocolate, and bit lazily into it. Heaven. And the meal had been heaven too. Actually, it wouldn't have mattered had it been egg and chips - it was the fact somebody else had cooked it that made it such a treat. She'd started with carrot and orange sorbet, gone on to roast leg of lamb, and finished with summer pudding; Len had chosen spiced Cumberland soup, halibut, and Irish coffee pudding, and both of them had gasped at the prices on the menu.

'Shall I ask for the menu as a momento of our visit?' she suggested, and they both laughed. When Major Pratt had phoned earlier to pass on a few selected praises from Madame Lesage (not *too* expansively; one didn't want the paid staff thinking they were indispensable) he had emphasised the impact last night's menu appeared to have made. 'I don't know what you served,' he commented grudgingly, 'But it seems to have made a lasting impression. And she appreciated being given the menu as a momento, so they could show everyone at the Catering College what they'd had for dessert...'

Kate had brought the camera to record the occasion, as this would be the one and only time they'd eat here. She took a photo of Len reaching for his brandy, he took one of her biting into yet another strawberry, and they used up the last of the film to photograph the rays of the setting sun slanting across mulberry velvet hills onto a lake of golden champagne.

The proprietor approached and enquired if they'd enjoyed their meal.

'Thank you, yes,' replied Kate. 'It was fantastic!'

'Good. Anything else you'd like, to round the evening off?'

Len smiled, swilled his brandy round the glass, and raised it in a silent toast to Kate.

There was, but that would come later.

THREE: A JOB FOR EWAN

Len was in a restless mood.

It was the fatal combination of 'Sea Breezes' arriving that morning ('Sea Breezes' was a monthly shipping magazine to which he had subscribed for more years than he could remember), and a fresh, energising wind that whipped in from the west, chasing spectacular cloud formations and the odd squally shower across a brilliant blue sky. Each factor on its own would have stirred in him a longing to be near the sea; together the effect was irresistible, and he had to stifle an overpowering urge to flee The Office and drive, there and then, to the Mersey estuary.

Because there was no chance of satisfying his "lust for the sea", as Kate called it, in the near future. Their next day off, still five days away, was earmarked for a trip to Cash and Carry, and any thoughts of standing on the seashore by the Fort Perch Rock, facing out to the open sea and listening to the waves roar and crash on the rocks as the tide tumbled in, could be forgotten.

He could smell it.

He might be standing in the cell-like confines of The Office staring at baked beans, cheese spreads, and teabags, but the cleansing salty tang of the sea was actually in his nostrils.

Dud had pretended not to hear the belligerent tirade that had poured into his left eardrum for most of the journey, but even he couldn't ignore the imperious dig in the ribs from his pillion passenger that caused the Honda to swerve outwards in an arc into the oncoming traffic. A van careered past, horn blaring, the driver's face white with terror.

'Can't you bloody hear me? I said, pull in at those toilets!' bellowed Mona.

Dud muttered under his breath. They were cutting things fine for the Committee Meeting as it was, and everyone knew Major Pratt took a very dim view of tardiness. And there was another matter he wished to pursue before it started, concerning Anna.

'Can't you wait til we get there?'

'NO!'

Tch! *Another* delay while she heaved herself off the bike, peeled off waterproofs and overtrousers, and searched for a coin (which meant he'd have to peel off his waterproofs and overtrousers as well, because she wouldn't be able to find one). There'd be no time to waylay Anna, as planned, and reassure her that Mona was no threat, there was no need to be jealous.

Because one thing could be guaranteed; if Major Pratt was Chairing a Meeting scheduled to start at 8.30PM, that Meeting would start at 8.30PM. On the dot.

The Office was claustrophobic at the best of times, but tonight seemed more like a coffin than ever. And the knowledge that when he did emerge from it he'd spend the rest of the evening sitting through a stultifying Committee Meeting, during which Beckside's fate would be announced, made Len feel even more unsettled.

He flicked aimlessly to the adverts for maritime memorabilia at the back of 'Sea Breezes', stuck the "Back In A Moment" card in the window, and, with the stealth of an Indian brave reconnoitring a Wild West Fort swarming with Bluecoats, padded towards the front door. From the kitchen he heard Oliver's petulant whine: 'But why have Anna and I got to sit through this stupid Meeting?'

'I keep telling you,' Kate's voice explained wearily. 'It's regarded as a great honour for you to be invited.'

Silence.

Len smiled to himself. That fell on stony ground.

'And before you volunteer for Shop Duty to get out of it,' continued Kate. 'They give us a dispensation to shorten the shop hours for the evening, to allow us to attend.'

Yes, nodded Len wryly, opening the front door and sniffing the wind like a dog picking up a familiar and much-loved scent. We've all tried that one.

Major Pratt made up his bed, laid out his pyjamas neatly on the pillow, arranged his travelling clock, indigestion tablets, spare pair of reading glasses, and box of tissues on his bedside chair, then looked at his watch. 8.10PM. Just time for shower.

He strode briskly to the Men's Washroom, adjusting the personal headphone thing his daughter had given him for his last birthday and beating time against his thigh as 'The Liberty Bell' crashed joyously to its crescendo. Nothing like a bit of Souza to put a spring in the step! In fact he'd suggest, under Any Other Business, that Len played it every morning at 7.30AM on the Tannoy system. It was so *unnecessary,* the way half the hostel always trailed down late for breakfast. People needed something invigorating to wake up to, not namby-pamby classical guitar rubbish that was more likely to lull them back to sleep. There'd be no problems with tardy-risers after a good blast of Souza!

He glanced out of the corridor window at the clouds scudding over the fells; ideal sailing weather. The weekend had worked out well. He and Eloise had been invited by friends with a holiday cottage near Ambleside to join them for a spot of sailing on Windermere tomorrow afternoon. Which coincided nicely with the Committee Meeting at Beckside this evening. Which meant, of course, they could claim expenses for the trip.

He right-wheeled into the Washroom, toilet bag under arm.

A row of lavatory cubicles took up one wall, facing a line of washbasins which were all in use except one.

Major Pratt beamed in friendly approval at the fit, muscular young men attending to their ablutions. Nordic Vikings, from the look of them (and the buzz of conversation in some unfamiliar language, guttural but pleasant, which filled the room), come from their fiords and high mountains to visit our sceptred isle. An ideal opportunity to extend the hand of friendship, promote international goodwill and understanding. Hands across the sea and so on.

First things first, however; best nip in the shower while it was free. Plenty of time for the welcoming, how-nice-to-get-to-know-you, let-me-put-you-at-ease-and-help-with-any-language-problems-you-may-have chat when he came out, or somebody else might dive in and cause him to be late for the Meeting. And punctuality was a virtue Major Pratt promoted with vigour. He took a *very* dim view of tardiness.

He was vaguely aware of a voice calling something in the unfamiliar language: *'De douche werkt niet!'* (The shower is broken!) as he stepped into the shower cubicle and undressed, but assumed it was some communication between the group. He adjusted the temperature setting, and reached for his soap.

Then stood, paralysed with shock, as a deluge of cold water

86

cascaded down his back, searching out every fold and cranny before pouring down his legs to freeze his well-pedicured feet.

Len watched the ancient Morris Minor splutter unsteadily along the last few yards of road and (just) manage the turn into the drive. He was sympathetic; he knew the feeling. With detached curiosity he worked out the odds of the engine actually getting the car up the drive.

The little car struggled up the incline and stopped fifty yards away, steam billowing from its bonnet. The driver's head dropped forward onto hands that still gripped the steering wheel, and remained motionless.

There was something vaguely familiar about the slumped figure. Len peered more closely, grinned, and started down the steps to welcome the weary traveller.

Major Pratt snatched his towel, wrapped it around his corpulent middle, and staggered from the cubicle.

'THE SHOWER'S BROKEN!' he exploded.

'Yes,' agreed his neighbour mournfully, balancing on one foot as he clipped the toenails of the other into a washbasin.

Major Pratt stamped back into the cubicle and glared upwards. The shower head had been removed.

Damn foreigners, vandalising everything!

He frowned suspiciously at the line of robust outdoor-types, but had to admit they didn't look the sort to indulge in mindless destruction. They scrubbed their armpits with dedicated thoroughness, shaved, brushed teeth; none seemed to be convulsed with secret mirth at the result of a childish prank. The only other occupant was a wizened ancient in blue striped pyjamas, stooped over the washbasin at the far end, making hideous noises in his throat and taking no notice whatsoever of the proceedings. No, decided Major Pratt. He couldn't possibly be the culprit. He'd scarcely be able to reach the controls, let alone the shower head.

It was damned provoking. There he was, stark naked and in need of a shower... and by the time he got dressed and went in search of Len to mend it, there wouldn't be time for one. Tch! He'd have to make do with a quick wash and shave, and notify Len as soon as he went downstairs.

He headed to the vacant washbasin, between the gargling ancient and a youth with the physique of Hercules who was soaping his ample genitalia, and looked for somewhere to put his clothes. All the hooks were full. So were the chairs provided for the purpose. We need more hooks in here, he thought irritably, then remembered he'd used his casting vote against the extravagance, as it had seemed at the time, of Len's request to purchase more.

'OK to use your chair?' he approached his muscular neighbour. 'Uh?'

Major Pratt, tactfully averting his eyes (you had to be so careful in these situations; common courtesy demanded eye-contact, but you certainly didn't want anyone getting the wrong idea), draped his clothes over the mound already covering the chair, propped his shaving tackle behind the taps, and pressed the hot tap. Water shot into the bowl, swirled round in a torrent, and swished out again, soaking the ancient on the other side.

'Sorry,' muttered Major Pratt, looking for the plug. 'Damn plug's missing now! Anyone got a spare plug?'

The line of faces turned towards him with uncomprehending stares, and he tried to summon from his considerable French and German vocabulary the translation for plug. It eluded him.

'Hij heeft un stopper nodig,' (He wants a plug,) guessed one perceptive individual halfway along the line. *'Heeft iemand un stopper?'* (Has anyone got a plug?)

Heads shook politely, the line once more returned to their ablutions, the conversation resumed, the toothless ancient reproachfully wiped his pyjamas, and Major Pratt glared at his plugless basin. Good lord, was Len letting the place fall down around him? First no shower head, now no plug…Once again he was faced with either getting dressed to inform Len, who (knowing Len) would trail down to the store room and then not be able to find the dratted things anyway, or managing without one. He glanced at his watch. Nearly twenty past...

He commenced his shave, which, to Major Pratt, was a reassuring, unchanging ritual; one held one's soapdish in one's left hand as the right hand dipped the brush in the water, having first ensured it was exactly the required temperature and came to exactly the required level in the washbasin. In the present circumstances he had to press the tap with his right wrist whilst

88

trying simultaneously to wet the brush underneath it, and all he succeeded in doing was soaking his neighbour with a series of sudden gushes of water that hit him sideways on.

The young Dutchman on the other side winked.

'Uitdagingen maken het leven wel veel boeinder!' (Isn't life exciting when there's a challenge!) he remarked companionably.

Major Pratt, who had long since lost all desire to foster international friendship with hands-across-the-sea bonhomie and interested enquiries as to which distant land our welcome Viking visitors had journeyed from, turned on him a glare guaranteed to strike mute any squaddie stupid enough to prolong the pleasantries of visiting Royalty with matey egalitarian chatter, and gave a dismissive grunt.

For the first time in living memory the Chairman, renowned for his oft-repeated views on tardiness, was going to be late for his own Committee Meeting.

Kate, having spread tomorrow morning's bacon on catering trays, was covering it with clingfilm when Major Pratt blazed in.

'Ah.' He pulled up short and glared round. 'Where's Len?'

'In The Office.'

'No he's not!' Major Pratt's plump jowls quivered with disapproval. The whole thing was so *typical* of Len and Kate; one wandering off like the lost tribe of Israel, the other clueless as usual - and the Meeting due to start (he checked his watch) in less than a minute. 'And we've got a crisis on the plugs front!'

'Plugs front?' repeated Kate, mystified.

'Yes. Plugs, Kate, plugs! In the Men's Washroom. One of the plugs has gone. The shower head's disappeared as well!'

'Oh. Yes, it's amazing what people will take, isn't it.'

Major Pratt stared at her. 'Take? What d'you mean, take?'

'Well... Remove from the premises.'

'Don't be ridiculous Kate, hostellers don't "take" things! Anyway, what on earth would anyone want a shower head for? Or a washbasin plug?'

'I've no idea. They don't come and tell me they're taking things, or why,' retorted Kate, stung. She turned to Oliver, who was hovering by the cereal bins. 'Was the shower head there this morning when you cleaned the Washrooms?'

Oliver, who hadn't a clue whether it had been there or not,

assured her that it was.

'And all the plugs?'

'Definitely.'

Kate sighed. 'I'll tell Len.'

'Yes, do, Kate, because it doesn't give a very good impression, does it. Place full of foreigners up there, what must they think? Quite apart from which, it's delayed me. And you know my views on tardiness -' He broke off in irritated indignation as a tall figure sauntered in, and winked at Kate.

'Aye aye there Missus. You're looking good!'

Major Pratt stared. Who on earth was *this*, barging in as if he owned the place? With increasing disapproval he took in the pirate-like face and unruly grey locks.

Anna and Oliver were also regarding the newcomer with interest. As for Kate, greeting him with delighted surprise, one would almost think that matters of urgency like shower heads and sink plugs - to say nothing of the Committee Meeting which should have started (Major Pratt again looked ostentatiously at his watch) forty five seconds ago - had been flushed right out of her head by the arrival of this disreputable-looking individual.

He was right.

Len and Ewan had known each other since their teens, and could have attracted quite a following in the Liverpool Folk Scene (Len played guitar, Ewan mandolin) if Len hadn't kept on returning to sea and Ewan disappearing to Scotland.

As the years passed, they saw him at periodic intervals when he'd arrive out of the blue, taking up with easy humour where they'd left off before vanishing once more on some nomadic jaunt, some entrepreneurial venture, some money-making certainty, some eternal quest for the unfindable - from which, he freely admitted, he'd probably run a mile anyway if he ever found.

Ewan had been born and spent most of his early childhood in Glasgow, where his father, a Liverpool seaman, had married a local girl when his ship docked there. As the family grew they moved to Merseyside. Ewan left school at fifteen and started an apprenticeship at Cammell Lairds shipyard until, after one row too many with the foreman, he walked out and hitched a lift to Scotland to visit his relatives, one of whom was leaving to work in Aberdeen. Ewan tagged along. The next few years were spent roaming the Scottish Highlands, earning his living from whatever casual work presented itself. He picked soft fruit in the Angus glens, he went out with the fishing fleet at Mallaig, he worked in a papermill near Fort William, he joined a wood-cutting gang in Sutherland, he was a barman in Stornoway, he gutted fish in Lochinver, he lived in Inverness with a Canadian girl, and, when the grand passion fizzled out, he hitched to London and got a job in a fast-food joint.

He formed a guitar-and-mandolin folksinging duo with another Scot. They busked in the West End until a fight over a pitch landed him in hospital, where he fell in love with a nurse until they visited her brother in Brighton who made a pass at him. Time, as they say, for a quick exit, and he returned once more to Scotland.

Performing at a Fringe gig in the Edinburgh Festival he finally met the girl of his dreams (he thought) who was, of all things, a Civil Servant on holiday from Portsmouth. And with this most unlikely of partners, Ewan finally turned respectable, got married, and went to ground in deepest Hampshire, where he got a job at a Boating Marina. A few years elapsed with no sightings other than a yearly Christmas card, then everything blew up in a bitter divorce.

Ewan disappeared again. Australia this time, selling hot dogs on a beach, bar work, rickshaw-pedalling, busking, anything. He travelled around; a postcard would occasionally arrive from New Zealand or Fiji.

The next anyone heard was from London. Ewan's fortunes had picked up. He was now part owner of a night club, and having a passionate affair with a Country and Western singer, the exotically named Conchita. He told Len and Kate about her at a friend's party held to mark the Tall Ships Race in Liverpool in 1984. Naturally, they'd been dying of curiosity to see this fascinating siren, but she'd been unable to come owing to a gig in London.

And in fact she'd missed a truly memorable party. Quite apart from the setting, on the New Brighton side of the River Mersey - the garden sloped down to the promenade and river, which meant everyone had an unsurpassed view of the ships over the heads of crowds thronging Radio and TV Broadcasting vans, hot dog and ice-cream stalls, and street entertainers - it was an extremely successful mix of young and old, family and friends, and a carefree, carnival-like atmosphere enhanced the entire day.

The Tall Ships progressed with stately splendour down the river to the open sea, some spectacular and majestic, others quaint or unusual; the crowds followed, waving farewell until the last billowing sail was out of sight. The afternoon turned to evening, the evening to night, and as the lights twinkled across the river from Liverpool and it got colder, the older ones moved indoors, the younger generation commandeered the stereo system rigged up in the garden and took over, and somewhere along the way Ewan disappeared, and that was the last they'd seen of him.

Until now.

'This is Ewan,' Kate introduced him, as though that explained everything.

'Pleased to meet you.' Major Pratt sounded anything but pleased. 'And now do excuse Kate rushing off and leaving you, but -' Again he was interrupted, this time by Dud clumping in, unstrapping his crash helmet.

'This is a bit of luck! Thought the Meeting would have started by now. Just want a quiet word, Anna, before we go in.'

'Dud, we're already running late!' snapped Major Pratt. Good lord, what was the matter with them all? Even *Dud* arriving late!

'I've got to make a phone call.' Clearly indifferent to Major Pratt's exasperated sigh, Anna slipped from the kitchen.

One must be tolerant of Anna's unfamiliarity with established routines (obviously Len and Kate hadn't explained what an honour it was to attend a Committee Meeting), but Major Pratt, impatiently motioning Dud and Oliver ahead of him towards the Quiet Room before anything else caused yet more delay, felt obliged to reiterate his views on tardiness. He turned, assuming Kate was behind him, to remind her that he'd like refreshments at 10.30pm *prompt,* if she pleased.

She wasn't there.

Fingers itching to violently shake her, he swooped back to the kitchen. Look at this! Calmly pouring a mug of tea for the stranger! *Now*, of all times!

'I'll be there in a minute, I'm just -' began Kate.

'I should have thought you'd be there right now!' You do realise we'll be discussing Beckside's future tonight?'

'Yes.' Kate was suitably sombre and respectful.

He exhaled noisily. It was beneath one's dignity to have to *drag* the paid staff to a Meeting they should be only too grateful to attend, especially with this unknown stranger looking on... Well, it wouldn't matter too much if she missed the opening formalities for once, he supposed.

'I'll tell everyone you'll join us *in a moment.*' There was a warning gleam in his eye.

'Yes, all right,' nodded Kate, turning eagerly back to Ewan.

Once again Major Pratt had an uncomfortable suspicion she'd forget all about him the moment he turned away.

Once again, he was right.

The Quiet Room was intended to provide a retreat for those sensitive souls wishing to read, letter-write, or catalogue wild flowers and geological specimens, but ended up mainly being used by teenagers embarking on holiday romances.

For tonight's Meeting a variety of chairs had been arranged in horseshoe formation, at the open end of which sat Major Pratt, a small occasional table covered with papers in front of him. Oliver, wriggling in a lumpy fireside chair, recognised most of the Committee Members (who now sat respectfully waiting, each equipped with notebook and pen) except for two strangers; an almost spherical worthy submerged in a sagging armchair, and a bony-kneed brunette hunched over a notebook, face hidden by a curtain of lifeless hair.

Major Pratt was pompous and self-important, but not vindictive. Now that the Meeting was (at last) about to start, he made a genuine effort to banish all niggling irritations from mind as he finished shuffling his papers and looked up.

'Right. Good evening, everyone. Apologies for the delay, due to a most unsatisfactory state of affairs in the Men's Washroom, about which I'll be grilling Len in Any Other Business.'

'Not literally, I hope!' giggled Dud.

'Well, I think we might find barbecued Len for Apres-Meeting refreshments a little *too* tough to chew.' He paused as a ripple of amusement circulated at this pleasantry, then grew serious. 'Actually, they've been delayed; a friend has unexpectedly arrived. I gave Kate permission to miss the opening formalities, then Len collared me in the Reception Area. *He* wanted to miss them as well!' He shook his head. Such a difficult species to comprehend, even when one did possess unlimited patience.

Anna came in, her distinctive perfume issuing a subtle challenge to the fug of cigarette smoke forming above Mona and Dud. Mona's eyes narrowed. She didn't like the look of This One at all; she'd keep her eyes skinned here. However, she'd resolved to take to heart Bridie's latest homilies regarding the hauling in of the matrimonial fish. Which were, keep on that slippery sod's tail and don't let him out of sight for a minute - and *remember to curb the temper*. Easier said than bloody done with the likes of him, but she was right. To achieve the objective it was worth zipping her lip for the time being. Plenty time to unzip it later.

'Ah,' smiled the Chairman, 'Anna. For those of you who haven't met, let me introduce Oliver and Anna - the artist in our midst. Did everyone hear about the amazing coincidence? The picture Eloise bought for my birthday a fortnight ago was actually painted by Anna here!'

There was a chorus of admiration, from which Mona noticeably abstained. She fixed Anna with a menacing scowl as Major Pratt nodded in turn to the pot-bellied worthy and the note-taker.

'Leslie, and Dottie. You know everyone else, don't you. Now, before we start - as ever, a quick reminder - has everyone claimed travelling expenses?'

There was a murmur of assent. As ever, everyone had.

'Tch! I see Len's forgotten to tell Anna and Oliver to bring paper and pen in case they wish to make any notes...'

Eloise obligingly passed across a couple of pages from her filofax, together with spare ballpoints.

'Thank you darling. So, I formally declare this Meeting open.' During the pause for effect, Oliver noticed Leslie's breathing had grown increasingly relaxed. 'First, Opening Remarks. Now at the risk of repeating myself - because I've said it before and I'll say it again - I really do find the dedication and enthusiasm of this Committee tremendously gratifying!'

There was a murmur of abashed modesty, during which he added privately that he'd find it even more gratifying if Mona showed less dedication and enthusiasm and didn't turn up at all.

Since Dud had taken up with her (Major Pratt had no idea where they'd met; he wasn't in the least bit interested in Dud's unsavoury affairs) her main priority in life appeared to be a determination - some might say obsession - to become a "real" Committee member. And, as he was equally determined the ghastly creature would never serve on any Committee of which he was Chairman, he was obliged to continually sidestep her demands with vague prevarications.

'I agree, darling,' his wife was saying. 'And isn't it nice to see the Seasonal staff so keen to join in and take part.'

'Certainly is!' agreed Dud, growing bolder.

'Don't you bloody start!' Mona half rose from her chair, all good intentions regarding the temporary curbing of the less appealing aspects of her nature immediately forgotten.

Major Pratt cleared his throat.

'Got that, Dottie?' he checked briskly. 'Dedication and enthusiasm, that's right. Next, Apologies.' (So much for Kate's promise to be here directly, but then that was Len and Kate for you; give them an already generous mile and they'd take the entire motorway.) 'Any apologies to pass on, apart from Nigel and Marcia of course? Anyone heard from them since the wedding, by the way?'

Mona pricked up her ears. Weddings, was it? Oh. Could be a chance to slip in a sly dig here, then.

'Yes,' stammered Babs, blushing crimson. 'I got a postcard this morning.'

'Did you, Babs?' coaxed Eloise, who prided herself on putting awe-struck inferiors at their ease. 'What did it say?'

'Erm, they're having a lovely time. And the weather's nice.'

'They're enjoying the honeymoon then,' summed up Brian.

'So,' added Mona with crafty cunning. 'They can recommend marriage, can they?'

'Oh yes. They didn't get much sleep the first night, though.'

There was an embarrassed silence. Babs turned from crimson to deep magenta.

'I... I mean, people kept coming and going past them all night.'

'Coming and going?' questioned Oliver, intrigued. He wasn't sure whether the lower castes were actually permitted to speak, or were expected to merely sit in awed silence, but he couldn't just nod understandingly, as Wilf as doing, over this one. 'You mean there was a lot of traffic outside?'

'No, somebody in Nigel's dormitory had a weak bladder, he kept going to the... the Rest Room every half hour. And tripping over peoples' rucksacks every time he passed.'

Oliver wondered if he'd had a lapse of concentration and missed part of the conversation. 'Did you say, in his dormitory?'

'Yes.'

'I thought they'd gone on honeymoon?'

'Yes, they have.'

'In a *dormitory?*'

'Yes.'

'You mean they're staying in a *Youth Hostel?*'

'Lots of people spend their honeymoons Youth Hostelling,' Major Pratt informed him coldly.

'Well, I wouldn't know, meself.' Mona flicked ash from her cigarette onto the floor.

'Eloise and I are doing something similar for our Anniversary later in the year. A sort of second honeymoon.'

'All right for some, isn't it,' sniffed Mona. 'Some of us haven't even had one yet!'

'They're actually staying in a *Youth Hostel?* On their HONEYMOON?' Oliver was still incredulous. He'd heard of some weird weddings and honeymoons, but this was something new... Separate sex dormitories, with weak-bladdered old men shuffling past all night? What sort of people wanted a wedding night like that?

'I've already told you, lots of people do,' snapped Major Pratt. 'Incidentally - under Apologies, include Albert, would you Dottie. He still can't travel.'

From Leslie's chair floated a contented sigh, and the even breathing changed imperceptibly into a gentle but unmistakable snore. Anna, using her knee as a paper rest, tried out a few doodling strokes with the ballpoint; some diverting occupation would obviously be necessary if her brain was to survive the evening without atrophying to mush. Shielding the paper from view with her left hand, she began a hideous caricature of Dud.

Dud gazed, entranced, at Anna's dark eyelashes cast down upon flawless cheeks. She was so delightfully interested in it all, wasn't she; look at her, making her little notes on her piece of paper, bless her artistic, impractical nature! She may not have thought to provide notebook and pen, but was at least using her unorthodox stationery, which was more than could be said for Mona, going all broody at the mention of weddings (she could forget *that* lark!) and contributing nothing to the proceedings.

Major Pratt checked his watch. He could, of course, dispatch someone to fetch Len and Kate, but that was so... undignified, somehow. He'd give them another thirty seconds.

'Right. On to Minutes of the Last Meeting -'

Brian's hand shot into the air. 'Point of order, Mr. Chairman. Only a minor detail, but I must pick up on it... did Dud make a *towel* rack, or *tea* towel rack for Wayfarers Hostel? Because a towel rack implies it's intended for the Washrooms, whereas if it's a *tea* towel rack, it would presumably be for a kitchen?'

The snoring from Leslie's chair increased in resonance. Oliver watched, mesmerised, as the braces on the globe-like belly rose and fell with soporific rhythm, and wondered if anyone would notice an additional descant accompaniment; since the topic had moved on from Nigel and Marcia's wedding night, boredom had set in and his own eyelids were growing heavy. He glanced at Anna's paper. She was working her way round the Committee members, doing a thumbnail sketch of each. The one of Leslie showed the armchair, the top of his head, and his stomach. A series of little Zs rose in the air above the chair.

Major Pratt shuffled through the Minutes, and Dud, who felt he'd been silent long enough, at last had an opportunity to toss in his own invaluable contribution. Looking at Anna (she must have made more notes on her humble sheet of paper than all the rest of them in their notebooks!), he lifted a dirty carrier bag from which protruded four white wooden prongs of uneven lengths, festooned with dried paint drips.

'Yep. It is indeed a tea towel rack. And I -'

'Not yet, Dud,' broke in Major Pratt hastily, as Brian's hand again started to rise. 'We're still on Minutes of the Last Meeting. That's Matters Arising. So, subject to amendment, paragraph five, sub paragraph three, line four, could we - thank you darling. Seconded, Brian.'

From Leslie's chair rose a particularly vigorous snore, followed by a startled silence as he realised he'd woken himself up. He hoisted himself to a slightly more upright position.

'Now.' The Chairman, ignoring the interruption, looked at his watch. 'Matters Arising, and *still* no sign of that pair malingering in that damn kitchen. I'd better send someone to -'

But Dud was already rustling into his carrier bag. He proudly held aloft a roughly-cut wooden rectangular base from which four white wooden batons, each approximately a half metre long, jutted in irregular angles. 'As I was saying, it gives me great pleasure to donate this little beauty - which I made myself - to Beckside's Self-Caterers' Kitchen!'

The Committee appraised Dud's handiwork with appreciative, if slightly bemused, interest.

'I hope he puts a plaque under it so nobody'll think *I* made it,' muttered Oliver to Anna behind his hand.

'Did you say something, Oliver?' enquired Major Pratt smoothly. 'I should have pointed out, for the benefit of guests, that all remarks must be directed strictly *through the Chair.*'

Babs, who had been casting around for something complimentary to say about Dud's tea towel rack, finally came up with, 'It's saved us a lot of money, hasn't it?'

'Absolutely,' agreed Major Pratt, mentally postponing Len and Kate for yet *another* thirty seconds. 'Don't forget to claim expenses for the wood and so on... You already have? Good.' He turned his professional smile to Mona. 'And I understand Mona has sewn new curtains for Beckside's Quiet Room, the old ones having all but disintegrated. Is that right, Mona?'

'Do show us,' smiled Eloise, as Mona hauled a huge white paper parcel, enmeshed in string, from under her chair. Oliver, about to whisper something to Anna about Moby Dick trussed up in harpoon ropes, caught Major Pratt's eye and coughed instead.

'This is the material I chose for my suit,' she announced, slashing through the string with Dud's Swiss Army knife. 'I got a real bargain! I browbeat the fella til he reduced it.'

If she'd browbeaten him a bit more he'd probably have paid her to take it, thought Oliver, as a jarring and discordant plethora of multi-coloured daisies against a background of puce was revealed under the layers of paper.

The Committee stared in horrified silence. Eloise, as ever, took the situation in hand with gracious aplomb.

'*What* an... eye-catching design, Mona. So vibrant! But, er... I thought we agreed to co-ordinate with the colour scheme already in place; warm peach, and cream?'

'I don't want a peach and cream suit.' Mona dismissed such irrelevancies impatiently. 'I want something a bit cheerful like. I've brought the receipt to claim me expenses.'

'But they clash with the décor!' Brian pointed out nervously.

The understatement of all time, fumed Major Pratt, shuddering as the nausea-inducing additions to the "Quiet" Room were held aloft for all to admire.

'Not at all!' snapped Mona witheringly. 'They go with it lovely!'

She heaved herself onto a chair, unhooked the unassuming drapes which had complemented the restful aura of the Quiet Room for years, dropped them contemptuously onto the floor, hooked the replacements into place, and pulled them together with a triumphant flourish that almost wrenched the curtain pole from its fixtures.

A six inch gap appeared between curtains and sill, and window-frame at either end.

Faces registering a range of emotions from shock to terror (except for Oliver, who fought to keep his straight by masking hysterical giggles with a severe spasm of coughing, and Anna, surreptitiously sketching the scene), the Committee Members shrank into their chairs as Mona's blasphemous oaths, rising in crescendo like Hitler driving himself into a frenzy at a 1930s rally, compared Dud - who'd been given specific instructions to add on sufficient extra for hems when relaying the required measurements to the seamstress - to, among other less savoury portrayals, an impotent baboon.

Leslie, roused from his slumbers, yawned, snuffled, and levered himself stiffly out of his chair.

'Just resting my eyes,' he explained. 'Is it time for the refreshments now?'

Unaware of the bizarre events in the Quiet Room, the fugitives in the kitchen were pursuing their own agenda.

'Am I hearing right?' repeated Len in amazement. 'You? Work *here*?'

'What's so weird about that? You do.'

'We mightn't, after tonight.' Len paused. 'Anyway, there's no way they'd employ a third Assistant, even if you were serious -'

'I am serious.'

'- They've already cut us down from three to two seasonal staff this year.'

Ewan speared another potato. (Kate had hurriedly heated up a pan of left-over scouse.) 'D'you know of anything else going around here then? Casual kitchen porter? Anything at all?'

'I thought you were coining it in with your club in London? What d'you want a job peeling spuds and cleaning cludgies for?' Len looked at him shrewdly. 'You in trouble?'

'Yes and no.'

'Yes and no? Who's after you?'

'Nobody. Or at least, nobody who'd think of looking for me in a Youth Hostel in the middle of nowhere.'

'What does Conchita think about all this?' asked Kate.

Ewan looked sheepish. 'Let's just say she's not likely to find life so unbearable without me that she'll turn up asking for a job as well. It's her husband who's looking for me, actually. He's back on the scene -'

He broke off as, from the direction of the usually sedate Quiet Room, came sounds of escalating tumult followed by footsteps pounding towards the kitchen. Dud burst in, face beetroot red and sweating profusely. He ignored the newcomer apart from an instinctive curious glance; this was no time for introductions to Len's dubious-looking friends. Scapegoats were urgently needed in the Quiet Room, which was why he'd so readily obeyed Major Pratt's order to *please fetch Len and Kate from the kitchen, Dud.*

'Major Pratt,' he announced sternly, 'Is not a happy bunny. A few moments, he told you, to chat to your friend!'

'Surely that's not what all the shouting's about?' asked Kate incredulously. 'Us, being a couple of minutes late?'

'Just hurry up!' snapped Dud.

Len resignedly tossed the flat keys to Ewan. They'd got away with far longer than he'd hoped before the bloodhounds were dispatched to round them up, but there was no escape this time.

'Make yourself at home til we're finished,' he said, and then, conscious of the possible ironic double meaning, trailed obediently with Kate behind Dud to face short-term retribution, and, more seriously, possible long-term redundancy.

Heightened emotions in the Committee Meeting had subsided

to a rather forced entente cordiale when Eloise, with perfect-timing diplomacy, remembered that new curtains were needed in the Self-Caterers' Kitchen of the neighbouring hostel, Wayfarers, where the windows were slightly smaller than Beckside's Quiet Room. And as the walls had recently been emulsioned blue, the curtains might... er, co-ordinate more pleasingly, mightn't they. And might not such stimulating, invigorating colours be more appropriate for a kitchen than a Quiet Room?

Dottie was recording unanimous approval to this solution when Dud ushered in Kate and Len like truants delivered to the Headmaster's study by an avenging prefect.

'Ah. At last.' Major Pratt eyed the newcomers coldly. 'We've already disposed of - and moved on from - the Quiet Room Curtains, in addition to everything else you've missed through your unpunctuality. They'll be re-allocated to Wayfarers.'

There was an uncomfortable silence, and Kate's stomach turned to ice. Nobody puts new curtains in a hostel that is about to close; Beckside was obviously history.

'Does that all come under Matters Arising?' asked Dottie.

'I think so, dear,' Eloise nodded.

Leslie's snores grew louder. Brian tapped him discreetly on the shoulder. He jerked upright, then settled down comfortably once more, like a cat shifting position before resuming an interrupted sleep. Major Pratt gave an indulgent chuckle at this, to lighten the atmosphere and indicate that things could now progress to a far more agreeable topic - one he'd been looking forward to discussing all evening.

'Right,' he went on in the tone of one driven to the limits of patience but still valiantly plumbing reserves. 'Now you're here at last, we can move on to the next item: Beckside itself. Which I propose to bracket with Correspondence. Now, as we all know, the future of Beckside has been hanging in the balance -'

All eyes swivelled to Kate and Len, who stared stonily back.

'- And it's always sad when financial pressures force the closure of a hostel. Nobody *wants* to close hostels willy-nilly, despite what some people may think.' He glanced at Len. 'Particularly in the light of recent compliments regarding your creativity of menus instead of the usual unimaginative stereotype institutional fare. And, of course, such a glowing Inspection Report. Even the National Office wallahs agreed about that.' He paused, then added with a shrug, 'Frankly, I was surprised. I hadn't realised it was so impressive. Still, there we are.'

Len, aware of puzzled glances from Anna and Oliver (and Dud), avoided eye contact with all three.

'Now we lease the building - for a peppercorn rent, I might add - from an old gentleman in Glasgow. Must be pretty well off, this chappie, because if he charged us anything like its true value we'd have had to close years ago. Anyway, the point is -'

He paused, and Len's heart lurched. How would it feel to look at the dirty paving slabs of a shopping precinct, select a doorway, know this was your bed, your armchair, your wardrobe, your larder; know there's no fire to switch on when you're cold, no kettle to plug in for a hot drink? To sleep in your clothes every night on folded cardboard boxes as ground insulation against the cold? (Kate's feet were bad enough in a warm bed!) To stand, legs aching, hour after hour in the rain, selling "The Big Issue"? He always bought "The Issue" himself and felt it should be compulsory reading for all MPs, privatised industries fat cats, and management of huge business empires. Occasionally Kate brought vendors back to Beckside and provided them with a couple of square meals and the opportunity to shower and wash their clothes; how many erstwhile colleagues would do the same for them?

'- That not only is Mr. MacTavish agreeable to renewing the lease on the same extremely favourable terms,' Major Pratt smiled approvingly at Anna. (How nice to see *one* keen member of staff! Why, she must almost have filled her piece of paper with diligently jotted notes by now!) 'But Beckside has made sufficient profit - just - to quash, for the time being at any rate, all uncertainties and rumours regarding possible closure. So there we are! Good news, eh?'

There was a murmur of approval. Everyone on The Committee already knew unofficially anyway.

'Especially so, darling, when we remember that Beckside celebrates forty years as a Youth Hostel this September,' prompted Eloise.

'Yes. And...' Major Pratt paused again to give his next announcement greater impact, 'There's another reason why September is significant!'

The Committee pricked up their ears. This was something

they didn't know.

'I've discovered that it's Mr. MacTavish's seventieth birthday on the twenty-first.' Major Pratt sifted through his papers, selected a letter, tapped it with his pen. 'Now I know this will all sound rather sudden. And, of course, you may wish to throw the whole idea out of the window...' He glanced around. The Committee gazed respectfully back. Evidently they did not wish to throw their Chairman's idea out of the window. '...But we thought it might be rather fun to hold some sort of celebration to mark Beckside's Fortieth Year, now its future is secure. *Then* we thought - it was a sort of, you know, natural progression, really - as a tribute to Beckside's benefactor, why not mark his birthday as well? Incorporate both events into one, and invite him as Guest of Honour? A rather charming idea in my view, for which we have Eloise to thank.' He gestured towards Eloise, who acknowledged the tribute with a modest smile.

Kate flashed an apprehensive glance at Len.

'Do you think he'd attend?' asked Dottie doubtfully. 'After all, he's never accepted any previous invitations, has he? He never comes to England. None of us have ever met him!'

'All the more reason to bring off what would be rather a coup, don't you think? But obviously, before we could take the concept beyond the abstract idea, we had to consider his possible state of health, social calendar, and so on. So we, you know, rather anticipated your approval on this one. I couldn't foresee anyone objecting...?' Major Pratt looked round, eyebrows raised. He had anticipated correctly. Nobody objected. 'So we put out a few preliminary feelers via his solicitor -' He lifted the letter aloft triumphantly. 'Who has now replied, saying that Mr. MacTavish would be happy to accept our invitation.'

'Brilliant!' Dud punched the air with his hand.

Leslie's snores climaxed to a shuddering snort. The lolling head jerked upright; he looked around with an air of guilty alertness. 'Wha... what?'

'Normally we'd have far longer to organise an Event of this stature,' continued Major Pratt, ignoring the interruption. 'But of course the circumstances were somewhat unusual in that none of us knew whether the Hostel would actually survive. However - and I can't stress this enough - we've really got to pull out all the stops on this one, make up for lost time. Can't have Mr.

MacTavish turning up to some, you know, dismal second-rate affair smacking of untalented amateurs doing their best.' He glanced at Kate. 'So Eloise has kindly offered to supervise the choice of menu, table decoration and so on, so everything's done with, you know, élan, style, panache - no offence, Kate - and the date we've agreed on, as it very conveniently falls on a weekend, is Saturday the twenty first of September.'

'Oh no,' groaned Kate.

'What's wrong?' Major Pratt looked at her sharply.

'It's our Twenty-fifth Wedding Anniversary,' explained Len.

They didn't want a big fuss, a lavish party. What they did want was to wake up in a quiet hotel (Kate had sworn on pain of death not to set foot in Beckside's catering kitchen on her Silver Wedding), have lunch with Mike and Tony and their girlfriends, then drive north to spend a week far away from crowds, noise, and bustle, in a cottage on one of the more remote Hebridean islands. They'd already booked their week's leave.

'Is it really? Well,' said Major Pratt magnanimously. 'Seeing as it's a special occasion, I don't think there'd be any objection to, you know, combining your Anniversary with Beckside's, would there?' He looked around the Committee.

Kate closed her eyes and bit her lip. Oh God, no. Not their Silver Wedding. The one day in the year... the ONE DAY she truly couldn't bear to spend toiling in Beckside's sweltering kitchen...

'*What* a lovely idea, darling.' Eloise smiled at her husband, then turned to Kate. 'Especially since your life has been tied up with Beckside's for so long, Kate. Symbolic, really.'

There was a distinctly unenthusiastic pause. It was symbolic all right, thought Len, unable to meet Kate's eye. A day of stress, shredded nerves, and unremitting hard work. Everyone's dream Silver Wedding.

'A triple celebration!' fluttered Babs delightedly, wondering why Kate looked so downhearted. Surely she'd jump at the chance of combining their Silver Wedding with Beckside's Jubilee? Such a romantic, exciting idea! It would all be such *fun*!

'Yes,' agreed Eloise, 'And the first and most obvious decision is, sit-down meal or buffet? Personally, I feel a buffet would be the better option for the numbers involved. About a hundred, I should imagine. And I suggest a Scottish theme. Rather obvious, admittedly, but *safe*, bearing in mind we've never met the elusive Mr. MacTavish. Traditional Scottish fare... little plates of haggis and, er, neeps, whatever they are. Such a novelty! And oatcakes and bannocks and things. And, er, a... a cloutie dumpling. All terribly wholesome, and, you know, *Scottish*.'

There was a chorus of admiring enthusiasm.

'And then, tableware. I do love to see well-laundered crisp white linen tablecloths, don't you? And of course tartan loops and swags, with large bows tied on the corners, and baskets of cheese straws and so on with tartan ribbons on the handles -'

'They sell tartan serviettes in the tourist gift shop in the village,' suggested Babs helpfully.

There was a pause.

'*What* a quaint suggestion, Babs. But where we have tartan, it must be the authentic MacTavish tartan, mustn't it, not hideous mass-produced souvenirs for Japanese tourists. No, I think white linen napkins, dear.'

'We've already researched Mr MacTavish's tartan,' added Major Pratt. 'Which is predominantly green and blue, so we don't want horrid garish red things everywhere. Perhaps I should emphasise that we'll be inviting, you know, Anyone-Who's-Anyone. VIPs. Bigwigs in Conservation and Outdoor Pursuits. High-ranking officials from National Office. Possibly even minor Royalty, one never knows. Local dignitaries. The media, of course...'

'You mean, a classy do, like,' nodded Dud, scratching his crotch.

'I could wear me new suit,' mused Mona, eyeing Dud speculatively. She could (or rather, he could) lash out on a posh hat to go with it. Then inspiration struck - *why not use the occasion to announce the Engagement*? All the nobs in attendance - the very dab! Might be a reporter from "Hello!" magazine as well. And they'd do all right for wedding presents - everyone would be half cut. (Scottish theme, was it. Well, they'd have to lay on plenty of whisky then, wouldn't they. She was more partial to Bushmills herself, but Scotch'd do if that's all there was.) She could catch them unawares, spring the Wedding Present List on them and mark off the names against items there and then. ' - Because *I've* just had an idea for a celebration an' all! Yeah! A fourple - what is it - quadruple celebration!'

Major Pratt, hastily seizing back control before the whole thing degenerated into a rag-bag of personal celebrations for miscellaneous nonentities (there was some excuse for including Kate and Len's Silver Wedding. They'd *have* to be in attendance, or who would do the work?) deliberately ignored her. How dare that impudent slut think she could swarm aboard his bandwagon!

'So we must delegate responsibility for all the work, because Eloise and I are off to Tuscany for eight weeks next week.'

Ewan yawned, wondering how much longer Kate and Len would be incarcerated in the Quiet Room. He washed his plate and some utensils lying in the sink, and tossed up whether to look at the car or investigate job prospects in the village.

The decision didn't take long. The way his finances were, he wouldn't be able to do anything except "look" anyway.

He set off to the pub.

'… So *do* feel free to carry out any imaginative or charming ideas you may have, to enhance the flavour of Caledonian culture,' Eloise, extending this gracious invitation to Anna, had no idea that Anna wasn't listening to a word. 'And of course, souvenir programmes. We thought ruby red lettering on a vellum background. What do you think, Anna?'

Anna, having filled her paper with doodles and caricatures, was gazing out of the window, chin cupped in hand. Her cash wasn't accumulating quite as rapidly as she'd anticipated, and she was considering a second outlet. She was vaguely aware of her name being spoken, faces turning expectantly towards her. Obviously somebody had asked her opinion about something.

'Um...' she hedged non-committally.

'Perhaps *you* might volunteer to do that for us?'

'Er...'

'And then, napkins. Had it been a sit-down meal we'd have some sort of napkin art, waterlilies or something. But as it's a buffet, simplicity is the key.' Eloise smiled encouragingly at Kate. (*So* important to make one's helpers feel part of the thing from the outset!) 'Which brings me to Table Accoutrements. Now, I usually place a rosebud with the ladies' napkins when I give a dinner party. I thought maybe we could do the same thing, with thistles, of course, in honour of Scotland? If some kind soul would divest them of prickles...?'

Dud unhesitatingly volunteered. (Tailor-made excuse to transport the manufactured goods to Anna, after delegating the tedious chore to Mona.) Mona, about to snap that her prospective bridegroom would be too busy running pre-nuptual errands to have time for any of that bloody nonsense, remembered Bridie's advice and clamped her mouth firmly shut. This was perhaps not the moment to tell him he'd be fully occupied with Wedding arrangements; guest list, photographer, cake, and so on. Not that he'd have any say in anything, they'd all be her decisions, but he'd better be on hand for her to inform him of them.

So it was duly noted that Anna would undertake artistic embellishments, whilst Eloise devised the menu and informed Kate of those tasks she wished to be carried out; the donkey work, the thankless, behind-the-scenes, unglamorous slog.

Kate had learned the hard way, from countless battles over the years which she'd lost through voicing honest opposition to the many unfair, unjust, or simply unworkable harebrained schemes and crackpot directives from above, that there was no point in outright objections.

'Well, I'll co-operate gladly, of course.' Her tone was a blend of readiness tempered with doubt, willingness mixed with regret. 'But, you see, we've still got the day-to-day work to do, and the staffing level's been cut. What we really need,' she added slowly, 'Is another pair of hands.'

'Oh, the other wives will rally round, Kate, and help,' Major Pratt promised vaguely. 'And Eloise will take care of the more, you know, exacting challenges - flower arrangements and so on.'

'We can't run the place efficiently as it is,' Len immediately backed up his wife. 'We really do need another member of staff.'

'Absolutely not. Sorry Len, no can do,' said Major Pratt firmly.

Support, however, came unexpectedly from Anna, who had no intention of spending any off-duty time on Jubilee artwork but was quite prepared to do it in the time normally allocated to, say, vegetable preparing or pan scrubbing. An extra member of staff would be very welcome as far as she was concerned. She smiled composedly at Eloise, and pointed out that she hadn't - she *really* hadn't - sufficient time to ensure that her contributions were of the standard she would wish to be associated with her reputation, and professional pride forbade donating to the Event anything which fell even slightly below the exacting standards she set herself.

'Well, we don't want to put you under any pressure, Anna,' reconsidered Major Pratt immediately. 'I tell you what, Len. If a reasonably personable backpacker was willing to help in return for a free stay two or three nights a week, I'm sure the Committee would have no objection to that?'

'And where would he go for the other four or five nights?' murmured Len.

'Hm. I take your point, Len. All right then. Should a suitable candidate present herself - or himself of course, mustn't be sexist - to help with odd jobs in return for staying free of charge, fine. But you're not wheedling a *proper* member of staff out of us. There'd be no pay.' Major Pratt prided himself on being a skilled negotiator. (You needed to be, in his position. They'd run rings round you if they thought they could get away with it.)

Kate and Len exchanged glances.

It wasn't much, but it was more than they'd expected before the Meeting, which was nothing at all.

The barman was from Devon, with a West country burr. Yes, he said, they needed part-time bar staff.

The only thing was, they had no staff accommodation other than the caravan he lived in, and that wasn't big enough to share. They wanted someone local. Wasn't much point in asking Mrs. Reynolds about it if he had nowhere to live, was there.

True, agreed Ewan, sipping his pint philosophically.

Oh well. He'd leave the car at Beckside and hitch up to Scotland in the morning; aim for Edinburgh or Inverness, try for kitchen porter work in one of the hotels.

'... And finally,' Major Pratt tapped his filofax. 'Entertainment. With the relevant Scottish flavour. And we must include something nautical, as well; sea shanties or hornpipes or something. He's apparently something of an old sea-dog. '

Brian knew a Folk Group who sang shanties, and offered to book them.

'Yes, do,' nodded Major Pratt, pleased. 'And we must rustle up a piper from somewhere.'

'What about Gavin's piper?' suggested Eloise. 'You know, the chap who pipes New Year in at their annual Hogmanay party?'

'Hm... I don't know, darling. He charges. We don't want some professional who'd cost the earth, do we.' Major Pratt looked round hopefully.

'I know one,' said Len slowly.

'Do you, Len? D'you think he'd do it for us? As, you know, a sort of generous gesture?'

'In other words, without payment?' translated Brian.

'I'd have to ask him.'

'Could you ring him now? Get it organised?'

'He's not on the phone.'

'Well where does he live?'

'Liverpool.' There was no need to add that it was a pretty safe bet the friend in question was at this moment propping up the village pub bar.

'Hm,' said Major Pratt. 'That means a letter, doesn't it.'

'He's hopeless at answering letters,' said Len truthfully.

There was a pause. Nobody else offered a piper. It would have to be Len's friend, or pay for one.

'We *could* drive down tomorrow,' offered Len in his prepared-to-undertake-a-tedious-chore-with-unflagging-devotion-to-duty voice. 'Anna and Oliver could manage til we got back if we were slightly late, couldn't you?'

'I could stay on and help,' offered Dud immediately.

'So could I,' added Mona with a snake-like smile.

'Hm. We wouldn't be prepared to pay travelling expenses,' Major Pratt warned primly. 'But very well, if you think you could persuade him to do it for nothing...'

He put a neat tick against PIPER as Len nodded obediently. It was all starting to come together.

Major Pratt's voice droned ceaselessly on. There was a word to describe it, thought Len, trying to remember it. Turgid? The meaning wasn't exactly right (although apt enough) but the sound certainly was. Tur-gid. Think of a word, see how many others you can make from it. Grid, dirt, dig, tug...

'- And *tasteful* Scottish Country Dancing, ladies in white dresses and tartan sashes, men in kilts. No roistering or boisterousness -'

'With audience participation?' Dottie chewed her pen.

'Better not,' considered Major Pratt. 'We're dicing with the unknown to a certain extent. There'll be over a hundred people; we can't vet everybody, and you know what the press is like. We can't risk the hooligan element rearing its ugly head. No. We'll stick to a Demonstration.'

'But Mr. MacTavish might like to join in,' suggested Babs brightly.

'Quite!' shuddered Major Pratt. 'He'll be seventy, Babs! Suppose his heart gave out and he died, there and then on the lawn?'

'Is there a Mrs MacTavish?' wondered Kate, dreading a crusty old misogynist complaining incessantly throughout his stay. Unless (hopefully) he was far too grand to stay at a Youth Hostel, and would book into one of the local upmarket hotels along with the usual clutch of high-ranking Officials junketing up from National Office for the Event.

'There was. He's been a widower for years. All terribly tragic, I gather,' answered Major Pratt.

The discussion moved on to the seating arrangements. It would be *so* much more fun if the entire thing were al fresco, but against that were flies and wasps and weather, because September being September one never knew. It was finally decided that the main Event (and Engagement Announcement) would take place on the lawn outside the Dining Room, with the buffet inside, and the Common Room kept in reserve for wet weather contingency plans.

Len caught Kate's eye. She stared bleakly back. He gave an encouraging wink; they still had a job, and a home, and if they hadn't got Ewan proper employment at least they'd managed a temporary refuge for him. *And* they'd got away with the Inspection Report scam! Ex-seaman Liverpudlian savvy one, juggernauts of power nil.

And - an unexpected and fortuitous bonus - they were off to the Mersey estuary tomorrow!

Major Pratt listened as the Committee indulged in the inconsequential small talk that always followed any Meeting. You could never tell which direction a Committee Meeting would take, and Minutes, no matter how meticulously recorded,

110

took no account of unvoiced undercurrents. But his own impression was that, after the initial infuriating delays and that unspeakable woman's outburst over the curtains, it had subsided to an almost unrealistically tame affair. As if half the participants - noteably Guests, not bona fide Committee Members of course - were preoccupied with some private agenda of their own. Look at Kate for instance, sitting there glum-faced and silent for the rest of the Meeting, in spite of the fact he'd offered the wretched creature the opportunity to share her Silver Wedding with Beckside's glittering Jubilee! Good lord, what *did* it take to put a smile on her face?

Yet Len had been uncharacteristically malleable, particularly over the staffing arrangements. Hardly any objections at all! And what a pleasant surprise to hear him offer constructive help for once. Volunteering a trip to Liverpool to book this piper... Must be mellowing in his old age!

Anna, of course, hadn't actively contributed much, but she'd been industriously making notes and setting out preliminary sketches for the programme design on her sheet of paper for most of the evening. And when she'd filled hers, she'd used the doltish Oliver's as well.

As for Mona, he'd been on Red Alert all evening to quell any more unseemly eruptions. Some people were prone to Road Rage; Mona was affected by Anything-At-All Rage, and reminded him of an unpredictable, brooding, menacing volcano likely to spew out a deadly torrent of vitriol at any moment. But as the Meeting progressed she too had seemed increasingly preoccupied and engrossed in some secret project of her own.

Altogether most curious...

He gathered his papers, replaced them in his briefcase, and looked at his watch. Ten thirty *prompt* Kate, he'd instructed, for the apres-Meeting refreshments. It was now ten thirty-five. No doubt when the glorious hosts trumpeted across the sky announcing the last minute of the Last Day, Len and Kate would still be dawdling in that damn kitchen...

Beyond redemption, the pair of them.

Certainly beyond him!

Major Pratt wasn't the only one reflecting on tonight's Meeting and looking forward to bringing plans to fruition at the Jubilee.

Mona, lighting another cigarette, eyed him with contempt. Thought he could brush her aside as though she were of no account and that'd be the end of it, did he? Well, he was going to learn otherwise. The Jubilee would be the perfect venue to announce her and Dud's Engagement, and the Engagement was *going* to be announced at the Jubilee whether Major Bloody Pratt liked it or not.

And whether Dud liked it or not, for that matter.

'No point in going on about it, love,' said Len quietly. 'It could have been a lot worse. We mightn't have had a job at all.'

'I know.' Kate, guilty and wretched, lifted sausage rolls and quiche from the oven.

Anna and Oliver silently loaded sandwiches, scones, and chocolate cake onto trays, and set off to the Quiet Room. Ewan, filling teapots, also remained silent. Kate and Len obviously had more to worry about than the fact that he hadn't found a job.

'All right, we've lost the Anniversary itself,' admitted Len. 'But we'll get a day in lieu tagged on to the end of the holiday. And look what we're gaining on the deal. A trip to Liverpool tomorrow, and a job for Ewan -'

'What did you say?' said Ewan.

'Don't get too excited, it's unpaid. But if a room and food'll do for the time being, til you find something better -'

'A room and food'll do very nicely,' grinned Ewan. 'They want a part-time barman at the pub, but there's no accommodation. So that'd work out great. Thanks!'

Kate forlornly arranged a sprig of parsley on the sausage rolls. She was grateful Beckside wouldn't close, pleased they'd got some good news for Ewan, glad Len could visit his beloved Mersey Estuary, but... but. Some Silver Wedding, stuck in here. They'd probably end the day filing for divorce.

'What did you say about the Pool tomorrow?' went on Ewan.

'Oh yes. The Jubilee is going to have a Scottish theme; wall-to-wall tartan, bagpipes, and haggis, all done with élan, style, and panache, no offence Kate. And *tasteful* Scottish Country Dancing, none of yer Scots Wha-hae and the hooligan element. They want a piper. Can you do it?'

'Aye, sure,' said Ewan goodnaturedly. 'But what's that got to do with skiving off to Liverpool?'

'You're losing your touch mate. Kate and I are having our own private Staff Outing tomorrow. A day away from this place. We're off to Liverpool. To book you to play the bagpipes.'

Ewan laughed, and headed for the phone. 'Better ring the pub. Clinch the job before they get someone else.'

Kate and Len were alone.

'You and I will hold our own private Silver Wedding celebrations the minute it's over, Kate,' he promised quietly, enfolding her in his arms.

'Yes, but -'

Oliver came in to remind them of Eloise's specific request for her cocoa to be made with *milk,* if they'd be so kind. Len, indicating the sausage rolls and quiche with a jerk of his head, unceremoniously motioned him out again.

And Oliver, who had a healthy sense of self-preservation, speedily obeyed. Because it was quite clear that the last thing on Len's mind was Eloise's cocoa.

In fact not only Eloise's cocoa but the entire Committee, together with their Meeting and their post-Meeting refreshments, had all receded to another dimension.

Len, gently kissing Kate's forehead and caressing a tendril of her hair, was murmuring a private promise about deserted Hebridean beaches and warm September afternoons. The Jubilee itself would, admittedly, be a nightmare, but they'd faced lots of nightmares over the years and survived them; they'd survive this one as well. And the minute it was over, he'd make it up to her.

And Kate, feeling like one of those Disney characters whose faces melt into a grin of pure delight as they blink, blush, and bashfully twist their hands in rapture, marvelled at the unaccountable effects of love on the human species. All through the Meeting she'd longed for bed, and sleep. Now, suddenly wide awake, her face transformed by a smile of radiance that would have amazed and astounded Major Pratt had he seen it, the longing for bed had increased a hundredfold as desire for sleep was replaced by desire for Len.

He was right, as always. Stuff the Jubilee.

They had more interesting things to think about tonight.

FOUR: A HOTBED OF WEEDS

The following morning started badly for Oliver.

Catapulted into wakefulness by a military band exploding without warning over the tannoy system, he lay, panic-stricken and disorientated, squinting at the alarm clock.

7.30AM.

Omigod... He should have started work at 6.45AM.

The alarm had obviously gone off, because the Stop button had been pressed, although he had no recollection of thumping the thing silent. He hopped into the half inside-out jeans lying on the floor and hurtled downstairs to the kitchen, pulling a teeshirt over his head.

'Sorry, I overslept!' he gabbled.

Kate, cursing a tray of sausages Len had got on special offer (and which, despite a liberal coating of oil, had fused to the base and were now systematically splitting themselves open to expose innards of a lurid and unnatural fluorescent pink), wrenched a sausage from its anchorage of grease with the tongs.

'We'd all like to oversleep, Oliver. *We're paid not to.*'

Anna continued silently breaking eggs into the frying pan. The eggs said it all. Crack-splash, crack-splash, accuse-reproach.

He ripped open a sliced loaf, spread ten pieces under the grill, began filling the milk jugs, and was making a surreptitious attempt to comb his hair with his fingers when Major Pratt breezed in, resplendent in navy blazer, white trousers, and immaculately folded cravat.

''Morning, all!' he boomed, rubbing his hands. 'Everything A-OK?'

''Morning. Yes, fine, thank you,' replied Kate automatically.

'Well there you are, you see, Kate. What did I tell you? Good blast of Souza, and one thing I can safely guarantee you'll have no problems with *this* morning is, anybody oversleeping!'

Oliver tried unsuccessfully to hide a yawn by keeping his mouth closed. Major Pratt, catching the facial contortions, studied him critically. Rumpled teeshirt, crumpled jeans - good lord, the lad didn't even look as if he'd combed his hair! The smile faded. What on earth was Kate doing, tolerating this unkempt hobo in a catering kitchen? Look at him, scratching his head all over the milk jugs!

'Kate,' he began sternly, then sniffed and glanced at the grill, from which a thickening cloud of smoke was starting to billow. 'Who's supposed to be looking after that toast?'

Oliver instinctively looked at the grill. The jug overflowed. Milk swamped the table, setting up a steady drip to the floor. He darted to the grill, and tipped ten smoking heaps of carbon into the bin.

'Look at this!' gasped Major Pratt, horrified, 'Chucking half a loaf away in one go! And he's wasted almost a pint of milk! No wonder Beckside's in financial difficulties if this is the sort of -'

Oliver fumbled in the loaf-wrapper for a replacement handful, and dropped a slice on the floor. Under Major Pratt's gimlet-eyed frown he retrieved it, then fingered it nervously; did he follow the rules of hygiene and throw it away, or heed the views on thrift Major Pratt had just expressed? Whatever he did was bound to be wrong... Flicking ineffectually to remove any particles of dust, he shoved it under the grill and hoped for the best.

'Kate, are you so preoccupied with those damn sausages you're unaware of what's happening around you?' barked Major Pratt immediately. 'He doesn't even seem to know the first rule of hygiene! He's just picked that bread *off the floor!*'

Kate, gritting her teeth as she plucked at a sausage that was twisting itself into a circular inside-out black pudding, burned her wrist on the metal tray.

There was a knock at the door. Major Pratt, poised to embark on a galvanising pep talk encompassing the importance of both thrift and hygiene, paused as it opened to reveal a wailing child.

'I've dropped my scrunchy down the loo!'

He immediately took charge of the situation.

'Oh dear! Never mind, poppet,' he comforted, wondering what a scrunchy was. (Whatever it turned out to be, he'd delegate this particular crisis to the paid staff.) 'Tell Len to see to it for her, would you Anna.' Then, raising his voice above the overheating fat and spitting eggs, he turned his attention back to the kitchen, strolling deliberately towards Oliver to carry out a more thorough inspection; good heavens, the lad didn't look as though he'd even washed his face!

Oliver evaded the scrutiny by dodging across to the sink for a dishcloth. Major Pratt stalked after him, hands behind back.

'I must say, Kate, I'm most concerned -'

Oliver detoured to the grill. Major Pratt also changed course, and the gap narrowed.

'- About the level of efficiency in this kit-'

'Ow! OW!'

A volley of splashes from the frying pan, by now a seething cauldron of erupting fat and exploding eggs, caught Oliver on the chin as he doubled back to mop up the milk on the table.

Major Pratt shook his head. The place was like a bear garden! And as for this ludicrous game of cat and mouse, pursuing the lad from pillar to post around the kitchen to ascertain whether he'd attended to the most fundamental of personal grooming... The whole matter needed looking into in more depth.

He watched Kate subdue the rioting eggs.

'I think we'd better have a chat after breakfast, Kate,' he promised grimly. '... If anyone actually *gets* any breakfast this morning!'

Dud sneaked up to Beckside's small washroom on the top landing (too many interested eyes in the main one), pushed back the navy blue yachtsman's cap to a slightly more jaunty angle, and adjusted the red and white neckerchief knotted at his throat. Nice little nautical touch, that. If you were going to change your image, you may as well do the job properly. No point spoiling the ship for a hap'orth of tar - as the Nautical Set might say.

The idea had materialised after Anna had made such a big thing out of that clown rowing across the Atlantic. Not that *he* had any such notions, but the image of the sailing fraternity sipping G-and-Ts outside the Yacht Club was an appealing one, and Dud fancied being part of it. So during the week he'd visited an upmarket sports shop - discount and cheap-skate stores would henceforth become things of the past - and bought denims, a blue and white striped matelot top, rope-soled deck shoes, and a vaguely skipper-like navy blue corduroy cap. Lastly, as a spur of the moment extravagance befitting the easy-come easy-go Jolly Tar image, he'd thrown in the carefree-looking neckerchief.

The next phase was dropping subtle hints to Major Pratt, who periodically nipped off with a few cronies for a spot of sailing.

Sailing, he mused nonchalantly. He'd always liked the sound of that. Must give it a whirl one of these days. In fact - that was a thought - didn't Major Pratt say he and Eloise were going sailing this weekend, come to think of it? On Sunday? Oh. That was nice. With friends? Tim and Lucinda, was it?

But Major Pratt could be extraordinarily obtuse at times, so Dud had given up subtlety and gone straight for the jugular. How about him joining them for a bit of a trip round the lake, like?

When Major Pratt made some fatuous comment about a young blade like Dud surely not wanting to join a boatload of old fogeys when he could spend his time with Mona, Dud assured him he'd be only too delighted. But even Dud had to eventually admit he was flogging a dead horse with this one, and his thoughts turned instead to a 'For Sale' sign fixed to the mast of one of the boats moored off the jetty. "Sultry Nights", she was called. He liked the sound of that. Very promising!

Might be a better proposition, come to think of it. By-pass the Major Pratt route altogether, and blaze down a more direct avenue to the world he intended to inhabit, a world where people hobnobbed at Yacht Clubs, and went to posh new restaurants before anyone else had ever heard of them. He'd burst on the scene, a fully fledged member of the yachting fraternity with his own boat; an irresistible lure for Anna, given this weird penchant she had for Atlantic rowers. He pictured himself, wearing his matelot top and jeans, leaping athletically in and out of it, coiling a few ropes and things, or whatever people did.

'Anna?' he'd murmur into the phone as he leaned back with his feet up on the desk, idly doodling on the jotter, 'Book me in for the weekend, there's a sweetie. Thought we might go for a sail. Couple of bottles of champagne and a picnic, pull in at one of those bays you can only get to by boat -'

'Oh Dud!' she'd breathe shyly, 'Are you... are you inviting *me*?'

He winked confidently at his reflection, then frowned as an unwelcome spectre flitted across this pleasant scenario. There was always *one* horrible great bluebottle in the ointment.

Mona.

She held him back from the world of sophistication awaiting him; she prevented sailing party invitations from Major Pratt; and she was the sole reason for Anna's reluctance to become An

Item. High time he unloaded her... although he'd planned on her de-prickling the thistles first, because if anyone's fingers were going to be torn to ribbons they may as well be hers.

He considered the options. Tell her tonight, as he dropped her at home? Wait until she was levering herself off the Honda, one leg on the pavement and the other over the pillion seat, then solemnly launch into After Giving It A Lot Of Thought, Mona... And then roar off (praying the Honda wouldn't break down), leaving her incandescent with rage on the pavement? Or allow her a few more days to get all the tedious thistle-work done?

Hmm. Perhaps he'd let Fate take its course for today. If the opportunity arose to end the relationship, he'd take it; if not, the minute she'd done the thistles she'd be history, and he'd move in on Anna, straight for the kill, no holds barred, and she wouldn't know what had hit her.

Anyway, the immediate problem was, how to sneak off on his own this morning to buy the boat without Mona knowing anything about it. "Sultry Nights" was part of his glittering future with the *Beau Monde*, and that future didn't include Mona. She was never going to set foot aboard.

They were supposed to be joining the rest of The Committee for a walk today. Well - he winked at the mirror - it wasn't beyond a razor-sharp mind to invent some complicated mechanical problem with the Honda which meant he'd have to go and get a spare part, insisting she went with the group and they'd meet up later. Which reminded him. Another bonus to the post-Mona era: not having to cart her stupid primus stove all over the place. Mona didn't like flask tea, but didn't believe in lugging the apparatus for a freshly made brew herself; she expected Muggins to do that. So it'd be good riddance to paraffin and primus as well as Mona, and he'd be equally glad to see the back of all three.

In fact he'd dump the stuff right now. He'd never liked the idea of driving the Honda with a bottle of paraffin in his rucksack. He'd pour it down the loo now, while he thought about it.

He practised the jaunty wink once more, replaced cap and neckerchief in the carrier bag with the rest of his maritime ensemble still in its virginal cellophane, returned to the dormitory, hid it under his bunk, collected the paraffin, nipped back upstairs, and emptied it down the lavatory pan.

To Oliver's relief Kate and Len set off as soon as possible after breakfast (apparently an early start would be necessary to secure the services of this mysterious piper in Liverpool), which meant there wasn't time for Major Pratt to discuss the junior member of staff as he'd so obviously intended.

'Ring me tonight,' he'd instructed as Len started the car, 'To confirm you've booked the fellow. Another matter I want to discuss, as well.' He'd looked directly at Oliver, and made a note in his filofax.

Oliver was more worried than he was prepared to admit about this. The thought of confirming his father's doubts about his ability to keep a job, even as a menial skivvy in what he scathingly referred to as "some two-bit Backpackers' Doss-house", was not a pleasant one, so it suited Oliver for Len and Kate to be gallivanting in Liverpool rather than itemising his shortcomings with Major Pratt, even if it did mean extra work for the other staff. Not that he personally had done much; if the newcomer, Ewan, was willing to take over the most unpopular chores such as scrubbing greasy breakfast catering trays and pans, then cleaning the dormitories and washrooms etc, while Oliver assumed Len's physically less arduous role in The Office, who was Oliver to stop him? It seemed Ewan's new boss wanted him to start in the pub at lunch time, but he'd offered to work here this morning so Len and Kate could make the trip to Liverpool.

He glanced at his watch. 10.30AM. The Hostel should have closed thirty minutes ago. And if Len had been here, he admitted privately as a horde of Belles-of-St-Trinians lookalikes surged around The Shop, it would have done.

Len's parting words: 'That's worked out well! Most people have gone early today. Just these few kids left. They'll be gone in ten minutes,' echoed mockingly in his ears because they were still here an hour and a half later, leaderless and lawless, and he was sick of the sight of them; he couldn't get his breakfast until they'd gone. There'd been no time to eat anything other than a snatched piece of toast because of oversleeping, and he was ravenous.

Even more alarming, however, was that a slightly disturbing trend had crept into his hitherto wholly innocent banter with the little girls. A precociousness, a vying for his attention; not actually flirting with him, not actually baiting him, but an indefinable and uncomfortable mixture of the two. An insidious shift in power had somehow taken place without him being aware of it happening, and he no longer felt quite in control. He saw his future CV: "Reason for Leaving Last Job: Sexually harassed by eight-year-old children", and a prospective employer (who looked just like his father) sitting behind a desk reading it, convulsed with laughter.

A newcomer, one hand behind her back obviously hiding something, sidled up. There was some furtive whispering, giggling, and sidelong looks in his direction, which he pretended not to see, then one child, emboldened by the digs in the ribs and hissed encouragements, became more daring.

'Tara found this in the Ladies' Washroom,' she announced as the newcomer whipped from behind her back a huge once-white nylon bra with a distinct whiff of underarm perspiration. 'She wants to hand it in to Lost Property.'

It was the signal for the cackles and hoots to begin in earnest.

'Will you go around trying it on to see who it fits, like the prince with Cinderella's slipper?' sniggered Tara, who obviously had a reputation for outrageousness to uphold.

'Wouldn't be any point in trying to fit it on any of you lot, would there,' retorted Oliver, and immediately regretted it, remembering Len's oft-repeated warning that you never, but NEVER, made any comment to minors which could possibly be misinterpreted at the fond homecoming. He could already hear the outraged parents: "He said *what*? He wanted to go around measuring left-behind bras on little girls?" as Head Office was dialled and an extremely serious complaint lodged.

He wished another adult would appear so that things would revert to normal, and scanned the Reception Area for an ally. But hurrying towards him instead of the hoped-for responsible figure of authority was Babs, who had volunteered to sweep the front doorstep, a look of concern on her face. Which probably meant she'd trodden on an ant and wanted advice on how much to donate to Greenpeace in reparation, thought Oliver irritably. Infant Lolitas, and now Babs.

'Oliver -' she began hesitantly.

'Have you lost your bra?' Tara, sensing a natural victim,

swung the item provocatively to and fro.

'No, it's not hers, it's too big!'

Ten pairs of eyes assessed with ruthless curiosity the size of Babs' slender chest. She blushed crimson and tried to shrink into herself. There was another chorus of sniggers and cackles of glee, and Oliver felt his authority evaporate even further. He felt a pang of sympathy for Babs; timid and self-conscious at the best of times, she stood as much chance against these tormentors as a baby rabbit about to be devoured by a pack of alsatians.

Babs recognised the object Tara was dangling in front of her. Mona had been wearing it last night when she undressed in the Ladies' Washroom.

'I, I think it belongs to Mona.' The news she'd come to impart was embarrassing enough, without this added torture. She took a deep breath, and plunged resolutely on. 'Oliver, there's a bird fallen down the... er... the outside loo.'

This produced another round of hysterical giggles.

'Is she stuck down the bog?' Tara enquired.

'Not a *girl*.' It was Babs' turn to scan the Reception Area for a capable adult who would take control and assume responsibility for the rescue operation. But she, like Oliver, had to make do with the material available, and she turned resignedly back to him. 'A real bird.'

'A bird?'

'Yes. I went in to sweep it out, and there's a bird stuck in the... down the...' Babs' distress was obvious and genuine, and the mood sobered. Oliver as potential sex symbol was instantly dismissed from the fickle minds of his juvenile fan club, together with snigger-worthy items of lost property.

'Aah! Poor thing!'

'How did it get in?'

'Can you rescue it, Oliver?' implored Babs.

'*Me?*' Oliver stared at her. How was he supposed to get the thing out?

'Yes. Hurry!' Babs was already caught up in the excited army of liberators surging to rescue the hapless victim from its unfamiliar habitat. 'We need somebody brave and strong!'

Too true, thought Oliver. I know just the man. He headed to the stairs and yelled: 'Dud!'

Faintly the reply echoed: 'What?'

'Some bird's got stuck in the outside loo!' Oliver grinned to himself. 'Can you help? I can't leave The Office!'

Mona lay on the bunk and lit a cigarette. A German girl, fastening the straps of an outsize rucksack, looked primly across.

'It is *verboten* to smoke!'

'Sod off,' growled Mona.

The German hauled on the rucksack and scuttled out, leaving the door open. Through it, Mona heard the commotion. Apparently some emergency was taking place outside. She heard Dud call to Major Pratt that he, Dud, was needed to sort it out, and Major Pratt's peevish reply as he emerged from the Men's Washroom, followed by his entourage of acolytes: 'Yes. So I heard. Although one of the ladies would be the obvious choice in the circumstances, I would have thought. Where's Babs, or Mona?'

Babs or bloody Mona is it, thought Mona, inhaling. Well, I don't know where Babs is, but Mona's staying right here. And that goes for all the offers to "help" made by Major Bloody Bigmouth, as well. Let them clean the place themselves if they were all so keen. Not that she could imagine Eloise rolling up her sleeves and mopping up the suspicious-looking puddle in one of the toilet cubicles in the Ladies' Washroom. And if Eloise wouldn't be sullying her hands with a floorcloth, why should Mona? As for the men, their idea of "cleaning" was just another unofficial Inspection, snooping around searching out faulty toilet-roll holders and dripping taps. Bad enough having to trek round the lake with them while Dud skedaddled off for *more* spare parts for that bloody motorbike - because she'd intended a romantic saunter on their own, to the jewellery shop in the village - without doing her back in hauling up some stupid bitch who'd fallen down the lav as well.

She settled more comfortably on the bed, inhaled, and flicked another scattering of ash over the floor for Arty-farty Anna to sweep up.

The River Mersey, once so alive and bustling, now stretched empty and quiet to the open sea. No longer a working river; a ghost river, a theme park for visitors, a watery museum where ferry boats (now for the most part carrying tourists rather than commuters travelling to work in the shipping offices of Liverpool) blared old Beatles and Spinners hits. And, to add to the Disney atmosphere, a recorded metallic voice told of ships proudly launched from Cammell Lairds shipyard, now eerily silent, to be greeted on their maiden voyage by the sirens and hooters of other river traffic, similarly welcomed back to their home port throughout their lives, and bid a sad farewell at the end of their days.

Len remembered being taken as a child to see one of the last great working sailing ships make her way proudly and defiantly upriver, sails furled for the last time, to end her life in the breaker's yard. Thousands of miles, thousands of adventures, thousands of stories of the sea and the men who had sailed in her - the end of an era. Now, of course, there wasn't even a breaker's yard. There was nothing left to break up. New ships, old ships, large, small, happy, tragic ships - they'd all gone.

He sauntered, hands in pockets, along the New Brighton shore, his footsteps leaving an undulating trail in the sand as he avoided the waves lapping lazily in at low water mark. The tide was on the turn; soon the waves would increase in strength and vigour, but for now they were gentle, placid, quiet.

It had been such a noisy river in his childhood. Even the tide had its own distinctive sound as it raced exuberantly in past dredgers clanking in the deep channel, fishing boats and small pleasure craft moored near the pier, and the lifeboat bobbing a little way off. As a small child he'd learnt to tell whether the tide was ebbing or flowing from these boats because they, like the seagulls that settled in flocks above the submerged mudflats and sandbanks, always faced the incoming or outgoing tide.

Len's childhood playground had been the Mersey shore, and he, like many a Merseyside urchin, could glance up from a game of football at a ship sailing upriver, and (long before they'd even heard the word 'geography' at school) tell you which country she'd arrived from and what cargo she carried - especially if that cargo was foodstuffs. The 'Fyffe Line' boats, laden with bananas, were greeted with particularly keen anticipation in Len's post-war childhood. So was any ship coming from the United States: "My Dad/big brother/Uncle's on that ship - I hope he's brought me something from America!"

He remembered the loud bangs, clatterings, and muffled

thumps from the shipyards and repair basins upriver, the strange unidentifiable rumbles and clanks that periodically echoed over the water from the Liverpool docks, ships' sirens greeting each other as they sailed out to, or in from, all the ports of the world. And always the regular river traffic - the Pilot boat racing out to meet a homeward-bound ship at the bar, the Isle of Man packet sailing prompt at 11AM every day, the tugs tearing bossily around huge passenger liners, the cargo vessels, lighters, small coastal tramps, and of course the ferries ploughing perpetually back and forth in the midst of them all. Len recalled the praise and adulation heaped on one of the Royal Family by the media some years ago when he'd brought his Royal Navy ship safely alongside a landing stage somewhere. The Mersey Ferries did the same thing six times every hour during rush hours (when there'd been rush hours), in every possible weather and tidal condition from Force Ten gale and racing tide to impenetrable fog, while dodging other traffic travelling up or downriver at the same time.

A faint explosion sounded from the far side of the river. Len looked across at the miles of docks, once seething with activity and bustle. Now they too lay deserted and silent. Except for the Albert Dock, of course, where new life had been breathed into the rat-infested derelict warehouses grouped round an expanse of filthy stagnant river water, and tourists now strolled by dockside shops, cafes, the Maritime Museum, and Salthouse Dock.

Salthouse Dock. He stopped, prodding gently with his foot an enormous jellyfish left stranded by the tide, remembering the occasion when he and Ewan had sung in some decaying old cargo boat which had been turned into a floating Folk Club in Salthouse Dock, then legged it with guitar and mandolin through Canning Place and Paradise Street to their second venue, Jackie and Bridie's Folk Club. Two bookings in one night - next stop superstardom! Ewan, strangely enough, had in later years become one of the 'Hattonistas' as they were known locally - he'd worked for a short period on the Albert Dock Complex during its reclamation, during one of his sojourns in Liverpool after arriving home, broke, from Australia and the far east.

Len had wandered further along the deserted shore than he realised, and almost reached the Fort Perch Rock. Detouring inland, he sat down on the rocks in the lee of the wind, which, during the night, had veered round to the east, and leaned against the massive red sandstone blocks of the Fort, staring out to sea.

He picked up a discarded dogfish's egg case, moving it slowly from side to side so it caught the sun. Brittle, dark green-brown, the umbilical attaching twine still in place in each corner; Mermaid's purses, they'd called them in his childhood. He launched it across a rock pool, watching as the disturbance set a shoal of Jack Sharps darting with maniacal speed to find cover under a slight overhang of rock.

The ripples gradually subsided. The private lives of the rock pool inhabitants resumed once more. A seagull wheeled above, assessing his likelihood as a possible food source, then flew off to join its companions.

Peace. Warmth. The sun sparkled on the water.

The nearness of the sea, the movement, the sound, the smell of it, satisfied a need in his soul. Gradually his eyes closed.

Ewan opened the window to clear the smell of feet and body odour, then started sweeping the dormitory. The brush knocked against something soft under the corner bunk. He drew out a carrier bag containing a navy blue yachting cap, red neckerchief, rope-soled deck shoes, and, in unopened cellophane with price tickets still attached, a blue and white matelot top and denims.

Nobody who had stayed here last night was returning to this dormitory tonight; the bag had obviously been forgotten. He started to take it downstairs, then glanced at his watch - better hurry if he wanted a shower before going to the pub. He finished tidying the dormitory. This section of the building was now all done, except for the small washroom on the top landing, which hadn't been in use last night. He sprinted upstairs, glanced briefly in. Yes, it was OK. No need to spend any time here.

He stowed the bag in the Lost Property Box (which wasn't a box at all but an understairs cupboard on the first floor landing), knowing Oliver would look there when its owner called in person, wrote, or phoned to claim it, and went for his shower.

Dud staggered into the kitchen, forefinger held up like an Old Testament patriarch prophesying plague and pestilence.

'Blasted thing bit me!'

Anna looked up from slicing cooking apples into a bowl.

'What did?'

'That horrible thing in the toilet!'

She gaped at Oliver, who had followed him in and was ripping open a packet of chocolate biscuits.

'A bird fell down the outside loo,' he enlightened her.

'Oh, poor thing.'

'Well I don't mind admitting, it hurts like hell,' nodded Dud. 'And I can't stand the sight of blood, I -'

'Not you, the bird. What sort was it?'

'A hawk-type thing with a beak like a chain saw. And I -'

'Is it all right?'

'No! I keep telling you, it's really painful! And I can't -'

'I meant the bird.'

'*Never mind the bird, what about me?*'

'You had a rabies inoculation lately?' asked Oliver, mouth crammed full of biscuit.

'Rabies?' repeated Dud, startled.

'Yes. Birds of prey eat rats and things, don't they. People catch rabies from them, on the Continent.'

'We're not on the Continent, we're in England!'

'I know, but it might have just flown in from the Continent, mightn't it, and eaten a nice juicy rat before it left. I'm not trying to worry you or anything,' Oliver assured him maliciously (nice to see he wasn't the only one who'd had a rotten morning!) as he took the antiseptic solution from the First Aid cupboard. 'But it might be wise to clean it. In case it goes septic and poisons your bloodstream as well, you know?'

Major Pratt strode in, followed by Brian.

'Well, the patient seems to have recovered somewhat, now!'

'Oh, I'll be all right,' nodded Dud stoically. There was a character in a book he'd read once - James Bond or someone - who'd let a brave little smile play about his lips while his wounds were dressed by some luscious nurse. Dud had always liked the sound of that. He let a brave little smile play about *his* lips. 'It's just that I can't stand the sight of blood, I -'

'Ah, Dud.' Major Pratt looked at him curiously. Why was his mouth twitching like that? 'Yes. Sorry. I meant, you know, the bird.'

'It's on the roof now, recovering from its ordeal,' added Brian, as Oliver poured boiling water into a bowl and placed it on the table.

Dud, fighting the very real terror of infection, felt that the bird had had more than its fair share of attention. Time some sympathy was directed at the heroic rescuer.

'Well, I'm still trying to recover from *my* ordeal,' he reminded them, straining to keep the jocularity in his voice.

'Yes. We must get that wound thoroughly cleaned straight away.' Major Pratt, who prided himself upon being scrupulously fair-minded, decided to offer Oliver the opportunity to redeem previous deficiencies by demonstrating other skills he may possess. 'Wasn't there something in your CV about a First Aid course, Oliver?'

'I've applied to go on one. I haven't actually been on it yet.'

'Well, if you're keen to learn, here's an excellent opportunity to practice.'

Oliver, eager to take advantage of this PR Damage Limitation Exercise, said, 'Oh, right,' gave a confident smile, and plunged Dud's finger into the bowl.

'OWW!' screamed Dud, as, in addition to the original wound, his finger was scalded to the knuckle.

'Didn't you check the temperature first?' Brian asked incredulously as Oliver, muttering an embarrassed apology, scurried to add cold water to the bowl. 'I think you'd *better* go on a First Aid Course!

'Quite frankly, I think it would be a waste of time, Brian. He's obviously *non compos mentis*,' murmured Major Pratt. This latest display of inanity reinforced his earlier opinion; the lad was neither use nor ornament. He'd discuss the situation with Len tonight.

Fortunately for Oliver, The Shop bell rang. Major Pratt watched disapprovingly as he hurried from the room, then, as Dud gingerly lowered his hand into the tepid water, continued with a more congenial subject. 'Never actually seen a sparrowhawk close to before. Beautiful specimen, wasn't it.'

'Oh yes,' agreed Brian readily.

'Interesting story about sparrowhawks, actually.' He was looking forward to narrating the anecdote to Tim and Lucinda this afternoon. ("Yes, beautiful specimen. Must have flown in after a small bird, stunned itself on the wall, and dropped into the pan. One of our Committee chappies got it out. Nearly got his finger bitten off for his pains!")

'Really?' encouraged Brian respectfully.

'Yes. Apparently when they built Crystal Palace a flock of sparrows got trapped inside. Didn't know how to get rid of them. Couldn't shoot them, of course.'

'No, quite.'

'So Queen Victoria asked the Duke of Wellington, I think it was, what he suggested.'

Brian cocked his head in anticipation. 'Which was -?'

'*A sparrowhawk, Ma'am!*' Major Pratt delivered the punchline with triumphant emphasis, and Dud, fidgeting in his chair, became increasingly resentful. Here he was, the hero of the hour who'd just risked life and limb, ministered to by that clot Oliver who'd made matters worse, and virtually ignored while Major Pratt rambled on about Queen Victoria and the know-it-all Duke of Wellington!

Heavy feet in high heels clumped towards them. Mona, who had no intention of remaining out of circulation any longer than was necessary, and having judged enough time had elapsed for work to be done and emergencies dealt with, paused in the doorway, taking in the First Aid Box and Dud's hand immersed in the bowl of water.

'What's up wit' yer?'

'Nothing.'

'Nothing? Must be something wrong, sitting there with a face on yer like a slapped arse!'

'I'll be all right.' The brave little smile once more played about Dud's lips.

'What's the matter wit' yer mouth? Yer got toothache?'

'No!'

'Well what's it twitchin' for?'

The brave little smile vanished abruptly.

'And what's wrong wit' yer hand?'

'I rescued a sparrowhawk stuck down the outside toilet,' said Dud sulkily. 'And it bit me.'

Oh. So that was it. Every picture tells a story, and the look of aggrieved indignation on Dud's face clearly told his. The Mutual Admiration Society weren't coming up with the goods - the requisite praise and flattery. Well, wasn't she the very one to step in and press home her advantage, thank you very much.

128

'Ah now, wouldn't that put Saint Francis of Assisi himself to shame!' she gushed, and, before Dud could realise her intention and take evasive action, rammed his face into her unyielding bosom with fingers that felt like a network of steel hawsers on the back of his skull. His glasses bit deep into the bridge of his nose; his air supply was blocked completely.

'I hope youse'll be telling everyone about this in yer Committee bumf?' She glared at Major Pratt, the maternal lioness standing alone against the world, defending her cub.

'Of course we will!' snapped Major Pratt. Good lord, the dratted woman was actually threatening him!

'Good.' Mona patted the frizzy ginger head. 'Ah God love him, isn't he a treasure!'

The sort of treasure best kept safely in an underground vault together with its jailor, agreed Anna silently, as Dud poked at the rolls of flesh surrounding Mona's waist to signal surrender.

She unexpectedly loosened her grip. He surfaced, massaged his pulverised nose, sucked his bitten and scalded finger, and gazed soulfully at Anna. Talk about star-crossed lovers, torn apart by cruel Fate... because obviously he couldn't dump Mona tonight, after *this* display of besotted adoration, without branding himself a heartless cad, thereby alienating his fellow Committee members and scuppering any chance of eventual election to high office. He'd have to postpone ditching Mona for the time being.

'Are we ready to go now, children?' squeaked the teacher in charge of the eight-year-olds ingratiatingly.

The realisation that they were finally leaving struck home, with unexpected results. Tara, calculating the effectiveness of open rebellion against tears, grabbed a handful of postcards and flung them at her.

'Tara dear! Whatever's the matter?'

'I don't want to go home!'

The uprising was contagious. Abigail, impressed by the consternation Tara's announcement produced, quickly followed suit.

'Nor do I!'

The teacher blinked. 'But Tara dear, you've wanted nothing else *but* to go home ever since we arrived!'

The effect of this logic was to fan Tara's peevishness into full-blown fury. The postcard rack was ripped from its stand, the contents scattered over the floor.

'Stop her!' panicked Oliver, anticipating Len's wrath on his return. ("You mean some eight-year old brat decided to destroy a hundred pounds worth of postcards, and you just stood there and let her?")

'Tara, you're being rather naughty,' chided the teacher hesitantly, and explained to Oliver: 'Her mother says she must be allowed to express her feelings. And she'd have me for assault if I so much as touch her arm.'

Abigail made her own bid for the starring role with a heartrending sob, and the kitchen door was flung open. Major Pratt glared ferociously around. What the devil was going on out here? His eye alighted on Oliver in the midst of the commotion.

'YOU! What d'you think you're doing, upsetting these poor mites?' He strode across, inbred authority that had subdued countless squaddies turned fully on Oliver.

'*Me*?'

'Yes, you! Different when the boot's on the other foot, isn't it! Bullying little thug!'

'The reason they're crying is because they don't want to go home!' explained Oliver desperately, looking at the teacher for confirmation. The teacher nodded.

Major Pratt blinked uncertainly. Eloise immediately took the situation in hand, murmuring with smooth diplomacy: 'Darling, do you think perhaps we could make the children's departure a little bit special?' She smiled graciously around, and sobs of rage subsided to token snuffles. 'Everyone take home a small momento of Beckside? A postcard and badge... Perhaps a chocolate bar?'

Major Pratt, rehearsing another anecdote for Lucinda and Tim, nodded enthusiastically. (..."Crying their little hearts out! Didn't want to leave, apparently. Never know what I'll have to cope with next as Chairman..." Might come in handy for the Annual Christmas After-Dinner Speech too, come to think of it.)

'Who's going to pay for all this?' asked Oliver, as neither Major Pratt or Eloise made any move to do so. The Father Christmas smile and Ho-ho-ho act was the easy part; Oliver knew who'd be blamed if the books failed to balance.

'Oh, tell Len I've sanctioned the expense.' Major Pratt waved such details aside as he jovially distributed Mars Bars to the clamouring hands.

Oliver, watching the same hands craftily held out more than once in the crush, made a mental note to also tell Len that Major Pratt forgot to count them first. May as well take advantage of this spontaneous generosity to salt away an extra one or twenty for himself... He rescued the postcard rack, now irretrievably dented and minus most of its paint, and gathered the postcards scattered around the floor.

'Now - badges,' beamed Major Pratt, thoroughly enjoying himself. *This* was better! Much more in keeping with how one saw oneself.

'Will you write to me, Oliver?' wheedled Tara.

Oliver hesitated.

'Of course he will,' promised Major Pratt expansively.

'And me?' sniffed her arch rival.

'He'll write to all of you. Won't you, Oliver.'

Oliver swallowed, wondering how to justify what must appear an ill-mannered reluctance to correspond with the small tearstained faces, now radiating unworldly innocence.

'Oliver?' prompted Major Pratt warningly.

'If I've got time.'

'I don't think you quite understand.' Major Pratt's voice was icy. 'These young people are tomorrow's clientele; we're trying to increase revenue, not appear indifferent whether they return or not. So I suggest you *make* time... Now, postcards. And Oliver will autograph them all for you!'

Major Pratt's stern views on tardiness obviously didn't apply when it came to him vacating the premises, noticed Oliver bitterly. But then, having recently partaken of Full English Breakfast, and safely wrapped in an invisible cloak of Diplomatic Immunity which rendered the wearer incapable of fault, the thought that his own tardiness in departing might delay the paid staff's breakfast never occurred to him.

'And he'll write to you, care of the school. *Won't you, Oliver?*'

And Oliver, who'd reached the point of agreeing to write to Lucifer in Hell if it meant they'd all go away and let him get something to eat, nodded miserably.

The sun went behind a cloud. Len opened his eyes and sat for a few moments listening to the hypnotic lapping of waves against seaweed-covered rocks, then stood up and stretched.

Kate was visiting a cousin. He'd arranged to meet her there, but there was something he wanted to do first.

Oliver locked the front door with heartfelt relief. Only a few weeks ago he'd refused to play his tapes at anything less than maximum decibels; now, to his amazement, he was discovering that the sound of silence could actually be quite pleasant.

The school party had (at last) left in the minibus, followed by Major Pratt and Eloise purring down the drive in the Rover, followed by a small cluster of Committee Members trudging down to the lake to take part in a ramble before dispersing later that afternoon. The hostel was now empty; he could finally relax and get something to eat.

There was a loud burp on the stairs. He spun round, startled.

'Dud!'

'The one and only, Ol ol' pal.'

'The others have just left. You'll be able to catch them up if you hurry,' hinted Oliver politely.

'I don't want to catch them up. I was waiting til they'd gone, to ask if anything's been handed in to Lost Property this morning?'

'Yes,' replied Oliver. 'But I don't think it's yours.'

'Well that's where you're wrong, Ol, because it is.'

'No,' Oliver started to explain. 'It's a -'

'I know what it is,' Dud interrupted. 'And it's mine. When you get to know me a bit better, Ol, you'll find I'm full of surprises.'

Oliver looked down at the bra handed in by Tara, which he'd dropped without further thought into the waste bin. (Surely nobody would actually want to claim the grotesque thing?)

'You'd cause a few surprises if you went out wearing that!'

'Actually, I think I'll look quite good in it,' winked Dud.

'Oh, you'd look irresistible in it!'

'Hey up, Ol, you'll be saying Hello Sailor next!' gurgled Dud. 'No, seriously, I'll be wearing a lot more of this sort of thing in future. But I don't want to Come Out, as it were, just yet. I've got something else to buy first.'

The grin froze on Oliver's face. Surely the poxy gorilla couldn't actually be serious?

Dud leaned towards him conspiratorially. 'I don't want Mona

to know anything about it. You won't tell her, will you?'

'No,' Oliver promised faintly.

'Good lad. Keep it under the counter 'til I get back. I'll pick it up then,' arranged Dud. 'I don't want Anna to know about it yet, either. OK?'

'No. I mean, yes.'

Dud winked and swaggered to the front door.

And Oliver stared at the hideous article in the bin. What on earth was he supposed to do now? Dud's revelations didn't exactly enhance the sleaze-free image of outdoor wholesomeness the Association wished to project. Should he report it? And if so, to whom? And if he did report it, would *he* be censured for a discriminatory attitude towards cross-dressing Committee Members?

Trust Len to be nowhere in sight. Len was like the proverbial policeman - never there when you wanted one. And always there when you didn't.

Ewan arrived at the pub to meet Mrs. Reynolds coming out.

'Sorry about this,' she said, 'But I'll have to pop out for half an hour. Someone's interested in an old boat we've had up for sale for ages. Go on in, Tom will show you what wants doing.'

'I'm not exaggerating, this has been the worst morning of my entire life!' groaned Oliver, chomping into a hunk of bread and cheese as he collapsed into a chair.

Anna, checking a delivery of fresh fruit and vegetables against a list, didn't bother to reply. Every morning was the worst of Oliver's entire life.

'Quite apart from oversleeping, Major Pratt listing all my sins in his poxy filofax, and juvenile terrorists who'll probably get me arrested as a potential child-molester, d'you know what I've just discovered about Dud?'

'No. And I don't want to.' Anna was examining a box of apples. 'They've made a mistake with these - sent expensive ones and made out the invoice for those cheap red things.'

'Oh yippee, let's have a party to celebrate,' muttered Oliver sulkily, then looked up. 'Actually, that's not a bad idea. I deserve a treat after the morning I've had. And we've got the place to ourselves.' He wandered across to the apples, ferreted amongst the tissue paper wrapping the topmost row, picked out the largest one. 'Why not invite a few friends round?'

'Who did you have in mind, exactly?'

'Well... Seasonal Assistants from other Hostels in the area?'

Anna smiled. 'This wouldn't have anything to do with Josephine, would it?'

Oliver pretended to examine a bruise on the apple. Of course it had something to do with Josephine, who was small, pretty, and shy, and had just started work at Wayfarers.

Anna considered. It was a bit windy for outdoor painting, and it wasn't as if she had anything else planned.

'OK,' she agreed. 'It's probably too short notice, but we can ring round a few Hostels, see if anyone's free. What sort of party? Spur of the moment, Come-As-You-Are-Job?'

Oliver hadn't got as far as thinking about party themes. An image of Dud wearing his repulsive female undergarments flitted across his imagination; a Guy Fawkes party, perhaps?

'How about a "Come as a Committee Member" party?' he suggested, and they both grinned.

'Yes. Beautiful specimen,' repeated Major Pratt, stirring his coffee. Luncheon had been excellent, but then luncheon at this exclusive country club always was. 'One of our Committee chappies got it out eventually. Nearly got his finger taken off for his pains!'

There was companionable laughter, then Tim said, 'Coming back to this Scottish Event you mentioned - there's a book about clans and tartans and things at the cottage. The previous owner left loads of books behind, we keep meaning to get rid of them. Would it be of any use? We could call for it later, if you like.'

'Oh, how kind!' enthused Eloise. '*What* a good idea, Tim. Isn't it, darling? We could pop it in at Beckside for Anna to design programmes and napkin rings and things, before we go home.'

'Splendid!' agreed Major Pratt. 'Yes, we'll take you up on that, Tim.'

Eloise clapped her hand to her forehead. 'Oh *no*! I've just had a horrid thought! *Could* we be perfect nuisances and get it now, rather than later? We've got that Charity Safari Supper tonight, darling. I managed to wangle the cheeseboard to give us as much time as possible, but we're still going to have to rush back.'

134

'Of course,' nodded Lucinda, handing the cointreau truffles round once more. 'We'll whizz back and get it now, so you can drop it off before we go sailing.'

Brian examined his find with delight. A sheep's skull, bleached white, the horns still intact. He'd been hoping to find one of these things for years. Just right for that space on the bookcase, next to the piece of driftwood that looked like an alligator.

It would have to be sterilised first, of course. His fellow ramblers, huddled together out of the wind in the shelter of a dry stone wall, grateful for the unscheduled stop, were not slow to make helpful suggestions.

'Len's got an old pan he uses for dyeing things in,' panted Leslie.

'Has he? Oh. That's useful.' Brian stared meditatively at the skull. In that case, he might go back and boil it at Beckside instead of finishing the walk, because he certainly didn't want it near any of *his* pans. After all, since Major Pratt wasn't here to impress, the walk would be non-productive anyway from that point of view (when he'd agreed to take part, he hadn't known the Major would be spending the afternoon sailing). And if it wasn't going to enhance his standing with Major Pratt, he had more rewarding things to do than continue it.

'I think I'll go back and boil this little beauty,' he decided.

Although they hadn't yet covered two miles, enthusiasm for the walk had petered out amongst the others as well. They milled restlessly around.

'I'm pooped,' wheezed Leslie, wiping his brow. 'It's this wind! I think I'll come back with you, Brian.'

'These bloody corns are giving me gyp,' grumbled Mona. 'Bugger this, I'll come back an' all, wait for Dud there.'

'Has anybody got anything to put my sheep's skull in?' Brian held it gingerly at arm's length. It would make a fabulous focal point on the bookcase - terribly aesthetic - but he didn't want to actually be in physical contact with it any longer than necessary. Babs promptly produced the neatly folded carrier bag she always carried for emergencies, and the grisly souvenir was placed inside.

'Wilf and I may as well come back as well,' she said. 'It seems a bit pointless, the two of us struggling along on our own. Doesn't it, Wilf?'

Wilf nodded mournfully, and the entire contingent turned to trudge back to Beckside.

The figure accompanying Mrs. Reynolds along the corridor to complete the financial transactions in her office was discussing the mooring arrangements for "Sultry Nights" as they passed the open door of the kitchen.

'Yes,' he decided. 'I'll leave it - I mean, her - where she is for now. It's a surprise for my girlfriend, like.'

Ewan, immediately recognizing the voice, suspected the new owner's maiden voyage might turn out to be an even bigger surprise for other boat-users on the lake.

He finished mopping the floor. It had been a long hard morning, and a long hard lunchtime, and he was looking forward to putting his feet up in the garden at Beckside, with a couple of cold cans for company, for the rest of the afternoon.

The party was going well.

The common denominator of slavedriving wardens provided a ready source of conversation to break any initial ice, and Anna listened, amused, as a competition evolved to establish who worked for the worst, or nuttiest, warden.

'Ours keeps us in a permanent state of semi-starvation to break our spirits and force us into submission,' Oliver was complaining, chocolate biscuit in one hand and bag of crisps in the other. He stood bare legged in a baby-doll nightie from Lost Property, a child's wig of long silverfoil strips on his head and a shorthand notebook tied around his waist. He'd come as Dottie.

'Ours suffers from delusions of grandeur,' said Josephine. She'd tied a football around her middle, donned a striped pyjama top, huge grey flannel trousers and braces (also from Lost Property), and come as Leslie. 'He's reinvented himself as proprietor of a five-star hotel!'

'They're all as bad as each other,' nodded Bill, who'd stuffed a rolled-up pillow down his front, found some fluorescent orange waterproof trousers, teamed them with a shocking pink blouse from Lost Property, fashioned a home-made wig out of a dozen yellow plastic pan-scrubs, and come as Mona.

136

Stuart had come as Dud: dirty shorts held together by a safety-pin, shirt buttoned up wrongly, pullover unravelling from the waist, and smeary glasses. Tom minced around in a flowery pink dress, Grade One haircut peeping from under a wide pink bow, and sturdy muscular legs (he was a fell-runner, and had just spent three years in the Army) encased in pink ankle socks: Babs. His co-assistant, Alison, too weary to devise Fancy Dress costume, had come as herself - an exhausted Seasonal Assistant in tee shirt and jeans.

Anna's choice of party identity was Eloise, in an over-the-top travesty of sailing ensemble; brand new matelot top and denims Oliver had discovered in Lost Property. Normally she refused to even touch anything from Lost Property, but this cache, still hermetically sealed in cellophane, was so obviously uncontaminated she made an exception. Not enough of an exception to don the accompanying red neckerchief and navy cap, however. She'd added one of her own Hermes scarves instead.

But the real star of the show was Simon, who was a walking caricature of Major Pratt. He'd bought a spray-on hair colour in distinguished grey, donned navy blue blazer and cavalry twill trousers, ripped up an old paisley-patterned pyjama top to make a cravat, and, in an extremely accurate imitation of Major Pratt's public school accent, periodically boomed, 'Make a note of that would you, Dottie,' and 'What d'you think, darling?'

Everyone had contributed food; there was left-over quiche, risotto, cold apple pie, crisps and savouries, and a glut of chocolate biscuits (unknowingly provided by Len). Anna had prepared a vast salad, with crusty bread, a variety of cheeses, and a large bowl of fruit. And of course they'd all brought a bottle or six-pack.

'Ours goes round collecting leftover jam, then sells it to people by the eggcupful,' continued Oliver, returning to the absorbing subject of barmy Wardens.

'He doesn't!' laughed Josephine.

'He does,' Oliver assured her. 'And he steams off unfranked stamps to use again!'

'Mine's like that. He's unhinged, if you ask me,' said Simon.

There was a chorus of sympathetic and knowing grunts. *Everybody's* warden was unhinged, if you asked them.

'He's in a really foul mood today,' he went on. 'I was glad to get out. The dog's bitten the next door neighbour, and the next door neighbour's threatened to poison it.'

'Tell him to come over and get a plateful of our mushroom stroganoff. That should do the trick,' advised Stuart, and they all laughed and drifted out through the back door.

Ewan smiled to himself. A huge, off-white nylon bra with discoloured patches under the armpits was attached to the front door handle as a fluttering pennant, and a piece of cardboard bore scrawled directions:

"SEASONAL ASSISTANTS' ORGY - Round the back."

Diplomacy dictated that, as a friend of Len's who would probably be regarded as a spy, he keep well clear of this particular party. Anyway, they'd all probably be about eighteen, and Ewan had no intention of turning up in their midst as the token Oldest Swinger in Town. He'd forego the cans in the garden and, instead, make some tea and take it to his room.

He was pouring boiling water into a mug as Oliver, Anna, and Alison came in the back door.

He looked at Oliver's attire with interest.

'We're, er, just having a few friends round,' explained Oliver shortly. 'It's a fancy dress party.'

'You don't say,' grinned Ewan, leering at the nightie.

Before Oliver could reply, the front doorbell rang.

'More guests?' wondered Alison. 'Why don't they just come round the back?'

'Ewan probably knocked the notice off as he came in,' grumbled Oliver, setting off to the front door.

It was only as he was unlocking it the thought occurred to him: what if it *wasn't* a guest? If this was a hosteller, he was going to look a bit silly dressed like this. The thought made him wary. Instead of opening the door fully, he cautiously inched it ajar and peeped round.

Then froze.

Dud, grinning chummily on the doorstep and naturally assuming the door would open to admit him, stepped forward. Oliver saw him advance in unreal slow motion, like the murderer

138

in a horror movie whose victim stands petrified with terror. With no time to formulate a coherent defence strategy, he did the next best thing - instinctively slammed the door in Dud's stupefied face and fled back to the kitchen, tearing off the glittering headdress.

'*Omigod I don't believe it, it's Dud!*' he gabbled.

The doorbell immediately rang again, indignant, threatening, furious. Simultaneously, a melee of panic-stricken revellers tumbled in the back door.

'*The Committee's coming up the drive!*' Tom was frenziedly ripping off his pink bow. 'A whole gang of them! The *real* ones!'

'But, but they've gone for a walk round the lake!' gibbered Oliver. 'What are they all doing back here?'

Everyone was too busy divesting themselves of incriminating items of clothing to guess.

'Back to the dole queue!' groaned Simon, almost throttling himself as he yanked off the home-made paisley cravat. 'And we won't even get any dole money after this!'

Ewan, who wasn't without experience of parties disbanding abruptly and revellers dispersing stealthily into the night, found himself directing the evacuation.

'Just calm down! Hide this grub in the larder, then go upstairs and get changed. I'll stall them.'

'What about Dud?' panicked Oliver.

Ewan had already thought of that. He turned to Anna. 'Since you don't need to get changed, could you keep him talking at the front door? Some ammunition which might help - he's buying a boat as a surprise for his girlfriend. Spin it out for as long as possible!'

Dud, fuming on the doorstep, vowed vengeance and retribution on that clot Oliver. Who did he think he was, *daring* to slam the door in the face of a Committee Member? Just wait until Major Pratt heard about this. And what was that stupid headdress thing on his head? And, come to think of it, what had he actually been wearing? It looked like... it had looked, from the little he could see, like a woman's frilly nightie! Just what was going on here? He hammered angrily on the door, which suddenly and unexpectedly opened.

'WHAT D'YOU THINK YOU'RE -?' he spluttered, then

realised he was waving Mona's bra under the nose of the very woman he planned to seduce, and hastily stuffed it behind his back. Trust *Anna*, of *all* people, to see him brandishing the thing around like a semaphore! The irony of the situation didn't escape him. All the times he'd tried, without success, to manoeuvre a couple of minutes privacy with her... And now, when at long last he'd finally got her on her own, he had to waste the occasion explaining away Mona's underwear in his hand!

'I found it hanging on the knocker!' he explained distractedly. In normal circumstances he'd have made some hilarious reference to bras and knockers, but he was in no mood for witticisms now. He could *kill* that fool Oliver. Quite apart from the fact the gormless twit could have smashed his glasses and broken his nose (which hadn't recovered from being rammed into Mona's chest yet), there was the unbelievable insult of the paid staff actually closing the door on him!

'Oh really?' Her voice was cool, remote. She seemed more interested in picking up a piece of cardboard on the doorstep.

'*Yes!* I don't know what it was doing there. But I want to explain -'

'It's really none of my business,' she murmured politely, folding the cardboard in two. Some hitch-hiker's old destination card, he supposed, wishing she'd stop fiddling with it and give him her undivided attention.

'I didn't mean, explain what I was doing with Mona's bra!' Dud was so intent on impressing Anna with the sincerity of his words he forgot he was still clutching it in his hand as he gesticulated wildly to emphasise the point. 'No, what I've been trying to tell you for ages is, she means nothing to me, Anna!'

Anna looked pointedly at the inelegant object dangling from his hand.

'It was hanging on the front door!' Hysteria rose in his voice as once again he concealed the awful thing behind his back. 'There's nothing between me and her, honestly!'

Anna glanced over her shoulder, and Dud heard what sounded like a herd of elephants charging upstairs. He peered curiously around her. She held the door even more firmly, blocking his view.

'Well, that makes your generosity in buying a boat as a surprise for her all the more spectacular, doesn't it.'

140

Dud's jaw dropped; the herd of elephants was immediately forgotten.

'How did you know about -'

'Oh sorry, I forgot. It's supposed to be a surprise, isn't it. Well don't worry, I won't say anything.'

He stared at her. Amazement dissolving the fury that had engulfed him, he took in, for the first time, what she was actually wearing. Blue and white striped matelot top and navy denims... Why, they were identical to the ones *he'd* bought! His'n'Hers outfits, like. All she needed was a red and white neckerchief instead of that floaty scarf thing, and...

He experienced a thunderbolt of revelation so profound, so earth-shaking in its intensity that he was momentarily deprived of speech. *She knew about the boat!* He didn't know how, but obviously she'd made it her business to find out all she could about him, in those devious ways only a woman in love employs. *That's* why she was being a bit prickly! *That's* why she'd been fidgeting with that bit of cardboard he'd been tempted to snatch from her hand! *That's* why she kept glancing inside, hoping nobody would appear and disturb them! And *that's* why she'd deliberately dressed in this nautical attire: it was a secret message for him, and him alone, in a code only he could understand... She was signalling her desire for him by her outfit, without saying a word!

Brilliant. That was Class, that was.

His face broke into a knowing smile.

'Don't worry, babe.' He winked and reached for her hand. 'You're going to get what you've secretly wanted all along, very soon. I know it's hard, waiting. It's the same for me!'

She recoiled. 'What on earth are you talking about?'

'Oh, I think you know what I'm talking about.' He nodded archly, then became aware of voices approaching up the drive, and glared round in annoyance. Trust a gang of hikers to arrive just as he and Anna were sharing their first intimate moment together! He'd give them a piece of his mind. Didn't they know Hostels were out of bounds to everyone (except him of course) during Closed Hours?

'The Hostel's closed!' he yelled impatiently, then recognised his fellow Committee Members waving cheerily in greeting.

'It's all right, dearheart!' called Mona. 'It's only us!'

'Oh, isn't that nice, Mona.' Babs' voice floated happily towards him. 'Dud's back from the garage. You'll be able to spend the afternoon together after all!'

Dud closed his eyes. What were *they* doing here? They should be at the far end of the lake by now. Which was why he'd sneaked back to catch Anna alone.

When he opened them, Anna had been joined by Ewan.

'We're all ready now, Anna,' he was saying.

'What are you doing still here?' snapped Dud. 'Ready for what?'

'I'm the new Part-time Assistant. We're ready to start weeding,' explained Ewan pleasantly.

'Weeding?' Dud gaped at him.

'Yes. Haven't you told him, Anna? We're forming a Seasonal Assistants' Gardening Club. This is our first Meeting. We've invited a few others round to help.'

Dud digested this information in silence, then, once more forgetting what he held in his hand, absently scratched his head.

'Would you look at that now,' simpered Mona to the bemused audience as her intimate undergarment was displayed for all to see. 'He can't bear to be separated from me even for a moment. Besotted! See? When we're apart he even pinches me brassiere to carry around with him wherever he goes!'

The Weeding Party, consisting of Babs, Brian, Wilf, Leslie, and Mona (Dud, who needed to compose himself, had mumbled an excuse and bolted to the small washroom on the top floor for a quick fag to sedate his overwrought nerves), unenthusiastically inspected the overgrown flower bed which was the Gardening Club's first target, and adjourned to the kitchen for the obligatory pre-weeding cup of tea. It seemed the rest of the Gardening Club members, having assembled for the very purpose of tackling the job, had all suddenly remembered that, unfortunately, they were required to return early to their respective Hostels on this first occasion.

'Stupid sods!' raged Mona. 'Are youse all too thick to realise you've got to allow enough time to do the bloody *work*?'

Yes, rather badly organised, Ewan admitted, shouldering the blame. At their next meeting they must remember to allow sufficient time to actually do some gardening, rather than merely discuss the programme.

So the Gardening Club melted apologetically away, with murmured regrets and profuse offers of help in the future. All of them carried bulging carrier bags, presumably containing their unused gardening clothes.

'I think it was a marvellous idea, Ewan. Major Pratt will be really pleased when he hears about it. And now that the walk is off and we're at a loose end, we can all help, can't we,' offered Babs.

'Well, I don't know about that,' frowned Brian, and added, as though the thought had just occurred to him, 'By the way, I believe Len's got an old pan somewhere that he uses to dye things in?'

Oliver dug out the ancient discoloured pan from its customary niche, and Brian bumbled off to the Self-Caterers' kitchen.

Mona smirked at Anna. 'Isn't it romantic, Dud carrying my brassicre around with him like that!'

'The very thought of it leaves one weak with disbelief,' replied Anna evenly.

Oliver and Babs, each preferring to forget the arrival of this particular item of Lost Property, avoided eye contact.

'I bet *your* boyfriend wouldn't carry a thing like that around with him, would he,' continued Mona smugly. 'If you had one, like.'

'No,' agreed Anna. 'I can assure you he wouldn't.'

Mona's congratulatory self-satisfaction was abruptly interrupted by a muffled explosion, followed by a blood-chilling scream, which appeared to come from the top floor...

'Ah, Anna. Let me introduce Tim and Lucinda. We've just popped in to leave a book on tartans for the Jubilee preparations,' smiled Eloise as Anna opened the front door, then recoiled in horror. 'Heavens! What's that smell?'

The door opened more fully. They stared in amazement; Dud was being carried downstairs on an old wooden door serving as an improvised stretcher, held by Ewan at the front and Oliver at the rear. The rest of The Committee trailed behind in a concerned but impotent procession.

'What on earth's happened?' Major Pratt immediately strode inside to assume control, then faltered as he too sniffed the air.

143

Good lord, what *was* that appalling stench?

'There's been an accident,' explained Ewan. 'Dud's strained his ankle.'

Oliver, as usual in times of crisis, appeared to have been overcome by a fit of coughing, face averted politely from the company, shoulders shaking as he clutched the unorthodox stretcher.

'Have you phoned the doctor?' enquired Major Pratt crisply. 'We'd better have it checked in case it's broken.' He'd already seen Oliver's attempts at rudimentary First Aid; Dud could end up permanently injured if the lad saw himself as a skilled paramedic and made matters worse by twisting the ankle in the opposite direction in a misguided attempt to correct the injury. Better get qualified medical attention, and quickly, from the look of things.

'No, don't bother the doctor,' insisted Dud bravely from his palanquin.

'Rubbish!' declared Major Pratt. 'I'm not having you being a martyr, Dud. We'll have you looked over properly. Sorry about this,' he added to Tim and Lucinda. 'Come in while I sort this emergency out.'

Tim and Lucinda stepped gingerly over the threshold, sniffed, and stepped back out again.

'We'll wait out here,' decided Lucinda.

The stench appeared to emanate from the Self-Caterers' Kitchen.

'What *is* that diabolical smell?' demanded Major Pratt, and was astounded to see Brian - of all people - loping towards them carrying a blackened pan, from which belched a cloud of asphyxiating smoke. The Committee members braked in an undignified cluster as Ewan halted the cavalcade to allow him clear passage to the front door.

As the pan was whisked under her nose on its way outside, Eloise was horrified to see, nestling in its blackened depths, what looked like the skull of a goat or sheep, the horns still intact. What on earth had been taking place? Had they interrupted some obscene black magic ritual? She grabbed Major Pratt's arm in consternation as Brian rushed past with the grisly remains.

'It's all right, darling,' said Major Pratt grimly, fanning the air

144

with the book of Scottish clans and tartans, and turning to Ewan and Oliver. 'I think our two friends here have some explaining to do. What exactly has been going on?'

Len brought the car to a halt, switched off the engine, and yawned. Although it had been a long drive, he didn't feel stressed; he was pleasantly tired, mellow, relaxed. The world was bathed in a golden glow of serenity and well-being.

'Why are all the windows open?' wondered Kate curiously.

He glanced across. Sure enough, every window in the building was flung wide. Strange. The weather wasn't particularly hot.

Anna, who had seen the car approach, came out to meet them.

'Place still standing then,' Len greeted her, opening the car door.

'Oh yes,' she agreed. 'The building's still standing.'

Kate looked at her sharply. That was a strange remark to make; almost as though, by implication, something else *wasn't* still standing...

'Major Pratt left this for you,' Anna went on, handing them a sheet of Beckside's printed notepaper.

Len scanned it briefly. '"Have another engagement tonight, so won't have time to discuss Oliver's suitability for the job as intended..."' He smiled, knowing the matter would slip Major Pratt's mind tomorrow, and that he and Eloise would be safely in Italy for eight weeks in a few days time. '"...Inform me IMMEDIATELY, underlined three times, via Answerphone, re the piper. Also, Dud has left his motorbike in the Bike Shed. He'll pick it up when he's able to ride." Able to ride? It'll be here a long time then!'

'He means, physically able. He's strained his ankle,' explained Anna.

'He's always straining something. Usually my patience,' grunted Len, and carried on reading. '"Have sanctioned chocolate, badges, and postcards for a school party... Was much impressed by Ewan's initiative in forming the Seasonal Assistants' Gardening Club ..."' His eyes lifted to Anna's face in amazement.

'Gardening Club? Ewan? *Gardening Club?*' There was something extremely suspicious here. Ewan, who couldn't tell a daffodil from a daisy and hadn't the slightest interest in the

145

difference anyway, was the last person on earth to be overtaken by the desire to start a Gardening Club.

'Yes.' Anna nodded calmly. 'Anyway, tell us about your day.'

Len, who knew a cunning attempt at subject-changing when he heard one, brushed the enquiry aside.

'How about you telling us about yours? Everything go OK?'

'Well, yes and no,' answered Anna.

'That wouldn't be another way of saying, what would we like first, the good news or bad, would it?'

'Yes,' admitted Anna.

'Let's have the good news first.' Kate looked uneasily at the open windows.

'Well, the plumber's been.' Anna's voice was expressionless. 'He charged a bit extra because it's Sunday, but he's sorted everything out upstairs.'

There was a pause.

'Ah,' nodded Len, golden glow of well-being disintegrating like a puffball mushroom under a Size Twelve boot. 'I see we've come to the bad news, have we. Like, what exactly was the plumber sorting out upstairs?'

'Well,' Anna inhaled. 'Dud blew up a lavatory pan, and -'

'He WHAT?'

'- And while everyone was upstairs rescuing him - because he was, er... it was in use at the time - Brian's sheep's skull boiled dry in your dyeing pan. That's why there's a bit of a niff.'

Len looked at Kate.

Welcome to the House of Fun.

'Who icl it?' Bridie fumbled impatiently with the receiver.

'It's me!' bellowed Mona. 'I'm staying at Dud's tonight, ma.'

'What? Where are you? I've been worried click!' Bridie's voice was querulous. 'Liclten, wait yet til I get me teeth in!'

Her slippers flopped into the distance, then returned. 'God love us, where've you been 'til this time? Yer dinner's all dried up in the oven!'

'Dud's had an accident. I'm staying the night. To nurse him,' explained Mona, with a sickly smile at Dud's mum, glowering in the corner.

There was a loud sigh of exasperation. 'What's the stupid sod done now?'

Mona hastily covered the receiver with her hand.

'He's strained his ankle.'

'He's strained his what?'

'HIS ANKLE!'

'Oh God love us, is that all?' Bridie sounded disgusted. There was some indistinct muttering, then: 'He hasn't strained anything else, has he? If you get my meaning?'

Mona, once again covering the receiver as Bridie's penetrating voice echoed across the room, directed another sycophantic grimace at Dud's mum.

'Are you there, mavourneen?'

'Yes! Hush, ma!'

'It's all right, they can't hear me, I'm down the phone. How did the soft git manage that?'

Mona hesitated. 'The toilet blew up under him.'

'The what blew up under him?'

'The TOILET blew up under him!'

There was a scream of laughter.

Mona directed another appeasing smile at Dud's mum, who scowled back.

'How in the name o' God -?' Bridie cackled helplessly down the phone.

'*Hush*, ma, will you!' Mona slammed the phone down. Wouldn't it make you weep! Here she was, giving the Ministering Angel performance of a lifetime (everyone knew men only had to clap eyes on a nurse's uniform and they were down on one knee proposing; she didn't have the nurse's uniform, but then he needn't bother with the down-on-one knee bit under the circumstances), and Bridie ruining everything, roaring with laughter down the phone!

Eloise nibbled absently at a sliver of Wensleydale with apricots, and tried to concentrate on the conversation taking place around her.

'All right for hacking around...' Penelope was describing a new addition to the stable.

Eloise excused herself from the Safari Supper for a few moments, to massage a little more lavender oil into her temples. Her nerves were still jangling after that awful, *awful* journey home.

147

They'd had to abandon the afternoon's sailing with Tim and Lucinda, of course.

Dud had refused point blank to be examined by the local GP, and hobbled, supported by Brian on one side and Major Pratt on the other, to Major Pratt's Rover to be chauffeured home. They'd had to endure for the entire journey Mona's cloying solicitude for his various injuries, and her nerves had been pulverised to the consistency of wire wool listening to Dud's Sultan-like acceptance of this unnatural homage.

She returned to the drawing room, and made a conscious effort to focus her attention on the saga currently being related. The new addition to the stable had, it seemed, cantered off and resisted all attempts at re-capture until somebody suggested a stallion. An unwelcome picture of Mona, whispering into Dud's ear as he sniggered in the back seat, superimposed itself onto the image Penelope was now describing in graphic detail.

Eloise shuddered, and determinedly banished the entire distasteful concept from mind.

Len was entering his report in the Accident Book.

Ewan and Oliver, it seemed, had been first on the scene, and discovered the undignified aftermath in the cubicle. Ewan, fearing for Oliver's job (and possibly life) if the lad was seen convulsed with laughter, hastily dispatched him in search of a suitable stretcher.

Anna, meanwhile, answered the front doorbell, which rang immediately after the explosion. Then Brian, alerted by the smell permeating through the building, remembered his sheep's skull in the Self-Caterers' Kitchen and raced downstairs to find the pan boiled dry.

"'The injury occurred as a result of the casualty, whilst sitting...'" er, no. "'The casualty dropped his cigarette butt into the lavatory pan,'" Len phrased his report aloud for the others to monitor its accuracy. "'Which ignited the residue of paraffin he'd emptied into it earlier in the day. The injury sustained thereby was unfortunately aggravated when the younger stretcher-bearer found the thought of the lavatory exploding under the casualty so amusing, he let go one end and dropped the patient on the floor -'"

A small party of late-arriving mountain bikers, wishing to

book in and getting no response to their increasingly frenzied bell-ringing at The Office, opened the kitchen door to investigate, and discovered Beckside's entire staff rolling around the kitchen table helpless with mirth, having apparently collectively overdosed on laughing gas.

Dud lay back on the bed, allowing Mona to fuss around him and plump the pillows up. Ironic, really. Just as he was on the point of dumping her, she was falling over herself to show she'd finally learned her place. Those Arabs had the right idea. Keep 'em in a harem, with the older ones marshalled into a workforce as they got past it. Take the thistles, for example. She'd tried getting a bit bolshie at first - "It's yer ankle that's strained, not yer bloody wrist!" - but gone all lovey-dovey when he'd reminded her how people would admire the artwork at the Jubilee. Not that she'd be there to see it.

But enough of Mona.

His eyes grew misty at the thought of Anna, signalling her unmistakable desire for him in her blue and white matelot top and denims. (He'd forgotten to pick up the carrier bag containing his ensemble in all the trauma. Must ring Len, tell him to keep everything safe until his next visit.) He hadn't missed her aroused confusion at his nearness; he'd finally broken through that shell of reserve, and she'd let him know, by her ingenious use of nautical attire which made words unnecessary, that underneath the facade of cool aloofness she was seething with lust for him.

Only a matter of time now. She was waiting for him, ready to fall into his arms like a delicious, perfectly formed plum.

Just think of her, there at Beckside, her little heart beating wildly as she imagined his next visit...

Len slipped outside to join Kate, who liked to stand for a few moments on clear evenings to look at the stars.

'I've got a Present from New Brighton for you,' he told her, and brought from his pocket two unspectacular, nondescript pebbles. She looked at them, unimpressed. Pebbles? What sort of a present was that?

'And you accuse *me* of being unromantic!' mocked Len. 'It's a pledge, Kate. A promise of things to come.' He imitated Eloise's voice. 'Symbolic, don't you think?'

'Symbolic of you all right,' snorted Kate. 'Pebbles! Too tightfisted to buy a proper present!'

He brought something else from his pocket; a small bag bearing the name of a Merseyside jeweller. He'd had time - or rather, made time - to go to the shops before joining her. She drew out a package. It contained a silver bracelet set with small polished stones.

It also held four photograghs: *Amhuinnsuidhe, Huisinis, Losgaintir*, and their own favourite beach in south Harris, on the back of which he'd written a message about other pebbles they'd collect as they strolled along a deserted shore of pure white sand washed by a turquoise and azure sea. And other ways to enjoy the backdrop of mountains, sky, and sea, after a picnic on a rug as the waves lapped gently beside them.

And just in case the warm September sunshine didn't materialise, or the wind blew too energetically, the cottage they'd booked was two minutes walk across the *machair* from the beach.

And it had an open fire.

He'd earmarked a dead apple tree that needed chopping down, so they'd take a sack of spicily aromatic logs with them for log fires, buy some peat, and collect driftwood. For those occasions when it would not be necessary for her to be adorned in anything other than the bracelet, he'd provide plenty fuel to warm her. And not just the sort in the fireplace.

Who needed oysters? Or any other kind of aphrodisiac?

FIVE: THE DUMMY RUN

There are times when weather patterns produce a very accurate reflection of life; bouts of turbulent activity subsiding into long troughs of monotony, when both sky and life appear to consist of nothing but a spiritless, insipid blanket of grey. So it was at Beckside as July dragged wearily towards August.

Days merged into an exhausting pattern of physical and mental drudgery; demoralising, repetitive, and at times completely pointless, reminding Oliver of the piles of straw spun nightly into gold by Rumpelstiltskin only to appear as straw again next morning to be done all over again.

This summer had been particularly trying because of cutbacks in staff, and all of them had cause to be grateful to Ewan, not only for the workload he unstintingly took on, but for his irreverent sense of humour, which had defused several potentially explosive outbursts of tension.

When August arrived Len, sensing they were all in dire need of a psychological boost, implemented a small but heartening Survival Strategy: a ritual defacement of the calendar each and every evening at 5 o'clock, when the date was ceremoniously crossed through. This was a gesture of defiance during the first week, a talisman to cling to during the second, a gleam of hope as the third trundled into the fourth, and a vital crutch for anyone who didn't expect to make the final week into September.

One good thing about August, pointed out Kate in an effort to find a positive aspect of the hated month, was the almost total absence of Committee Members, who, being creatures of habit, always took their own holidays then. (The other, Oliver reminded everyone *ad nauseum*, was that as soon as it finished it was his birthday, so would they all please note: HE WANTED 1ST SEPTEMBER OFF!)

Of course, it didn't always follow that Beckside in August could be guaranteed a Committee-free zone, as Dud proved when he unexpectedly hobbled in.

Following his unfortunate experience with the paraffin he'd taken to ringing Anna, becoming increasingly frustrated to find on each occasion that he was unable to speak to her. 'She's out,' Oliver would explain as Anna indicated she had no intention of coming to the phone. Or she was "not available".

'What d'you mean, "not available"?' he demanded indignantly, until Len finally lost patience and told him: 'Exactly that!'

So, a couple of weeks after his accident he set off by public transport to see her, like an eel battling instinctively to its spawning ground in the Sargasso Sea. Unfortunately, he picked the one weekend she'd taken Time Off In Lieu, hired a car, and driven up to visit a friend in Edinburgh.

After this unproductive episode he waited, nerves fraying, for a return phone call or Get Well card. When neither materialised he took to ringing his local Post Office and berating them for their monumental inefficiency in losing half his mail every day. (All right, you couldn't expect somebody of Anna's caste to do all the running, but she *must* have sent a Get Well card!)

Depression set in. He became so dispirited at having to put his plans concerning Anna on hold that he couldn't even summon up the energy to finish with Mona.

And Mona certainly hadn't finished with him.

As well as descending on him at regular intervals with interminable clumps of thistles ("Therapy, dearheart - it'll give yer something to do!"), she and Bridie decided things had drifted on long enough. As Dud hadn't got around to proposing voluntarily, they'd have to take matters into their own hands. Various ways of springing the Engagement trap were discussed, and when a Wedding Invitation arrived from a relative in London, it seemed like an gift from Fate.

'The very dab!' Bridie crowed. 'Get him down there and get him paraded. You'll come back engaged, mavourneen.'

'Bernadette's wedding?' frowned Mona. 'He won't want to go to that.'

'Never mind what he wants.' Bridie reached for the cigarettes, lit up, and exhaled. 'Nothing like one Wedding for getting another on the go, it's a well-known fact.'

Mona was still doubtful. 'What about his ankle?'

'Bugger his ankle!'

'But he'll use the thing as his excuse.'

'Tell him, when Bernadette and Sean go on honeymoon, you

152

and he can have the flat for the week.' Bridie tapped ash into the overflowing ashtray and squinted at the letter accompanying the invitation. 'See, she says here. No point in the place lying empty, they've still got to stump up the rent. He won't turn his nose up at a free holiday in London, will he?'

She'd guessed correctly. Dud didn't turn up his nose at a free holiday in London.

At first, as they'd expected, he was warily unenthusiastic about the wedding itself, but Bridie focused on the free holiday, and that, combined with the boredom of waiting for his ankle to heal, swayed the decision. Because Dud had his own reasons for finding the prospect of visiting London an appealing one.

During his convalescence he'd indulged in numerous daydreams featuring Anna, one of which was whisking her off for a romantic weekend in the capital and escorting her around the smartest eateries and nightclubs, brushing off obsequious club owners who rushed to greet him and usher him to the best tables. The uncomfortable reality, however, was that she'd suss within five minutes that he was an unsophisticated hick from the north who'd never been to London in his life.

So this wedding could provide the opportunity to familiarise himself with the In Scene; case a few cultural joints, Art Exhibitions, stuff like that. He'd find out where all these Galleries and things were. Didn't want to appear the archetypal bumpkin gawping round, clueless.

He was still free to ditch the bitch afterwards. After all, a week in London hardly constituted a proposal of marriage, did it?

Of course what they hadn't told him was, the flat was in Stepney, miles from the fashionable haunts he'd thought of as "London".

He'd envisaged "the flat" as a trendy penthouse overlooking the Houses of Parliament, all black leather settees and plush white carpets, from which he could nip out to Harrods for a spot of shopping whenever the mood took him. The reality turned out to be the back bedroom of the most dilapidated in a row of terraced houses, with a boarded-up shop on one corner, a boarded-up pub on the other, and a derelict factory opposite. The shared "kitchen", in which lingered a mysterious and ever-present smell of boiled cabbage, comprised of a filthy cooker, a rickety table, and a glass-fronted crockery cabinet, the pane cracked but held together by congealed grease, on the landing. Of the other resident in the front bedroom there was no sign, although from the street could be seen a light bulb shining continuously behind drawn curtains. Dud wondered whether the occupant had died, and decided that if the curtains hadn't moved by the end of the stay he'd better investigate.

A group of Africans shared the ground floor. The building vibrated to the thump of drums and wild laughter, and there was much coming and going and banging of doors, mainly at night.

Bridie was billeted nearby with one of her numerous cousins who'd colonised the area and established a network of bases for an itinerant population of relatives.

They arrived the evening before the Wedding, in time for The Stag Night. Dud, eagerly anticipating wild and riotous debauchery in Soho and the West End, found himself instead in the local pub, where by 10PM the entire contingent was legless and engaged in a maudlin, never-ending chorus of "Danny Boy", which the Hen Night at the pub over the road drowned out with an increasingly boisterous rendering of, "Oh This Year We're Off To Sunny Spain!"

Dud, who had a healthy appetite, waited for the 'eats' to be wheeled out. As the night wore on, however, it became obvious that the only buffet he could expect was the landlord's strategically placed bowls of thirst-inducing salted peanuts. Eventually he slipped out unnoticed to a take-away down the road, which someone had told him was run by a family from Chile. ("I know this amazing little gem of Chilean Cuisine off the tourist trail, Anna...") Adopting a worldly air, he pointed to an intriguing item under the glass showcase.

It looked appetising; a golden triangle, presumably of pastry, containing what appeared to be minced meat. He took a large bite. His mouth started to burn. He chewed gamely on. His eyes watered. He swallowed, clutched at his throat, threw the Chilean Cuisine over a wall, and blundered into the Hen Party where the bride-to-be, in raucous partnership with Mona, drew him into the midst of a group of wildly applauding women, unbuttoned his shirt, unfastened his trousers, and lowered them slowly to his ankles as her entourage roared ribald encouragement.

He was vaguely aware of Mona slobbering over his lips and a

series of blinding flashes as a battery of cameras clicked and snapped from all angles...

They lost interest in him as "Wimoweh", thumping from the bar, heralded the arrival of Tarzan, his glistening muscles, and his baby oil. Dud, buttoning his shirt and restoring his modesty, tottered back to the Stag Night pub where he was welcomed with bleary-eyed sentimentality by the Danny Boy contingent. His hoarse request for a glass of water was greeted with gales of laughter; he was plied with more - and more - Guinness. He noticed a jug of tepid water covered with a layer of dust on the bar, glanced furtively around, took a large gulp, turned pale, and ran into the Gents to throw up. Eventually, supported by a couple of indistinguishable Uncles with straggly grey hair and identical light blue suits, he was escorted back to the flat and left, snoring, on the landing floor.

So the day of the wedding passed, for Dud, in a blur of African drums throbbing in time with his hangover as he crawled feebly to the communal lavatory with diarrhea.

Bridie was philosophical.

'Ah, who cares if he doesn't show up at this one? It's the next one that matters. And there'll be no wriggling out of that when he's seen the photos of himself grinning like a Halloween turnip, keks round his ankles and drunk as a skunk, proposing marriage in front of the whole Hen Night... And if his memory goes a bit blank, like, there'll be a pubful of witnesses queuing up to remind him, at the Engagement Party on Monday night!'

Dud, unaware his fate had not only been sealed but formally announced at Bernadette's Reception (where his absence was excused with unconscious irony: "He's not too clever today...") gradually recovered, and by Monday felt well enough to escape African drums, Mona, Bridie, and the wearisome relatives who'd appeared at spasmodic intervals to grin at him, mutter 'Congratulations', (he'd found that a bit puzzling, but put it down to surviving the Stag Night) and find highly amusing his sudden urgent needs to commandeer the bathroom.

'By, we put some stuff away last night, didn't we,' he greeted the first half dozen, before the novelty of trying to make conversation with Mona's monosyllabic male relatives wore off. So that took care of any social obligations he owed her, and from now on it was time for the real purpose of the trip to London.

Mona was unexpectedly amenable when he suggested getting out from under her feet for a bit, on his own.

'So you can have a nice chat with your relatives,' he offered.

'So we can prepare for the Engagement Party tonight,' nodded Bridie with satisfaction.

Dud made some lighthearted reply, wondering who was getting engaged. Probably the youngsters Bridie said needed a bucket of cold water throwing over them, making a holy show of themselves like that at the wedding. Not that it mattered; he'd escaped their clutches, and was now free to enjoy himself. The holiday starts here, boys - let the good times roll.

He made his way to the West End where he spent a fascinated ten minutes gazing in the window of a Ladies' Underwear boutique near Leicester Square, he watched street entertainers in Covent Garden, he viewed Buckingham Palace, Downing Street, and Westminster Bridge, and he chatted up a couple of French girls at Trafalgar Square, who, in an effort to get rid of him, pointed to the National Gallery and recommended a visit. ("Oh, is *that* where it is? I've been searching for it all over London!") He prowled knowingly around Soho, but drew the line at being enticed into any of the dives by skimpily-clad hostesses - they needn't think *he* was some goggle-eyed peasant who'd pay £100 for watered-down coca cola!

Eventually he realised it was getting late.

He'd leave Anna Territory, Sloane Square and so on, until tomorrow. Better not overdo it and put the kybosh on his ankle, which was starting to throb. Didn't want to spend the rest of the week held captive in Stepney, listening to African drums.

When he returned to the flat he was greeted by uproar.

The bride and groom, it seemed, had had a blazing row, and the groom was now being treated in Outpatients after being knocked unconscious by the bride. The officiating priest had been instructed to petition the Pope for an Annulment, and the honeymoon had been cancelled; the groom wanted his flat back, and wished to rid it of all traces of his bride, including her freeloading relatives. A couple of female cousins or aunties - older, fatter versions of Mona - were distractedly stuffing the wedding presents from the bride's side into an assortment of carrier bags and binliners.

'And where've *you* been til now?' demanded Mona.

'I got lost,' lied Dud, surveying the half-prepared buffet dumped in an unappetising jumble on the table. Sliced white bread with wedges of hard red cheese, several bags of own-label crisps, and a soggy flan, the pastry sunk into itself on one side and overcooked on the other. Whoever this Engagement Party was for, if the banquet plighting their troth was anything to go by, it didn't say much for the heights of wedded bliss waiting ahead.

Mona's voice gatecrashed his train of thought.

'Sorry, dearheart?'

'I said, the Engagement Party's cancelled. We're going home.'

'Home?' repeated Dud, stunned. He hadn't explored Anna Territory yet!

'Yes, home!' snapped Mona. 'Get your bags packed, quick.'

'What, now?'

'*Yes, now!* And bloody hurry up!'

So Dud's first and only trip to London ended with an abrupt decampment. As he struggled downstairs with two suitcases and three carrier bags, the door of one of the downstairs rooms creaked open. He attempted a conciliatory smile at the scowling face that appeared, tripped over a shoe lying on the bottom stair, dropped the heaviest suitcase on his damaged ankle, and tottered into the street.

The light was still on and curtains drawn in the front bedroom.

Dud gulped, turned away, and limped down the street after Mona.

When Major Pratt and Eloise returned from Tuscany, amongst the post that had accumulated in their absence was a memo informing them that, so far, there almost a hundred acceptances for Beckside's Jubilee.

Pleased, Major Pratt consulted his notes regarding who'd been delegated which tasks, and rang the relevant Committee Members for a progress report. The first was Brian, marked "Sea Shanties". Shouldn't be any problem there; Brian was on the ball and extremely keen.

After the opening pleasantries he directed the conversation to the business in question - and was astounded when Brian calmly informed him that as he'd now taken up stamp collecting, he hadn't had time to organise any shanty-singing. Yes, he supposed it was a bit of a drawback, but there we were. Such was Life.

Fuming (it was aggravating enough to be let down, without inane philosophical observations thrown in), Major Pratt phoned Babs. At least he could be certain *she'd* have diligently accomplished her allocated task.

But Babs, stammering with confusion, confessed she hadn't organised the Scottish Dance Demonstration Team because her friend was "expecting" and had retired from the world of energetic social pursuits to await the Happy Event.

Eloise, eavesdropping in the background, tutted in annoyance. One had enough on one's plate as it was with table decorations and flower arrangements, without these extra crises at this stage in the proceedings.

'Honestly!' she exclaimed. 'Isn't it *irksome!* How on earth are we supposed to find replacements before 21st September?'

'I could wring their necks!' thundered Major Pratt. 'The whole damn lot of them, incapable of doing anything unless I stand over them with a whip! It's farcical. We'll probably hear from Len that the piper's cancelled next!'

Before they phoned Beckside to ascertain the state of affairs there, however, Eloise had an idea.

'Darling, would Gavin and Isabelle be able to help, do you think? They're always rushing up to Scotland for St. Andrews Night Balls and things.'

So she rang Isabelle, who was sympathetic but dubious about the chances of providing a Demonstration Team at such short notice, and suggested, as a sort of safety-net in case she didn't find one, that if they could rustle up a few volunteers she'd sort out instructions and music for one or two simple dances which, with sufficient practice, would get them by.

'Rustle up a few volunteers?' repeated Major Pratt, aghast. 'Doesn't she understand this is a formal Display? We're not trying to find a vaudeville turn for a Gang Show!'

'Darling, it's just a precaution,' Eloise chided gently.

'It'd turn the Association into a laughing stock!'

'Darling, I'm sure you needn't worry,' soothed Eloise again.

'Needn't worry?' Major Pratt, who had been advised by a

doctor friend they met up with in Tuscany to take several deep breaths and proceed serenely to some calming, relaxing hobby - gardening, for example - whenever he felt the onset of stress, started viciously dead-heading the geraniums on the window ledge. 'A hundred VIPs turning up expecting a professional Display of Scottish Culture and Flavour of the Sea, and finding some ridiculous DIY pantomime - and I *needn't worry?*'

'Do calm down, darling. Gavin and Isabelle *will* find a replacement; this is merely a precaution, just in case. And I'm sure we can find someone who knows a few sea shanties. If the worst comes to the worst, Len might. He's a Liverpudlian.'

Major Pratt almost snipped off a cluster of buds in his agitation. 'Oh be sensible, darling! Beckside's Jubilee, turned into some ludicrous burlesque by Len trying to sing Sea Shanties?'

Eloise sighed. Really, the whole thing was too bad. She'd expected to devote her energies to those pleasurable finishing touches at which she so excelled; purchasing candlesticks and tartan ribbons, ensuring the laundering of the tablecloths had been done to her satisfaction, that sort of thing. And now here they were with less than a month to go, having to organise Scottish Country Dancing and Sea Shanties.

Major Pratt piled dead geranium heads into a heap for Mrs D to clear away. 'I suppose we could get away with *one* Event being withdrawn...' He eyed the withered petals with ill-humour. 'If necessary, we'll drop Sea Shanties. Concentrate on Scottish Country Dancing. At least we'd have our hands on the reins for that. We'll arrange the practice for this weekend.'

The next stumbling block was that none of their own circle of friends could manage this weekend, because it was Bank Holiday.

'It's *got* to be this weekend,' insisted Major Pratt as Eloise worked her way through the address book and drew a blank at each call. 'It's the Golf Club AGM on September 7th.'

'Well, the 14th is definitely out. That's Toby's Christening.' Eloise leafed through her diary, hesitated, then, in desperation, suggested Beckside's staff for the emergency rehearsal.

Her husband groaned and held his head in his hands.

'Do remember it's only for an absolute emergency, darling,' said Eloise tartly. 'I'm trying to be constructive. Who else can we

159

practise with at such short notice?'

'I don't know, but not them!'

'Darling, the point is, we'll be in control, supervising everything. All they've got to do is follow instructions.'

'The point is,' corrected Major Pratt. 'They haven't got sufficient mental capacity to follow instructions. Imagine it! Len blundering around, tripping over his own feet...' He dead-headed another cluster of blooms, then wished he hadn't. The thing was starting to look like a collection of bare stalks. 'And as for that nincompoop Oliver...'

It was at this point Dud phoned.

Added to his irritation at having to abandon reconnoitring the London In-Scene was an even more disturbing worry; Dud still hadn't managed to find the right opportunity to offload Mona. Instinct for self-preservation had prevailed on the train journey home, where - rather alarming, this - he had the distinct impression both old hags appeared to think the London trip had in some way clinched some deal, consolidated Mona's position.

It made him very uneasy.

However, as August progressed, things started to look up. His ankle was recovering, and this morning he strode confidently into the Doctor's Surgery to be given a clean bill of health (then, on the way out, tripped over an umbrella propped against a wall to drip, causing a titter of amusement to ripple through the habitués of the waiting room). At last, the time had arrived for his and Anna's long-delayed consummation of mutual passion aboard "Sultry Nights".

He dialled Major Pratt's number. Eloise answered.

Yes, his ankle had taken longer to heal than expected, but it was better now, thank you. And yes, the thistles were all done. Oh, they could rely on him, though he did say so himself. Not everyone was a sneaky self-centred Judas like Brian. In fact, as he'd recently embraced all things nautical, they'd be relieved to know that *he* could save their bacon and step into the Sea Shanty breach himself! Yes, no problem. So, were they by any chance going to Beckside in the near future? Oh, this weekend? It was just that he couldn't take the thistles himself, you see, having no transport. Yes, the Honda was still there. Nuisance, wasn't it. He'd have to find some way of getting there to collect it...

Mona? Oh, he hadn't seen her for ages. No. No, she wouldn't be coming with him. Yes, he was quite sure. Scottish Country Dancing? Was that this sword-dancing lark? Oh, a set of eight, like. No, he hadn't done any of that. Mind you, it was pretty easy to get the hang of, he supposed. He'd been to a Barn Dance once.

Major Pratt, in the background, muttered something about Fred Karno's Circus.

'Darling,' comforted Eloise as she replaced the receiver. 'It's only in case of the *direst* emergency.'

'Just as long as he doesn't bring that appalling woman with him!'

'Oh, he said that was more or less over. I think he's letting it die a natural death. Babs will stand in,' Eloise reassured him as he dialled Beckside.

Oliver answered.

'Is Len there?' barked Major Pratt brusquely. (No point trying to hold an intelligent conversation with this nincompoop.)

'He's, er, talking to a school groups organiser at the moment,' Oliver explained, as Len, who'd just sat down with a mug of tea and his paper, indicated through the kitchen door that he wasn't available.

'Well tell him we're coming up this weekend to hold the Jubilee Dummy Run. We're bringing Dud and Babs. Got that?'

Oliver grunted a brief acknowledgement.

'I said, have you got that?'

'*Yes!*'

'And tell him,' boomed Major Pratt. 'We've got no Scottish Country Dancers for the Demonstration. We're all going to have to pitch in with a DIY effort. We'll practise it tomorrow night.'

The phone was replaced with an abrupt clunk.

'There! Good riddance!' said Kate, crossing through the 31st with relish. The dragon was slain at long last, the whole of August now obliterated.

'Not quite,' Anna reminded her. 'We've got tonight to get through yet.'

'Yes,' Oliver added bitterly. 'The poxy Dummy Run. Prancing round doing Scottish Country Dancing! I'm warning you, if anyone ever tells any of my friends about this I'll set fire to the place. I'm serious.' He glared at Kate. 'And you've known all summer I wanted the first of September off for my birthday!'

'Don't start that again,' sighed Kate. 'You know Len would let you have the day off if he could.'

'I'm amazed you've got enough energy to celebrate anything anyway,' remarked Anna with feeling. July and August had taken their toll; dark smudges had appeared under her eyes, and her hair had lost some of its lustre. She hadn't made as much money from her paintings as she'd anticipated, mainly because she hadn't had time, energy, or inclination to produce quality work. Although other artists enjoyed painting out of doors in August, she personally found it an uninspiring month and disliked the all-pervading green that swamped the countryside. Quite apart from which, physical exhaustion effectively drained away creative urges.

'Whether or not I've got any energy to celebrate it isn't the point,' argued Oliver, as Len came into the kitchen. 'The point is, I shouldn't have to work on my birthday.'

'I've told you,' said Len, 'If I could let you have the day off, I would. You knew at the interview you'd have to work without a day off some weeks.'

'Yes, but not on my *birthday!*'

'Oh, stop harping on about it. I spent my twenty-first chipping ice off freezing davits in the North Atlantic... Anyway, there's a sink blocked in the Men's Washroom. Can you take over in The Office, while I see to it?'

'I suppose I'll have to,' sulked Oliver.

'Not at all,' said Len pleasantly. 'You can unblock the sink if you'd prefer?'

A broad-shouldered giant wearing a light-coloured belted mac was whipping off dark glasses as he strode towards The Office.

'Israeli Security,' he introduced himself, flashing an ID card. 'You are...?'

'I'm the Assistant Warden,' blinked Oliver.

'The *Assistant* Warden?' Israeli Security was obviously not used to dealing with underlings. 'Where's the Warden?'

'Unblocking a sink.'

Israeli Security stared at him. He was obviously not used to staying at places with blocked sinks, either.

'Our coach party has arrived. I had expected to be greeted with a degree of professionalism, by someone in authority. *Would you please bring a more senior member of staff at once.*'

The tone was utterly scathing, and it was one provocation too many for Oliver, who was tired, stressed, and still boiling with resentment about having to work on his birthday (especially as the reason for it was standing in front of him complaining about being booked in by inferiors of unacceptable rank).

For a few seconds he stared silently at the man, then, still without a word, locked The Office, ran up the stairs, went to his room, picked up a bottle of Jack Daniels whisky, trotted down the back stairs, and slipped out the back door.

'Where's Oliver?' demanded Kate.

'That's what I'd like to know,' said Len grimly. 'But if he's wise he'll stay hidden. And not just from me; Mossad's probably got a contract out on him.' He explained how he'd discovered a fuming Israeli pacing the Reception Area, waiting for either the Warden or his Assistant to appear.

'You and Mossad can join the queue. He's got the wrong sausages out of the freezer for the toad-in-the-hole. *Pork! For Israelis!*'

Len looked at the sausages laid out to defrost, and touched a couple at random. They were partly thawed; returning them to the freezer wasn't an option.

'Why not just make more batter and camouflage them? There's probably no pork in the things anyway, they're all gristle and sawdust...'

The subject was discreetly dropped as Major Pratt bustled in, followed by Dud carrying a music centre.

'Len, we'll plug this by the Dining Room french windows, so we'll need an extension cable for it to go outside,' announced Major Pratt. 'Can you oblige?'

As he was speaking, Israeli Security padded stealthily into the kitchen, like a feared member of the KGB. Kate instinctively attempted to position herself between him and the sausages.

'Ah. *Shalom!*' greeted Major Pratt.

Israeli Security nodded briefly, eyes flicking around the kitchen, taking in the position of the back door, larder, and utility room. Kate, contriving to block the sausages from view, edged furtively along the table.

'Salaam aleikum,' added Dud knowledgeably. (Major Pratt wasn't the only one who could show off a few foreign lingos!)

The Israeli broke off his scrutiny of the kitchen to stare at him.

'That's Arabic, Dud!' hissed Major Pratt.

Kate mouthed to Len: 'Get him out of here, quick!'

'Right. The extension cable. Yes. It's in The Office.' Len flung the door open to distract attention from the sausages - then swiftly closed it again before Major Pratt saw the farce being enacted in full view on the stairs. Ewan, supporting Oliver's weight as he heaved him bodily upstairs, was unsuccessfully trying to smother the inebriated giggle following each hiccup.

'Er... actually, I think it's in here,' he explained lamely.

'It's in The Office, where it always is!' ground Kate between clenched teeth as she hovered in front of the sausages.

Israeli Security listened to this exchange impatiently, as though trying to decide which of them possessed least intelligence; Len, his half-witted Assistant who'd set off to fetch him and hadn't been seen since, or his wife with her peculiar habit of patrolling the kitchen table.

'I won't bother you any longer. You will appreciate it is necessary to check over the entire building.' He turned to go.

'So, everything all right then?' Len blocked his way.

Major Pratt looked at him in amazement. What on earth was he playing at? It was quite obvious the Israeli wished to leave!

'Any problems, just let me know,' went on Len helpfully.

'You can be sure I will.' The Israeli advanced to the door, forcing him to abandon delaying tactics and open it.

Len exhaled with relief.

The stairs were empty. Ewan had made it.

Dud smiled complacently as he connected the extension lead to the music centre. Oh yes, Anna might fool everyone else with that cool, impersonal façade she displayed towards him in public, but she didn't fool him. And tomorrow, when she was alone with him aboard "Sultry Nights", and she dropped that sweet little pretence of indifference, and they were -

Hell's teeth... Surely that wasn't *Mona's* voice?

'I thought I'd surprise you, dearheart! I rang yer mam, who said you'd volunteered to help with some emergency here this weekend.'

164

Dud darted an embarrassed glance at Major Pratt. 'Er, yes. We've been let down over the Scottish Country Dancing Display for the Jubilee.'

'Dancing Display? Ah God love us, why didn't you tell me? Yer problems are over, dearheart. I'll organise a few Irish jigs for youse!'

Major Pratt closed his eyes.

Irish jigs. For a Scottish Theme.

Was there *no* escape from the dratted woman?

Ewan, elbows propped on The Office counter, was discreetly informing Len how he'd found Oliver sitting amongst the dustbins, giggling into a whisky bottle, when a stooped figure in a crumpled suit opened the front door and looked around the Reception Area with interest.

'Good evening,' Len welcomed the stranger. 'Can I help you?'

'I got a lift from Stranraer, the lorry dropped me in Carlisle. Someone picked me up who was coming this way; he told me to get a bed here for the night. I'm on me way to visit me sister in Manchester,' confided the newcomer trustingly. 'Because I'm on the look-out for a wife.'

Dud, approaching from the Dining Room just in time to hear this intriguing information, eyed the man with interest.

The man apparently felt among friends because he continued, 'Me mother, God rest her, passed away, so I'm needing a bit of help on the farm now. I can't manage on me own.'

'So you're looking for a wife, eh?' nodded Dud encouragingly.

'Yeah.'

'And, er, what sort of wife are you looking for, like?'

'Well, she's got to be a worker,' considered the prospective wife-seeker.

'Oh yes,' agreed Dud wholeheartedly. What use was one that wasn't?

'And she's got to be good on the bog.'

Good on the... Well, Mona was that all right. She was never away from the place.

'Well, friend,' he nodded solemnly, like a genie having weighed up the request and decided to grant the wish, 'It's a strange thing, Fate. Maybe you've been directed here by Destiny, and you'll find the woman of your dreams right here, this very night! And I'm in a generous mood, so I tell you what I'll do. I'll treat you to your stay. Book him in, Len! On me!'

'Isn't that the kindest thing you ever heard, now,' marvelled the wife-seeker, taken aback by this unexpected generosity.

'Oh, I'm like that.' Dud brushed aside the man's gratitude.

'If I can ever do a return favour for you,' offered the stranger earnestly, holding out his hand, 'I will. Me name's Eamon.'

'Well actually, there is something, Eamon,' Dud told him, shaking it. 'Did you say Oliver's not well and gone to bed, Len?'

'Yes. He's, er, had to go and lie down.'

'Well, we're having a little dance later on,' Dud told the newcomer, who was still dazzled by his unforeseen welcome and good fortune. 'And we're a man short. Would you like to take his place?'

The dancers were assembled on the lawn.

Eloise looked up from the opening chapter of a booklet entitled "101 Scottish Country Dances" which they'd borrowed from Gavin and Isabelle, along with a handful of tapes, and appraised with misgivings the raw material from which she had committed herself to produce a moderately convincing Demonstration Team.

'I thought it might be rather nice to start with a little background information and history of the dance,' she suggested brightly to the unenthusiastic faces awaiting the coming lecture.

Oh dear. This was obviously going to be heavy weather.

She'd managed to marshal them into some semblance of a Scottish Country Dance Set; two lines of four facing each other (and even *that* seemed like a major achievement), with Major Pratt and herself as first couple, Kate and Len second, Dud and Mona third, and Babs, teamed with the unlikely stranger Dud had mysteriously produced, fourth. Anna had earlier explained that, as she was in mourning for a family friend who had died during the week - failing to mention that the friend in question was her aunt's cat - she felt frivolity was unseemly and volunteered instead for Shop Duty.

'Good lord, who's this?' Major Pratt had hissed in a horrified aside as Dud wheeled out the new recruit in his crumpled suit to meet the dancers.

'This is Eamon,' announced Dud, pushing his protégé forward.

'He's offered to take Oliver's place.'

'Oh. How kind,' murmured Eloise faintly.

She had to admit that the novice Dance Team was, at best, uninspiring. Mona ferreted in a dirty plastic handbag for her cigarettes, Kate and Len stared like trapped animals at a heron flapping lazily overhead, Eamon smiled vacantly at the grass, and Dud was studiously ignoring Mona. He was beginning to find her presence increasingly menacing; there was something weird about the way she kept appearing from nowhere like some horrible clinging leech. (Nothing worse than a besotted admirer who won't take no for an answer, is there!)

'Because it *would* be rather fun to learn a little about it, don't you think?' Eloise appealed to the conscripted dancers.

Only Babs nodded in happy anticipation.

'So I'll just read this short excerpt, if I may.' Eloise glanced at her husband rifling through the tapes, then quoted resonantly: '"Scottish technique and presentation…" Is everything all right, darling?'

'No it isn't!' The tapes clattered as Major Pratt inspected the reverse sides once more. 'Gavin's left one out!'

'Oh no!' groaned Eloise. They'd spent an entire evening selecting the programme with Gavin and Isabelle; three dances which satisfied the criteria of aptly sea-flavoured titles, yet were simple enough to be picked up by beginners. 'Are you sure?'

'Of course I'm sure!' Major Pratt's voice was peevish. He hadn't missed the alacrity with which Len and Kate seemed ready to escape the formation.

'Oh, how aggravating. Well, we'll have to eliminate that one. Erm... where was I?'

'Scottish technique and presentation,' Kate reminded her dully.

'Oh yes. "The dancing in its elegance and carefully detailed steps -"'

Major Pratt made a gesture of impatience. Thoughtfully included snippets of history were wasted on these philistines; he was more concerned with assessing the realistic possibility of a Demonstration Team, which he personally doubted. Gavin and Isabelle had promised that if they couldn't find a genuine Display Team they would themselves take part on the day, so it was a case of which participants to reject and which (if any) to include as a workable unit. So they may as well get on with it.

167

He took the book from Eloise.

'Thank you, darling. Most interesting. We'll run through the actual dance instructions now, shall we. And the first thing we need to know -'

He looked up to emphasise the first thing they needed to know, and found all eyes had swivelled to the Dining Room french window steps, where two Americans, carrying plates of toad-in-the-hole retrieved from the waste bucket, were settling down to munch their scavenged meal.

Major Pratt, horrified, was about to stride across and castigate them, then decided it might be wiser to ignore the matter. Perhaps they were penniless. There again, perhaps they'd so enjoyed tonight's meal they couldn't resist purloining more. It *had* been unusually tasty. Lots of batter in the toad-in-the-hole. Much more than usual. He'd meant to compliment Kate at the time, but Israeli Security had been doing the same thing and one didn't want to overdo it.

He tapped the instruction book to reclaim the dancers' attention.

'Now, we want to incorporate Mr. MacTavish's seafaring days in our tribute to him, don't we, so we're going to start with a dance called "The Sailor".'

His eye alighted on Babs, who nodded docilely.

'Eloise will demonstrate the steps. First, the pas-de-basque. This is what you do when I call "Set!" So, if you'd like to try...?'

Eloise demonstrated the step to the best of her limited ability, and the rest awkwardly attempted to follow. Len, who hadn't been near a dance floor since his Cavern days, resentfully felt like the token elephant brought in to boost the confidence of the others.

'Now, if you've got that,' continued Major Pratt, unimpressed by this display (obviously they hadn't, but he couldn't spend all night on one simple step - there was the entire dance to drum into them yet), 'We'll try the dance itself. Let me read the instructions. "First four bars: First Couple cross over giving right hands." Like this.' He deposited Eloise between Len and Dud, and positioned himself between Kate and Mona. 'Then we join nearer hands... like this... to form a St. Andrew's cross. Double triangles! You see? Now, "set"!'

There was a collective ungainly hop.

Major Pratt tutted irritably. 'Try again.'

They all trooped back to the starting position. Once more he passed Eloise courteously across. She grabbed the relevant hands and executed a graceful pas-de-basque, and Len and Dud attempted a self-conscious shambling bob. If the situation were not so urgent, thought Major Pratt, it would be downright laughable; a collection of inept clodhoppers murdering a graceful, stylised dance.

'Now.' He again checked his instructions. 'The first lady - Eloise - casts round the second man - that's you, Len - to stand between the second couple facing *down*, while the first man - me - casts around the third woman - that's you, Mona - to stand between the third couple, facing *up*.' He looked around, seeking confirmation his directions had been intelligently assimilated. Six faces gaped uncomprehendingly back.

'Perhaps we'd better walk it through. One tip our Scottish friends gave us was, always remember: the lady goes *up*, and the man goes *down* -'

There was an eruption of vulgar sniggers from the Dining Room steps. Major Pratt glared across, but decided to ignore it. He and Eloise solemnly paced into position.

'Now - all set!'

The entire group sprang jerkily in an uncoordinated leap.

'No no no!' Major Pratt closed his eyes and held his hand in front of him like a policeman directing traffic. 'When I say, "all set", I don't mean *all* set. Bottom couple, you don't actually take part at this point.'

A loud burp erupted. 'Pardon,' muttered Mona.

Major Pratt sighed.

'We'll move on to the next phase. Which is...' he consulted the instructions. 'Yes, here we are. Reels across the dance.'

He looked up. This was where the fun really began.

When Leslie arrived, wheezing, perspiring, and clutching the counter for support, Anna hastily brought him the stool from inside The Office.

'I've come to help with the Dance Practise,' he gasped, sagging onto it.

Anna, suspecting the Dance Practise might have enough problems as it was without a possible heart attack as well, suggested he just sat and watched.

'No! I've come to take part, not watch! I used to be hot stuff in my day... D'you remember Ivy Benson and her All Girl Band?'

'No,' said Anna.

'Well, they -' A hornpipe started up in the distance. Leslie paused to listen. It got as far as bar ten, and stopped.

'Oh. I didn't realise it was this square dancing lark. I can do my stuff with the waltz and valeta, but I can't give them much help with that. I didn't know it was square dancing.'

'It's Scottish Country Dancing,' explained Anna.

'Oh,' said Leslie, none the wiser. 'I must have dozed off for a second during the Committee Meeting, when they were discussing it. I wouldn't have come if I'd known. Not my cup of tea, that lark.'

'Just sit and watch,' advised Anna.

'Oh no,' protested Leslie. 'I like to take an active part. Just let me get my breath back...'

The phone rang. Ewan, stacking yesterday's delivery of tinned goods on the shelves, answered it.

'Good evening. Could I pass on a message to Major Pratt?' requested a cultured male voice. 'Tell him, Gavin has some good news. We've found a Demonstration Team for the 21st!'

Word spread like wildfire of the free cabaret on the lawn, and the space beside the Americans had filled up with an assortment of curious spectators. Every time a sequence was performed correctly there was an ironic cheer, and each mistake was greeted with ribald hoots and cackles of glee. Major Pratt, having airily invited everyone with whom he came into contact to come and watch, now had to restrain himself from ordering the multiplying hordes to clear off.

He frowned at his lacklustre Demonstration Team. Look at them! Not one of them (with the exception of Babs smiling shyly at her dour-faced partner) making the slightest effort to master the intricacies of the steps! Mona's eyes followed Dud like a lizard about to flick its tongue at an insect, Dud fidgeted restlessly, and Kate and Len stood, captive participants with a total and obvious lack of interest in the entire proceedings.

The chord sounded.

'Double triangles!' prompted Major Pratt. 'And remember -'

170

In what was an extremely unfamiliar experience for Major Pratt, his words were drowned by the hooligan element joyously roaring its own unorthodox instructions: "*And remember - the lady goes* UP, *and the man goes* DOWN!"

Ewan, on his way to pass on Gavin's phone message to Major Pratt, stepped from the workaday world of harsh fluorescent light into a fairyland of ethereal evening sunlight. It was as though Helios, the sun god, had used the sky as a canvas for the entire spectrum of his celestial paintbox.

Even as he stood entranced on the doorstep the god-artist intensified the effect. You think this is exquisite? Just look what I can do with a little more darkening here, a subtle lightening there.

Ewan, staring at the majestic glory spread above the darkening Lakeland hills as the sun dipped behind them, decided Major Pratt could wait for his phone message until Nature had bid the world this magnificent adieu.

'It's perfectly simple,' Major Pratt upbraided his perspiring dance team through clenched teeth. 'We'll try again - if you feel up to it, darling?'

This was met with more coarse guffaws. Then, as Major Pratt glared threateningly across, Leslie tottered out and reduced the onlookers to near hysteria by offering to teach the dancers the waltz and quickstep if they liked. Major Pratt seriously considered abandoning the whole thing there and then - he'd *warned* Eloise it would be a disaster - but what if Gavin and Isabelle failed to come up with a Display Team for the 21st? No. They couldn't give up.

With iron control he forced his voice to stay level.

'If we could all just pay attention, we'd find it's perfectly straightforward. I'll read it again.' He studied his instruction book and quoted sternly: "'The leading dancer begins the figure by passing the dancer he is facing with right shoulder and the third dancer comes in to pass him with left shoulder." There you are. *Now* do you understand?'

Babs, cheeks crimson with mortification, eyes staring like a rodent hypnotised by a cobra's swaying head, didn't know which was more terrifying: to admit she hadn't a clue what he was talking about, or for the eagerly awaiting spectators to find out for themselves when the music started again and it became obvious.

'N... er, yes, I...'

Major Pratt had long since accepted that the entire group (except for himself and Eloise, of course) were geographically challenged, but good heavens, surely they could distinguish between right and left?

Ewan approached across the lawn, grinning. 'I've got -'

Major Pratt's parade-ground roar annihilated the rest of the sentence; the appearance of a legitimate target on which to unleash his bottled-up fury couldn't be better timed.

'I think we can do without unhelpful comments from you, thank you!'

'But I've got -'

'Did you hear me?' The cheek of the fellow, daring to continue when it had been made abundantly clear that neither he nor his smart-alec humour were welcome!

Ewan tried again. 'Yes. But I've got -'

Major Pratt held up an authoritative hand. *'I will not tolerate any further interruptions!* GO AWAY!!'

Ewan shrugged, and turned obediently back to the hostel.

And Major Pratt, watching the enemy retire trounced and defeated to lick his wounds, mentally dusted his hands. Such a *satisfying* feeling, disposing of an irritating buzzing insect with a good swipe from a rolled-up newspaper!

Dud's protegé, who, after his initial burst of friendliness had lapsed into brooding silence, suddenly announced: 'I'll have to go now. I've got to ring somebody,' and stumped off just as they were on the point of launching into the next sequence.

Major Pratt, despite his irritation, heaved a sigh of relief. He'd found the presence of the surly, smelly individual with his habit of staring silently at them all most unnerving. Moreover, it was an opportunity for everybody to have a break. (Heaven knew *he* needed one!) So he dismissed the formation with a slightly self-conscious: 'Take five, everybody.'

'Now you've got no excuse, Anna!' Dud wagged his finger roguishly as he approached The Office.

'No excuse for what?' Anna looked up from the nightly balancing-of-books with an irritated frown.

Oh, she was in one of her hoity-toity moods, was she. Well, that was understandable. He knew what was bugging her. Mona. This hard-as-nails act was just a defence mechanism against the jealousy and pain of having to watch him dance with another woman; her love-rival. Also, he must bear in mind that she was so used to keeping her feelings hidden, she'd probably become deeply inhibited and would need his sensitive reassurance to help her relax, and admit the truth.

'For this ice-maiden act you put on in front of others.' He smiled at her tenderly. 'But you can drop it now, Anna. We're all alone. We're free to release all that pent-up passion at last!'

Ewan, stacking cans of soup on the shelf under the counter, listened with interest to this highly original romantic overture. Update your manual, Casanova. A lesson for us all here.

'Yes, I think it's time we gave up the pretence,' nodded Dud solemnly. 'Time you and I had a talk, Anna.' The finger again wagged mischievously. 'And I think you know what about.'

'I haven't a clue what -'

'Haven't a clue, eh? Would you like me to give you one then?' Suddenly realising what he'd said, Dud giggled. 'A clue, I mean. For now. Blue and white striped matelot top and denims...?'

'*I don't know what* -'

'That was brilliant, Anna. Just like this Ice Maiden act you put on in public!' He regarded her knowingly from under half-closed eyelids. 'But it's time for the ice to melt now. Oh yes. Once I get you alone aboard "Sultry Nights" you'll be like a polar bear on heat, and -'

'*I beg your pardon?*'

Dud's voice was a low growl. 'Oh, it's not my pardon you'll be begging for, Anna!'

Ewan settled back in pure enjoyment. This was better than an England-Scotland at Murrayfield.

Dud smirked confidently. Under that cool exterior she was as nervous as a kitten. Look at her, shuffling her feet and lowering her eyes to hide the confusion and excitement he'd aroused!

Anna glared down at Ewan. She should have sold ringside seats for this, with a block booking for Len, Kate, Oliver, and the entire Assistants' Gardening Club. They'd all be splitting their sides. But she wasn't splitting hers. Exhausted by the worst August she'd ever experienced, Anna was in no mood to find this ludicrous conversation with its smutty double meanings and offensive innuendoes - or indeed, Dud's tiresome fixation for her - in the least bit amusing. You read about these things in the papers; someone became infatuated, and then couldn't, or wouldn't, accept that the idol not only didn't reciprocate the adoration but was totally oblivious of the smitten one's existence. Or, as in her case, couldn't stand the sight of him.

Well, she'd tolerated it for long enough. When she first started at Beckside he'd been merely a joke, a self-important figure of ridicule nobody could take seriously. Now she was heartily sick of the whole unpalatable nonsense. He'd get his talk all right, but it wouldn't be what he was expecting to hear. At this point in the season it no longer mattered if he turned spiteful or vindictive; she'd safely won her bet. Autumn was already in the air. The mornings were getting colder, leaves starting to turn golden, swallows instinctively gathering on the telephone wires. In another four weeks she'd be gone as well.

'... Yes, the time has finally come, my sexy Goddess of Ice and Fire, for the iceberg to thaw.' (They always found the dominant caveman approach irresistible. Even the PC In-Yer-Face militant feminists at the office secretly craved Arab sheikhs on stallions carrying them off to desert tents, no matter how much they pretended otherwise.)

What sounded like a muffled snort erupted from below the counter. Dud looked at Anna, puzzled. Anna prodded Ewan sharply with her foot.

'- And the flames leap from smouldering lust, which we've both had to pretend for so long didn't exist, to white hot unbridled all-inhibitions-cast-off action -'

Another snort exploded from the region of Anna's feet. Dud stared at her. He wasn't imagining things this time.

He peered over the counter - and saw Ewan sprawled against a pile of cardboard boxes, fist rammed into his mouth in a futile attempt to stifle convulsions of helpless mirth.

Major Pratt, awaiting Dud's return with his depleted Dance Team, tutted impatiently.

'What on earth is Dud doing? Go and chivvy him up, would

you, Babs? Tell him we're waiting. We *must* perfect at least *one* dance!'

Dud was desperately casting his mind back, trying to remember exactly what he'd said. To think this guffawing pig had been lurking out of sight, listening to every word! And what was he doing, anyway, scrabbling around Anna's feet? Outraged eyes held Ewan's like a boxer before a fight, glinting dislike bordering on hatred.

'Has this pain-in-the-neck been annoying you, Anna?'

'Yes, you have,' replied Anna evenly.

Babs peeped hesitantly round the front door.

'Dud, Major Pratt says, erm, are we ready to try again now?'

'Tell him there's a phone message, Babs,' said Anna. 'His friend rang. He's got a Demonstration Team for the 21st.'

Dud stared at her. First *he'd* heard about any phone message!

'Oh, how lovely!' breathed Babs, delighted.

'Why didn't you tell me?' demanded Dud.

'I couldn't get a word in. Neither could Ewan, when he tried to tell Major Pratt ten minutes ago, and was told to stop interrupting and go away.'

Dud looked at Ewan sharply. Ewan nodded.

Totally unaware of the animosity crackling around the Reception Area, Babs prattled happily on.

'Major Pratt will be so relieved, won't he! Oh, come on Dud, let's go and tell him!' She took his wrist in a gesture of naïve enthusiasm, and, before his traumatised brain could recover sufficiently to react and snatch it back, skipped lightheartedly down the Reception Area and danced him outside.

Anna and Ewan looked at each other, both fully aware that Babs' childlike innocence had just averted an explosion of wrath so venomous it could easily have resulted in manslaughter.

(As to whose, Anna knew which of them *her* money would be on as survivor in any fight...)

The audience had got bored waiting for a succession of absconding dancers, and drifted away. All that now remained on the steps, apart from chocolate wrappers, crisp packets and cigarette ends, was a yawning Israeli posted as look-out to report any upsurge in activity making it worthwhile for the rest to return, and Leslie, propped up against somebody's rucksack, snoring gently.

Major Pratt, almost hopping with impatient vexation, was about to set off himself to drag each and every truant dancer back outside when Babs at last appeared with Dud, who looked pale and agitated.

'Good news!' she called. 'Your friend telephoned and left a message. He's got a Demonstration Team after all, Major Pratt!'

And Major Pratt closed his eyes, uttered a brief prayer of thanks, and snapped shut "101 Scottish Country Dances" with such heartfelt relief that, when Len broke out of the formation like a weary beach donkey at last unharnessed, he didn't even utter a rebuke.

Chambers' Twentieth Century Dictionary defines "infatuation" as "To turn to folly; to deprive of judgement; to inspire with foolish passion."

Dud's definition, as his infatuation for Anna shrivelled like a deflating balloon, was far simpler: What did I ever see in the stuck-up cow? She'd *known* Ewan was there, listening to every word and killing himself laughing, yet she'd allowed him to go on humiliating himself by saying all those things to her!

To think he'd wasted all that time plotting and planning and worshipping from afar, indulging in pleasurable daydreams about romantic weekends in London and trips to secluded coves in "Sultry Nights"!

Well, all he could say was, he had a lot of time to make up. And there was no time like the present to start. As for Ewan, who was after all the lowest of the low (didn't even qualify as paid staff!) and not worth sullying his hands on, a quiet word to Major Pratt about disrespect to his superiors on The Committee would soon sort *him* out, and send him, tail between his legs and referenceless, off to the Job Centre where he and his like belonged.

When "Hava Nagila" suddenly blared forth and Israelis poured out of the Dining Room, overrunning the Scottish Country Dancers on the lawn, Major Pratt was at first highly indignant.

'Who gave these people permission to dance out here?'

'Oh darling, does it matter?' smiled Eloise tolerant.

176

Major Pratt frowned, considering. No, he supposed it didn't. ('The whole hostel often gets together for, you know, impromptu Ceilidhs and things,' he'd laugh good-naturedly when chatting to Mr. MacTavish.) He duly extended a slightly belated invitation to the Israelis to join his Multi-Cultural Hands-Across-The-Sea Folk Dancing Evening; they could demonstrate Israeli dancing to the other hostellers, and the other hostellers - he'd noticed a couple of Germans booking in earlier (lederhosen and thigh-slapping), and a carload of Italians (Opera, hopefully), and of course there were the Americans (hillbilly ho-down) - could contribute their national flavour to the proceedings. There were some Canadians as well; they could sing 'Rosemarie' or recite 'Hiawatha' or something. The English contingent could, er... well, they'd think of something.

Rubbing his hands at the prospect of organising the Ceilidh, he instructed Kate and Len to rustle up a few nibbles. Nothing spectacular, just a few, you know, sandwiches and so on. And cakes. And lots of tea, and coffee, and fruit juice; everyone would appreciate a drink, wouldn't they. So rewarding, meeting other nationalities, exchanging views, fostering understanding, wasn't it?

Babs smiled delightedly. He was right. There'd be no strife, no discord, no wars in the world if everyone would just get to know each other, hold Folk-Dancing Evenings...

Dud liked the sound of this Ceilidh thing. One of those Israeli bints, the buxom one with dark eyes he'd noticed earlier chatting to Israeli Security, looked OK. And he could let Miss Snooty-Keks see she was now irrevocably classified in the 'Discarded' category along with Mona, as far as he was concerned. Pastures New were waiting to be conquered - and next time it wouldn't be an artist, either. He'd had quite enough of artistic temperament, thank you very much.

Even better - he'd seen Mona, adorned in her war-paint (she obviously meant business; undercoat, top coat, and high-gloss enamel finish) marching Eamon down the drive to the pub. The fickleness of the female sex! One minute all over you - yes Dud, no Dud, three bags full Dud - and then, as soon as they thought your back was turned, seducing the snake-in-the-grass you'd befriended! Well, as Mona herself would say, bad cess to the pair of them.

It felt so good to be free, slip the leash, unlock the shackles, and go on the prowl once more. Thank heavens he'd seen the light about Anna before she'd had time to really sink her fangs in, or he'd have had *her* to shake off as well as Mona - and look at the trouble he was having doing that!

Yes, it was true what they said. The chase was far more exciting than possessing the trophy.

The dancers swooped around rhythmically in a large circle, dipping knees and clapping over their heads every few bars.

Although the Germans hadn't shown up (neither had the Italians, Americans or Canadians for that matter) Major Pratt was enjoying his Ceilidh. He stood, deep in conversation with Israeli Security, bemoaning the burdens of responsibility.

When a small contingent of Israelis unceremoniously interrupted him, he was astounded. He was even more astounded when his companion held up a hand to stem him in mid-flow, listened as they gabbled something in their own language, excused himself offhandedly, and strode towards the hostel as though Major Pratt were some inconsequential nonentity!

Major Pratt, who was accustomed to brushing others carelessly aside, but had never actually experienced anyone doing the same thing to him, stared at the Israelis with increasing dislike and disapproval.

Ill-mannered lot!

'Corporal Clott and his UN Peace-keeping Initiative can wait until we've all heard what the sexy Goddess of Ice and Fire said to the Committee Member,' grinned Kate as the paid staff (including Oliver, who drifted in to announce dolefully that he'd just been sick, but felt better now) gathered round the kitchen table to produce the refreshments.

There was a businesslike tap at the door.

'We have all decided to eat out tomorrow evening,' announced Israeli Security. 'No reflection on your cooking,' His eyes flickered briefly towards Kate. 'We all enjoyed tonight's meal. Very tasty, those sausages. But it's someone's birthday. So we want a full refund on tomorrow's evening meals.'

Len looked at his Seasonal Assistant's head, drooped onto his chest. It was Oliver's birthday tomorrow, too. And Oliver wasn't the only one who needed the respite of a relatively easy day; they were all nearing exhaustion.

The Association, however, was not keen on parting with any money once paid, and refunds were always frowned upon. Especially one this size, and for a reason as flimsy as this. Len knew perfectly well that he was expected to argue most strongly against a refund, and that he could find himself in trouble for agreeing to one without prior sanction from above.

'I'll try to arrange it,' he said slowly. 'If a way presents itself.'

'Good.' The Israeli gave a curt nod. 'I'll leave you to get on with the refreshments then.' He looked pointedly at the empty table, and closed the door.

Oliver listed slowly towards Len, who stuck out a hand to prop him up.

'Oliver...'

'Urgh...?'

Len had been eighteen too, once.

'Go back to bed and get some sleep, son. We're half way to getting you a day off tomorrow.'

Major Pratt and Eloise were holding a discussion with a group of young Israelis on the merits of the kibbutz system.

'Very similar to Youth Hostels, in their way,' pontificated Major Pratt. 'Both, you know, foster international friendship and -'

His philosophical theories were abruptly cut short by raised voices. Spinning round to investigate, Major Pratt saw a dark, buxom girl complaining to Israeli Security and gesticulating angrily at Dud, who was rubbing a red weal on his cheek.

'What on earth's going on?' he demanded, striding across.

'She just slapped me across the face!' gasped Dud.

'And I'll do the same thing, but a lot harder,' Israeli Security threatened coolly, 'If he sexually harasses my fiancee again.'

Len and Ewan, emerging to re-fill teapots and replenish cakes, saw that all was not going quite to plan with the International Hands-Across-The-Sea Folk Dancing Ceilidh.

The Israelis, radiating tangible animosity and aggression, were huddled together glaring at Dud as Major Pratt moved amongst them, hands spread in a gesture of cajoling camaraderie, proclaiming: '*Shalom!* Peace! PEACE!'

'What's happened?' asked Len in amazement.

'Dud evidently insulted his fiancee,' groaned Major Pratt. 'And they've accused him of sexual harassment! Delicate one, this, Len.'

'Oh. Yes. You're right. Very delicate,' agreed Len. 'I wonder,' he suggested slowly, 'If a gesture of conciliation might help? They were asking about a meals refund for tomorrow night...'

There was a pause.

'Hm. I don't know about that.' Major Pratt frowned. 'Damage Limitation is one thing, but we don't want them to think they've got us by the, you know...'

'True,' agreed Len. Time to turn the screw a little. 'I hope they don't leak it to the media. We don't want it trumpeted all over the tabloids, do we? Especially with the Jubilee coming up.'

Major Pratt looked as though he was about to have a seizure. Good lord, he hadn't thought of that!

'Of course,' continued Len, 'I explained that a refund was out of the question. But... well, this sort of thing hardly fits the wholesome outdoor-organisation image we're trying to project, does it? Especially as the complaint is against a Committee Member...' He tailed off, allowing this discomforting seed to germinate and take root.

Ewan, meanwhile, strolled across to Dud, hands in pockets. Major Pratt, who hadn't been aware of any friendship between them - in fact he thought they hated one another - strained to hear what was being said as intriguing snippets drifted across, then concentrated on the infinitely more urgent matter in hand.

'Hm,' he capitulated eventually. 'You might just have something there, Len. And I must say, it's most unselfish of you to offer to make this sacrifice on your meals profits.' Perhaps he'd misjudged old Len. A bit bolshie at times, admittedly, but the fellow meant well at heart. '...Er, as long as they understand we want the whole thing treated with the utmost discretion...?'

Len gave a leave-it-to-me nod.

'Right then. I'll authorise things so there'll be no come-back from National Office about the refund.' Major Pratt paused, and lowered his voice. 'By the way... What on earth's Ewan talking about, to Dud? Pub regulars would enjoy hearing all about sexy Ice-Maidens and *polar bears on heat* if he were to lose his job?

What does he mean? Have you any idea?'

'About as much as Dud,' said Len, face expressionless.

Major Pratt shook his head, mystified. No accounting for the vagaries of mankind.

And mankind didn't come much more vagarious than Ewan.

September 1st was grey, nondescript, uninspiring.

Oliver's parents had come up for the day, and taken him for a pub lunch. Anna was delivering another batch of paintings to the Gallery. Ewan was working at the pub.

In the midst of a heaving Lake District Bank Holiday weekend, the hedged-off portion of garden at Beckside was - for a couple of hours anyway - a quiet haven of seclusion and peace.

Len yawned, dropped his paper.

'Think I'll go upstairs for a lie down.' He smiled lazily at Kate. 'You look as though you could do with a bit of a lie-down as well. A bit tired, you're looking.'

'Well gee, thanks for the compliment!'

Len narrowed his eyes with exaggerated mock lust and leered at her: 'All right then. What does, "Come upstairs, my sexy Goddess of Ice and Fire, my little polar bear on heat, and let the flames leap from smouldering lust to white hot unbridled all-inhibitions-cast-off action," do for you then?'

'Makes the idea of a life of celibacy increasingly attractive.'

'Kate.' Len's voice was quiet as he helped her up and held the door open for her. 'We've survived another August; it's finished, at long last. That's something to celebrate. In the nicest way possible in the whole wide world. And as I can't give you a choice of exotic world destinations to celebrate it in - will our bedroom do?'

And Kate, who enjoyed countless daydreams choosing which paradise islands to visit if money were no object, replied truthfully that there was nowhere on earth she would rather be at this very moment than wherever he was.

Which happened to be right here.

But the bedroom sounded even better.

Danny MacTavish finished dusting the sideboard and started on the mantelpiece. He gently wiped the framed snapshot of Jeannie taken on their brief honeymoon in Dunoon, then moved on to the clock, behind which was the invitation printed in gold lettering on authentic MacTavish tartan card (someone had obviously been extremely thorough!). He fingered the envelope, wondering once more how he'd let himself be talked into this - and, more importantly, since the event was due to take place tomorrow, how he could talk himself out of it again at such short notice. He re-read the typewritten transport directions pinned to the card.

"If travelling by car, take ..."

There were no directions for if not travelling by car. Presumably it hadn't occurred to the writer that the Honoured Guest might be arriving by public transport, so that a local bus timetable would be of more use than a photocopied map of the area detailing the location of Beckside, which he already knew.

His gaze returned to the photograph of Jeannie.

Changed days, Jeannie. This was dragging up the past, and the past should be left to rest in peace. Which was what he felt like doing. He was seventy, or would be tomorrow, and now that the Event which in June had seemed so reassuringly far away was actually upon him, wished he'd shown a bit more sense. No fool like an old fool, Jeannie, and this old fool had agreed to traipse across half the country to be feted by strangers who knew nothing about him other than that he owned Beckside and therefore fitted the bill as Guest of Honour. A VIP to impress, a figurehead to revolve their festivities around. Aye, he'd seen plenty of occasions like this in his time. And plenty of pompous Guests of Honour as well.

Which was, if he was strictly honest with himself, one of the reasons he'd acted so out of character and accepted this unexpected invitation; from a sense of sheer mischief. He knew perfectly well the sort of person they'd be expecting, and the sort of person they'd be expecting bore no resemblance whatsoever to the sort of person he was.

Also, he'd shown the invitation to Molly. A widow, a kindly

soul who lived a few doors away, they'd been on nodding terms until one rainy November day several years ago when, selling Remembrance Day poppies in the Govan Road, he'd become chilled to the bone, and she'd brought him out a mug of steaming hot tea. Deeper friendship had blossomed, and as neither had any desire to remarry it was an easy, comfortable relationship, providing companionship and warmth for both of them.

When the invitation arrived he'd said he had no intention of going, and she'd chided him and said that he should, because they obviously wanted to thank him for giving a lot of people a lot of pleasure over the years. So he'd asked her to join him (the invitation included "partner"), but she said her knees wouldn't allow her to travel that far and instead offered to keep an eye on the place for him, switch the light on in the evening to deter burglars, feed Cabbage the cat, and get in a loaf and a pint of milk for his return. She'd look forward to hearing all about it when they walked to the library together on Tuesday.

And the third reason he accepted was that the invitation happened to arrive on a particularly poignant date on his calendar.

His Wedding Anniversary.

He'd never actually shared a Wedding Anniversary with Jeannie while she was alive. They'd been married less than a year before the full might of the German Luftwaffe had shown Govan what its bombers could do, and one of them, who had either misjudged the target - which would have been difficult, because Glasgow couldn't have been more clearly illuminated from the fires raging downriver in Clydebank if the inhabitants had lit guiding beacons themselves - or, more likely, had excess bombs to dispose of and unloaded the remainder of his cargo as he turned for home, carelessly wiping out the two lives that meant more to Danny than his own; Jeannie, and his baby daughter, Elizabeth.

He sometimes wondered about the man who had deprived him of her babyhood (or at least, sharing it second-hand through Jeannie's letters until the war ended), childhood, and, as the future unfolded, watching her grow from adolescence to a beautiful young woman and walking down the aisle with her on his arm, giving her away with love and pride on her Wedding Day. Had he survived the war? Had he married, raised a family?

183

Had he sat with his own grandchildren on his knee, arms around them as they recited nursery rhymes in childish German voices? Had he told them the well-loved stories that have been told to children down the ages? Did they have a German version of Cinderella? Jack and the Beanstalk? (The Night Grandfather Bombed Govan?)

The ironic thing was, it was Jeannie who worried about him being killed, not the other way around. When he'd held her at the station and kissed her for the last time, lovingly stroking her stomach in both greeting and farewell to any new life that might be beginning inside, it never occurred to either of them that she would be the casualty, or that their child's life would be snuffed out, the infant buried in her tiny casket before he'd even seen her.

So every year he marked his Wedding Anniversary, his daughter's birthday, Jeannie's birthday, and the anniversary of their deaths, by placing a posy of flowers on their joint grave. During his years at sea he had taken the choicest bloom from one of the table displays in the Dining Room and released it over the side, watching sombrely as it was churned around in the turbulence of the bow wave.

And this year, partly as a reaction to the melancholy that always assailed him around each of these dates, and partly... oh, who knew, Jeannie, he was almost seventy, maybe it was time to lay to rest ghosts unable to find peace - he'd decided to accept the invitation to Beckside.

And now he wished he hadn't.

He stared at the photo of Jeannie, and she smiled back at him. How vivid, how clear were the memories…

You only had to say, 'Ah'm frae Govan!' to have strangers roaring with laughter since comedians and TV sitcoms had brought the place to the world's attention, but his mother hadn't had much to laugh about when she gave birth to him in a room-and-kitchen in Rathlin Street. He didn't have a Paw. He didn't know why he didn't have one; he just didn't have one. After his Maw died when he was six years old they'd taken him to the Orphanage. He couldn't remember much about that, except that it was a frightening place, full of strange rules and regulations, so he'd stayed quiet and unobtrusive in the background, careful not to draw attention to himself in any way. Lonely, miserable, and wanting his mother, he learned to cry silently at night, when darkness brought the only privacy to be had.

Then they farmed him out to "the hielans", which, to Danny, meant a smallholding a few miles from the village of Struy in Strathglass, run by a middle-aged childless couple, stern, pious, and humourless: Danny never heard either of them laugh during all the years he was there. He was expected to show gratitude to his benefactors who had performed their charitable duty (as they reminded him frequently) by working each day from 6.00AM at a weaving loom in the byre before he went to school, and again in the evenings after he'd completed his other chores around the place, until he left school at fourteen and went to work at a hunting lodge in Glen Affaric.

Enough to eat, and a working environment out of doors in all weathers; he began to fill out. The hard physical work developed his muscles, and gradually he changed from a pale, undersized child in hand-me-down jacket and threadbare trousers to a young man, still extremely sensitive and shy, but strong and fit, with a pleasant, weatherbeaten face, blue eyes, and dark hair. Kind-hearted and generous, he had an unsentimental affection for the wildlife that shared his working environment; deer, otter, wildcat, pine marten, and the birds of the Highlands, crossbills, siskins, grey wagtails, corncrakes, and the golden eagles that soared over *Mam Sodhail* and *Carn Eige* towards Loch Mullardoch and the lonely peaks of *Sgurr na Lappaich* in the north.

Life seemed mapped out for him, uneventful but not unhappy. Then in 1939 war broke out, and off marched Danny to fight for his country with the Cameron Highlanders.

Seven days embarkation leave... and nowhere to go.

Glen Affaric held little appeal; most of his former workmates had, like himself, joined up and were away. So when one of his new Army pals suggested visiting his brother in Glasgow, Danny readily agreed.

After the first couple of nights roistering, and the initial novelty of life in a huge and sprawling city wore off, he found himself at a loose end. So he decided to visit the place where he'd been born, with a vague, undefined - and yet once the seed

185

had been planted, increasingly insistent - notion of trying to find out who he was, where he'd sprung from.

So on the third day he boarded the Govan tram.

It was crammed with shipyard workers going on shift, most of whom were watching in amusement as a tiny clippie, no more than five foot high, was confronting a burly six-foot docker who'd obviously underpaid his fare.

'Ach, haud yer wheest, wumman!' The docker nodded at the notice advising passengers that spitting was prohibited. '- Or Ah'll spit oan yer tram!'

'You spit oan mah tram and ye'll get doon oan yer knees and clean it!' came the instant retort, and the man paid his fare with grudging ill-humour amidst the laughter of his mates.

Danny managed to find a seat, the unexpected small drama taking his mind momentarily off what he was actually going to do when he arrived at his destination. Approach complete strangers and ask if they happened to remember his mother? He stared through a fug of cigarette smoke at the cranes and shipyard equipment jutting starkly into the sky, common-sense warning that this was going to be an extremely painful disaster, intuition fully agreeing, yet powerless to abandon the project.

The tram clattered onwards... He got off, walked along the Govan Road as far as Rathlin Street, stood for a few moments on the corner, then continued on as far as the shipyard, where he vaguely remembered two formidable men carved into the wall on either side of massive doors, one standing in the prow of a boat, the other at a ship's wheel. They were still there, impassive, disinterested, and no help at all.

He turned away, wondering what had compelled him to make this harrowing and completely futile journey, and retraced his steps until a return tram headed towards him.

The same clippie was on it, and this time it was empty. They got talking. He told her his reasons for making this pilgrimage to Govan, and quickly discovered that the wee slip of a girl who'd stood up to a man with the physique of a bare-knuckle fighter - and won - was warm hearted, compassionate, and had the nicest, merriest laugh he'd ever heard. She lived in Howat Street (which was the next one along from Rathlin Street) with her family, she finished her shift at the end of this run, and he was welcome to come home with her and meet Maw and Paw who had lived in the locality all their lives, and so might remember his mother and help him throw some light on his past, if he wanted.

He did want. Very much.

Danny had fallen deeply and irrevocably in love, and wanted nothing but to spend the remainder of his leave in her company; to listen to her voice, low, husky, and enchanting; to watch her face, animated and expressive as she chatted. Captivated by her enthusiasm for life, her bubbling vitality, he worried that she'd find him uninteresting and dull.

In fact it was his very gentleness that endeared him to Jeannie. There was a quietness about him, a steadiness that spoke of integrity, honourableness, and unfailing loyalty. Both of them found themselves dreading the end of his leave, and on his last day she swapped shifts with someone so they could spend an entire day together.

It was a still January day with a sharp frost and clear sunlight. They took the train out to Balloch and walked along the River Leven to Loch Lomond, then wandered to a small shingly bay, skimmed stones over the water, and sat close together to eat the sandwiches Jeannie had packed. Danny stroked back the auburn hair framing her face, looked into her amber eyes, and told her truthfully that for as long as he lived he would love her.

And only her.

He knew he'd miss her sorely when it was time to go, but hadn't bargained for the sense of sheer desolation that engulfed him as the train rumbled southwards and the miles between them increased; the old cliché about feeling as if a part of his own body was missing, he discovered, was actually true. The urge to write to her was overwhelming, but he held back. Just because he loved her with a depth he hadn't believed possible didn't necessarily mean that she loved him in return. Suppose his imagination had allowed him to believe what he wanted to believe? Suppose he'd read more into the situation than was really there, on her side? Suppose... oh dear God, suppose she had just been being kind to him? She and her family were warmhearted Glaswegians who would bestow on anyone the same generosity and hospitality they'd shown him, a soldier with no family of his own, searching for his roots in their city. They'd tried to help, made enquiries with everyone they knew, but had drawn a blank. His beginnings would remain shrouded in mystery, but he now understood the strange compulsion that had driven him to undertake the quest. Fate, Destiny, call it what you like; he was meant to meet Jeannie.

And it didn't matter that he'd known her for less than a week, or that his pals laughed and said not to be so stupid, there were plenty to choose from for a bit of fun, and what he needed wasn't getting hitched but getting inside the next dancehall quick. Marrying a lassie you'd known for less than a week - or anyone else in wartime, for that matter - was about as wise as building a lighthouse on quicksand.

None of it mattered. He loved her. It was as simple as that.

Which was why he had to give her the opportunity to pull back. Now that he'd gone, allowing the intensity of their relationship some breathing space, it was possible she would see things differently. And he'd rather she didn't write at all than out of a sense of obligation, or, even worse, compassion.

Or so he tried to convince himself.

They marched from the barracks to entrain for France, the pipers playing "*Ho Ro Nighean Dhonn Bhoidheach*", and a week later her letter arrived. As soon as he read the first line, demanding to know why he hadn't written before now, he burst out laughing with sheer relief. His heart flooded with joy; all doubts dispelled, all inertia sloughed off, he replied there and then, the words he'd held in check tumbling freely out - how precious, how valued was every moment they'd spent together to him, how he was only half alive without her, how he ached, longed to be with her, how he'd feared it was all one-sided because he couldn't credit she would ever feel for him what he felt for her. He'd expected to feel self-conscious, knowing his most intimate thoughts would be read by a censor, but the censor faded to nothing against the need to tell her what she meant to him - which was, quite simply, everything. He would willingly give his life for her. He loved her with all his heart, and he wanted her, and only her, for his wife, his closest and truest friend, his soulmate, his love, for the rest of his life. He told her he'd wanted to propose to her properly, with flowers and a ring, as they sat by Loch Lomond, but was frightened of pressuring her, or worrying Maw and Paw who might have suspected he was some fly-by-night smoothie who'd ruin her life with a whirlwind wartime romance, a hot-air relationship which would blow itself out and end within six months.

It wouldn't end within six months. It wouldn't end, at least from his side, until he stopped breathing. He was hers, and only hers, until the moment his life ended.

There was a feeling of release, of deep inner peace once his feelings had been poured onto paper and the envelope addressed and posted; if he lost his life tomorrow, she would know that every minute of that life until the moment he met her had been merely a half-alive existence, experienced solely for the purpose of comparison with those precious-beyond-words few days they had spent together.

No longer was Danny conscious of being the only one who never got any mail. Now he too had someone who wrote to him, and he waited as eagerly as the others for the mail from home to arrive. Sometimes Maw wrote too, saying that as she was dropping a few lines to Alec and Hughie in the Merchant Navy she thought she'd say hello to him at the same time, let him know they were thinking of him.

And in fact it was as he was reading a letter from Maw that the news came through. King Leopold of Belgium had capitulated. Both flanks were now open; the 1st. Division in the Ypres/Dixmunde area was all that remained to oppose the full weight of the oncoming, and seemingly unstoppable, German Army.

In the turmoil of the next few days they moved, drenched by torrential rain, from the French frontier to Rexpoede, then on to Dunkirk where they were told that the Camerons would hold the line of the Dunkirk-Furnes Canal until the evacuation had been completed.

Then all previous orders were cancelled; they were to embark that night.

Just before midnight, still proudly wearing the kilt (the only Highland Battalion to do so), in the face of screaming German dive-bombers and murderous gunfire, they waded into the sea, filed aboard the troop carrier, and crossed the English Channel, and on 1st June 1940 Danny found himself one of eighty thousand men of the BEF who landed at Ramsgate. Many were injured; some, sadly, died aboard ship; all were battle-weary and exhausted. He remembered little of the actual crossing, other than someone pressing a packet of Woodbines on him in recognition of the Camerons at La Bassee who had (still wearing kilts, against Army regulations) held out for two days, thereby turning what might have been a demoralising defeat into a well-disciplined fighting finish. He'd fallen into a deep sleep after the initial amazing sight of the Little Ships - hundreds upon hundreds of them, from ferryboats to pleasure craft crewed by volunteers - ploughing across the Channel to play their part in the miracle of Dunkirk.

He filed off the ship, was given tea and a sandwich by the WVS, and a luggage label (the standard-issue postcards had run out) on which he wrote the two words allowed to everyone: "Am safe", signed it "Danny" and addressed it to Jeannie as his next-of-kin.

While the Camerons were taken to a reception camp in Derbyshire, Jeannie organised the wedding and special licence. They were married as soon as he got back to Glasgow, and so began the happiest period of Danny's life. He, who had no relatives of his own, suddenly found himself surrounded by a close, loving, extended family, and although Jeannie's elder brothers couldn't make the wedding (Alec was bound for North America in convoy, Hughie to Archangel in Russia), he was warmly welcomed by aunts, uncles, cousins, weans, and grandparents, and after the wedding he and Jeannie set off for Dunoon and booked into a small hotel for two nights.

Jeannie had heard of a vacant room-and-kitchen, and scrubbed it out with her sister, Lizzie, arranging the bits of furniture she'd been given or bought at the second-hand shop so that she and Danny could have a couple of days in their own home after the honeymoon.

The Camerons were detached to Yorkshire, where they were responsible for the defence of Withernsea. And it was there the letter arrived that filled Danny with such love and pride and happiness that he thought his heart would burst.

Jeannie was expecting a baby.

He ached to be with her, to cosset and cherish her, to await the arrival of their child together. He thought about the infant growing inside her; an embryo human being who would be a blend, a combination - in temperament, in looks, in everything - of Jeannie and himself. Strange thought. An adult who was part him, part her would one day be living somewhere on this earth. Would that person be female? A woman, with Jeannie's eyes? Her mouth? Her voice? Her mannerisms? A man, with his slightly bandy legs? His dark hair?

But first there would be childhood. And no child would ever have more love lavished upon it, or be surrounded by more warm protective family bonds, than this one. This child would never know what it felt like to be alone in the world, to have nobody of its own, to be at the mercy of officials in an impersonal Orphanage, to be farmed out and exploited as an unpaid servant, perhaps be treated even more callously than he had been... he remembered a young lass at school, her face a thin mask of misery, her eyes eternally red from crying, silent, withdrawn. He'd heard the rumours. Everybody had.

This child would never wear threadbare hand-me-downs already owned by a multitude of other children, and obvious as such. Or go barefoot to school, as he had done. He personally would make sure of that, by working every hour God sent to provide for Jeannie and his wean. When the war was over and he could go home... ("home" - he saw the room-and-kitchen smelling of wax polish and freshly-made stovies) he'd work night and day if necessary, no matter how rotten the job, how poor the conditions, to make sure his family had a roof, nourishing food, NEW clothes, and a patch of grass for the wean to play on. If it was a girl he'd buy her a dolly's pram. When he'd been small he had hankered after a dolly's pram; the problems that would have arisen for a wee boy pushing a dolly's pram around Govan, he realised when he was older, had been safely averted by the fact that his mother could barely afford to feed them, let alone buy toys for him.

And then, as he or she grew older, they'd go tramping the hills together, and he would pass on his knowledge of wildlife, his love of nature...

He was kept abreast of developments by Jeannie's letters. She had a relatively trouble-free pregnancy; everything was going well. Then, one blustery day in February, came the news he'd been longing for. Jeannie had given birth to the most beautiful wee girl in the world, and mother and child were fine. The baby was healthy, perfectly formed, had a few tufts of dark hair, and looked just like him. She even had his blue eyes! Jeannie would take her to the photographers and send a picture to him as soon as she was able.

They'd already discussed names, and the infant was duly christened Elizabeth. He learned, via Jeannie's letters, that she had a healthy appetite but didn't sleep well at nights - she needed feeding every three hours. Maw had made a wee teddybear which was tucked in Elizabeth's cot (which was in fact one of the drawers from the chest-of-drawers) every night, but Jeannie always ended up taking her into their bed where it was easier to feed her, and the pair of them would doze off, the child snuggled up to its mother.

Danny couldn't wait to hold her in his arms and talk to her, to tell her how much he loved her, and how she was going to be the happiest wee girl in the world, as he carried her around the room-and-kitchen, gently soothing her to sleep...

Then the letter arrived from Paw. It was terse, and had plainly been written in the depths of agony and despair; it broke Paw's heart to have to tell him but there was no easy way. A nine-hour blitz on March 13th. Two hundred and sixty bombers. They'd set Clydebank blazing and then headed for the Glasgow shipyards, Fairfields and Yarrows, and the main target, John Brown's. Over a thousand people slaughtered, almost three thousand seriously injured. They'd tried to cause as much chaos and destruction for the firefighters as they could, and that included torching the streets and tenements in the vicinity for good measure. Maw had persuaded Jeannie to stay with them for the first week of the baby's life, but she'd wanted to be back in her own home, and when she didn't appear in the shelter they'd hoped she was with a friend in a neighbouring one. But, for some reason they'd never know, she hadn't gone down to a shelter that night.

Maw was laid low, it had knocked the feet from under her. They'd had word just the week before that Alec's ship had been torpedoed, and had sunk within three minutes. Alec had been trapped below the water line in the engine room, and Maw couldn't rid her mind of unbearable pictures - the thought of her son's terror as the water surged in, the knowledge that there was no escape. She saw filthy oily water fill his mouth, his nose, his lungs; she saw his body floating amongst the scum and flotsam, sloshing against the machinery and bulkheads of the engine room. And now Jeannie and the wean, defenceless under the bombers - it was too much for her to bear. It was too much for any of them to bear.

Danny, given three days compassionate leave, returned to Glasgow to find the tenement that had housed his and Jeannie's room-and-kitchen a heap of rubble and broken masonry from which there still arose a miasma of smoke and dust.

He thought of Jeannie, alone with her baby, hearing the bombs scream down and explode around her, the tumult as neighbouring buildings collapsed and fires roared out of control. Nine hours of it. Dear God almighty, what had it been like for her? What had prevented her from going to the shelter? Had Elizabeth been sick? He contemplated the heightened terror of a mother that her new-born child could suffer horrendous injuries at any moment, the tiny fragile lungs caving in as the infant was entombed under rubble, the soft bones crushed as the building fell in on top of them, while not just one, but wave upon wave of aircraft - two hundred and sixty of them - flew overhead opening their bomb doors.

And this barely three weeks after you'd given birth.

He stared at the ruins of the tenement on the opposite side of the road, its outer wall ripped away, the room-and-kitchen facing their own now mercilessly exposed to the world. Its ceiling drooped unsupported at one end, and torn shreds of wallpaper still adhered to the jagged edges of the inner walls. He knew exactly how the building felt; he shared its shock, its sense of violation as surely as if they'd ripped open his own body and left him there broken and defiled, his internal organs exposed for all the world to see.

He found himself thinking like Maw, going over and over the last few minutes, the final seconds of her life. Had she somehow known... had she identified the actual bomb that would kill her and Elizabeth as it hurtled down? Had it sounded different from the rest? Were its acoustics clearer, more pronounced? Had she called to him, screamed for him, frantic, as it descended from the bomb door and plummeted towards her?

Bastards!

White hot rage caused him to shake. He should have been here. He should have been here with her, protecting them with his own body, dying instead of them.

He looked at where his home had been, and saw superimposed on the smoking rubble a small, shabbily-furnished room that had witnessed love, tenderness, gentleness, laughter, security - everything that made life worth living. He saw himself sitting in the fireside chair, a book propped under its broken leg, Jeannie snuggled on his knee, his arms around her, telling of a poem he'd learned at school that expressed exactly how he felt about her, quoting the beautiful words from "The Song of Hiawatha":

"Does not all the blood within me
Leap to meet thee, leap to meet thee,
As the springs to meet the sunshine
In the moon when nights are brightest?"

The vision faded. Reality reasserted itself. Everything that was precious to him - in fact, everything he had - destroyed in the wake of the brave Luftwaffe warriors returning to the Fatherland to celebrate their success. Jeannie hadn't even had time to get a photograph of wee Elizabeth. Not that it could have survived this, even if she had. He had nothing; nothing of his wife, nothing of his daughter, nothing of his home.

Danny, gentle by nature, teased by his pals because he found it impossible to swat a fly, swore to put to good use against the German war machine whatever time was left to him before the last unwanted breath was knocked from his body.

As things turned out, however, he didn't get the chance to carry out his own personal retaliation against the Luftwaffe. The Queen's Own Cameron Highlanders continued to move around Yorkshire until they embarked, in April 1942 at Liverpool, for India, and in 1943 were ordered to Assam to face the Japanese pouring over the Burma border into Manipur State.

For the "Forgotten Army" still fighting in Burma, VE Day came and went. So did 1946. And so did 1947, because even after the war in the Far East had formally ended, the Camerons were selected as part of the British Brigade of the Commonwealth Occupation Forces in Japan. So it wasn't until March 1948 that Danny's Battalion finally sailed from Singapore.

It was ironic, thought Danny, staring at the silvery wake stretching astern as the ship steamed through the night; so many millions throughout the world, to whom life had been precious, and had wanted so desperately to live, had perished. Yet he, who had no wish whatsoever to be alive, had survived safe and whole.

In Japan alone the toll of British POWs who had died in agony from beatings and torture, or been starved to death in the camps, or been worked to death on the railway, was heartbreaking. When he saw the men emerging from the prison camps (those who could actually walk), Danny had been mute with shock and pity. The Japanese nation may never have felt the need to apologise for such deliberate brutality, but he personally would not have been able to live with himself if he'd ever inflicted on any human being - and that included the bomber who'd killed his wife and child - even a fraction of the cold-blooded cruelty the prison guards had enjoyed meting out with such relish.

He made his way back to Glasgow and did what he could to help Maw and Paw, who had shrivelled from fun-loving, cheerful Glaswegians with a seemingly indestructible resilience, to wraith-like husks whose spirits had finally been broken by the slaughter of Jeannie and Elizabeth in their own city, and two sons drowned at sea.

They were particularly bitter at the lack of recognition of their sons' sacrifice in the Merchant Navy. Hughie's ship had been torpedoed in the Barents Sea in the winter of 1943. Once again Maw had been unable to rid herself of the images. She saw her second son, nineteen years old, who had been delicate as a child and always hated the cold, immersed in black, ice-cold water, his very lifeblood literally freezing in his veins, and her agony in imagining his last moments had been terrible to watch.

Paw referred to the Merchant Navy as the Poor Bloody Infantry of the Sea. He'd framed a newspaper cutting and hung it above the mantelpiece as a poignant tribute to his sons; the only Campaign Medal, the only honour their country had awarded this civilian force of brave Merchant Seamen:

195

"He is usually dressed rather like a tramp. His sweater is worn, his trouser frayed, while what was once a cap is perched askew on his tanned face. He wears no gold braid or gold buttons; neither does he jump to the salute briskly. Nobody goes out of his way to call him a 'hero' ,or pin medals on his breast.

He is just a seaman of the British Merchant Service."

Danny became firm friends with Jeannie's two sisters and surviving brother Eddie, who had followed his elder brothers into the Merchant Navy, not from any romantic notions about life at sea but simply because there was so little else around. After a few months Danny, who couldn't settle in Glasgow and found it impossible to shake off the depression that weighed him down, yet was reluctant to return to his old life in Glen Affaric, spoke to him about becoming a seafarer himself. He learned that the *"Duchess of Bedford"* had returned to the Scottish yards for a major refit following her wartime career as troop carrier, to be renamed *"Empress of France"* and become a luxury liner once more.

The CPR boats had a poor reputation among seamen; pay and conditions didn't compare well with other lines. However, the *"Duchess of Bedford"* was regarded a lucky ship almost from the moment her keel was laid. During the war she'd sunk a German U boat with the 6inch gun on her stern, survived being shot at and bombed, taken part in the invasions of North Africa, Anzio, and Salerno, and was the last ship to leave Singapore in January 1942, crammed with women and children escaping the Japanese who were already pouring into the city - and she'd come through all this without losing a life. So when the *"Empress of France"*, newly painted white and carrying the CPR house-flag on her two funnels, resumed her regular Liverpool (or Greenock) Quebec-Montreal run, Danny was on board as Dining Room Steward. And, as things turned out, she proved to be a lucky ship for him as well. He met Miss Sankey.

Miss Sankey was a remote and private figure who crossed the Atlantic at regular intervals, choosing not to mingle with other passengers and preferring solitude to company. She always requested a table in his section of the Dining Room, and over the years their mutual respect and affection deepened. She was a good deal older than he was - he never knew her age but guessed she must be at least thirty years his senior - and he mourned her, and missed her, when he heard that she had died. Nobody could have been more astounded than he was when a letter arrived from her solicitor, informing him she had bequeathed to him her home in Westmorland.

He didn't know what to do with it. He travelled up to look around it during his next shore leave, and was amazed by its size. He thought of his and Jeannie's room-and-kitchen, of people he knew who'd raised families of six, seven, ten children (sixteen in one case) in a couple of rooms that could easily be fitted into Beckside's Entrance Hall, the weans all sharing one bed. And he thought of himself sitting in those vast rooms, all alone.

He made a token attempt to sell it, but felt vaguely guilty; his heart wasn't in selling Miss Sankey's childhood home, and he was secretly relieved when a prospective buyer pulled out. He withdrew it from the market. It was sad and wasteful to see the house lying empty, however, and he wondered to what use he could put it. He'd heard of Youth Hostels, and the idea of Beckside welcoming young people with very little money who sought temporary escape from foundries, factories, coalmines, heavy engineering works, shops, and offices of the cities to explore the countryside, appealed to him. He had no child of his own to take tramping in the hills and pass on his love of their beauty and grandeur, but perhaps he could help other youngsters by making the house available for them to stay in.

So he asked Miss Sankey's solicitor to make the necessary arrangements and, once the lease had been agreed - he had insisted on a rent which, even at that time, was way below the current market value - put Beckside out of mind and returned to sea, until the "*Empress of France*" sailed up the Mersey for the last time in December 1960.

Danny left the sea. But Glasgow and its memories were somehow still too painful, and he returned to Strathglass, where there was a job going as cook at the Forestry Hostel in Cannich. During each successive summer he watched, with interest and sometimes private amusement, the comings and goings at the adjoining Youth Hostel, and wondered whether any of the hostellers who stayed there had also visited Beckside in the Lake

District - and, if they had, what they'd think if they knew it was owned by the small, insignificant, shabbily-dressed man who didn't even warrant a second glance from most of them.

There was a succession of wardens as the years went by; some he got on well with, some he definitely didn't miss when they left - and with one he struck up a particularly close friendship. The young Scouser, back in the early 1970s.

Strange, how Life sometimes tosses together the most improbable of kindred spirits, and unexpected friendships can develop to an undreamed-of depth of affection. A quietly spoken old man and a young lass nearly thirty years his junior - shades of Miss Sankey, with him the older one this time. She was just as he imagined Elizabeth would be at that age, and in a surprisingly short space of time grew to love her as the daughter he'd never had. On the face of things they had little in common, yet the bonds of affinity between them were strong, and deep, and true. She'd touched a chord in his life, and he in hers.

Neither of them, of course, had expected this to happen at their first meeting, when she'd knocked at the Forestry kitchen door, drenched from head to toe, hair plastered wetly around her face. A soldered join had blown apart in the overhead water pipe when she switched the stop cock on, and she'd tried to hold the pipes together whilst her friend attempted to turn the water off, but it had jammed open and water continued to pour down, flooding the place. The friend was now trying to hold the pipes together while she sought help to cut the supply off. Did he know where the nearest plumber was, please?

When he'd stopped laughing, he accompanied her back to the Hostel. Sure enough there was the friend, gasping for air, arms aloft in a valiant but futile attempt to hold the pipes together as the flood spread throughout the building.

We're going to have an interesting summer here, he thought privately, and he'd been right. Thinking back, it wasn't surprising that eyebrows were raised as the pair of them meandered by the river together, he in his shabby old jacket, pockets misshapen from frequent 'cairry-oots' of Dewars Whisky, or sat in her kitchen, drinking tea and giggling at some amusing incident. Not that either of them cared about the gossip which may have misconstrued their relationship. What mattered was the friendship, the affection, the gift of love itself, not what others thought about it, or regarded as a subject for gossip.

Aye. You'd have liked her, Jeannie...

Aye well, enough of melancholy. The past belongs in the past, eh. That's what you'd say, isnae it?

He gently replaced Jeannie's photo and moved on to the other photograph on the mantelpiece. There he was, standing proudly next to his wee Scouser, beautiful in her white wedding dress outside the church. Having lost her own parents some years earlier, she had asked him to give her away, a duty he had regarded as an honour, and been delighted and thrilled to perform - especially as he had grown very fond of the young man who was to become her husband, knew they'd be happy together, and that it would prove a good marriage for them both.

Aye well, that was the dusting finished - time to get the kettle on for a wee cuppee tea, because Molly would be in any minute to hear all the news from New Zealand. (He must remember to buy a new Airmail pad to reply, because his wee Scouser would want to hear all the gossip about the Event at Beckside as soon as he returned from it... Must let her know he'd booked his ticket for Christmas, too, because she'd said the children were already excitedly preparing treats and excursions for his visit.)

He picked up the bulky Airmail envelope lying on the sideboard and, as Molly came in with a couple of freshly baked scones, unfolded the additional letters from the children, together with the accompanying brightly coloured childish paintings which their mother had enclosed with her own letter, and spread them out on the table for her to read and admire.

They were good letters; interesting, lively, and fun.

But the nicest and most precious thing about them was all the love they sent their Honorary Grandad, and all the hugs and kisses as they told him how they couldn't wait for his next visit, how Christmas and New Year wouldn't be the same without him. Christmas was the time for families to be together.

And Danny was a much-loved part of theirs.

SEVEN: THE SOCIAL EVENT OF THE YEAR.

The explosion occurred at 5AM.

Len, who had finally crawled to bed at 2AM after issuing mops, buckets, and a terse invitation to fifty over-excited schoolchildren (whose teachers had abandoned all attempts to control them and withdrawn to the Quiet Room to succumb to nervous hysteria) to utilise their energy constructively until the desire for sleep overtook them - which it instantly did - cranked up a notch from almost-comatose to semi-conscious as the flat door buckled under an onslaught of hammering.

'Urrgh?' he croaked.

There was no doubting the urgency in the voice shrieking through the keyhole. 'I said, WE'RE UNDER ATTACK FROM TERRORISTS!'

Len looked at the sleep-sodden, uncomprehending face of his wife. Only his and Kate's Silver Wedding could be launched by a terrorist attack at 5AM... Happy Anniversary, darling.

It was also, of course, Beckside's Big Day. And if the dawn heralding it was any indication, the odds on the rest of it unfolding as a smooth-running triumph of success seemed about as long as an aimless stroll around the globe and back.

Dud woke early. Just as well; give him time to check the filters on the Honda. Couldn't risk the thing breaking down today of all days, with the latest Notch on the Bedpost - well, not *quite* on the bedpost, but she would be, by tomorrow - perched pillion on her way to be flaunted under the snooty conk of Miss Classy-Knickers at Beckside.

Thelma, her name was. New barmaid at his local. A bit dim, but she had plenty up front, which was where it mattered. He'd had quite enough of intellectual bints, thank you very much. Especially flat-chested ones with an answer for everything and a way of looking at you as though you were something the cat had vomited on the settee. But Thelma - now *that* was what you *called* a woman! So he'd invited her to the Big Bash, promising they'd go for a sail in his boat the following day.

200

He still didn't have a car, which tarnished the image a bit. He'd like to have roared up the drive in a sports job, splaying gravel everywhere as his stunning companion poured from the passenger seat. As it was he'd be chugging up on the Honda as usual - assuming the filters behaved themselves on the way - but although nobody could describe Thelma as stunning, she was touchingly awestruck at the notion of the boat. She'd never been sailing before, she confided (neither had he, but there was no need to enlighten her about that), so he'd waved aside any reservations on that score by trotting out a few nautical terms he'd overheard: "Stepping up the mast," and so on. He could always have a quick shufti at the instructions before they set off. Bound to be a booklet with the thing that told you how to start it, how to steer, and how to stop it again.

'Trusty old girl, "Sultry Nights",' he'd assured her with a sentimental smile which implied that although he'd owned hundreds of boats in his time he remained loyal to his old favourite, and she relaxed slightly and said she was looking forward to it.

'Yes,' he'd agreed, eyes gleaming. So was he, but for a different reason.

How did the song go? "I've got a beautiful fee-ling, everything's going my way..." It was all so simple really. You see, the secret was, you told Fate exactly what you expected it to do, then gave it a helping shove. The puppetmaster jerked the Mona/Eamon strings to bring about a gradual fading from the scene, avoiding outright confrontation whilst still allowing him to flit from flower to flower like a pollinating bee.

Although actually, Mona had been surprisingly docile of late. Obviously accepted at last there was no tying down this demon lover who juggled his women with debonair caddishness, this stallion who stood no nonsense from his harem. He wondered fleetingly whose life she'd be making a misery this weekend.

Not that it mattered, as long as it wasn't his.

Investigations revealed that the explosion had been caused not by international terrorists but by someone switching on the boiler without first turning on the tap supplying water to it. By the time Kate had calmed panicking hostellers and quashed the more outrageous rumours, and Len had cleared away the mangled wreckage, and the unofficial Courts of Enquiry clustered in the Reception Area dispersed, it was well after 6AM and there was no point in returning to bed. They trudged to the kitchen, to be joined at 7AM by Anna, who had no intention of being prised from her bed a moment before it was necessary by terrorists or anyone else, and Oliver, who had slept soundly through the entire proceedings.

Matters weren't helped when, just as breakfast was about to be served, Oliver dropped a tray of twenty fried eggs which coated the floor with a treacherous mix of grease and egg yolk. Things could only get worse: the school party lost their list with names entered against relevant choices. Half the children couldn't remember what they'd ordered; the rest used the excuse to change their minds and opt for something else.

'I ordered beans on toast,' insisted one child Len distinctly remembered putting up his hand for Full English Breakfast.

'And I definitely said croissants,' nodded an accomplice, who had demanded boiled eggs and toast.

Kate closed her eyes. The pressure and worry of the last few days meant her nerves were already drum tight, without an added traumatic 5AM awakening after less than three hours sleep, followed by mayhem over breakfast choices. Fortunately, deliverance (or at least, a couple of seconds respite) was provided by the postman battling through the queue. She quickly flipped through the mail for two greetings card envelopes addressed in their sons' writing.

They weren't there.

They'd forgotten.

Both of them.

No pleasurable anticipation, then, to counter a morning which had started abysmally and was worsening by the hour; no token of affection to mark a special day, no message of love and congratulation to savour during a quiet respite when she and Len finally opened the Anniversary cards they'd normally have exchanged in bed. She pushed the bundle under the counter, blinked back tears of sheer fatigue, and resumed serving. It wasn't even 9AM yet, and already she felt near breaking point.

A day of bleak and endless exhaustion stretched ahead; by the time the main Event started at 2PM her nerves would doubtless have snapped altogether, and horrified guests would witness a snarling, shaking creature working her way along the buffet table pelting the Guest of Honour, VIPs, National Office hierarchy, Major Pratt, and the entire Committee with haggis, trifle, Jubilee cake, and anything else to hand...

As Silver Weddings went, this one looked like having few equals.

Danny MacTavish walked reluctantly to the bus stop, seriously considering ringing Beckside with the first excuse that sprang to mind. He should never have agreed to this. He saw himself, marooned helplessly amidst a clique of in-crowd revellers - and there were few places on earth more lonely than that. You could be far lonelier in a crowd than you could ever be on your own. Oh, there'd be plenty hearty welcomes and inconsequential small talk, of that he had no doubt, but should this be one of those occasions from which your instinctive reaction was to flee the moment you stepped over the threshold - and he suspected it would - there was no escape.

If he'd had a car he could, after a reasonable time had elapsed, have driven to some unfashionable backwater and enjoyed a solitary walk. During the 1950s he'd spent some shore leave camping in Westmorland and Cumberland, and grown particularly fond of the area around Ullswater where you could tramp all day and not see a soul except for the occasional shepherd. Once, near the summit of Place Fell, he'd come across someone sketching the hills for a book he was writing for walkers - unassuming chap, pleasant and interesting; they'd chatted for half an hour until the rain gradually obscured Skiddaw and Blencathra, then Danny had gone on his way. He'd bought the book when it was published in 1957. Wainwright, the chap's name had been.

He'd brought it with him. When he'd written accepting the invitation, which included overnight hospitality at Beckside, he thought he might include a visit to a few old haunts. If there were any old haunts left. Judging by the tourist brochure he'd sent away for, the Lake District was now one giant theme park of Attractions.

The bus was approaching. Decision time, Danny. Get on it, or phone them with a pack of apologetic lies?

And face Molly and admit he'd taken the coward's way out?

Ach, no. He'd told them he was coming, and they'd have everything prepared by now. It would be selfish and childish to announce, at this stage, that he couldn't make it after all. It wasn't their fault he regretted committing himself to this ordeal.

He boarded the bus.

He'd go through with it with as much grace as he could muster, and escape as soon as possible.

Kate was slumped at the table with a throbbing head and a hot flush, feet plonked on Len's knees, moodily sipping tea, when Major Pratt strode into the kitchen. Although this was the respite she'd craved since 5AM - five minutes privacy with her husband, to open Anniversary cards and gifts they'd normally have exchanged in bed after making love - by now neither of them were in the mood for a sentimental opening of cards, even if they'd had any from their sons to open.

'Well! All right for some, isn't it!' remarked Major Pratt acidly. Look at this! The pair of them sprawling around as though there was nothing to do! 'Chop chop, Kate, there's a hundred and one things to get done!'

'We've only just sat down, we've -' began Len.

'Oh, I've heard it all before, Len.' Major Pratt waved him impatiently aside. 'Although actually, it might be an idea to have a brief run through things as you're here. I think I can safely say Eloise and I *deserve* a cup of tea; we've been on the go since the very *crack* of dawn!'

'Yes,' confirmed Babs, trotting in behind him. 'I stayed overnight, so Eloise had to cope with three different choices of breakfast!'

'Oh, Eloise takes it all in her stride.' Major Pratt pulled out a chair and sat down. 'No, the worst of it was, we got woken up early. I set the alarm for eight-thirty, but the dratted thing went off at eight o'clock!'

'Yes. Poor Eloise hasn't had her full quota of sleep,' frowned Babs worriedly. 'And there she was, heroically catering for *three* of us! D'you know what I had for breakfast, Kate? A plate arranged with sliced grapes, kiwi fruit, strawberries, and bananas! I thought, ooh, wouldn't this be a nice option to add to Beckside's breakfast menu? Another item for hostellers to choose from?'

Kate managed a grunt of courteous interest.

'Ah, here you are, darling,' greeted Major Pratt as his wife appeared in the doorway, elegant and cool.

'Good morning!' Eloise smiled graciously around.

'I was just telling them, darling,' continued Major Pratt, directing another critical stare at the dark rings under Kate's eyes and tendrils of damp hair plastered to her forehead. '*What* a morning *we've* had!'

Mona came out of the hairdressers pleased with the result. She'd had the young assistant almost in tears, demanded someone was brought who knew what they were doing instead of this silly kid who hadn't a clue, and had the lot of them running around bringing cups of tea and fussing and patting and getting the hair exactly as she wanted it. And the result was just right. Dyed jet black (time to change the dizzy blonde image now she was getting engaged), lots of backcombing and height.

As the puce-and-daisy suit she'd originally planned to wear had run into production difficulties when the sewing machine supplier threatened court action following non-appearance of either payment or returned machine, she'd bought a pillar-box red blouse (nice and tight over the bust - if you've got it, flaunt it), and a scarlet mini skirt. And to set the whole thing off lovely, a wide-brimmed crimson hat. The white high heels she already had. They were a bit scuffed, but nobody'd notice, and they were already moulded around her bunions so they were nice and comfy. No point in crucifying yourself in new ones.

Bridie had chosen a buttercup yellow zig-zag patterned dress and a pink hat, and all that remained now was to make sure Eamon was ready on time as well.

He'd needed a bit of firm handling at first, but he was coming round nicely to her and Bridie's way of doing things. And they were doing things in style today. Mona had planned on getting a taxi to the Bus Station, but Bridie had gone one better and got one of her cronies down the Irish Club, who had his own taxi business, to do her a special deal and run them all the way to Beckside, so they'd arrive at the same time as all the Bigwigs and La-de-Dahs at two o'clock.

She turned her head to admire the hairdo as she passed a shop window, and patted the laquered mass. All in all the day was going nicely to plan.

And it had better continue to go nicely to plan as well.

Lack of sleep caused Kate's eyelids to grow heavy as the monologue progressed. The "brief run-through" was (surprise surprise) developing into an interminable celebration of Major Pratt's own voice.

'...So you will keep an eye on that, won't you Len. Lots of fruit juice and minerals, and, you know, Highland Spring Water...'

Her thoughts drifted to Mike and Tony. Both had said, months ago, they'd make it home for this weekend - but that was before Beckside's Fortieth Jubilee circus had been arranged for the same day. Then they'd both gone a bit cagey, and said they mightn't be able to get away after all. And she couldn't blame them. Who wanted to spend an afternoon making polite small-talk with pompous VIPs?

'...Filo parcels of feta cheese and spinach,' droned Major Pratt.

'Ah. That's Wayfarers.' Eloise consulted her soft leather filofax. 'They're doing the Atholl Broze Ice Cream as well. She suggested Summer Pudding to follow the Ruby theme, but I said no, we don't want *too* much red dominating everything. Nothing worse than a plethora of reds all clashing with each other.' Eloise gave a delicate shudder. 'I think strategically placed cake trays overflowing with redcurrants and things are far more effective. Which reminds me. Salads. Now, the mayonnaise -'

'We've got jars of the stuff,' said Len, and added pointedly, 'It was on special offer at Cash and Carry.'

There was a pained silence.

'Not *bottled* mayonnaise, Len,' rebuked Eloise gently.

'Eloise makes her own,' explained Babs. 'She made a special trip to a shop in Edinburgh for the ingredients.'

Len choked on his tea.

'Oh, it was no bother, really. We had to go anyway for the venison and smoked salmon.'

Kate shot Len a warning glance. It would achieve nothing to question how an organisation that was (according to memos constantly churned out exhorting staff to pursue the most stringent economies in every possible sphere) struggling for its very survival, could suddenly afford this veritable cornucopia of money-no-object delicacies.

'And Beluga caviar?'

Len's contempt was unmistakable, and Eloise's look of strained patience implied that she hoped he wasn't going to be in one of his awkward moods today of all days, because they had more important things to do than placate Len's peculiar foibles about expenditure. All terribly commendable of course, but good heavens, didn't he realise this wasn't some tuppence ha'penny parish picnic for the hoi polloi?

'It's like some privatised industry or huge business empire!' Len, having set fire to his boat, tossed the oars on the funeral pyre. 'People at the bottom losing jobs while High-Up Fat Cats and Executives get their snouts stuck in the trough -'

'Yes. Thank you for that irrelevant observation,' snapped Major Pratt. He had a number of shares in privatised industries, and they were doing very well. 'But to get back to the point...'

He paused. A good Chairman needed plenty of tact at times (and dealing with Len was one of them) because there was always *one* grumbling underling to mollify. He adopted a man-to-man confidentiality. 'We can't offer, you know, Anyone-Who's-Anyone a few sandwiches on paper plates, can we?'

'Why not?'

A vein began to throb in Major Pratt's temple. 'Good lord, all these infantile sulks and vapours over a few -'

'Len,' cut in Eloise smoothly, '*Would* you be an angel and pop out to the car for the table linen and tartan swags. And could you manage the tussie mussies as well?'

'*Tussie mussies?*'

Len instantly knew in that one ridiculous utterance he'd capitulated unconditionally. The rebel had taken on a 15inch gun with a child's catapult; the pebbles had clattered futilely against it and now he stood before the gunner, impotent, emasculated, the fetcher of tussie-mussies.

'Little nosegays to hang everywhere. I got my florist to do them,' Eloise told him as he stood mute, face expressionless.

The rebellion had been safely crushed; the lower orders gently but firmly put in their place.

Mona knew something was wrong the moment she opened the front door.

In the kitchen, the new skirt was draped on the ironing board, an iron-shaped hole edged by brown singe marks right in the middle of the front.

'*What happened?*' she screeched, although the upright iron, its base coated in brilliant scarlet, provided a reasonable clue.

'I went for a quick pee,' explained Bridie, picking dementedly at the solidified strands of crimplene radiating from the iron's base. 'And when I got back he'd stuck the iron down on it.'

'Didn't I tell you I'm not much of a one for the ironing,' confessed Eamon mournfully. 'Me mother, God rest her, used to do all the women's work. The likes of me don't know about temperatures and settings and all that palaver.'

Mona held the skirt up and inspected the hole, so perfectly mirroring the shape of the iron.

'Put a patch on it. Nobody'll notice,' suggested Eamon optimistically, then flinched as the iron flew past his shoulder and embedded itself in a pile of bridal magazines on the sideboard.

He sighed. Look at the pair of them! Pre-Engagement nerves, he supposed. Still, once his new bride was installed on the farm with his accumulated stack of washing to keep her busy (she'd need an iron then all right!) there'd be no time for any feminine caperings and histrionics. He'd been right to steer well clear of womankind for as many years as he had, but with Ma passing on he needed a replacement for the farm chores and peat cutting, and now he'd found an unpaid housekeeper at last he didn't want to go through all this performance again to ensnare another one. He drew a wad of grimy notes from his back pocket.

'Here,' he offered with another conciliatory sigh. 'Will this be enough for a new one?'

Bridie's scowl crinkled into an ingratiating bearing of gums. 'Ah God love him, hicl heart'cl in the right place, icln't it now Mona?'

Mona grunted. Never mind where his heart was, it was where his wallet was that mattered. And as long as that was within easy reach...

'Right, that takes care of the food. I knew the haggis would arrive safely. They're a reputable firm, export all over the world,' said Major Pratt, and added as an afterthought, 'You did bring that book of Rabbie Burns' poems for me to quote that thing about, you know, its honest sonsie face or whatever it is, didn't you darling?'

'Yes, I asked Babs to pick it up as we came out, didn't I dear?' smiled Eloise.

Babs turned brick red, then ashen, then increasingly suicidal with guilt as Major Pratt dialled the local library and every bookshop within a twenty mile radius, barking his staccato questions into the phone: 'You got an edition of Rabbie Burns' poems in stock? *Are you sure*? HAVE YOU CHECKED?'

The library informed him they could order a copy but it might take a couple of weeks, all the book stores in turn said much the same thing, and the local second-hand bookshop told him there wasn't much call for Burns' poems in the Lake District and, in an effort to be helpful, suggested he might have more luck in Ayr.

No sooner had his colour subsided from violent heliotrope to its usual plum red when Len discovered "To A Haggis" printed on the inside lid of the haggis boxes, than it deepened again as a group of Seasonal Assistants arrived with their Hostels' contributions to the feast, and one of them dropped a trifle in a particularly ornate crystal bowl on the front doorstep.

'Is the entire world populated by imbeciles and nincompoops?' thundered Major Pratt as he set off to oversee Operation Clean-Up. 'And could we please have lunch at noon *on the dot* for once, Kate!'

A belch from the doorway announced Dud's arrival. He winked and grinned, indicating a vacant-looking girl waddling upstairs with a make-up bag. 'What d'you think of that then, Len? Bit of an improvement on Mona, isn't she?'

Len, shredding cabbage into a bowl for the coleslaw, agreed politely, leaving unspoken the obvious. Anything was an improvement on Mona.

Dud continued to extol the attributes of his pneumatic companion. 'Wait til you see her properly. Like this, she is!' He demonstrated his meaning by forming his hands into claws in front of his chest.

'Oh. Got rheumatism, has she?'

'No, seriously, she could win a wet tee-shirt competition, Len! Thought I'd get one printed for her to wear this weekend: "I've eaten one of Kate's Disasters - and lived!" or something, ha!'

'Have you thought of, "But if I'd eaten one of my own I

209

probably wouldn't," on the back?' murmured Len.

Major Pratt bustled back into the kitchen, followed by Babs.

'Ah, Dud, hello. Brought a companion, eh?' His voice lowered confidentially. 'Glad Mona's off the scene at last... Now,' he turned to Kate. 'Eloise's just had an idea. When we went to the Garden Party at Buckingham Palace, one detail we thought was an extremely nice little touch -'

Voices sounded in the Reception Area. Major Pratt, who didn't like missing anything, paused to listen.

Dud's guest appeared at the door.

'There's a bloke out here,' she announced, indicating an unseen presence behind her, 'Wants to know if you hire out rooms by the half-hour?'

There was a blank silence.

'Half-hour?' repeated Major Pratt suspiciously.

'Yes. It's for him and his girlfriend,' elaborated the girl.

A swarthy-skinned individual with greasy hair peered round the door.

'Is OK? You let us have a room?' he wheedled in a heavily accented hoarse voice.

An unmentionable suspicion was worming its way into Major Pratt's head. Did... did this character actually mean...? No, surely not, the idea was preposterous. He must be imagining things. This was an English Youth Hostel, for heaven's sake!

Len had no such doubts. He'd been in the job too long.

'No,' he said shortly.

Babs, so horrified by this brusqueness that she battled with her own paralysing shyness to show the visitor a more favourable side of British hospitality, enquired apologetically whether a dormitory would be acceptable to his - erm, race and creed, hastening to explain lest such inquisitiveness should cause offence: 'You see, Youth Hostels have dormitories. Not rooms. Erm... What did you want a room for half-an-hour for, exactly?'

Len covered his eyes with his hand.

Immediately scenting weakness submitting to dominance, the man sidled with increasing confidence into the kitchen. 'Use your imagination, uh?' he winked.

Instantly on his feet, Len forced him to retreat to the door. Babs was shocked. A guest to our shores, requesting hospitality - how *could* Len be so rude?

Len briskly escorted the guest to our shores, together with the woman, to the front door. As he returned, Anna was coming out of the Dining Room.

'The Seasonal Assistant from Cragside says, some of the vol-au-vents are burnt underneath, so can we make sure to arrange -'

He waved her quiet. Babs' voice was quavering tearfully from the kitchen: 'But *why* was Len so cross because the man wanted a room for half-an-hour?'

Len grinned to himself. Get out of that one, Major Pratt.

And as six pairs of eyes looked curiously towards him, Major Pratt did the unthinkable. He turned on Babs, whose irritating saintliness was apt to grate on his nerves every bit as much as Len's unwelcome outspokenness at times.

'Because the purpose of Youth Hostels is not to facilitate carnal lust, Babs,' he said sharply. 'Now, to get back to this garden party at Buckingham Palace...'

It was 1.55PM.

Guests, VIPs, and dignitaries were arriving, and Dud had assumed control of parking arrangements on the grassy area down by the gate.

Major Pratt, glancing out of the window on his way downstairs to welcome the early arrivals, halted in amazement as he saw Dud suddenly perform a classic double-take, plunge into the shrubbery, and lope, bent almost double, towards the kitchen door. His frown deepened as a red hatchback joined the queue of cars, overtook a dozen waiting vehicles, and swept up the drive, the occupant of its passenger seat waving an imperious arm to direct the driver into the parking spot reserved for Mr. MacTavish.

What was the nincompoop doing, indulging in this theatrical cloak-and-dagger nonsense as cars piled up unsupervised by the gate? (And, more importantly, delaying him from taking up his position with Eloise to welcome the guests, because of course he would now have to investigate what all this was about.) He hurried downstairs and confronted the fugitive in the kitchen.

'Dud! What on earth are you *doing*?'

Instinctively attempting to keep the presence of this unwelcome gatecrasher from Major Pratt (not that there was any likelihood of *her* merging into anonymity for the afternoon; he'd be lucky if she remained unnoticed for five minutes, regardless of the new jet-black hairdo), Dud gave an unconvincing shrug.

'Nothing. I just popped in to... er -'

Major Pratt checked his watch. 1.56PM. This was no time for a tactful drawing out of some delicate problem, a gentle coaxing of reluctant confidences.

'Come on Dud, we haven't got all day. Who's in that car?'

'Er... er, Mona.'

Major Pratt stared at him. That dratted woman? *Turning up here*? TODAY?

'Mona? What's she doing here?'

Dud shook his head worriedly. That was what he'd like to know as well.

Major Pratt closed his eyes. If Dud *must* surround himself with these dreadful camp followers he picked up heaven knew where, the least he could do was keep them well clear of Officers-and-their-Ladies occasions such as this. That inane barmaid he'd foisted on them was bad enough, got up like some French onion-seller's strumpet and sunning herself on the lawn, but never in his wildest nightmares had it occurred to him that this trollop would turn up as well. What if they started a catfight on the lawn, tearing each others' hair out in the middle of somebody's speech? (His, for example?)

He checked his watch. Three minutes, to assess the problem, form a strategy to overcome it, and effect a result. His Army training had equipped him to deal decisively with unexpected emergencies, but the problem with this particular problem was - there was no solution to it. He'd order Len to get rid of her if he thought it would do any good, but the fact Mona hadn't been sent an invitation didn't mean she'd obediently go away just because Len told her to; it meant an attention-drawing scene if he dared try. The blasted woman had engineered a fait accompli. And it wasn't just Mona on her own - a grisly enough prospect - but, judging from the car, a tribe of appalling relatives as well.

'But I thought that relationship finished ages ago?'

'It did,' lied Dud worriedly. Well, he thought it had.

1.58PM.

Major Pratt had orchestrated every detail of Beckside's Jubilee so that it would be remembered as the most outstandingly successful Event of all time. Now, with two minutes to go to the

Grand Opening, and faced with a predicament he couldn't possibly have foreseen or made contingency plans for, it was more likely to be remembered as the most outstanding Farcical Disaster of all time.

And there was absolutely nothing he could do about it.

Mona emerged from the car, smoothed down the replacement lurid purple mini skirt, and looked smugly around. So much for the La-Di-Dahs; she and Bridie were got up as posh as any of them. Or would be, as soon as Bridie put her teeth in.

Eamon eased himself stiffly out of the back seat.

'God, I nearly got taken short there,' he whined. 'Where's the lav again?'

Nobody answered. Mona was too busy making sure the title of "Hello!" magazine, which she'd pinched from the hairdressers, was prominently displayed - they might have a reporter here this afternoon, interviewing guests at random and selecting subjects cognizant with the publication - and Dud, who'd been instructed to make sure the driver vacated his unauthorised parking place forthwith, fretted impatiently as Bridie rummaged in a scuffed plastic handbag for her teeth.

Major Pratt, in place as Official Welcomer on the steps, darted an agonised glance at Eloise and increased the volume of his voice as the first guest approached; a tall man in a blazer bearing a regimental badge, accompanied by a lady in a flowery dress.

Major Pratt shook his hand. '*Ave fratre!* Jolly nice of you to come. You remember Eloise, don't you?'

Bridie, usually acutely hard-of-hearing, had no problem in picking up Major Pratt's hearty greeting.

'That fella muclt be one o' them diclfrocked priecltcl,' she deduced.

'Never mind him, where's the lav?' persisted Eamon urgently.

Dud, in a cold sweat lest Mr. MacTavish should arrive and find nowhere to park, hustled Bridie from the car and, knowing Eloise would mask her dismay under a more convincing veneer of surprised delight than her husband, steered his outlandish cargo towards her.

'Mona's, er, come to the party. And this is her mother, Bridie.'

And Eloise, as ever, rose gallantly to the occasion.

'*What* a lovely surprise!' She extended a gloved hand

graciously. '*How* kind of you all to come!'

'And, er, you remember Eamon, don't you.'

'Of course,' murmured Eloise smoothly. 'How are you, Eamon?'

'I've got prostrate glands, I need the lav!'

'Oh dear, poor you. Well, Dud will show you where everything is, won't you Dud.' She turned, with a regal smile, to the next guest.

But Bridie was not going to be shunted to one side. She had come to socialize, and she may as well begin with Major Domo here, since they had something in common - he was obviously One Of The Flock. The Latin was the give-away (unless he was a doctor or chemist, but even then she could throw in enough snatches for him to appreciate that here was a woman of intelligence, culture, and education). She'd set the ball rolling by taking a friendly interest in the gentleman in the military blazer with the regimental badge.

'Icl he an ecl-prieclt?' she accosted Major Pratt.

'I beg your pardon?' Major Pratt turned to face what, to him, appeared to be a Les Dawson impersonator who had just won a girning competition.

'Him.' Bridie nodded at the man, who was making his way to the bar accompanied by his companion.

'What about him?'

'She says, is he an ex-priest?' translated Mona, adding a cursory explanation: 'She hasn't got her teeth in yet.'

'No he isn't,' said Major Pratt shortly.

'Ah now, he needn't worry, poor man.' Bridie gave a confidential tap to the side of her nose. 'There'cl loadcl of them in Ireland. If they get up to... clome little micldemeanour, you know what I mean -'

Major Pratt stared fixedly at the tree behind her.

'- They get clent back there for a bit, 'til thingcl have quietened down. They tell the pariclionercl they've gone on a Retreat. What'cl thicl one done?'

'He hasn't done anything, he's not a priest!'

'No, no,' soothed Bridie. 'Well, he needn't worry, we won't crack on to nobody.'

Major Pratt turned pointedly to greet the next guest, hoping she wasn't too thick-skinned - or merely thick - to take the hint.

214

'Better keep him off the communion wine, hadn't we!' Bridie gave him a jocular poke in the ribs.

'I really -'

'I alwaycl thought it wacl a micltake to get rid of the Latin, wacln't it,' went on Bridie, enjoying this satisfying theological discussion with a like-minded ally. They obviously shared religious convictions; they could start on politics next. Northern Ireland or something. That was always a good ice-breaker.

'Quite,' replied Major Pratt, edging away.

'Never been the clame clincle, hacl it,' continued Bridie, edging after him.

'No,' agreed Major Pratt distantly. 'Well, nice to have met you. You must be in need of a nice cup of tea after your journey.' He turned to Dud, an unmistakable glint in his eye. '*Dud will take care of all that for you.*' He nodded, clearly signalling dismissal, and turned away once more.

'I'm in need of a bloody good piss. And if someone doesn't tell me where the lav is,' threatened Eamon, effectively annihilating Eloise's genteel pleasantries with the Lady Mayoress. 'I'll be doing it here and now in the shrubbery!'

Had Major Pratt looked out of the landing window half an hour later he would have seen another fugitive intent on avoiding detection. A slight figure in a well-worn houndstooth jacket, trousers pressed and clean although far from new, shoes highly polished, had slipped past while the gatekeeper's attention was taken up with berating a driver who'd reversed into the parking notice, and was padding warily up the drive.

He hesitated, taking in the crowd of expensively-dressed women greeting each other with shrill hoots of laughter, the confidently chatting men. And then, very quietly, turned and retraced his steps.

He'd known all along this would happen. What he should have done, of course, was write a polite note thanking them for the invitation but regretting that he had a prior engagement. But he hadn't - some of us never learn, Jeannie - and now look at him, creeping shamefacedly away, physically unable to proceed any further up the drive because his own personal demon stood there barring the way. Loneliness, his demon was called. It didn't attack often, but when it did... well, we all have our failings,

Jeannie, and his meant that right now all he wanted to do was escape that poised, confident, alien group of people.

His pace quickened. He'd noticed a track as he came along the road from the village, and it obviously led up to the fells. His eyes instinctively turned to the hills - *"I will lift mine eyes to the hills"* - and immediately felt reassured, confident, and happy to be on his own.

No, not on his own. Jeannie was beside him, holding his hand, and the demon evaporated like a lungful of exhaled cigarette smoke that has fouled the air but is dispersed by a clean, pure wind, dispatched back to its lair in a cold, misty, inhospitable land far beyond the sea.

It was 2.45PM and the Guest of Honour still hadn't arrived.

Major Pratt considered cutting the welcoming speeches short if he didn't turn up soon; nobody would be inconsolable at the curtailment of long-winded babbling by a clutch of National Office officials who'd junketed up for the Event. But it was widely accepted that he did have a particular flair, a gift, for the oratory, and it would be a pity to deprive Mr. MacTavish of hearing it. Hearing it in full, that was.

Another niggling item on his list of Things To Keep An Eye On: the haggis. If he left it to those nincompoops in that damn kitchen he'd probably find, at the very moment it was due to be borne ceremoniously outside behind the piper, that the dratted things were still sitting in their boxes, completely forgotten. And that was another thing. Where *was* this mysterious piper Len had assured him they'd booked? He'd seen neither hide nor hair of any brawny, kilt-attired, bearded Scotsman swinging up the drive with a set of bagpipes.

Better check on that side of things...

'Repulsive old hag!' fumed Anna, returning from the garden with a pot of tea rejected by Bridie. 'She's decided she'll try Lapsang Souchong now!'

Major Pratt had insisted there should be an all-encompassing selection of Indian, Chinese, fruit, and herbal teas on offer. Anna would act as waitress, Kate brew pots of the required tea whilst attending to her other chores in the kitchen, and Ewan collect the dirty crockery ("And remember, the key word is *unobtrusive...*")

and wash up.

Kate dropped a couple of "Special Offer Cash and Carry 1000 Catering Teabags for £1" teabags into a pot and filled it.

'Here. Give her this, with my compliments.'

Major Pratt bustled into the kitchen, allowing Anna to pass with her tray. 'Everything A-OK, Kate? Read the instructions re cooking the haggis, have you?'

Kate indicated a large pan bubbling on the cooker.

'Ah. Good. Not too complicated then?'

'Not unless they're different from every other haggis I've ever cooked. We often eat haggis.'

Major Pratt, who had no interest in whatever rubbish Len and Kate chose to eat as long as it wasn't haunch of venison or brace of pheasant, strode across to the pan, lifted the lid, recoiled from the steam, and peered at the curious heathenish objects submerged inside. Presumably this was how the things were supposed to look?

'Good girl,' he praised, as though encouraging a four-year-old who'd made a valiant attempt at a jigsaw. 'Now what I - yes, what is it, Babs?'

Babs peeped around the door, obviously searching for him with news to impart. 'I'm awfully sorry, but there's been a prang down by the gate.'

'Oh God!' groaned Major Pratt. 'Don't tell me some idiot's ploughed into Mr. MacTavish?'

'No. Nobody's hurt, but someone's reversed into the parking notice and knocked it down.' Babs conscientiously relayed the message verbatim.

'Well why hasn't Dud put it back up again?'

'I don't know,' blinked Babs.

'Can't Len deal with it?'

'You said any emergencies were to be reported direct to you.'

Major Pratt sighed. Yes. So he had. How infinitely easier life would be if the earth's population included a few others who possessed sufficient intelligence to deal with all those problems only *he* seemed capable of sorting out...

'Tch! We'll have to leave the haggis for the moment, Kate. I must go down to the gate.'

He was gone, Babs scurrying after him. Ewan, watching this self-important departure, misquoted irreverently:

"'I must go down to the gate again,

"To the lonely gate, and the cars.

"And all I ask is a haggis that's cooked,

"To shove up MacTavish's -'"

'SHUSH!' warned Kate sharply as Major Pratt's distinctive footsteps strode briskly once more towards the kitchen.

It appeared that Len, having been issued with strict instructions to inform Major Pratt the *instant* Thelma awoke, had duly reported that she'd opened her eyes and yawned just as he was about to rush down and sort out whatever crisis was taking place at the gate. So Major Pratt had decided to delegate Ewan to assist Dud, because obviously the crisis about to erupt on the lawn took urgent priority, and his presence at the nerve-centre of Ops would be infinitely more vital there than fiddling about with some parking notice down at the gate.

Thelma sat up and looked around at the guests, chatting and laughing in the warm September sunshine. Some stood with drinks, others sat in groups at tables dotted around the lawn, and a queue had formed at the bar. She realised with surprise that she'd been asleep for almost an hour.

There was no sign of Dud - popped down to check on the boat, probably. She surveyed the group nearest to her, slumped around a patio table discussing tea; a man of late middle-age in a crumpled blue suit, a fat woman with dyed frizzy black hair and pasty overweight legs, and an older, even fatter version in a canary yellow dress and pink hat.

'Now this is better, this Lapsong Shoeshine,' the old woman was remarking.

'Oh, try the bloody lot ma, seeing we haven't them to pay for. Give that stuck-up bitch something to do,' Mona answered, then caught Thelma's eye. 'Ah, hello dear. Woken up, have you?'

'Yes,' yawned Thelma.

'And who exactly are you, like?' Mona always favoured the direct approach. Might as well find out at the outset whether they were worth the bother of turning on the Irish charm for.

'My name's Thelma. I'm a guest of someone called Dudley.'

Mona stiffened. *Dudley*? DUDLEY? By God, if he'd dared - if he'd DARED bring this floosie... 'Dudley, did you say?'

'Yes,' went on Thelma innocently. 'He must have popped

down to see his boat while I was asleep.'

A moment of uncertainty, a stay of execution.

'His boat?'

'Yes.'

Mona's boiling blood subsided to its usual sulphurous simmering. Whoever this Dudley was the girl had come with, it couldn't be the one she was thinking of. He didn't know one end of a boat from the other.

'Had it long, has he, this boat?' she probed, eyes narrowed, to make absolutely certain.

'Oh, he's had it for years,' said Thelma confidently. 'We're going for a sail in it tomorrow.'

Bloodshed had been averted. Out of a gathering of over a hundred, it was, after all, quite possible for more than one person to be called Dudley.

'Ah now, isn't that lovely!' In an impetuous burst of sisterhood spirit once it was safely established the girl wasn't laying claim to any of her possessions, Mona discussed her own plans for the following day. 'I wish I had time to go sailing, but there's so much to get done for the Wedding.'

'Oh.' Thelma nodded understandingly. 'Big do, is it?'

'Ah, we'll be making a bit of a splash, you know. As a matter of fact we'll be making one here, this afternoon, as well. We're announcing the Engagement.'

'Oh, what a nice idea!' smiled Thelma, then looked up in surprise to see Major Pratt and Eloise homing in on them at a businesslike trot.

'Well now, and how are you all enjoying yourselves?' Major Pratt bared his teeth in a hyena-like smile. 'Kate looking after you, is she? Would you like some more tea?'

'Ah, I never say no... to anything!' cackled Bridie archly. 'Nice drop o' tea, this Hoo Flung Dung. They serve it down the Irish Club too, you know.'

'Oh really?' Major Pratt wondered how long one could spin out a subject as relatively incombustible as tea. Obviously they'd arrived in time and the touchpaper hadn't been ignited, or the ensuing conflagration would have consumed the entire Event by now. But they couldn't afford to be complacent; the barmaid was a naked flame hovering next to a petrol tanker, and had to be got away as speedily as possible. 'Can I order you another pot?'

'Depends what else is on offer,' she considered with a leering wink. 'I like a bit of variety, you know.'

'Ah. Good idea,' rejoined Major Pratt vaguely. He glanced at Eloise. That was the preliminaries over - down to business. And Eloise, as ever, came up with the goods.

'Thelma,' she begged with her most beguiling smile, '*Could* we beg the most *enormous* favour of you?'

Thelma blinked in surprise.

'Len, who is nobly attempting to master the art of being barman for the day,' confided Eloise flatteringly, 'Is getting rather swamped, I fear, and we wondered - as you are such an expert in that particular field - *would* you be a positive angel and help him out?'

'Doesn't look all that busy to me,' remarked Mona, then an expression of cunning flitted across her face; keeping That Other One run off her feet with pots of different tea was all very well in its way, but what *she* wouldn't say no to was getting stuck in at the hard stuff. 'But I'll give him a hand an' all if he can't cope.'

Major Pratt's mouth went dry. Mona, matily teaming up with Dud's new bimbo to form a duo of Barmaids from Hell?

'Not at all, Mona,' said Eloise firmly. 'You must look after your mother. I'm sure she'd like to look around the gardens, wouldn't you Bridie?'

'What for?' Bridie could see them perfectly well from here.

Eloise swallowed. 'Mona, didn't you say your mother was terribly interested in -' She cast her eye towards the nearest overgrown flower bed, where a jungle of suckers swarmed over a few greenfly-ridden blooms. '- Tea roses?'

Thelma, meanwhile, had taken the opportunity to assess the bar staff. The bronzed, muscular Wayfarers Seasonal Assistant scored ten out of ten and a gold star on the Phwoar Factor, and she remembered now - she'd been a bit confused when she'd first woken up - Dud hadn't gone to see his boat. He'd been stationed on duty at the gate as car park attendant. Well, that didn't mean she had to spend the afternoon like a nun, did it.

She smoothed her hair. 'I'll go and help in the bar then.'

'Oh *would* you?' smiled Eloise, as Mona and Eamon hauled Bridie out of her chair for the tour of the gardens. 'How kind... Now, Mona, tell us all your news. What have you been doing with yourself these past weeks?'

'Oh, she's been busy getting the wedding organised,' Thelma informed her chattily as she set off. 'They're going to announce the Engagement here, this afternoon. Isn't that nice?'

Major Pratt gaped at Eloise, thunderstruck. Engagement? *Here*? NICE?

Danny smiled to himself. He'd slipped in unnoticed while the bouncer, presumably posted to deter undesirables, was distracted by someone reversing into the parking notice, and it looked as though his luck would hold for the exit as well; there was a mini riot taking place now. The gatekeeper was encircled by a flock of enraged OAPs, and even if he noticed Danny sneaking past he'd be unlikely to challenge what, to him, would merely appear to be one of their number who'd got a bit confused due to his age, and was going the wrong way.

Major Pratt's face outpurpled Mona's skirt as it waddled along behind Eloise, who, Pied-Piper-like, lured her garden-viewing party safely into the distance. Blasted woman! It beggared belief, turning up here uninvited with her nauseating entourage and hatching some diabolical plot to upstage him! There might have been some excuse had the engagement been to a Committee Member - although even that he would have regarded as the height of bad manners - but to use the occasion to... to what, exactly? Was this some sort of public retribution against Dud? Because surely she didn't think anyone else would be interested in her sordid affairs?

He was distracted by a posse of OAPs marching up the drive. He saw them stop at the bar. They spoke to Len, who pointed towards him. He groaned. *Now* what?

The spokesman announced that they were the Scottish Country Dance Display Team (Major Pratt blinked in surprise; he'd expected youthful Andy Stewarts and wholesome Moira Andersons in their primes, not a collection of decrepit geriatrics) and they wished to make a complaint. "Some self-important little Hitler" had waved their cars to the marshy area right at the bottom of the field, and one of the ladies had dropped her white dress in the mud. Fortunately it was in a plastic bag, but that wasn't the point. The point was, they were doing him a favour, and shouldn't be expected to park so far away with kilts and dresses and things to lug around.

Major Pratt immediately assumed the mantle of all-powerful Dispenser of Retribution. He personally would have that insolent Scouse-Scotsman, Ewan, thrown off the premises forthwith.

'Not him!' The spokesman shook his head impatiently. 'If it hadn't been for Ewan sorting things out we'd have all driven straight home again. No, this bullying tyrant was called Dud!'

Major Pratt instinctively looked around for Eloise, but Eloise was fully occupied in enticing her charges towards the furthest reaches of the grounds. Anna, however, possessed sufficient charm to sooth the dancers' ruffled feathers, show them to the dormitories set aside for their use, and instruct Kate to go into overdrive with the tea. He beckoned her across, noticing, out of the corner of his eye, Ewan sneaking towards the back door with an elderly man in a houndstooth jacket. Good lord, was *that* the piper? (Where were they all coming from? Was it National Geriatric Week?) He'd expected a brawny giant with red hair and a beard down to his chest, the sort you saw tossing cabers at Highland Games. This one didn't look capable of tossing a pine cone. Small and wiry, but straight back, and clean - ex-Services, at a guess. Probably been a piper in the Liverpool Scottish or something. Where the kilt and pipes were heaven only knew; doubtless that would be the next crisis he'd have to sort out, when the piper realised he'd left them on the bus...

Anna, meanwhile, was mollifying the Display team. The leader turned out to be a gregarious individual, ready to chat, especially when Major Pratt commented stiffly that he'd expected the dancers to be a little younger.

'Yes, that's what everyone says,' he agreed complacently. 'Guess how old I am?'

'Sixty?' hazarded Anna.

'Seventy two!' announced the man proudly.

'No!' grinned Anna, immediately taking to the twinkling eyes and ready smile.

Major Pratt, interjecting admiring noises at the correct intervals while keeping one eye on Ewan and the slight figure accompanying him, was astounded to see Ewan detour to the bar, have a quick word with Len, pick up a bottle of Glenmorangie, and usher the piper towards the back door. His jaw dropped. *Look at this*! The kitchen riff-raff, calmly snaffling malt whisky! He murmured an excuse to Anna and her flock, and turned towards the kitchen for a long overdue confrontation with that silver-tongued con merchant.

As for the other old trollop, forewarned is forearmed. They'd had a narrow escape - his blood ran cold at the thought of Mona taking the bemused audience by surprise as she hauled the luckless Eamon in front of them to announce their engagement - but thank heavens that vacuous barmaid had let the cat out of the bag. At least now he could counter-attack. Dud might be no match for her, but Major Pratt certainly was, and he had no intention of allowing her to turn Beckside's Jubilee into some absurd farce.

He summoned Oliver across.

Mona had had enough.

When they'd reached the furthest point of the so-called "vegetable garden", Oliver had approached and mumbled something about a phone call, and Eloise excused herself in her la-de-dah way and skedaddled off back to the land of the bloody living while he took over and unconvincingly assured them how he'd love to conduct them around in her place.

She didn't know what their game was, hoiking the three of them out of sight up here like a gang of bloody lepers, but there was something bloody fishy going on, because nobody else was traipsing round viewing the unspectacular expanse of grass and an unkempt vegetable allotment that comprised "the gardens", or being dragged all round Len's stringy rhubarb and acres of overgrown mint. And her picking her way through brambles and nettles in white high heels, with the new tights hanging round her legs in shreds!

Yes, by God. She'd had enough of this.

Her bunions were playing up, Bridie needed to sit on an old stone bench to get her breath back, and Eamon was whining that he was sick of the sight of vegetables, he saw enough of the things at home. Meanwhile, the speeches could start any minute, and here she was, stuck up here with this halfwitted gossoon!

'Listen, you!' she jabbed a finger into Oliver's chest. 'We're going back. And don't you give me no crap about "But we haven't seen the apple trees yet," or I'll...!'

Oliver dodged hastily out of physical reach. Major Pratt had told him to show them every living organism in the plant world, and spin it out for as long as possible. But what was he supposed to do if Mona didn't find of riveting interest every slug-eaten lettuce, every shrivelled cabbage, every overgrown row of potatoes? If she insisted on returning to the party, how exactly was he supposed to stop her? And why should he? Why should he be the fall-guy, saddled with this horticultural Mission Impossible? If Major Pratt wished to keep these three unhinged old bats in purdah up here, then Major Pratt could do it himself.

He obediently quickened his pace.

Just as Major Pratt was about to pounce on the thieving wretches in the kitchen, Wilf arrived, pained and aggrieved. He'd waited for Dud to call for him on the Honda, but Dud had whizzed past with a girl on the pillion, and he'd had to make his own way by public transport.

'Oh, how aggravating,' sympathised Eloise, still panting slightly from her expedition. 'Never mind. Mr. MacTavish hasn't arrived yet.'

'No. Anyway, I'm glad you're here, Wilf, because we've got what one might call rather a delicate problem,' confided Major Pratt. 'That ghastly woman-friend of Dud's has arrived, and -'

He was interrupted by a shriek.

Babs was flapping at her chest. 'There's a wasp gone down my... Oh! OH! It's crawling -'

Major Pratt immediately took control. 'Undo your blouse and set it free, Babs,' he instructed crisply.

'Undo my...?' Babs stared at him, aghast. Undo her blouse - in front of all these people? She'd rather endure a thousand wasp stings and die!

Eloise drew her to the porch, where she modestly unfastened the top three buttons. As the wasp flew off, Major Pratt caught sight of Len, taking advantage of the distraction to slip quietly towards the back door to join the clandestine drinking den in the kitchen.

Et tu, eh, Len?

And you think you're going to get away with it, do you?

Laughter echoed from the kitchen (how appropriate - the Thieves' Kitchen!) as Major Pratt strode grimly towards it to confront the nest of pilfering vipers inside. He let the door swing open. The chatter stopped abruptly. He advanced, hands behind back, eyes swivelling knowingly from the Glenmorangie on the table to the staff sitting around it, and on to the stranger.

He took in the jacket with its frayed cuffs, the hands, weatherbeaten but well-shaped and clean, the trousers neatly pressed. His eyes flickered upwards. The facial muscles were taut - very little sagging around the cheeks, no fleshy jowls. Clear blue eyes, kindly but wary.

The man returned his appraisal with a slightly guilty air.

'How do you do. I assume Len would have got around to introducing you in due course,' began Major Pratt smoothly.

Nobody spoke. The only way Ewan had been able to coax the old man to set foot in the building at all was by promising not to reveal his identity to anyone other than Kate and Len, and guaranteeing an escape route any moment he chose to leave.

'I take it they're looking after you satisfactorily?' went on Major Pratt, glancing pointedly at the bottle. The audacity of it! Dishing out malt whisky - to the *piper,* if you please! A cup of tea and a biscuit, yes, but...

It suddenly registered; they were drinking tea. Couldn't very well order Ewan off the premises for misappropriating a mere thimbleful of party fare, unfortunately. There was hardly any whisky gone from the bottle - unless they'd already cunningly re-filled it with water - but what *was* missing was obviously only in the piper's tea. To give the fellow his due, he had the grace to look ill-at-ease and guilty. As well he might.

Len started to say something. Major Pratt raised his hand; he hadn't time to listen to a string of predictable excuses about the piper being unable to play until he'd had a wee dram. He had to get back to his post. Mr. MacTavish could arrive any moment.

'We're not quite ready for you yet,' he addressed the stranger. 'But very briefly - you've seen the programme, have you?'

The man nodded.

'Good. Welcoming Speeches 3 o'clock, Scottish Country Dancing Display immediately afterwards, then Shanty Singing, that's Dud - and then you pipe the haggis out. Or rather, *in,* which I understand is the correct expression, even though it will actually be carried outside, so the Buffet proper can begin. And then we thought it would be rather nice if you could, you know, sort of play in the background while everyone's tucking in?'

The wariness relaxed, the blue eyes twinkled. Major Pratt frowned. How much whisky had the fellow got through? Was he sozzled already? The prospect of a drunken piper was too hideous even to contemplate.

'Where's your, you know, kilt and things?'

'Ah havenae got a kilt.'

Major Pratt stared at him. Surely - SURELY - he didn't think he was going to pipe in the haggis dressed like that? If you booked a piper, it was taken for granted he'd wear a kilt, with all the appropriate regalia (unless, of course, you booked one through Len. He should have known they'd end up with another fiasco if he trusted that bungling oaf!) He thought quickly. The Scottish Country Dancers had kilts. The piper could borrow one of theirs. Not the spokesman's, obviously; that would come down to the old boy's ankles, but -

Len was again saying something.

'What?' snapped Major Pratt impatiently.

'I said, he's not the piper.'

'Not the - ?' The vein in Major Pratt's forehead began to throb. 'I thought you told me you'd booked a piper?'

'I did.'

'Well where is he?'

'He rang up to say he's ill, he can't come.'

Major Pratt was incapable of speech. "He's ill, he can't come!" - and Len, gossiping unconcernedly in here instead of urgently relaying this latest catastrophic bombshell!

'Don't worry,' Len continued, 'Ewan's offered to step in as replacement.'

DON'T WORRY? Which was worse, no piper at all, or that buffoon turning the occasion into a burlesque pantomime?

'He's a very good piper,' said Len quietly.

There was no doubting the sincerity. Major Pratt anxiously checked his watch. If Mr. MacTavish arrived now, and witnessed this humiliating disorganisation...

'Has he got, you know, a kilt and -'

'Yes.'

The same calm tone of equanimity. If he didn't know Len better, he'd have suspected the whole thing had been pre-arranged, and he'd been... duped in some way. But Len wasn't capable of duping anyone, least of all him, and, although it was damned provoking to be obligated to that lout, what other option was there? In the meantime (his eyes flickered to the unknown visitor silently observing proceedings; presumably some relative or friend of Ewan's, going from the easy camaraderie between them which was plainly evident) they could continue their cosy reunion later - they were paid to work, not skulk in here holding their own private party - and he could return to his post, to present a dignified welcome for Mr. MacTavish.

'Hm. Well in that case, you'll be anxious to clear the dirty dishes before you take up your duties as piper, won't you. And I think we'll just put this back where it belongs, as well,' he added silkily, scooping up the bottle. 'Perhaps your friend here would like to finish his drink outside while we all attend to, you know, our *orthodox* guests.' He smiled, the distant, impersonal smile of Authority confident that every order will be instantly and unquestioningly obeyed.

Decision time again, Danny. Either he revealed his identity now or he didn't reveal it at all. He'd guessed straight away the irate sleuth investigating goings-on in the kitchen must be Major Pratt; from Ewan's description he couldn't be anyone else. And if the non-appearance of the piper had almost caused a seizure, the non-appearance of the Guest of Honour could finish him off altogether.

He sighed, reached inside his jacket pocket for the invitation and original solicitor's approach letter, and handed them to Major Pratt.

'Ah'm sorry. Ah shoulda said earlier. Ah'm Danny MacTavish. Pleased tae meet ye.'

No matter how unlikely, unusual, or bizarre the circumstance, Eloise's immeasurable expertise guaranteed a faultless response, and she was now injecting warmth into the slightly strained welcome proffered by her husband. Wilf was sent to rouse Leslie from his slumbers in the Quiet Room, where he'd gone to ground on his arrival, and Babs ran to inform Dud that the Guest of Honour had arrived.

'What d'you mean, he's arrived?' challenged Dud. 'He hasn't come past me, I've checked every car!'

'Well that's what Major Pratt said.' Babs' voice was a nervous squeak. 'He said he's in the kitchen now.'

'In the *kitchen*?'

'Yes. Major Pratt said he's -'

'*He can't be!*'

'Well Major Pratt said he's -'

'What on earth's he doing there?'

'Well all I know is, Major Pratt said he's -'

Dud turned away with an impatient tut. How the Guest of Honour had managed to get past him was a mystery, but as there was now no longer any excuse for him to be stationed at the gate, he was (in theory) free to concentrate on, and make up lost time with, his own nubile guest. And although that was going to take some doing under Mona's all-seeing Evil Eye, even he, Treat-'Em-Rough-They-Love-It-Really Dud, couldn't leave her on her own all afternoon just because Mona had turned up.

Major Pratt, meanwhile, felt that the Guest of Honour was labouring the point slightly. Yes, it was fortunate Ewan had happened by the gate while there was "a wee bit stramash" going on. And yes, it was *so* kind of him to act as piper, especially at such short notice. And he was delighted to hear that Len and Kate had been so welcoming (God help them if they hadn't). But there were far more praiseworthy aspects to eulogise about than Kate's tea. The brains behind the whole thing, for instance.

This wasn't how he'd imagined things at all. He'd envisaged the staff lined up in the kitchen in order of importance, presenting each in turn to a suitably remote figure who'd bestow a few pleasantries, like Royalty greeting the artistes at the Command Performance, after mingling with the more important guests outside.

He cleared his throat to cut short another tribute to Kate's hospitality.

'Yes. Well now...' He checked his watch with polite concern. 'D'you think we're ready to, you know...?'

'Kate will make more tea later, won't you Kate,' Eloise added reassuringly. 'Nothing quite like a cup of tea to revive one after an arduous journey, is there. Poor you! No wonder you were exhausted when you arrived. All that way, by public transport!'

Len glanced at Ewan. So that was the official line to explain the Guest of Honour's unorthodox back door arrival - he was exhausted, poor old chap. And a bit confused. He was seventy, after all.

Major Pratt nodded encouragingly. 'So! Ready for the fray?'

Ewan couldn't look at the old man. What price betrayal? Thirty pieces of silver, masquerading as a tot of Glenmorangie? Proud of yourself are you, big man? Because Danny was not ready for this particular fray, and never would be. And the very things he'd been unable to face, and run away from - being the focus of attention for curious onlookers and fawning officials, listening to speeches, and, even worse, being expected to make his own - Ewan had blundered along, swept him up, and dropped him right back in the midst of it all.

He felt Danny's steady gaze and looked up. Danny shook his head slowly and smiled, a smile of wry resignation.

Unspoken communication transmitted between both pairs of eyes - the confession: "I never meant for this to happen, Danny. I'm truly sorry."

And the immediate, unhesitating absolution: "Ach ferget it, son. It's ma fault anyway, no' yours."

The news spread like wildfire; the Guest of Honour had arrived incognito. One of those eccentric multi-millionaires who book into top hotels carrying battered suitcases tied up with string, you know. Yes, he was in the kitchen now apparently, recovering from his journey.

The crowd quietened as Major Pratt and Eloise emerged from the Dining Room french windows, guiding a slight figure by the elbow with over-elaborate concern. Major Pratt waited for complete silence, then began.

'Good afternoon everyone, and welcome! Lovely to see you all!' He smiled around. 'And I'd like you to join me in extending a particularly warm welcome to our Guest of Honour, Mr Danny MacTavish -'

There was a round of enthusiastic applause.

'- Without whose generosity dear old Beckside could not have offered its world-renowned hospitality to all those devotees of the Great Outdoors who've tramped across its welcoming portals these past forty years -'

Another round of applause.

'- And whose special milestone birthday we are delighted, and indeed honoured, to be able to celebrate with him here today, because... well, as you all know, he is *seventy years young!*'

More good-natured applause.

'Now, I always say a good speech is like a lady's gown; long enough to cover the subject but short enough to be interesting -'

A ripple of appreciative chuckles, provided, in the main, by the stalwarts in the front row.

'And whilst I don't intend boring anyone -'

The chuckles immediately faded to murmurs of protest; perish the thought the Chairman's speeches could ever be boring!

'I do just want to say a few words - yes, that's right, gather round, all you good people there at the back, if you can't hear - to briefly explain, for any of you not too *au fait* with our aims, our purposes, our *raison d'etre*, a little about the wonderful work done by the Association...'

At last, everything was falling into place. Yes, it had been worth shouldering the tedious burden of responsibility to feel the audience in the palm of his hand like this, to know the occasion was going to be a glittering triumph - HIS glittering triumph!

Out of the corner of his eye he saw Mona and her entourage moving into range, and permitted himself a smile of quiet triumph.

Too late, my dear.

He'd successfully seen off any grubby little schemes from *that* quarter.

Dud, who heard the news of Mona's Engagement from Leslie in the Men's Washroom, skipped downstairs and out into the sunlight, punching the air elatedly. YES! It had worked. She'd sunk her fangs into the unsuspecting morsel of bait he'd impaled on the hook, and he'd wriggled off the line for good.

As for Major Pratt's indignation about her plans to announce the coming nuptials during Beckside's Jubilee, well, Major Pratt knew as well as he did what an unstable, unfathomable species women were. The only thing anyone knew for certain about them was that nobody knew what they'd do next, and he couldn't be held accountable for every discarded conquest who turned up to boast about dragging some pathetic victim down the aisle. He was free, and that was all he cared about. Free to concentrate on the first of many seductions aboard "Sultry Nights" (and, incidentally, shove Thelma under Miss Snooty-Keks' conk, to let her see she wasn't the only bint in the casbah).

He cast an anticipatory glance in Anna's direction and saw, beyond her, Mona lumbering towards the crowd, with Bridie and Eamon puffing along behind, and Oliver skulking in the distance. She appeared to be heading straight for him. Obviously going to be some sort of sentimental farewell: "Forgive us dearheart, this thing was bigger than both of us..." Well, he'd happily play along, the rejected suitor magnanimously shaking the victor's hand and trotting out philosophical platitudes: To the conqueror, the spoils, etc.

'A little bird tells me -' he began, then blinked in amazement as a fat hand slid, python-like, around his elbow and he was propelled forward, so completely taken by surprise that he'd almost reached the Dining Room steps before it occurred to him to put up any resistance. In dreamlike slow motion, as he was frog-marched helplessly up the steps to whatever unknown doom awaited, he became acutely aware of irrelevant details; a fag-end and half-eaten sausage roll tossed into a flower arrangement, one of the tussie mussies hanging tipsily over a window lintel where Len hadn't secured it properly.

'I know the Major here won't mind me just butting in for a minute,' simpered Mona, calmly taking over as the thunderstruck Chairman faltered in sheer disbelief.

'*You* -' spluttered Major Pratt.

'Dud and I had a romantic few days in London not long ago,' Mona informed the stunned onlookers in a tone of playful roguishness, totally ignoring him.

Some of the audience tittered uncertainly. Was this some publicity stunt in aid of charity? The laughter quickly dried up - one look at the apoplectic fury on Major Pratt's face assured them it wasn't.

'And at me cousin's Hen Night -' She fished a photograph wallet from her bag and pressed a selection of photos onto the main players on the steps, who had no option but to take them. Some were blurred, some taken from a distance through a crowd, some close-up, but all featured the same unmistakable subject - Dud, grinning lasciviously, trousers half-mast round his ankles as he and Mona shared a slobbering kiss. '- He PROPOSED!'

Colour drained from Dud's face as though someone had turned

231

on a tap in his feet.

'But not in the usual, boring, run-of-the-mill English way. No, Dud wanted the moment to be really special, didn't you dearheart, so he chose the method that he knew would mean the most to me. This is what us romantic Celts call a traditional Celtic proposal: a public declaration of his love, for all the world to see!' In a grotesque parody of maidenly coyness she waved one of the horrifying images in front of Eloise, who blanched, shuddered, and looked away.

A greenish tinge had appeared on either side of Dud's gaping mouth. He prop...? *He prop...?* HE WHAT? Since when did a snogging session at a Hen Night constitute a proposal of marriage? No normal, rational person could possibly mistake... He risked a sideways glance at Mona, and his insides shivered in real fright. Mona, as he had subconsciously feared all along, was not normal, or rational.

For once even Eloise was lost for words. (*Dud* had proposed? She thought it was Eamon. Had they both proposed then?)

To Major Pratt, incandescent with rage and conscious of a hundred guests witnessing the whole unspeakable debacle, it was a matter of supreme indifference who had proposed to whom, or in what manner, as long as he regained control of the situation.

'*Get off these steps, or I'll -*' he threatened in a vitriolic hiss.

'Now some people flash romantic messages on football scoreboards or trail banners behind planes -' Mona scornfully disposed of this attempt to gag her. (What would they rather listen to, the wonderful work done by the Association, or whether she'd accept Dud's proposal?)

Dud listened to the loathsome voice in mute paralysis. We all have an inbuilt mechanism for self-preservation, but there are occasions - usually when it is particularly vital for the adrenalin to race and a razor-sharp mind effectively counter-attack imminent catastrophe - that the brain decelerates to a sluggish mush resembling the contents of a stationary concrete mixer, and focuses instead on trivialities; in this case a word floating aggravatingly just out of reach of his tongue.

'- But I knew what you'd prefer, dearheart. So I'm giving you me answer here today, so we can share our happiness with all these lovely people!' The pause for effect was brief, lest Major Pratt rally his reeling forces. 'It's YES, dearheart!'

A terrifying surge of electricity activated the concrete mixer, sending it spinning into overdrive.

'And we've got another bit of news for yer, as well,' Mona promised the spellbound crowd, and burped. 'Pardon. Cupid shot his arrow at Eamon recently. Him and me mother are gettin' hitched an' all! It's a double wedding!'

Two distinct perceptions leapt into vivid relief against the turmoil of half-formed thoughts crackling around Dud's brain. The first was the word he'd been groping for, which floated into consciousness just as he was losing that very state.

Poleaxed.

And the second was, that old cliche about the ground spinning up to meet you when you were about to faint was true.

It did.

As he watched Babs run to the bar for a bottle of Highland Spring Water, Major Pratt thought uncharitably that it was just as well Dud was stretched out unconscious at his feet; the temptation to knock both his and Mona's heads together to render the pair of them incapable of further chaos might well have proved irresistible.

And Dud, faced with a choice of Mona's gloating triumph six inches from his nose on one side and Major Pratt's fury on the other the moment he opened his eyes, deliberately delayed revival by pretending to drift back into unconsciousness.

No matter how drunk he'd been at that Stag Night, he knew perfectly well he had never, but NEVER, proposed marriage to Mona - by mysterious "traditional Celtic" ritual (what nutcase could interpret a clinch at a Hen Night as a marriage proposal?) (Only the one he was now apparently engaged to!), or any other way. He willed his befuddled brain to formulate some sort of strategy for a Great Escape from this mess.

That was it - The Great Escape! He'd often fancied himself as Steve McQueen, revving up the bike for that Do-Or-Die leap to freedom. He had the motorbike (well, the Honda). And he had the field (well, Beckside's lawn). A few devil-may-care revs, and blaze down the drive to freedom - with one addition. 'Get on, woman!' he'd shout, veering the bike with a swashbuckling flourish towards the heartbroken Thelma.

There was no other way. Things had got completely out of

hand, and whether he went along with the Engagement for today and tried to extricate himself later (No thank you - been there, done that, got the current nightmare to prove it), or brazened it out now in front of the goggling audience, the damage was irreparably done as far as prospects of higher office on The Committee were concerned.

On the plus side, though, it wouldn't do any harm to his image of a man oozing with the potent aura of danger so irresistible to women. "Yes," he'd laugh to his new circle of friends in the Yacht Club, the men guffawing jovially, the women vying to catch the eye of such a popular and amusing raconteur. "I just roared off down the drive and left them to it!"

Why not? Why not discard this now obsolete phase of his life like a snake shedding an outgrown skin? And when he got home, he'd ask Brian if there were any openings for Committee Members at the Philatelic Club.

There was only one way to handle a situation like this.

You turned to the Guest of Honour with an expression of unflappable nonchalance - and you used any means you could to create an eclipsing diversion. For example, one comment Danny made as they came through the Dining Room might prove useful; it was Kate and Len's Silver Wedding today. Major Pratt had forgotten about that. Well, one bit of blatant upstaging deserves another, wouldn't you say - and what could be more piquant than keeping to the theme of wedded bliss? Play down the impact of Mona's bombshell by focusing on the part Beckside had, over the years, played in so *many* romantic interludes; this timeless backdrop had witnessed so *many* moments of drama and emotion - if only these walls could talk etc. Which led nicely to the wonderful work done by the Association. Which led nicely to the wonderful work done by Major Pratt. He'd spent hours poring over this speech and they were going to hear it, come hell, high water, thunder-stealing Engagement announcements, or Dud swooning like some Victorian virgin.

He flashed a kindly, paternal smile at the audience awaiting the next theatrical extravaganza as, with a sympathetic nod at Dud (still slumped on a chair, mutely enduring the ministrations of his prospective in-laws) he drew Kate and Len onto the steps.

234

'Never a dull moment, eh! But while Dud, understandably overwhelmed by his good fortune, takes a few moments to adjust to being officially betrothed, and before *we* resume the festivities and return to the aims of the Association - because we mustn't let ourselves get so carried away with all the excitement that we loose track of the main purpose of our little Event - can I mention another little celebration? Today, as well as being special for Beckside, Dud and Mona, and our Guest of Honour -'

The kindly, paternal smile froze; Kate quite obviously wasn't listening to a word he said. Her eyes were following a battered old Vauxhall as it bumped its way up the drive and stopped outside the front door. A young man in jeans and tee-shirt got out, laughing at something his companion said as he held the passenger seat forward for two girls to clamber out.

Major Pratt faltered in surprise as Kate's customary expression of deadened resignation blossomed into one of transparent joy. The distraction cost him dear; by momentarily losing concentration, he also lost the attention of the crowd, who instinctively turned to inspect the unknown gatecrashers. Because it was obvious the grins lighting the faces of Kate and Len were caused by the arrival of the occupants of the car rather than the prospect of hearing an itemised catalogue of the wonderful work done by the Association.

'- Is also Kate's and Len's Silver Wedding Anniversary,' he finished lamely.

Quite frankly, there were occasions when one was tempted to let this particular Chairmanship lapse, and concentrate solely on the Golf Club.

At last, something was going right.

The Scottish Country Dancers performed a faultless display, briefly explained the symbolism and intricacies of the movements, demonstrated a simple reel ideally suited to beginners, invited audience participation, and patiently and expertly guided volunteers through the dance.

Major Pratt beamed affably, clapping in time to the music, and, taking an apt cue on the merits of dogged perseverance from Robert the Bruce and his spider, mentally re-phrased Rabbie Burns' "To a Haggis" to incorporate the wonderful work done by the Association: "And speaking of Puddings, we like to ensure that all our catering staff regularly attend updating courses..."

Eloise, meanwhile, had discovered that Danny lived, at one time, next door to Cannich Youth Hostel in the Highlands, and reclaimed her husband's wandering attention with the news.

'Did you indeed,' boomed Major Pratt, good humour fully restored. 'Did a bit of walking in that area myself, once. Rained, unfortunately.'

'But isn't it the most *incredible* incidence!' marvelled Eloise, diplomatically steering the topic from the weather lest the Honoured Guest felt personally responsible. She'd unearthed a conversational nugget of pure gold; the opportunities for sentimental reminiscences were limitless.

'Yes,' went on Major Pratt. 'You see, the plan was to leave the car there and walk to the coast, returning via Cluanie, taking in a few, you know, Munros on the way. Kintail and so on.'

Danny nodded, thinking wistfully of Len's and Kate's family gathering in the kitchen. (Under the guise of "just popping to check on the haggis", they, their sons and their girlfriends had made their escape. Kate had shot him an apologetic smile as they went; the captive VIP who must consort only with his fellow luminaries.)

'Well, I looked at the sky and thought, hmm. Better take the car. Just as well I did. After a mile the heavens opened!'

Danny had heard it all before. He shook his head courteously at Major Pratt's description of ceaseless, bone-chilling rain. He knew what Highland rain was like. He'd worked in it for years.

'...Well, I got wetter and wetter...'

Again Danny tutted with the sympathy he was obviously expected to display. The same rain swept the hills, drenching the men as they planted trees, exposed to wind and rain tearing viciously into their faces for a full eight hour shift. There was no shelter for them.

'...But I plodded on for another half a mile...'

Again Danny nodded dutifully.

'Then I thought, no. Turned round, drove to Inverness. Wild place, Glen Affric. Totally barren.' Major Pratt shuddered, then noticed Anna weaving her way through the crowd towards them, and leaned forward, playfully conspiratorial. 'Yes, Anna, and what can we do for you?'

236

Anna diplomatically translated Kate's caustic message from the kitchen into an enquiry of polite concern. 'Kate wondered when the Shanty Singing scheduled for 3.45PM might actually start, as you ordered the haggis to be ready at 4PM *on the dot.*'

Major Pratt blinked, and checked his watch. Five past four! It *couldn't* be! It was only a couple of minutes ago - surely? - since Dud, assuring them he was now fully recovered, had set off to get changed for his Sea Shanty debut. What on earth had happened to him?

'Listen. Get that bloody fella back out here,' Bridie advised her daughter grimly. 'People'll think there's something peculiar, him vanishing off to one o' them dormitories all this time!'

'Ah, he just wants to change into his sailor suit,' said Eamon.

'Yeah. And I just want him out here where I can keep an eye on him. Slippery as a bloody eel, that one!' Mona flicked another fag-end into a nearby flower arrangement, and stood up.

'And listen,' suggested Bridie as sudden inspiration struck. 'Tell him you'll sing along with him! Wouldn't that be lovely now, the lovebirds doing a little duet!'

'Isn't it supposed to be Sea Shanties?' ventured Eamon.

'Ah, who wants to listen to that bloody old rubbish!' dismissed Bridie witheringly. 'Our Mona's got a voice on her like an angel, God love her! She won a talent contest once, when she was a kid, with that song Ruby Murray used to sing.'

'I always liked "When Irish Eyes Are Smiling" meself,' recalled Eamon with a sentimental sigh.

'Here, you've just given me an idea!' It was Mona's turn for inspiration to strike. 'We'll all join in!' She paused as Major Pratt's response to the news that his meticulously-organised schedule had just been fouled up by the Shanty Singer's tardiness wafted across, and smirked at Bridie. 'Ma, go on over and tell that snotty git Mona will get Dud out here for him. Say, as *a future Member of his Committee,* like, I'm right behind him. And tell him we'll put on a bit of a singsong an' all!'

She departed to find her fiance, and Bridie waddled across to reassure Major Pratt that not only would Mona produce his missing singer, she'd thought up a couple of nice little improvements for his Entertainment programme as well. Instead of boring old Sea Shanties, Dud and Eamon would form the backing group for two honey-voiced female vocalists who'd provide a nice little singalong for the guests.

There now! *That* had put the twinkle back in his eye, hadn't it?

Phase One of The Great Escape had been successfully executed; Dud had reached his dormitory under the pretext of changing for the Shanty Singing, collected his things, and was slinking under cover of the shrubbery back to the Bike Shed.

Unfortunately, the shrubbery skirted "the bar", and as he crept past the crates at the back he overheard Thelma, almost hysterical with laughter, telling that smarmy Assistant from Wayfarers who seemed to spend his life showing off his biceps how she couldn't wait to get back to the pub to tell everyone about Dud's Engagement.

Couldn't wait, eh? Well, the traitorous slag would be waiting longer than she thought, because she was going to find *she'd* been dumped as well as the manipulating hag who considered herself his fiancee.

He reached the Bike Shed safely, and was congratulating himself on this not inconsiderable achievement and psyching himself for the exhilarating dash to freedom when the sledgehammer blow fell. The Honda's battery was dead.

He carried a few tools for emergencies, but all the tools in the world couldn't recharge a flat battery. *Hell's bleeding teeth...*

No wonder people referred to anything with an engine as 'she' and gave it a woman's name! Look at the collection he was surrounded by - one calmly announcing they'd got engaged, another splitting her sides laughing about it, and now this Whore of Babylon conking out just when he needed a loyal escape vehicle! The whole lot of them were the same. Useless. From now on he'd make sure all any of the 'fair' (huh!) sex got out of him was a Happy Hour bowl of crisps on the bar. Never again would any female take *him* for a ride. (Quite apart, that was, from the Honda, which obviously wouldn't.)

No matter how violently Major Pratt's fingers itched to wring Bridie's flabby neck, he couldn't risk another public scandal with the bat-eared outdoors magazine editor hovering interestedly nearby. This particular cat had to be skinned quietly.

And the most convenient scalpel was Anna, still waiting for

his decision on whether to keep to the programme even though it meant running ever later, or trying to catch up with the timetable even though it meant dropping the Shanty Singing. Well, this decided the issue; he'd order the haggis to be piped out immediately, and include in his speech a fatherly concern for Dud: "Out of consideration for our Shanty Singer's earlier incapacity, resulting from his heightened emotional state, I felt it would be kinder to postpone that particular slot..."

And then ensure it stayed postponed.

'How kind, Bridie, but actually the haggis is ready. I was just about to tell Anna to give the kitchen staff the go-ahead.'

'Where *is* Dud, anyway?' wondered Eloise, as Anna departed to relay the instructions.

And more to the point, where was he at 3.45PM, seethed Major Pratt. Because if he'd been where he was supposed to have been when he was supposed to have been there, this slobbering crone wouldn't be here now, sending his blood pressure spiralling to clog-popping level at the thought of SingalongaBridie'n'Mona's All-Time Favourites.

Lurking indefinitely in the Bike Shed was obviously not an option. Either Dud abandoned the Honda and attempted to sneak unnoticed through a hundred or so guests, including Mona & Co, towards the gate, carrying his assorted clutter and crash helmet, or he abandoned The Great Escape. Which meant, in addition to all his other problems, he'd now have incurred Major Pratt's wrath over a tardy start to the Shanty Singing.

And that was another thing. He hadn't the first clue about Shanty Singing; he'd volunteered on impulse after hearing at the weekly Amateur Talent Nite at his local an undiscovered hopeful (as yet still undiscovered) yowling an endless dirge comprising almost entirely of "Ranzo! Oh Ranzo me boys, Ranzo!" who had agreed to write out the words for him, such as they were. If that was all there was to this Shanty Singing lark, reasoned Dud, he could yowl as loud as the next man.

He rifled frantically through his carrier bags for the words, then, rigid with horror, realised he'd left them in the Men's Lavs when he'd nipped in for a quick fag earlier.

He struggled into the matelot top, denims, and red neckerchief, kicked his things into the corner, and crept back towards the Hostel (You could get away with 90% of "Ranzo me boys, Ranzo!" in a selection of different keys and sound as though you knew what you were doing, but still needed to throw in the occasional 10% of salty-sounding rubbish every now and then, and he was past making it up as he went along) - then froze as Major Pratt's malevolent eye blazed accusingly into his own.

There was only one course to take, and Dud took it. Play the sympathy card again. He crossed his eyes and slithered to the ground once more, croaking with theatrical pathos:

'Shanty Singing... stage fright... nerves...'

The haggis earmarked for the piping-in ceremony was being prepared for its final journey, and Kate was garnishing the mashed potato and parsnips surrounding it with fresh parsley when Leslie's blood-suffused face peered round the door.

'Len,' he wheezed, 'We've got *another* emergency outside!'

The latest crisis involved not just one, but two casualties, in distinctly rival camps. Major Pratt was wilting on a straight-backed kitchen chair as Eloise, Babs, and Wilf fanned him with programmes, while Mona, Bridie and Eamon ministered to Dud, supine on the grass.

'God love him!' Mona held a glass devotedly to her fiance's quivering lips. 'Would you look at the state the poor sod's been driven to, all this pressure on him to sing Sea Shanties! You're all right now, dearheart. Mona's here to make sure they don't take no more advantage of you.' She glared across at the Major Pratt camp, the vigilant lioness guarding her cub from a pack of merciless predators.

Dud choked and spluttered; water dribbled down his chin.

Major Pratt also choked and spluttered. How dare that overblown trollop imply he would exploit anyone! Why, look how he'd allowed Kate and Len to combine their special Day with Beckside's Jubilee! Proof enough for anybody!

'Len,' whispered Eloise in an urgent aside. 'What on earth are we going to do? He simply can't take any more disasters!'

Her husband, grey-faced and haggard, stared unseeingly ahead. His prestigious Event had been sabotaged once too often, and was now beyond repair. There was nothing anyone - least of all Len, for heaven's sake - could do about it.

Len took in the situation without comment. Some seventieth

birthday this was turning out to be for Beckside's benefactor; an old war veteran, a fellow seaman, and a man who'd given so much to countless others over the years.

And clearly none of the Committee Members were about to risk what could turn out to be a wrong move. Far safer to let someone else take control of the situation, and stay uninvolved on the sidelines. "Len, what on earth are we going to do?" Translation: "Len, you cope with it - and be the scapegoat we can hold responsible if further disaster occurs, while we remain beyond reproach, free to criticise and pass judgement."

'Dud,' he began carefully, 'You're obviously not very well, are you. Would you like Mona to take you to lie down quietly in a dormitory for a while?'

Dud managed a slightly more robust groan. No, he certainly would not like Mona to take him to lie down quietly in a dormitory, thank you. That wouldn't hasten his recovery at all.

Very well. If compromise in the form of temporary banishment was rejected, it would have to be all-out war for higher stakes; all four of them departing for home. Because Danny wasn't going to have his party until the Event resumed, and the Event wasn't going to resume until Major Pratt recovered, and Major Pratt wasn't going to recover until Mona's coven of witches and warlocks was out of his sight.

Fortunately, she'd just spent the last five minutes unknowingly hoisting Dud by his own petard. He shifted direction.

'Mona, I think you were right about poor Dud being put under too much stress,' he agreed in the hushed, respectful tones of an undertaker.

There was a collective sharp intake of breath from the Major Pratt camp.

'- Because this is the second time he's fainted, isn't it?'

'It is, Len. Yes.' The tone was righteously indignant as Mona obligingly hoisted the petard ever higher. 'Poor sod's got himself in such a state of nerves over this bloody Shanty Singing, it's making him ill!'

'You're right, Mona. We should be ashamed of ourselves for selfishly putting our desire to hear him sing Sea Shanties before poor old Dud's own wellbeing. How thoughtless! We should be doing what's best for the patient, not for us - and that is, to remove him as far as possible from the cause, the source, of his stress, isn't it?'

Mona blinked uncertainly, and Len went on guilelessly: 'Because obviously all the worry about Shanty Singing, on top of the excitement about you accepting his proposal, has been too much for him, hasn't it. He's soldiered valiantly on, determined not to let us down, like the reliable and loyal and true friend he is, but... I agree with you, Mona. It's obvious, isn't it; what he really needs is to just go home and rest.'

'Go home?' Mona rounded on him indignantly. 'You expect the poor sod to get on his Honda and drive home, in this state?'

'Well no. Obviously I thought you and Bridie, having his welfare at heart, would want to take him in the car.'

Mona gaped at him. What did he think he was bloody doing, hustling them off before they'd softened up the rich-bitch guests for the Engagement Present cheques? Also, she'd calculated that the flower arrangements, if kept watered, might just last the necessary three weeks til the wedding, and the tussie mussies would do nicely for the church porch... Oh no. They wouldn't be leaving just yet, by God.

Dud was in a state of panic. Here was Len calmly arranging a legalised kidnapping, the victim to be abducted by Mona's *Ton Ton Macoute* under the unsuspecting noses of the entire audience - and the Chairman of the Committee, by his silence, implicitly sanctioning it! Talk about Cosa Nostra and "Omerta"!

'No! Honestly! I'll be fine!' he assured them desperately.

'Now Dud, stop being such a martyr. You've fainted *twice*. Obviously your poor nerves are completely overwrought,' insisted Len in his infuriating tone of patient concern, and nodded a pre-arranged signal to Oliver on the steps, who made a thumbs-up sign and vanished indoors. 'Mona was quite right about you being put under too much stress over the Shanty Singing. Wasn't she, Wilf?' he couldn't resist adding.

Wilf nodded, then, realising he was confirming the very exploitation his Chairman had so vehemently denied, loyally shook his head, only to realise he was now implying his fellow Committee Member was a malingering hypochondriac.

Surprisingly enough, it was Bridie who finally persuaded Mona to leave.

'Listen,' she whispered in her daughter's ear. 'I've got an idea. While we've got the car here, let's get him in it and round to the priest. Get all the arrangements made and the Banns organised while he's still a bit on the subdued side, if you get my meaning. And Father O'Rourke could -'

What Father O'Rourke could do was drowned by the sudden wail of bagpipes on the front doorstep.

And as all eyes turned towards the piper, Len, gently motioning aside Dud's frantic protests, helped Mona guide the overwrought Shanty Singer whose nerves had been so cruelly shredded by stage-fright towards the car, while Bridie located the driver and told him there'd been a change of plan; they were leaving early.

Looking back, that was the turning point, everyone agreed later.

Even Major Pratt, eyes locked on the piper in a mixture of critical appraisal and apprehensive dread, had to admit that Ewan made a striking figure in his kilt; tall, well-proportioned, muscular, and obviously a highly-skilled piper.

And Oliver, trailing behind bearing a huge meat plate on which nestled an outsize haggis in its artistic arrangement of mashed potato and parsnip, managed to get safely down the steps without both plate and contents hurtling into the adjacent bushes.

By the time the pair got to the bar, Major Pratt had recovered sufficiently to be helped to his feet by Eloise. When they reached the top buffet table in the Dining Room, he was in place to meet them, beaming genially.

The crowd applauded Ewan with enthusiasm. Major Pratt raised a modest hand, acknowledging it as *his* rightful due.

'No, really, The Show Must Go On, as Ralph Reader always used to say. I don't want any of you to be concerned on my account -'

'But we *are* concerned!' Babs assured him.

Major Pratt smiled fondly. 'So thoughtful, as ever, Babs. But... I'll be all right. Now I *must* just say a few words about the wonderful work done by the Association before I Address the Haggis -' He looked with distaste at the plate of steaming victuals Oliver was lowering onto the table. What a singularly unappetising sight! The most attractive thing about it was the parsley garnishing it. Eloise had been right in suggesting that a spoonful each might be more than adequate. After all, nobody would want to actually eat the disgusting-looking stuff (except possibly Kate, Len and Ewan; no accounting for *their* tastes). It was purely a gesture, thrown in for the look of the thing - terribly, you know, Rabbie Burnsish - but would be extremely embarrassing for guests to have to discreetly dispose of huge mounds of it. Even worse if anyone actually felt obliged to eat it! Yes, a miniscule portion was far more considerate.

'- But I wonder if our Guest of Honour might like to say a word or two first...?'

'Aye,' agreed Danny, to everyone's surprise. 'Ah would.'

Anticipating the traditional litany of compliments conferred on hosts by Guests of Honour from time immemorial, Major Pratt smiled complacently.

'Ah'd like tae thank Ewan for playing that particular tune.'

Major Pratt, hastily assuming the expression of a thoughtful host who'd spent hours selecting the appropriate tune (whatever it was), was taken aback. All very creditable to mention the piper of course - but good lord, surely he came way down the list?

Ewan, who'd chosen "The March of The Cameron Men" as a tribute to the Queen's Own Cameron Highlanders tie he'd noticed Danny wearing—the Cameron Highlanders had strong links with the Liverpool Scottish - winked in acknowledgement.

'And I want to thank Len and Kate for making me so welcome -'

Obviously going to be an Uncle Tom Cobleigh and All job, thought Major Pratt, nodding in solemn agreement and using the time until the Honoured Guest got down to the nitty-gritty (ie the indispensable input by the brain masterminding the occasion) to pinpoint the target area of the haggis in which to plunge the knife. Presumably one had to get it right first time or the thing would shoot off the plate and...

'Eh... Could Ah make a wee request?' Danny continued diffidently.

'Of course!' boomed Major Pratt. 'Another cup of tea?' He looked round for Len. 'Len, Mr. MacTavish would -'

'Eh, no...'

'Oh. Well, whatever it is, I'm sure Kate and Len will be only too delighted to comply. Won't you?' He flashed a confident smile at Len.

'Aye well, it's the rest of you I'm hoping will comply.'

This was more like it, thought Major Pratt, instantly alert. The Guest of Honour, impressed by today's Event - in particular the organisational brilliance behind it - would like them to accept a small donation... Ten thousand pounds? Twenty? Fifty? The deeds to Beckside itself, made over to the Association? He hurriedly improvised a spontaneous speech of thanks.

'If a few volunteers got together to help with the clearing up,' continued Danny. 'Maybe Kate and Len could have the rest of the day off to enjoy their Silver Wedding with their family?'

Kate sat back in the warm September sunshine, listening as Ewan played the pipes on the far lawn ('Yes, it's all terribly *Scottish* and so on,' complained Major Pratt, still extremely annoyed at being so completely taken by surprise by the Guest of Honour's request that he'd forgotten to Address the Haggis, 'But I can't hear myself speak! Is there any way of, you know, turning the volume down on the things?') content to be part of the group yet detached from it, listening as her family chatted and laughed with Danny.

Mike glanced across at her. She smiled, studying his face, seeing her own eyes - or to be more precise, her mother's eyes in his face - smile back in that slow, measured smile that had enchanted her since his babyhood.

Love and pride flowed through her. Sometimes it did you good to think about what you were fortunate enough to have in life rather than what you didn't, and although she and Len had worked hard for so many years and ended up with so little, well, that applied to lots of people. As did worries about redundancy.

But they had their health (strange how the stress-headache that had plagued her since the abrupt 5AM awakening had now faded so completely), and, more importantly, so did their two sons. She said a silent prayer of gratitude for that, and another for those families who had lost children, particularly in violent and unspeakably dreadful circumstances. That stopped you in your tracks when you grumbled about superficial problems in life. And made you appreciate how fortunate you were to have had the privilege of sharing your own children's childhood.

Childhood.

Did children actually have a childhood these days?

She'd once read an exceptionally moving book by Corrie ten Boom in which the author's father, a Dutch watchmaker, faced with his young daughter's innocent question: "What's sexsin?" had responded by asking her to pick up a bag laden with tools; when she protested it was too heavy, he gently and wisely explained that just as he'd be a poor sort of father to expect his little girl to pick up a heavy load before she was sufficiently old and strong enough, so it was with knowledge. Some knowledge was too heavy for children to bear; it was the responsibility of the adult to carry it for them. (*See Acknowledgements Page 3*)

How shocked he'd be to know that youngsters now roamed housing estates like packs of animals, terrifying the weak and elderly cowering behind fortified doors. Or, for that matter, of the more "advantaged" variety, carted round "Art" exhibitions of Aids-contaminated blood, excrement, animals' innards, dead horses, and piles of bricks. Or spending evenings isolated in their rooms in front of their computer screen or personal TV, with as much notice taken of nine o'clock watersheds as Party Political Broadcasts.

What an ugly and frightening place the world must seem to grow up in, if you weren't near the top of either heap.

'Any empties?' trilled the Lady Mayoress as she collected dirty crockery on a tray.

When Major Pratt had, like a benevolent genie, promised to grant whatever request the Guest of Honour wished to make, he hadn't envisaged marshalling high-ranking officials and other prestigious guests into a washing-up squad. Especially as most of them, like him, had a 'treasure' who popped into their homes to stack dirty crockery in the dishwasher, press a couple of magic buttons, and hey presto. After an awkward pause (the paid staff have the rest of the day off? But who would do all the work?) Eloise, as ever, supplied the consummate *bon mot*.

'*What* a quaint idea, darling,' she said brightly, and turned to the Lady Mayoress, who had no option but to agree.

'Absolutely! All enter the spirit of the thing... er, just like the inmates! Is that what they do? All cheerfully muck in together with the chores?'

'They used to, before a lot of highly-paid officials got rid of all the original ideals.' Len was unable to resist the temptation.

Major Pratt, aware of the editor of the outdoors magazine hovering nearby, ears swivelling like radar antennae to pick up any controversial rumblings within the camp, was about to expound on the importance placed by The Association on fostering community spirit (out of deference to the Honoured Guest's request) while emphasising how we must all move with the times (to show support for the highly-paid officials responsible for current policy) when both he and the Guest of Honour were unceremoniously elbowed aside. Bridie, armed with a couple of ice-cream containers and a forest of carrier bags, was plundering the buffet in a last-minute trolley-dash before hurrying to the car.

Ignoring her, he changed the subject from Len's polemic and discomforting observations by spearing the minutest sample of haggis and neeps courtesy would allow, and watching the Guest of Honour devour his portion with obvious enjoyment.

'Well, tell me,' he enquired. 'What d'you think of Kate's efforts with the haggis? Did we Sassenachs manage to cook the things properly? What's the verdict?'

And Danny, who was a perceptive judge of character, replied that the haggis - just like everything else at Beckside - could not be more to his taste.

And as the rosy glow of self-satisfaction swelled and Major Pratt murmured modestly, 'Well, we try our best, you know,' Mona's taxi accelerated down the drive with Bridie devouring a huge slice of Jubilee cake in the passenger seat, and Dud, ashen-faced, wedged between Mona and Eamon in the back.

And the oppressive black cloud which had settled on his shoulders with her arrival finally lifted, to be replaced by a euphoria so ecstatic he would gladly have washed up a hundred dishes himself.

Well, almost.

Well at least, wandered in when they'd nearly finished and dried a couple of saucers.

Kate watched, fascinated, as the pages of Anna's sketchbook filled with lightning images of the day. An almost photographic image of the piper playing on the lawn was currently materialising under her skimming pencil.

Ewan had been quite happy to play requests, but for the most

247

part kept to his own particular choice, with something for each of the staff: "Up in the Morning Early" for Oliver, "The Dark Island" for Anna, "Song of the Somme" for Len - they'd often played it, slow time, on mandolin and guitar in the old days in Liverpool Folk Clubs - and an air of haunting wistfulness, which Danny (who had made a polite excuse to Major Pratt and returned to chat with the paid staff) told her was called "My Home", for her own dearly-held dream that one day she'd live by the sea in a small house with a homely, cluttered kitchen, a garden for any future grandchildren to play in, and a west-facing window to watch the sunsets.

Major Pratt hovered agitatedly nearby with a pristine J Cloth. Look at this! The paid staff hogging the Guest of Honour *again*! Courteous respectfulness if and when Mr. MacTavish chose to address any of them was one thing, but monopolising him - especially when it was obvious that Mr. MacTavish would prefer to circulate with the more influential guests and, you know, high-ranking officials - was quite another. Heaven only knew what subversive rubbish Len was pouring into his ear while the Great and Good were drudging in the kitchen!

Duty bound to take matters in hand - the poor chap was obviously desperate to be rescued - he gave the J Cloth an ineffective flick at the neighbouring table, then, Cheerfully Mucking In With The Chores not only accomplished but seen to be accomplished, spoke to the Guest of Honour.

'I'm so sorry, we all seem to have abandoned you.'

'Don't worry aboot it. Ah'm enjoying masel',' smiled Danny.

'Well, we're almost finished now.' Major Pratt looked across to where two National Office officials were tipping the remainder of the egg sandwiches onto a plate of tuna and mayonnaise ones. 'And there's a couple of chaps I'm sure you'd be most interested to meet...'

'Ah'm jist fine whaur Ah am.'

'Oh, I'm sure Len and Kate have taken good care of you while we were busy,' Major Pratt agreed smoothly. 'But our Len can sometimes get a bit hot under the collar about some issues, isn't that right Len?'

'Ah'm the same,' said Danny equably. 'That's why Ah always got on wi' the Scousers when Ah used tae dock in Liverpool, when Ah wis seagoing.'

'Really,' acknowledged Major Pratt attentively.

'Aye. And it turns out Len and I were actually wi' the same Line.'

'Yes,' said Len. 'I was in the "*Empress of Canada*", Danny was in her sister ship, the "*Empress of France*".'

Danny? DANNY? *This* was good, wasn't it? The paid staff, on first name terms with the Guest of Honour! He didn't care if Len had sailed in the Empress of Timbuctoo, he knew perfectly well - or should do - that he had no business hobnobbing matily with Guests of Honour earmarked to hobnob matily with Major Pratt.

'Really,' he commented again, slightly distantly.

'Aye. It's been an unexpected birthday present for me, being able to have a wee blether with an ex-seafarer from a sister ship,' continued Danny quietly. 'That's why *I* asked *him* if I could join him and his family.'

'Oh, absolutely,' Major Pratt agreed easily. 'However, now you've finished your chat...'

'We havenae finished.' Danny's voice, though quiet, held a note of authority which caused Major Pratt to blink in surprise. After a slight pause, he continued. 'It's difficult to explain, but there's a strange attachment seagoing men have for each other that sets them apart. There's a kind of magic settles on a man who has earned his bread visiting distant places.'

If anyone else had said that, thought Kate, it would have sounded nauseatingly affected and phoney. Danny's simple dignity nullified any such accusations.

Major Pratt cleared his throat. He couldn't say *he'd* ever noticed any magic settling on Len, but Guests of Honour - especially Guests of Honour who owned the property and grounds on which they now stood - must be humoured and indulged. And if he preferred gossiping with the hoi polloi and traipsing down maudlin memory lanes with Len (of *all* people!) to a stimulating conversation with the intelligentsia, well...

Although naturally one hesitated to put it into words, it had been obvious from the start: the Guest of Honour was Not One Of Us.

'*Do* take care of your hands,' exhorted Eloise as Babs stoically unloaded another tray of dirty crockery into the sink.

'The irony is,' remarked Major Pratt, who had arrived to oversee the operation and stood, hands clasped behind back, ready to offer suggestions to improve efficiency, 'That Kate would probably rather be in here doing this herself. I mean, lounging around out there... it might give her a migraine or something. Inactivity can have that effect, you know.'

'Oh, I hope not!' Babs broke off scrubbing the cream from a cake plate in concern. 'We don't want any more casualties!'

'No. Shame old Dud wasn't very well. All that drama and excitement must have been too much for him,' wheezed Leslie, meticulously drying a cup.

'Well quite frankly,' observed Major Pratt drily, 'I would have thought that turning up with another young lady to the very function at which one's fiancee intended announcing your Engagement rather contributed *to* the drama and excitement.' He flicked at a fly settling on a half-eaten vol-au-vent. 'Quite apart from which, Eloise and I are now stuck with having to take that ghastly barmaid home.'

Babs sought reassurance. 'But Mona made the right decision to take Dud home for some peace and quiet, didn't she?'

'If I didn't know Len better,' Major Pratt's tone was thoughtful. 'I'd have said *he* somehow made the decision that Mona would take Dud home for some peace and quiet.'

'Oh nonsense, darling!' chided Eloise, laughing. 'How could *Len* possibly have engineered a thing like that?'

'True,' agreed Major Pratt, dismissing the thought. Eloise was right. Old Len was straight as a die. Might be a bit bolshie at times, but he was openly bolshie. Hadn't a devious bone in his body. And even if he had (comforting thought), the cerebral ability to carry through any wily schemes was quite obviously lacking.

'Oh, by the way, that reminds me,' added Eloise. 'He mentioned Oliver was leaving on Tuesday.'

'Hm. Can't say I'll miss him,' sniffed Major Pratt. 'Terribly immature.'

'Yes, that's just what I said. Len agreed that the qualities of more mature workers were often undervalued -'

'Well he would darling, wouldn't he!'

'- And tentatively suggested that Ewan might be prepared to join the paid staff full time in Oliver's place.'

Major Pratt stared at her. 'EWAN?'

'Yes, darling, you know, the piper. I said, what a marvellous idea! In fact, we both thought - I think Len actually suggested it - it might be wise get things formally agreed today, in case he changes his mind.'

'Did he indeed. In that case I suggest Ewan is brought in here to tackle these dishes right now, instead of us, in the hope that he does!'

Len's head peeped round the door. 'Sorry to interrupt, but Danny was just wondering - would you have any objections to Ewan playing a few more special requests for him?'

'...And finally,' Major Pratt smiled at his captive audience, 'Having whetted your appetite, it would be most remiss of me not to include a few words on the wonderful work done by the Association...'

He paused to savour the moment, basking in the reflected glory of the preceding item. The Shanty Singing had been a phenomenal success; a tribute to his inspired utilisation of emergency resources. He'd offered Len the opportunity of singing a couple of Shanties (on condition he did it, you know, *properly!*), and although at first this had met with typical Len-like truculence, Danny had made a specific request; would Len and Ewan consider singing "The Leaving of Liverpool" for him? Then mandolin and guitar had been produced, and one felt entitled to sit back and congratulate oneself.

Because they were surprisingly good.

He'd expected a carousing pub song, but they'd sung with moving empathy of a man embarking on a long voyage, not from some mawkish, sentimental love of the sea, but because he had no other way of earning a living. Then a selection of other shanties (even *his* feet tapped as they belted out "Oh you New York girls, Can't You Dance the Polka!"), finishing with the haunting, wistful "The Sailor's Farewell", before returning to the last verse of "Leaving of Liverpool" for the final encore:

"I'm bound for California
By way of the stormy Cape Horn,
And I'll write to you a letter, love,
When I am homeward bound."

All terribly, you know, emotional and *appropriate,* somehow.

Yes. All in all - despite Mona's Engagement debacle and then that nincompoop Dud with his scene-stealing swooning right, left, and centre - the Event looked like proving to be a runaway success, and he was looking forward to reading the accolades and tributes in the Newsletter, Outdoor Pursuits magazines, and local press.

Must remember to distribute copies of his speech to the reporters.

'- Well, very briefly...'

It was over.

Beckside's official Jubilee Celebrations had formally terminated hours ago; VIPs, assorted dignitaries and Anyone-who-was-Anyone long since departed.

Beckside's unofficial Jubilee Celebrations were now taking place around the kitchen table, which was laden with surplus goodies (including the Glenmorangie) from the main Event.

Danny had decided to stay on for a second night, and accept a lift with Len and Kate as they drove up to Glasgow. He was joining them, together with Anna, Oliver, Ewan, Tony, Mike, and their girlfriends, for a celebratory bar meal the next day, the venue for which was now being discussed.

'Somewhere well off the tourist trail,' stipulated Anna.

'Should I book a table?' wondered Kate. 'There'll be ten of us.'

Len surveyed the profusion of delicacies on the table. 'Couldn't you just make up a sort of picnic with all this lot?'

'Sure - *if you want to celebrate your Silver Wedding with a divorce?*'

'How about just making it a spur-of-the-moment thing? Like your visit.' Ewan turned to Mike.

Mike shook his head. 'It wasn't a spur of the moment thing. I wrote to let you know, instead of ringing, with being on nights. It should have arrived yesterday.'

Len shrugged. 'Never got it.'

'Didn't it arrive this morning, either?'

Len and Kate looked at each other. "This morning" was now so distant that trying to remember it was like regressing to a previous life.

'That's a point. Where *is* the post?' wondered Len.

'Must still be in the Dining Room,' admitted Kate sheepishly. 'I put it under the counter until we finished serving breakfast, then forgot all about it. I'll get it.'

'It's a typewritten brown envelope,' Mike called after her.

Oh. No wonder she hadn't noticed it. She'd been looking for handwritten, card-shaped ones.

She returned, rifling through the bundle of letters.

'Is this it?' She extracted a white envelope, then frowned, puzzled. It was typewritten, but addressed solely to her.

'Here, give us the bundle while you stand dithering!' Len flipped through the pile as she slit open the mystery envelope.

'This the one?' he asked his son, holding up a likely candidate.

Mike nodded.

He waved it at Kate, expecting her to reach eagerly for it as she always did when a letter from one of their sons arrived.

'Kate, it's here!'

No response. She was staring, transfixed, at the letter in her hand; the other hand moved instinctively to her mouth. Len looked at her in amazement. Either she was undergoing some deep charismatic religious experience, or Oliver had slipped a trip to Disneyland in tablet form into her wine as a farewell present.

'What is it, Mum?' Tony was getting to his feet in alarm.

Her eyes were shining, her face radiant; her hand shook as she handed the letter to Len, who skimmed through, blinked, read it again, and looked up at his wife, the grin of delight on his face widening to mirror hers.

Her play, re-submitted after much re-writing and editing, had been accepted by the Liverpool Playhouse.

It was ten past midnight. Beckside's day was finished; Kate and Len's just beginning.

As they staggered and stumbled upstairs to the flat, he supporting her, she leaning against him, knees pleasantly weak from the wine, he whispered a promise about the pleasurable First Item on their own private Celebration Programme... if the keyhole would just stay still long enough for him to unlock the door.

They fell inside. Kate detoured to the bathroom, then paused at the bedroom door, and smiled to herself.

Her husband was stretched out on the bed, stark naked. His eyes were closed, his breathing even. An Anniversary card, together with a package wrapped in Silver Wedding paper, lay on his chest, held loosely in one hand.

She gently drew them from his unresisting fingers, put them on the bedside table, eased the duvet from under him, covered him, and crawled in beside him.

'All talk, some men.' She lightly kissed his ear, snuggled up to the warmth of his body. Obviously the promised pleasurable First Item on their own private Silver Wedding Programme would now take place in the morning.

There was a slight movement beside her. One eye opened, regarded her lazily, smiled.

'Not this one.'

Correction: The *Second* pleasurable Item on their Silver Wedding Programme would take place in the morning.

THE END.